A Marriage on Paper

When his convenient bride
...becomes his real wife and lover!

A Marriage on Paper

THE MILLIONAIRE'S MARRIAGE

by
Catherine Spencer

MARRIAGE AT A PRICE

by
Miranda Lee

CHRISTOS'S PROMISE

by
Jane Porter

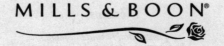

MILLS & BOON®

*MILLS & BOON and MILLS & BOON with the Rose Device
are registered trademarks of the publisher.
Harlequin Mills & Boon Limited,
Eton House, 18-24 Paradise Road, Richmond, Surrey, TW9 1SR*

A MARRIAGE ON PAPER
© by Harlequin Enterprises II B.V., 2005

The Millionaire's Marriage, Marriage at a Price and
Christos's Promise were first published in Great Britain by
Harlequin Mills & Boon Limited in separate, single volumes.

The Millionaire's Marriage © Kathy Garner 2001
Marriage at a Price © Miranda Lee 2001
Christos's Promise © Jane Porter 2001

ISBN 0 263 84471 4

05-0105

*Printed and bound in Spain
by Litografía Rosés S.A., Barcelona*

Catherine Spencer, once an English teacher, fell into writing through eavesdropping on a conversation about Mills & Boon romances. Within two months she changed careers and sold her first book to Mills & Boon in 1984. She moved to Canada from England thirty years ago and lives in Vancouver. She is married to a Canadian and has four grown children – two daughters and two sons – plus three dogs and a cat. In her spare time she plays the piano, collects antiques, and grows tropical shrubs.

Look out for the next sizzling read by Catherine Spencer:
THE ITALIAN DOCTOR'S MISTRESS
Coming in May 2005, in Modern Romance™!

THE MILLIONAIRE'S MARRIAGE
by
Catherine Spencer

CHAPTER ONE

"I'VE left word that you're expected. If I'm not home when you arrive, the concierge will let you in."

The words themselves were chillingly neutral but, even after all this time and despite everything, Max's husky baritone still had the power to make her break out in goose bumps. Holding the phone away from her mouth so that he couldn't hear how ragged her breathing had become, Gabriella fought the urge to beg him to be there himself to greet her and, matching his tone the best way she knew how, said, "Is it still Howard?"

"I'm surprised you remember, given the number of doormen who must have crossed your path in the last two years."

He made it sound as if she earned a living paying illicit visits to married men's hotel rooms! "There are few things about my life with you that I've forgotten, Max," she said stiffly. "Howard was one of the more pleasant aspects. It will be nice to see him again and know there's at least one friendly face in the building—unless, of course, you've poisoned his mind against me."

"Hardly," her estranged husband replied. "Your name rarely comes up in conversation, and then only in passing."

Though there was little doubt he was being his usual brutally direct self, even more regrettable was the fact that the truth should hurt so much. "Are you quite sure we can pull this off?" she said. "Two weeks of facing each other across the table at mealtimes might not be a long

5

time in the cosmic scheme of things, but I suspect it'll seem an eternity when it comes to living them second by second.''

''I can manage it, if you can. And I have no doubt that you can. It will be, after all, a lot like your life—a charade. And let's face it, Gabriella, you've always shown a talent for pretending. No doubt that explains your phenomenal latter-day success as a model. How else do all those glossy fashion magazines feature you as dewy virgin bride one day, sultry seductress the next, and beach bunny yet another?''

She'd made up her mind she wouldn't get drawn into the retaliation game, no matter how he might try to provoke her, but his scornful dismissal of the success she'd worked so hard to achieve spurred her to respond, ''Why, Max, I had no idea you followed my career so closely!''

''I don't,'' he said crushingly, ''but I'd have to be brain dead not to recognize that, technically at least, I'm married to the most famous face in North America and possibly the world. Given your unquestionable versatility when it comes to make-believe, plus the fact that you're an accomplished liar, I'm sure you can pull off the image of contented wife for a couple of weeks, especially since you have so much at stake and I plan to make myself as scarce as possible most of the time. All it'll take is a little civility in public, a few harmless demonstrations of affection. We've been married over two years, Gabriella. Your parents aren't going to expect us to act like besotted honeymooners.''

''Which is just as well, since a honeymoon's one thing I've never had the pleasure of experiencing.''

But she knew about heartbreak, and loneliness, and rejection. She knew how it felt to be a bride standing beside a groom who, when he looked at her at all, did so with a blank indifference touched with loathing. She knew what it was like to lie alone in the big marriage bed while her husband slept in the guest room—a pain only slightly less unbearable than the few times when primitive need had driven him to come silently to her in the night then, when his hunger was appeased, just as silently leave her again.

She knew what it was like to be married to a man who hated her all the more because, once in a very rare while, he couldn't resist her.

"Gabriella? Did you hear what I just said?"

Startled by his unabashed impatience, she jerked her attention back to the present. "Um...not exactly."

"I asked what time they land in Vancouver."

They: her aged parents who thought their only surviving child was blissfully happy with the grandson of a man they revered more than God! What if they saw past the subterfuge so carefully constructed for their benefit? What if her world-famous smile cracked, and she couldn't disguise the misery?

Suddenly, when it was too late to change anything, she wondered why she'd ever encouraged them to leave their native Hungary and visit Canada, or why she thought she could pull off such a monumental deception. "Three o'clock tomorrow."

"And you're in Los Angeles now?"

"Yes. I stayed with a friend last night but I'm flying out at ten. I expect to be at the penthouse by early afternoon."

"That should leave you enough time to unpack and reacquaint yourself with the place. And while I think of it, you might want to pick up a few supplies. The stuff in the refrigerator's pretty basic and unlikely to measure up to your gourmet standards."

Why did he do that? she wondered. Why imply that she

was impossible to please and needlessly extravagant? Whatever else she'd contributed to the failure of their marriage, overspending his money was not on the list, for all that he'd been convinced his bank account was what had made her chase him to the altar.

But taking issue with him now would lead only to more acrimony and she already had enough to handle. "Grocery shopping's at the top of my list of things to do," she said, then waited, hoping he'd volunteer the information she most needed to learn, and so spare her having to be the one to raise a topic he surely hadn't overlooked.

Once again, though, he disappointed her and with obvious relief said, "I guess that's it, then. If I don't see you today, I'll catch up with you tomorrow at breakfast."

"Before you go, Max…"

"Now what?" There it was again, the weary impatience she so easily inspired in him.

"Where am I… I mean…um, which room is…mine?"

So clearly taken aback by the question that she could practically *feel* his incredulous stare zinging down the phone line, he let a full thirty seconds of silence elapse before replying, "I thought the whole idea here is to convince your parents we're still happily married, despite what the tabloids say."

"It is."

"Then which room do you suppose, Gabriella?"

Feeling like a none-too-bright child being asked to put two and two together and come up with four, she muttered, "The master suite?"

"Bingo! And since all my stuff fits easily into one closet, I hope you're bringing enough clothes to fill the other, unless you want it to be patently obvious that, like your parents, you're merely visiting. I don't imagine, given your extensive wardrobe, that's a problem?"

"None at all," she said, recovering a trace of the haughty composure that had made her an overnight sensation as a model. "I have three large suitcases packed and waiting."

"I'm delighted to hear it. Any *more* questions?"

Indeed yes! But nothing would persuade her to come right out and ask, *Will we be sharing the same bed?*

She'd find out the answer to that soon enough!

She'd grown up in a palace—a small one, to be sure, and rather shabby around the edges, but a palace nonetheless. The Tokyo apartment she'd bought eighteen months ago, when she left Max, was small but exquisite. Her most recent acquisition, a house with a lovely little walled garden on the outskirts of Rome, was a gem of seventeenth-century elegance.

Still, as she stepped out of the private elevator on the twenty-first floor and stood under the hand-painted dome in the vestibule, the magnificence of Max's two-story penthouse took her breath away, just as it had the first time she'd set foot on its hand-set marble floor.

Leaving her luggage and the sacks of groceries in the foyer, she crossed the vast living room to the right of the winding staircase and slid back the glass doors to the terrace. Tubs of bougainvillea, hibiscus and tibouchina in full flower lent splashes of exotic color to the sprawling rooftop garden. Yellow roses climbed up the south wall. A miniature clematis with flowers the size of bumblebees rambled along the deep eaves. The raised swimming pool and hot tub shimmered in the drowsy heat of the late June afternoon. People who didn't know her real reason for taking up residence here again could be forgiven for thinking she'd entered paradise.

Beyond the parapet, the Vancouver skyline showed itself off in all its summer glory. Sunlight bounced off the glass walls of newly built office towers. Sailboats drifted on the calm waters of Georgia Strait. The graceful arc of the Lion's Gate Bridge rose from the green expanse of Stanley Park to span the First Narrows as far as the North Shore where snow-kissed mountain tips reared up against the deep blue sky.

It had been just such a day that she'd come here as a bride, with the air so hot and still that the tears she couldn't keep in check had dried on her cheeks almost as fast as they'd fallen. She'd been married all of forty-eight hours, and already knew how deeply her husband resented her. She'd stood in this very spot, long after sunset, and prayed for the hundredth time that she could make him love her. Or, if that was asking too much, that she could stop loving him.

Her prayers had gone unanswered on both counts, and remembering the weeks which had followed left her misty-eyed all over again.

Annoyed to find herself so soon falling back into old, bad habits, she gave herself a mental shake and returned to the cool, high-ceilinged living room. Like the city, it, too, had undergone some change, not by new additions but by the complete removal of anything that might have reminded Max of her.

"Do what you like with it. I don't care," he'd flung at her when, as a bride, she'd suggested softening the austerity of the decor with various wedding gifts and dowry items she'd brought with her from Hungary—lovely things like the antique tulip lamp, hunting prints and painted wall clock handed down from her grandparents, and the brass trivets and finely stitched linens from her godmother, all of which she'd left behind when she fled the marriage.

Now, the cherrywood accent pieces Max had chosen before he met her provided the only contrast to the oyster-white couches, carpets, walls and deep, carved moldings. Even the classic fireplace, swept scrupulously clean of ashes, looked incapable of warmth. He had erased every trace of her from his home as thoroughly as he'd erased her from his life and, while some might admire the severe elegance of the room, without the reminders of her childhood home and family, Gabriella found it cold and hostile.

Surely, he hadn't thrown away those treasures her family had managed to save from the ravages of the political upheaval which had reduced so many once-wealthy families to poverty? Surely, as she went about the business of—how was it he'd put it, when they'd spoken on the phone that morning?—*reacquainting* herself with her former home, she'd find they'd just been stashed away somewhere?

Returning to the foyer, she averted her gaze from the stairs which led to the bedrooms, and carried the grocery bags to the equally barren-looking kitchen. Max's claim that he had only basic supplies in stock had been, she shortly discovered, a masterpiece of understatement. Although the temperature-controlled wine cellar at one end of the room was well stocked, the refrigerator contained nothing but beer, a very old block of cheese, and a carton of grapefruit juice.

Apart from a couple of boxes of cereal and some canned soup, the lower cupboards were bare. The glass-fronted upper cabinets stood completely empty, the panes staring back at her like sightless eyes. Neither cup nor plate graced their shelves.

The copper-bottomed pots and pans hanging from a stainless-steel rack above the work island were linked by a fine network of cobwebs, giving testament to how infrequently they'd been taken down. As for the built-in range and double-wall ovens imported from France, Gabriella doubted either had been used since the last time she'd cooked dinner there, over eighteen months ago.

In fact, the entire main floor of the penthouse had the look of a showpiece owned by a man who stopped by only occasionally to check on his investment, and she had no reason to suppose the upstairs rooms would be any different. There was none of the casual clutter, no sense of the warmth that speaks of a home shared by a couple in love. Her father might be fooled into believing otherwise but, as things presently stood, her mother wouldn't be taken in for a minute.

Realizing she had a host of shopping still to do, she searched through the drawers for a notepad on which to list the items needed. She didn't find one. Instead, she came across a flowered apron with a ruffle around its hem, and a half-empty tube of hand cream.

The sight caused her stomach to plummet and left her feeling slightly sick. Neither had ever belonged to her and she couldn't imagine any circumstance which would have persuaded Max to make use of them—in which case, who had?

Don't do this to yourself, Gabriella, the voice of reason scolded. *It's going to be difficult enough to preserve your parents' peace of mind by letting them think your marriage is on solid ground so get on with the job at hand, because it's going to take you the rest of today to make the place look lived in.*

By nine that evening, her manicure was ruined but the transformation she'd effected throughout most of the rooms was worth every chip in her nail enamel.

The pantry and refrigerator fairly bulged at the seams

with delicacies. In the storage room under the stairs, she found boxes containing the missing heirlooms; also the Herend china she'd brought with her as a bride stowed alongside crates of wedding gift crystal and other reminders of her brief sojourn as lady of the penthouse.

Now, the china and elegant stemware and goblets were again on display in the glass-fronted upper cabinets. A pretty blue bowl filled with oranges, lemons and limes sat on the granite counter beside the brass trivets polished to a blinding shine. A braid of garlic hung next to the freshly washed copper-bottomed cookware, and pots of basil and oregano nestled in a wicker planter on the windowsill.

On a shelf at the very back of the storage room, she discovered the large, silver-framed formal portrait of her and Max on their wedding day. Surprised and grateful that he hadn't tossed it in the garbage, she'd dusted it off and set it on a side table in the living room, next to two small framed photographs she'd thought to bring with her, of her parents and the brother who'd died six years before she was born.

A fringed shawl she'd found in a bazaar in Indonesia lay draped across the back of one of the couches, its bronze and gold threadwork glowing like fire against the oyster-white upholstery. Flower arrangements blazed with color on the writing desk and sofa table, and filled the empty hearth.

She'd placed slender ivory tapers in the heavy Swarovski candlesticks on the dining room table. The antique sterling coffee service bequeathed to her by her great-aunt Zsuzsanna shone splendidly on the sideboard in whose top drawers lay the freshly ironed hand-worked linens.

Upstairs, the guest room and adjoining bathroom were prepared, with lavender sachets hanging in the closet, a vase of roses on the dresser, soaps and lotions arranged on the marble deck of the soaker tub. Monogrammed towels hung ready for use, the mirrors sparkled. Crisp percale linens covered the bed—that same bed where she'd found Max on their first night as husband and wife in North America.

She'd have thought the enormous emotional toll entailed in facing *that* room would have inured her to entering the other; the one in which she'd slept—and wept—for nearly six months before she'd found the courage to walk away from her loveless marriage. Yet, with the cool mauve light of dusk pooling around her, she found herself hesitating outside the door of the master suite, a clammy dew of apprehension pebbling her skin.

She was disgusted with herself. In view of everything she'd achieved since her marriage had fallen apart, how foolish of her now to fear four walls! *Things* could not hurt her. Only people had the power to do that—and even then, only if she let them.

Surely she'd laid those old ghosts to rest? And surely...*surely*...safeguarding her heart was a lesson she'd learned well since the last time Max had trampled all over it?

Still, she quaked inwardly as she pushed at the heavy door. It swung open in smooth, expensive silence, just as it used to do when, a lifetime ago, he'd paid those brief, late-night visits to her bed.

Inside the room, filmy floor-length curtains billowed in the evening breeze at the tall open windows. Avoiding the hulking mass of the bed itself, her gaze flitted instead from the bench at its foot where one of Max's ties and a paperback mystery lay, to a pair of his shoes sprawled crookedly next to a chair, and from there to a navy golf shirt and three wooden golf tees tossed carelessly on top of a chest of drawers.

It was a man's room; a room so devoid of a feminine presence that it might never have accommodated a bride. And yet the ghosts of yesterday sprang out at her from every corner, clamoring to be acknowledged.

Her first night there, she'd bathed in scented water, put on the gauzy peignoir trimmed with French lace that was part of her trousseau, sprayed a little perfume at her wrists and throat, and brushed her pale blond hair to satin smoothness against her shoulders. And waited for Max.

The sky had grown pearly with a new dawn before she'd finally accepted that he was not going to join her. And so, silly creature that she'd been then, she'd gone looking for him. And found him spread-eagled on the bed in the room across the hall, sleeping soundly with a sheet half covering him from the waist down.

For the longest time, she'd simply looked at him, bewitched all over again by his masculine beauty. Such skin, polished to bronze, such perfect symmetry of form, such sleek, honed strength!

Oh, how she'd ached to be enfolded in his arms, to be possessed by him! How she'd longed to feel his mouth on hers, claiming her soul; to hear his voice at her ear, hoarse with passion!

Driven by hunger and need and hope, she'd traced her fingertip along the curve of his eyebrow, smoothed her hand lightly over his dark hair. Made bold by the fact that he didn't stir, she'd bent down to lay her mouth on his when, suddenly, his eyes had shot open.

Instantly awake, suspicious, annoyed, he'd growled, "What the devil do you think you're doing?"

"Isn't it obvious?" she'd whispered, hoping the

warmth of her lips against his would ignite an answering fire in him.

Instead, he'd turned his face away so that her kiss missed its mark and landed on his cheek.

"Don't," she'd begged. "Please don't turn away from me. I need you, Max."

She might as well have appealed to a slab of stone for all the response she evoked. Ignoring her completely, he'd continued staring at the wall, and even all these months later, she grew hot with embarrassment at what had followed.

She'd pulled back the sheet and touched him—tentatively at first—beginning at his shoulders and continuing the length of his torso until she found the sleep-warm flesh between his thighs.

"It doesn't prove a thing, you know," he'd informed her with quiet fury when, despite himself, he'd grown hard against her hand. "It's a purely reflexive response—any woman could bring it about."

"But I'm not just any woman, Max. I'm your wife," she'd reminded him. "And I love you. Please let me show you how much."

And before he had time to realize her intention, she'd let her mouth slide over the muscled planes of his chest to his belly and then, with a daring born wholly of desperation, closed her lips softly over the silken tip of his manhood.

His breathing had quickened. He'd knotted his fingers in her hair and tried unsuccessfully to stifle a groan. Sensing victory, she'd slipped out of his hold and the peignoir in one swift move, and aligned her naked body, inch for inch, against his.

She'd seen the corded tension in his neck, tasted the film of sweat on his upper lip when he'd grudgingly let her turn his face to meet hers and succumbed to the sweeping caress of her tongue over the seam of his mouth.

She'd known a glorious tremor of expectation when, unable to hold out any longer, he'd hauled her to sit astride him and braced her so that, with the merest surge of his hips, he was buried inside her, tight and powerful. She'd felt the muscled flex of his abdomen, the steely strength of his thighs. Seen the rapid rise and fall of his chest.

He'd spanned her waist, framed the curve of her hips, drawn a line from her navel to her pubic bone, and then farther still, until he found the one tiny spot in her body most vulnerable to his measured seduction.

Sensation had engulfed her and left her body vibrating, from the tips of her toes to her scalp. Such pleasure! Such exquisite torture! She'd yearned toward him, wanting to prolong the delight only he could bring, but encroaching passion had slammed down with such vengeance that neither of them had been able to withstand it.

Caught in a maelstrom of emotion sharpened to dazzling brilliance by the spasms ravaging her body, she'd sensed her eyes growing heavy, slumberous almost. But his had remained wide open. Unblinking. Unmoved. As though to say, *You might wreak havoc with my body, but you'll never sway my heart or mind.*

''Satisfied?'' he'd said, when it was over. And, with that brief, indifferent question, managed to degrade their union to something so cheap and unlovely that she'd cringed.

Twenty-four months should have been time enough to lessen the hurt. A sensible woman would have forgotten it altogether. But she'd never been sensible where Max was concerned and if the tears scalding her cheeks now weren't proof enough of that, the dull, cold emptiness inside where once she'd known warmth and life and passion, should have been.

What would it take, she wondered, to cure her of Max Logan and heal the scars inflicted by her marriage? Would there ever come a time that she'd learn to love another man as she still loved him—and if so, would she love more wisely the next time?

Although dense silence greeted him when he stepped inside the penthouse, he knew at once that she was there. Quite apart from her suitcases still parked by the front door, and the scent of flowers everywhere, as well as a host of other clues that she'd made herself thoroughly at home, the atmosphere was different. Vibrant, electric, and unsettling as hell. A forewarning of trouble to come.

Dropping his briefcase on the desk in his office—one area, he was glad to see, that she hadn't tried to camouflage into something out of a happy homemaker magazine—he made a quick circuit through the rooms on the main floor before climbing the stairs. The thick carpet masked his footsteps thoroughly enough that she was completely unaware of him coming to a halt at the entrance to the master suite.

Shoving his hands in his pockets, he leaned against the door frame and watched her. She stood at the highboy dresser and appeared to be mopping her face with his golf shirt. But what struck him most forcibly was how thin she'd become. Not that she'd ever been fat or even close to it but, where once she'd been sweetly curved, she was now all sharp, elegant angles, at least from the rear. Her hips were narrow as a boy's, her waist matchstick slender.

Though probably a prerequisite for all successful fashion models, it wasn't a look that appealed to him. Even less did he like the air of fragility that went with this underfed version of the hellion he'd been coerced into marrying. It edged her too close to vulnerable, and once he started thinking along those lines, he was in trouble, as he very well knew from past experience.

"I'd appreciate it if you'd wipe your nose on something other than a piece of my clothing," he said, relishing how his voice suddenly breaking the silence almost had her jumping out of her skin.

But when she spun around, the expression on her face made short work of his moment of malicious pleasure. He'd forgotten how truly beautiful she was. In particular, he'd forgotten the impact of her incredible eyes and, suddenly, he was the one struggling for composure as memories of the night they'd first met in her father's house rushed back to haunt him.

"I'd like you to meet my daughter," Zoltan Siklossy had said, as footsteps approached along the flagstone path that ran the width of the front of the rambling old mausoleum of a place.

Max had turned and been transfixed, the impact of the city skyline beyond the Danube forgotten. Backlit by the late May sunset, she'd appeared touched with gold all over, from her pale hair to her honey-tinted skin. Only her eyes had been different, a startlingly light aquamarine, one moment more green than blue, and the next, the other way around.

Fringed with long, curling lashes and glowing with the fire of priceless jewels, they'd inspected him. He'd stared back, mesmerized, and said the first thing that came to mind. "I didn't know Magyars were blond. Somehow, I expected you'd all be dark."

A stupid, thoughtless remark which showed him for the ignorant foreigner he was, but she hadn't taken offence. Instead, she'd come forward and laughed as she took his hand. "Some of us are. But we Hungarians have a mixed ancestry and I, like many others in my country, favor our Finnish heritage."

Though accented, her English was perfect, thanks, he later discovered, to an aunt who'd studied in London years before. Her laughter hung like music in the still, warm evening. Her hand remained in his, light and cool. "Welcome to Budapest, Mr. Logan," she purred. "I hope you'll allow me to introduce you to our beautiful city."

"I'm counting on it," he'd replied, bowled over by her easy self-assurance. Although she looked no more than eighteen, he believed her when she told him she was twenty-seven. Why not? After all, her parents were well into their seventies.

In fact, she'd been just twenty-two and the most conniving creature he'd ever met—not something likely to have changed, he reminded himself now, even if she did look about ready to keel over in a dead faint at being caught off guard.

"I'm not wiping my nose," she whispered shakily, clutching the shirt to her breasts.

He strolled further into the room. "What were you doing, then? Sniffing to find evidence of another woman's perfume? Checking for lipstick stains?"

Something flared in her eyes. Guilt? Shame? Anger? "Should I be? Do you entertain many women here, Max, now that I'm no longer underfoot all the time?"

"If I do, that's certainly none of your business, my dear."

"As long as we're married—"

"You left the marriage."

"But I'm still your wife and whether or not you like it, you're still my husband."

He circled her slowly and noticed that her eyes were

suspiciously red-rimmed. "A fact which apparently causes you some grief. Have you been crying, Gabriella?"

"No," she said, even as a fresh flood of tears welled up and turned her irises to sparkling turquoise.

"You used to be a better liar. What happened? Not had enough practice lately?"

"I…" Battling for composure, she pressed slender fingers to her mouth.

Irked to find his mood dangerously inclining toward sympathy, he made a big production of tipping the loose change from his pockets onto the shelf of his mahogany valet stand. "Yes? Spit it out, whatever it is. After everything else we've been through, I'm sure I can take it."

Her voice, husky and uncertain, barely made it across the distance separating them. "I hoped we wouldn't…be like this with one another, Max. I hoped we'd be able to…"

She swallowed audibly and dribbled into another tremulous silence.

"What?" He swung back to face her, stoking the slow anger her distress threatened to extinguish. "Pick up where we left off? And exactly where was that, Gabriella? At each other's throats, as I recall!"

"I was hoping we could get past that. I think we *must,* if we're to convince my parents they need have no worries about me." She held out both hands in appeal. "I know you…hate me, Max, but for their sake, won't you please try to remember there was once a time when we liked each other and, for the next two weeks, focus on that instead?"

CHAPTER TWO

HER reminder touched a nerve. They *had* liked each other, in the beginning. He'd been dazzled by her effervescence, her zest for life. Only later had he come to see them for what they really were: a cover-up designed to hide her more devious objectives.

"My father treats me as if I were made of bone china," she'd confided, the day she took him on a walking tour on the Buda side of the Danube, some three weeks after he'd arrived in Hungary. "He thinks I need to be protected."

"Not surprising, surely?" he'd said. "You've had a very sheltered upbringing."

She'd batted her eyelashes provocatively. "But I'm a woman of the world now, Max, and quite able to look out for myself."

Later that afternoon though, when they'd run into some people she knew and been persuaded to join them for refreshments at a sidewalk café near Fishermen's Bastion, Max had seen why Zoltan Siklossy might be concerned. Although she made one glass of wine last the whole hour they were together, Gabriella's so-called friends—social-climbing opportunists, from what he'd observed—ordered round after round and showed no qualms about leaving her to pick up the tab when they finally moved on.

"Let me," Max had said, reaching for the bill.

"No, please! I can afford it," she'd replied. "And it's my pleasure to do so."

But he'd insisted. "Humor me, Gabriella. I'm one of

those dull, old-fashioned North Americans who thinks the man should pay.''

"Dull?" She'd turned her stunning sea-green eyes on him and he'd found himself drowning in their translucent depths. ''I find you rather wonderful.''

For a moment, he'd thought he caught a glimpse of something fragile beneath her vivacity. A wistful innocence almost, that belied her frequent implicit reference to previous lovers. It was gone so quickly that he decided he must have imagined it, but the impression, brief though it was, found its way through his defenses and touched him in ways he hadn't anticipated.

If she were anyone else and his sole reason for visiting Hungary had been a summer of fun in the sun, he'd have found her hard to resist. But there was no place in his plans for a serious involvement, and he hoped he had enough class not to engage in a sexual fling with his hosts' daughter.

The way Gabriella had studied him suggested she knew full well the thoughts chasing through his mind, and was determined to change them. Her usual worldly mask firmly in place again, she asked in a voice husky with promise, ''Do you like to dance, Max?''

''I can manage a two-step without crippling my partner,'' he said, half bewitched by her brazen flirting and half annoyed to find himself responding to it despite what his conscience was telling him.

''Would you like to dance with me?''

''Here?'' He'd glance at the hulking shadow of Mátyás Church, and the sunny square next to it, filled with camera-toting tourists. ''I don't think so, thanks!''

''Of course not *here!*'' She'd laughed and he was once again reminded of music, of wind chimes swaying in a summer breeze. Good sense be damned, he'd found himself gazing at her heart-shaped face with its perfect strawberry-ripe, cupid's-bow mouth and wondering how she would taste if he were to kiss her.

"My parents would like to throw a party for you," she went on, drawing his gaze down by crossing her long, lovely legs so that the hem of her skirt, short enough to begin with, rode a couple of inches farther up her thigh. "They hold your family in such esteem, as I'm sure you know. Your grandfather is a legend in this city."

"He took a few photographs." Max had shrugged, as much to dispel the enchantment she was weaving as to dispute her claim. "No big deal. That was how he earned a living."

"For the people of Budapest, he was a hero. He braved imprisonment to record our history when most men with his diplomatic immunity would have made their escape. As his grandson, you are our honored guest and it's our privilege to treat you accordingly."

"I'm here on business, Gabriella, not to make the social scene," he reminded her. "It was never my intention to impose on your family for more than an hour or two, just long enough to pay my respects. That your parents insisted I stay in their home when I had a perfectly good hotel room reserved—"

"Charles Logan's grandson stay in a hotel?" Her laughter had flowed over him again beguilingly. Her fingers grazed his forearm and lingered at his wrist, gently shackling him. "Out of the question! Neither my mother nor my father would allow such a thing. You're to stay with us as long as, and whenever, you're in Budapest"

A completely illogical prickle of foreboding had tracked the length of his spine and despite the bright hot sun, he'd felt a sudden chill. "I don't anticipate many return visits. Once I've concluded the terms and conditions of the property I'm interested in buying and have the necessary permits approved, I'll turn the entire restoration process over to my project manager and head back home.''

''All the more reason for us to entertain you royally while we have the chance then,'' she'd said, leaning forward so that, without having to try too hard, he was able to glimpse the lightly tanned cleavage revealed by the low neck of her summer dress. She hadn't been wearing a bra.

Responding to so shameless an invitation had been his first in a long line of mistakes that came to a head about a month later when the promised party took place. It seemed to him that half the population of Budapest showed up for the event and while he lost track of names almost immediately, everyone appeared to know not only of his grandfather but, surprisingly, of him, his purchase of the dilapidated old building across the river, and his plans to turn it into yet another of his chain of small, international luxury hotels.

''You see,'' Gabriella had cooed in his ear, slipping her hand under his elbow and leaning close enough for the sunlit scent of her pale gold hair to cloud his senses, ''it's not just Charles Logan's grandson they've come to meet. You're a celebrity in your own right, Max.''

She looked exquisite in a sleeveless flame-pink dress made all the more dramatic by its simple, fitted lines. The eye of every man in the place was drawn to her, and his had been no exception. ''I'm surprised people don't resent a foreigner snapping up their real estate,'' he'd said, tearing his gaze away and concentrating instead on the bubbles rising in his glass of champagne.

''You're creating work for people, bringing tourism here in greater numbers, helping to rebuild our economy.

What possible reason could anyone have to resent such a man?''

He'd been flattered, no doubt about it. What man wouldn't have been, with a roomful of Budapest's social elite smiling benignly at him and a stunningly beautiful woman hanging on his every word?

He should have been satisfied with that. Instead, he'd gone along with it when she'd monopolized him on the dance floor because hey, he was passing through town only, so what harm was there in letting her snuggle just a bit too close? Not until it was too late to change things had he seen that in being her passive conspirator, he'd contributed to the evening ending in a disaster that kept on going from bad to worse.

''*Didn't* we, Max?''

Glad to escape memories guaranteed to unleash nothing but shame and resentment, he stared at the too thin woman facing him; the woman who, despite the fact that they lived hundreds of miles apart and hadn't spent a night under the same roof in eighteen months, was still technically his wife. ''Didn't we what?''

''Like each other, at one time. Very much, in fact.''

''*At one time*, Gabriella, and *they* are the operative words,'' he said, steeling himself against the look of naked hope on her face. ''As far as I'm concerned, everything changed after that party you coerced your parents into hosting.''

''You're never going to forgive me for what I did that night, are you? Nothing I can say or do will ever convince you that I never intended to trap you into marriage.''

''No. You stooped to the lowest kind of deceit when you let me believe you'd had previous lovers.''

''I never actually said that.''

''You implied it, more than once.''

''You were a sophisticated, worldly North American and I wanted to impress you—be like the kind of women I thought you admired, instead of a dowdy Hungarian virgin who hadn't the first idea how to please a man.''

''My kind of woman wouldn't have behaved like a tramp.''

''I was desperate, Max—desperately in love with you. And foolish enough to think that giving myself to you might make you love me back.'' She bit her lip and fiddled with the thin gold chain on her wrist; the same gold chain she'd worn when she'd come sneaking through the darkened halls and let herself into his room while everyone else slept, himself included. ''Your time in Budapest was coming to an end. You were making plans to return to Canada, and I couldn't bear the thought of never seeing you again.''

''So you made sure you wouldn't have to by adding lies on top of lies.''

She flushed but her gaze, locked with his, didn't waver. ''No. When I told you I was pregnant, I believed it to be true.''

''How convenient that the ink had barely dried on the marriage certificate before you discovered otherwise.''

She gave a long drawn-out sigh. ''Oh, Max, what's the point of rehashing the past like this? You don't need to spell it out for me again. I already know how you feel.''

''You can't begin to know how I feel,'' he practically snarled, self-disgust sweeping over him afresh at the memory of how the night of the party had ended. Bad enough that he'd been duped into making love to a novice without the final humiliation of opening his door to hustle her back to her own room and coming face-to-face with her father.

''I thought I heard a noise and came to investigate,''

Zoltan had said, his voice trembling with suppressed anger at the sight of his guest standing there in a pair of briefs, and his daughter wearing a transparent negligee that showed off every detail of her anatomy. They couldn't have looked more guilty if they'd been caught stark naked! "I had no idea...*this*...is what I'd find."

Over the years, Max had made his share of mistakes, but none had filled him with the shame flooding over him that night. For the first time in his life, he hadn't been able to look another man in the eye.

"You could have told my father what really happened," Gabriella said now. "You didn't have to leave him with the impression that you'd lured me to your bed."

"Do you really think that would have made him feel any better, when the damage had been done already? His beloved child had been deflowered by a man he'd welcomed into his home and treated like a son. He thought the sun rose and set on you. Still does. What was to be gained by letting him know you'd come to my room uninvited? Why the devil would I have wanted to add to his misery by telling him that?"

"If it makes any difference at all, Max, he knew I was as much to blame as you, and he forgave both of us long ago."

"But I haven't forgiven myself. And I sure as hell haven't forgiven you."

She sank down on the bench at the foot of the bed, and he saw that the slump to her shoulders was not, as he'd first assumed, that she was dejected so much as utterly exhausted. "Then why did you agree to our pretending we're happily married?"

"Because I owe it to him. He's eighty-one years old, his health is failing, and I refuse to send him to his grave a day earlier than necessary by letting him in on the true state of our relationship.''

"He might be old, but he's not blind. If you're going to curl your lip in contempt every time you look at me, and recoil from any sort of physical contact, he'll figure out for himself within twenty-four hours of getting here that we're a long way from living in wedded bliss. And my mother won't take a tenth that long to arrive at the same conclusion.''

"What are you suggesting, my dear?'' he inquired scornfully. "That in order to continue bamboozling them, we practice married intimacy by holding an undress rehearsal tonight?''

Color rode up her neck, a pale apricot tint so delicious it almost made his mouth water. "We don't have to go quite that far, but would it be such a bad idea to practice being civil to one another?''

"Depends on your definition of 'civil.'''

"I won't initiate sex when you're not looking, if that's what's worrying you, Max. Subjecting myself to your outright rejection no longer holds any appeal for me.''

"I'd be more inclined to take that assurance seriously if we were occupying separate beds.''

He waited for the reproaches to follow, a variation on her old theme of *You don't even try to understand how I feel,* followed by a crying spell. Instead, she stood up and faced him, her spine poker-straight and her expression uncharacteristically flat. "I won't dignify that remark by trying to refute it. Believe whatever you like, do whatever you like. For myself, I haven't eaten since early this morning, so I'm going downstairs to fix myself a light supper.''

"You look as if you haven't eaten in a month or more, if you ask me,'' he shot back, irked by her snooty attitude. He wasn't used to being blown off like that, nor was he

about to put up with it. ''And if how you look now is
what being stylishly thin's all about, give me good, old-
fashioned chubby any day of the week.''

''I can't imagine why you'd care how I look, Max, and
I'm certainly not fool enough to think your remark stems
from concerns about my health.'' She brushed a surprisingly badly manicured hand over her outfit, a cotton
blouse and skirt which whispered alluringly over silky
underthings. ''What you apparently aren't able to accept
is that what you prefer in a woman is immaterial. I'd like
it better if we could be cordial with each other because
it's a lot less wearing than being disagreeable. But you
need to accept the fact that I'm long past the stage where
your approval is of the slightest consequence to me.''

If she'd slapped him, he couldn't have been more
stunned. The Gabriella he used to know would have
turned cartwheels through downtown Vancouver during
the afternoon rush hour, if she'd thought it would please
him. ''But you still need me, Gabriella,'' he reminded her.
''Why else are you here?''

''Only for the next two weeks. After that, I'll be as
happy to leave you to wallow in your own misery as
you'll be to see me go.''

Well, hell! Baffled, he shook his head as she stalked
out of the room. This new, underfed edition of the woman
he'd married didn't believe in mincing her words—or give
a flying fig about anything he might say or do as long as
he didn't blow her cover during her parents' visit.

On the surface at least, a lot more than just her dress
size had changed since she'd entered the world of international fashion. Unless it was just another act put on
solely for his benefit, his wife appeared to have developed
a little backbone since she'd flounced out of his life within
six months of forcing her way into it!

*   *   *

underfed version of the hellion he'd been coerced into marrying. It edged her too close to vulnerable, and once he started thinking along those lines, he was in trouble, as he very well knew from past experience.

"I'd appreciate it if you'd wipe your nose on something other than a piece of my clothing," he said, relishing how his voice suddenly breaking the silence almost had her jumping out of her skin.

But when she spun around, the expression on her face made short work of his moment of malicious pleasure. He'd forgotten how truly beautiful she was. In particular, he'd forgotten the impact of her incredible eyes and, suddenly, he was the one struggling for composure as memories of the night they'd first met in her father's house rushed back to haunt him.

"I'd like you to meet my daughter," Zoltan Siklossy had said, as footsteps approached along the flagstone path that ran the width of the front of the rambling old mausoleum of a place.

Max had turned and been transfixed, the impact of the city skyline beyond the Danube forgotten. Backlit by the late May sunset, she'd appeared touched with gold all over, from her pale hair to her honey-tinted skin. Only her eyes had been different, a startlingly light aquamarine, one moment more green than blue, and the next, the other way around.

Fringed with long, curling lashes and glowing with the fire of priceless jewels, they'd inspected him. He'd stared back, mesmerized, and said the first thing that came to mind. "I didn't know Magyars were blond. Somehow, I expected you'd all be dark."

A stupid, thoughtless remark which showed him for the ignorant foreigner he was, but she hadn't taken offence. Instead, she'd come forward and laughed as she took his hand. "Some of us are. But we Hungarians have a mixed ancestry and I, like many others in my country, favor our Finnish heritage."

Though accented, her English was perfect, thanks, he later discovered, to an aunt who'd studied in London years before. Her laughter hung like music in the still, warm evening. Her hand remained in his, light and cool. "Welcome to Budapest, Mr. Logan," she purred. "I hope you'll allow me to introduce you to our beautiful city."

"I'm counting on it," he'd replied, bowled over by her easy self-assurance. Although she looked no more than eighteen, he believed her when she told him she was twenty-seven. Why not? After all, her parents were well into their seventies.

In fact, she'd been just twenty-two and the most conniving creature he'd ever met—not something likely to have changed, he reminded himself now, even if she did look about ready to keel over in a dead faint at being caught off guard.

"I'm not wiping my nose," she whispered shakily, clutching the shirt to her breasts.

He strolled further into the room. "What were you doing, then? Sniffing to find evidence of another woman's perfume? Checking for lipstick stains?"

Something flared in her eyes. Guilt? Shame? Anger? "Should I be? Do you entertain many women here, Max, now that I'm no longer underfoot all the time?"

"If I do, that's certainly none of your business, my dear."

"As long as we're married—"

"You left the marriage."

"But I'm still your wife and whether or not you like it, you're still my husband."

He circled her slowly and noticed that her eyes were

She was shaking inside, her composure on the verge of collapse. Perhaps it was the cruel irony of the setting: the big marriage bed, so invitingly close they could have tumbled onto the mattress together in a matter of seconds if the mood had taken them, juxtaposed beside her finely tuned awareness of his unabashed animosity. Or perhaps it was as simple as his having shown up unexpectedly and taken her by surprise. In any event, she had to get away from him before she burst into tears of pure frustration.

Given that he'd acted as if she was the last person he wanted to spend time with, she didn't expect him to follow her downstairs, but he showed up in the kitchen about five minutes later to announce, "I've taken your luggage up to the bedroom."

"I could have managed it on my own, but thank you anyway," she said, laying out the French bread, cold barbecued chicken, olives, heart of palm salad, and mango salsa she'd purchased at the gourmet deli down the street.

He ambled over to inspect the food. "That chicken looks pretty good."

"Are you hinting you'd like some?" She pulled a chef's knife and fork from the wooden cutlery block next to the countertop cook surface and slid the chicken from its foil-lined bag to a cutting board.

"If you're offering, yes. Thanks." He helped himself to an olive and cast an appraising eye over the changes she'd made in the kitchen. "You've been busy. This place almost looks lived in."

Choosing her words carefully because, although she itched to ask him who owned the apron and hand lotion, she wasn't about to give him another opportunity to tell her to mind her own business, she said, "It had a somewhat unused look, I thought."

"Because I'd stored all the china and stuff you left

behind, you mean? Not everyone appreciates fine things, Gabriella, and knowing how you value yours and would eventually want to reclaim them, it seemed best not to leave them where they might get damaged.''

She managed an offhand shrug. ''But you were always very careful with them…unless, of course, you're referring to…other people?''

''What you're really asking is if I ever let another *woman* loose in here.'' He removed two of the wineglasses she'd arranged in the upper cabinet, then strolled behind her to the refrigerator. She heard him rummaging among its contents, and the clink of a bottle tapping the edge of a shelf before he swung the door closed. ''Well, as it happens, I did. For about a month, beginning the week after you left.''

Hearing him confirm her worst fears shocked Gabriella into betraying the kind of distress she'd sworn she'd never let him witness in her again. ''You mean to say you didn't even wait until the sheets had grown cold before you let another woman into my bed?'' she squeaked, and refusing to vent her outrage where it truly belonged—on him!— she accosted the hapless chicken, wielding the knife with savage intent. ''Why doesn't that surprise me, I wonder?''

''I didn't say that.'' Calmly, he rummaged in one of the drawers for a corkscrew.

''Not in so many words, perhaps, but the implication is clear enough! And so is the evidence!'' Brandishing the two-pronged fork, she gestured at the drawer. *That* drawer! ''I saw what's in there, so don't bother denying it.''

He laughed. ''And what is it that you saw, my dear? A body?''

''Don't you dare laugh at me!'' Hearing her voice threatening to soar to top C, she made a concerted effort to wrestle herself under control. "I found the apron and the hand lotion."

"Well, as long as you didn't also find high heels and panty hose, at least you don't need to worry you're married to a cross-dresser."

"*Worry?* About *you?*" she fairly screeched, aiming such a wild blow at the chicken carcass that a wing detached itself and slid crazily across the counter. "Let me assure you, Max Logan, that I can find better things to occupy my mind!"

Suddenly, shockingly, he was touching her, coming from behind to close one hand hard around her wrist, while the other firmly removed the knife from her grasp and placed it a safe distance away. "Keep that up and you'll be hacking your fingers off next."

"As if you'd care!"

"As a matter of fact, I would. I don't fancy little bits of you accidentally winding up on my plate."

"You heartless, insensitive *ape!*" She spun around, the dismay she'd fought so hard to suppress fomenting into blinding rage. "This is all one huge joke to you, isn't it? You don't care one iota about the hurt you inflict on others with your careless words."

"It's the hurt you were about to inflict on yourself that concerns me." As if he were the most domesticated husband on the face of the earth, he pushed her aside and started carving the chicken. "You're already worried your parents might guess we're not exactly nuts about each another, without your showing up at the airport tomorrow bandaged from stem to stern and giving them extra cause for concern."

"Don't exaggerate. I'm perfectly competent in a kitchen, as you very well know."

He jerked his head at the unopened bottle of Pouilly Fuissé. "Then make yourself useful and uncork that."

"Do it yourself," she snapped, the thought of how quickly he'd taken up with someone else once she'd vacated the scene rankling unbearably. *She* had honored her wedding vows. Why couldn't he have done the same?

"Now who's being unnecessarily hostile?"

She detected marked amusement in his voice. Deciding it was safest to keep her hands busy with something harmless lest she forgot herself so far as to take a meat cleaver to him, she began preparing a tray with plates, cutlery and serviettes. "At least," she said, "I haven't given you grounds for divorce."

"There are some who'd say a wife walking out on her husband is ample grounds for terminating a marriage."

"Then why haven't you taken steps to end ours?"

Finished with the chicken, he turned his attention to the wine. "Because we agreed there was no pressing need to formalize matters, especially given your parents' age, health and religious convictions." He angled a hooded glance her way. "Unless, of course, you've found some urgent reason...?"

"*I'm* not the one who went out shopping for a replacement within a week and had the bad taste to leave his possessions lying around for you to find!"

"Neither am I, Gabriella," he said mildly, his mood improving markedly as hers continued to deteriorate. "The woman you perceive to be such a threat was a fifty-nine-year-old housekeeper I hired to come in on a daily basis to keep the place clean and prepare my meals. The arrangement came to an end by mutual agreement after one month because there wasn't enough to keep her busy and she was a lousy cook. She must have left some of her stuff behind by mistake."

Feeling utterly foolish, Gabriella muttered, "Why didn't you say so in the first place?"

"Because you immediately assumed the worst before I had the chance to explain anything. Now that we've cleared up the misunderstanding, though, I suggest you take that pout off your face, smile for a change, and join me in a toast." He passed a glass of wine to her and lifted the other mockingly. "Here's to us, my dear wife. May your parents be taken in by appearances as easily as you are, and go home convinced their daughter and son-in-law are living in matrimonial clover!"

Twenty minutes later, they sat at the glass-topped patio table on the west side of the terrace. The Pouilly Fuissé stood neck-deep in a silver wine cooler. A hurricane lamp flickered in a sconce on the wall.

Outwardly, they might have been any of a hundred contented couples enjoying the mild, calm evening. Inwardly, however, Gabriella was a mess. Poking her fork into her barely touched meal, she finally braved the question which had been buzzing around in her mind like an angry wasp from the moment he'd misled her into thinking his housekeeper had been a lover. "Have you really never...been with another woman, Max? Since me, I mean?"

"Why don't you look at me when you ask that?" he replied in a hard voice.

Because, she could have told him, if she'd dared, *it hurts too much. You're too beautiful, too sexy, too... everything except what I most want you to be, which is* mine.

"Gabriella?"

Gathering her courage, she lifted her head and took stock of him, feature by feature. He leaned back in his chair, returning the favor with equal frankness, his eyes a dark, direct blue, his gaze steady.

His hair gleamed black as the Danube on a starless night. His skin glowed deep amber against the stark white of his shirt. He shifted one elbow, a slight movement only, but enough to draw attention to the width of his chest and the sculpted line of his shoulders.

Miserably, she acknowledged that everything about him was perfect—and most assuredly not hers to enjoy. She knew that as well as she knew her own name. Devouring him with her eyes brought her nothing but hopeless regret for what once might have been, and painful longing for something that now never could be.

Nonetheless, she forced herself to maintain her steady gaze and say serenely, "Well, I'm looking, Max, so why don't you answer the question? Have you been with anyone else?"

He compressed his gorgeous mouth. Just briefly, his gaze flickered. "You want me to tell you I've lived like a monk since you ran off to pursue a career?"

"I want you to tell me the truth."

He shook his head and stared out to where the last faint show of color from the sunset stained the sea a pale papaya-orange. "No, you don't, Gabriella. As I recall, you're not on very good terms with honesty and I doubt you'd know how to handle it in this instance."

She flinched, his reply shooting straight to her heart like a splinter of glass. Normally the most brutally candid man she'd ever met, his evasion amounted to nothing but an admission of guilt delivered as kindly as he knew how.

Unbidden, the night she'd lost her virginity rose up to haunt her, most particularly the exquisite pleasure he'd given her after he'd recovered from the shock of finding her in his bed and before he realized her duplicity. How practiced he'd been in the art of lovemaking; how knowing and generous and patient. And most of all, how passionate!

Had she really supposed all that masculine virility had lain dormant during her absence, or that he'd feel obligated to honor wedding promises he'd made under duress?

If she had, then she was a fool. Because what right had she to expect either when he'd never professed to love her? When she hadn't a reason in the world to think he might have missed her after she walked out on a marriage which had been a travesty from the start?

But the truth that hurt the most was the realization of how easy it would be to fall under his spell again. His tacit admission that there'd been another woman—possibly even women—was the only thing which pulled her back from the brink. Another minute, a different answer, and she'd have bared her soul to him!

Staggered by her near self-betrayal, she murmured shakily, "I see."

"I suspect not," he said, "but the real question is, does it matter to you, one way or the other?"

"Not in the slightest," she lied, the glass sliver driving deeper into her heart and shattering into a million arrows of pain.

"Should I take your indifference to mean there've been other men in your life?"

"No," she said forthrightly, unwilling to add further deceit to a heap already grown too heavy to bear. "I've never once been unfaithful, nor even tempted."

"Not even by those pretty plastic consorts you team up with in your photo shoots?"

"Certainly not."

He hefted the bottle from the cooler and splashed more wine in their glasses. "Why should I believe you?"

"Because I'm telling the truth."

A mirthless smile played over his mouth. "The way you were when you told me you were pregnant? The way you were when you intimated you'd had a string of lovers before me?"

"I'm not that person anymore."

"Of course you are, Gabriella. People never really change, not deep down inside where it matters. They just pretend to."

"When did you become so cynical, Max?" she asked him sadly. "Did I do that to you?"

"You?" he echoed cuttingly. "Don't flatter yourself!"

The pain inside was growing, roaring through her like a fire feeding on itself until there was nothing left but ashes. For all that she'd promised herself she wouldn't break down in front of him, the scalding pressure behind her eyes signaled how close the tears were, and to her horror she felt her bottom lip quiver uncontrollably.

He noticed. "Don't you dare!" he warned her, in a low, tense voice, starting up from his chair so violently that its metal legs screeched over the pebbled concrete of the terrace. "Don't you *dare* start with the waterworks just because I didn't give you the answers you came looking for! I know that, in the old days, tears always worked for you, but they aren't going to get you what you want this time, at least not from me, so save them for some other fool."

When she first started modeling, there'd been times that she'd found it near impossible to smile for the camera. Days when she'd missed Max so badly, it was all she could do to get out of bed and face another minute without him. Nights when she hadn't been able to sleep for wanting him, and mornings when she'd used so much concealer to hide the shadows under her eyes that her face had felt as if it were encased in mud.

But she'd learned a lot more in the last eighteen months than how to look good on command. She'd learned discipline, and become expert at closing off her emotions behind the remote elegance which had become her trademark.

She called on that discipline now and it did not fail her. The familiar mask slipped into place, not without effort, she had to admit, but well enough that she was able to keep her dignity intact.

"Sorry to disappoint you," she said, rising to her feet with fluid, practiced grace, "but I stopped crying over you so long ago that I've quite forgotten how."

"Don't hand me that. I know what I saw."

She executed a smooth half turn and tossed her parting remark over one provocatively tilted shoulder. "What you saw was a flicker of regret for the mistakes I've made in the past—a passing weakness only because weeping does terrible things to the complexion, especially when one's face is one's fortune. Good night, Max. I've worked hard enough for one day, so if you're feeling energetic, you might try loading our plates and cutlery into the dishwasher—always assuming, of course, that you remember how to open it. Oh, and one more thing. Please don't disturb me when you decide to turn in. I really do need to catch up on my beauty sleep."

CHAPTER THREE

IF THERE'D been any plausible alternative, he'd have spent the night anywhere but in the same room with her. Since he didn't have that option, he gave her a good two hours' head start before he went up to join her.

She was asleep—or pretending to be—perched so close to the far edge of the mattress, all it would have taken was a gust of air from the open window to topple her to the floor. Being scrupulously careful to leave enough space between them to accommodate a third body, he inched carefully between the sheets on his side of the bed.

Her breathing was light and regular, which made him think perhaps she really was out cold, and eventually he must have dozed off as well because the next thing he knew, it was four in the morning and somehow, while they slept, they'd gravitated toward each other. She lay spooned against him, with her back pressed to his front.

She was wearing a soft cotton nightshirt and it was either very short to begin with, or it had ridden a long way up from where it was supposed to be. He knew because his hand had found its way over her hip so that his fingers were splayed across the bare skin of her warm, taut little belly. A few inches higher and it would have been her breast he was fondling, a realization which put his nether regions onto instant and standing alert.

She stirred. Stretched a little, like a lean, pedigreed cat. Rolled over until she was half facing him. In the opaque light of predawn, he saw her eyes drift open. Then, as awareness chased away sleep, she grew very still and very, very wary.

For about half a second, they stared at one another, then simultaneously rolled away from each other. She retreated to her side of the bed again and he slunk off to the bathroom, telling himself his problem was that he had to pee.

It hadn't been the problem then, and it wasn't the problem three hours later when he found himself suffering the same physical reaction all over again at the sight of his wife—his *estranged* wife! he reminded himself for about the fiftieth time—presiding over the breakfast table and looking even more delicious than the food on his plate.

"Are you coming with me to the airport this afternoon?" she asked him, her tone suggesting she'd be hard-pressed to notice whether he did or not.

Regarding her over the top of the morning paper, Max had found himself wondering if there was something in the bottled drinking water she favored which allowed her to remain so cool and aloof, when it was all he could do not to break out in a sweat at the thought of the night just past.

"I wasn't planning on it," he said, trying to match her nonchalance. "It's been a while since your parents last saw you. I imagine they'd like to have you to themselves for a while."

Nonchalant? What a laugh! He sounded as stilted as a rank amateur trying out for a spot on some third-rate TV commercial! Not that she noticed. She simply gave that impassive little shrug of hers, waved the coffeepot under his nose, and said, "May I give you refill?"

He didn't know what time she'd slipped out of bed, but it must have been early. Not only had she ground fresh coffee beans and made fresh fruit syrup for his waffles, she'd also found time to repair her manicure. Her nails gleamed pale rose against the brushed steel of the carafe.

As for the rest of her…oh, brother! Sleek and elegant in a floor-length, blue-and-purple patterned thing which was neither bathrobe nor dress but something in between; with not a hair out of place and looking as fresh as the morning dew, she gave new meaning to the term "picture perfect."

"No," he said, slapping down the paper and shoving back from the table. "I have to get going." *Quickly, before his imagination ran riot feeding itself on memories of the night before and he made a further fool of himself!*

"When do you expect to be back?"

"As late as possible. That way, there'll be less risk of us screwing up the charade."

Her eyes, pure turquoise in the morning light, pinned him in an unwavering stare. "But you *will* join us for dinner?"

"Of course. That's part of our arrangement."

"And you will remember it's going to take more than just your putting in an appearance to carry all this off?"

"How much more?" he asked, more to annoy her than because he cared about her answer.

"As much as it takes," she said.

The remark stayed with him all day, a major but not, he was surprised to discover, unpleasant distraction. By the time he let himself into the penthouse late that afternoon, his dread at what the next two weeks might bring had been diluted by a peculiar anticipation. Damned if he understood why, but having Gabriella underfoot again charged his energy like nothing else had in months!

Stopping by his office to drop off his briefcase, he stood a moment at the partially open sliding doors, unnoticed by the threesome seated a few yards away at the table on the roof garden. He didn't need to understand the language to recognize a certain tension in the conversation taking place between his wife and his in-laws.

Still strikingly handsome despite failing health, Zoltan sat ramrod-straight in one of the cushioned chairs, his dark eyes watchful as Gabriella replied to something her mother had said. Maria Siklossy, a little heavier than she'd been two years ago, leaned forward, consternation written all over her face.

Gabriella, polished and perfect as ever in a dress which he'd have called washed-out green but which probably deserved a fancier description, traced her finger over the condensation beading her glass. From her stream of fluent Hungarian, only three words had meaning for Max: Tokyo, Rome, and Vancouver.

He didn't have to be a rocket scientist to figure she was trying to justify keeping three addresses while her husband made do with one, and that neither Zoltan nor Maria was buying any of it. Loosening his tie and rolling back the cuffs of his shirt, Max waded in to do his bit toward easing the old couple's concerns.

If the relief that washed over Gabriella's face when she saw him was any indication, he'd timed his entrance perfectly. Springing up from her chair like a greyhound let loose on the racetrack, she exclaimed, "You're home, Max! I didn't expect you until later."

"Missed you too much to stay away any longer, baby cakes," he said, immersing himself in his appointed role with gleeful relish.

Her mouth fell open. *"Baby cakes?"*

The opportunity was too good to pass up. Sweeping her into his arms, he planted a lengthy kiss on those deliciously parted lips. She smelled of wood violets and tasted of wild cherries.

Her eyes, wide open and startled, stared into his. Briefly, she resisted his embrace, then sort of collapsed against him. Her small firm breasts pressed against his chest. Their tips grew hard. Her cheeks flushed pink.

Fleetingly, he considered wallowing in the moment, if only to enjoy her disconcertion. Why not? He hadn't asked to be cast as the romantic hero in her little production, but since it had been thrust upon him anyway, he might as well get his kicks wherever he happened to find them.

At least, that's how he tried rationalizing his actions. But, just like the night before and the morning after, another part of his anatomy had different ideas and showed itself ready to play its part with animated enthusiasm. So, reluctantly, before she realized the state she'd reduced him to, he backed off slightly but kept her anchored next to him as he turned to greet her parents.

"Good to see you again, Zoltan," he said, shaking his father-in-law's hand. "You, too, Maria. Welcome to Canada."

He bent to kiss her cheek, peripherally aware of the tears in her eyes as she held his face between her palms and murmured approving little Hungarian noises, but most of his attention remained focused on Gabriella. Her waist, half spanned by his hand, felt shockingly frail. Though he didn't test the theory there and then, he was pretty sure he could have counted every rib through her clothes.

Pasting on his most affable expression to disguise his concern, he said, "So, what's everyone drinking?"

"Iced tea," Gabriella murmured faintly. "Would you like some?"

He smiled into her eyes which had a sort of glazed look to them. "We can celebrate your parents' arrival with something more exciting than that, surely? How about champagne—unless you'd prefer something stronger, Zoltan?''

''A glass of wine would be pleasant.''

He might have temporarily quieted Maria's suspicions, but he had a long way to go with the old man, Max realized. Zoltan was watching him like a hawk about to dine on a very fat mouse.

''Fine. I'll go do the honors.'' Suddenly feeling about as uncomfortable as he had the night he'd been discovered almost stark naked in the Siklossy palace, Max took off around the southeast corner of the terrace to the kitchen entrance, and left Gabriella to clear the iced tea paraphernalia off the table.

She followed soon after and plunked the tray of glasses on the kitchen counter with a clatter. ''What was *that* all about?'' she demanded, her color still high.

''Being a good host,'' he said, knowing damn well she wasn't referring to his suggesting champagne, but deciding to play dumb anyway. ''What are you serving for dinner?''

''Broiled salmon. But another stunt like the one you just pulled, and you might find yourself being the one shoved in the oven!''

''Your English gets better all the time, Gabriella,'' he remarked, hauling a nineteen ninety-seven Pol Roger out of the refrigerator and inspecting the label. ''Very idiomatic indeed. I'm impressed.''

''Well, I'm not! Who did you think you were fooling just now with that ridiculous exhibition?''

''Your mother, certainly. And if your father still has any doubts about us, I'll make short work of them, as well.''

''Not with a repeat performance like the one you just put on, I assure you.''

"Are you saying you didn't enjoy our little exchange?"

"Certainly not!" But she blushed an even deeper shade of pink.

"Keep telling fibs like this, Gabriella," he informed her genially, "and your nose will grow so long, you'll never model again. Come on, admit it. You practically fainted with pleasure when I kissed you."

"That wasn't pleasure, it was shock."

"Shock?" He rotated the bottle of champagne until the cork slipped out with a subdued and well-bred pop. "I fail to see why. Weren't you the one who lectured me just this morning on the need to act the part of besotted husband?"

"*Devoted,* Max, not besotted, and certainly not... *lecherous!* The next time you feel disposed to show your affection, don't get so carried away." She piled goose liver pâté and crackers on a square slab of glass which he now realized was some sort of serving dish but which he'd been using as a doorstop, dressed the whole works up with bits of parsley, and arranged a fan of cocktail napkins on the side. "And don't ever call me 'baby cakes' again! I've never heard anything so ridiculous in my life."

Scowling, he watched her march off. Blast the woman, anyway! She was as contrary as hell, and damned if he could read her mood from one minute to the next. Just when he thought he had a fix on her, she did an about-face that made him wonder if he'd ever scratch below her surface and find out what was really going on in her head.

Dinner was a never-ending nightmare, a minefield of disaster waiting to explode. Questions which would have been a breeze to answer if a person had nothing to hide required the most delicate handling, and the effort to appear happy and at ease taxed Gabriella to the limit.

As for Max—oh, she'd have cheerfully throttled *him*, if it weren't that he wasn't worth serving time in jail for! Smiling, urbane, doing and saying all the right things, without a single false step. Treating her mother as if she were a queen, deferring to her father in the choice of wines with the meal. And all the time sending her, his wife, glances brimming with mischief. Putting on a show that went above and beyond anything she'd had in mind when she'd persuaded him to take part in an undertaking which was turning out to be much more complicated than even she'd bargained for.

Her parents might have been charmed at the way he held out her chair at the dining table then, when she was least expecting it, leaned over and kissed the side of her neck, but she'd been so flustered she'd almost knocked the silver sauceboat of Béarnaise into her father's lap!

By the time she'd brought herself under control again, he was up to further mischief, flirting disgracefully with her mother. "Maria, I'm hurt you'd even ask!" he practically crooned, his sexy, Canadian baritone sliding the length of the table to wrap itself around Gabriella's senses like rich velvet. "Of course I'll be booking time off from work to take you sight-seeing. In fact, it occurred to me you might even like to travel a bit farther afield, once you're over your jet lag. What do you think, Gabriella? Shall we take them to Banff and show them the Rockies? I could charter a private jet to avoid the lengthy drive."

"What do I think?" she hissed, the minute she got him alone in the kitchen between courses. "I think you've lost your mind, that's what! Who are you trying to impress with all your talk of chartering a jet?"

"Why, who else but your parents, dear heart," he said

equably, attempting to feign injured innocence and succeeding only in looking as crafty as a wolf on the prowl. "I'm just trying to be helpful and live up to my end of our bargain."

"Stop trying so hard," she fairly spat.

He put down the second bottle of wine he'd just taken from the refrigerator and made for the swing door connecting to the dining room. "Okay. I'll go tell them I've had second thoughts and Banff in July isn't such a good idea. Too many flowers, too much sunshine—and too much you."

"You'll do no such thing, Max Logan!"

He paused with one hand poised to push open the door. "Hell, Gabriella, make up your mind. Do you want my help in getting through the next two weeks and sending your folks home happy, or not?"

"I want your help," she said feebly. The trouble was, she wanted a whole lot more than that, and being near him again—having him so close that she could smell his aftershave and the special scent of his skin and his hair, and the soap he used in the shower…oh, they filled her senses so thoroughly, she could barely think straight.

She wasn't completely stupid, though. She'd seen the way he'd sidled out of bed when he'd found her cuddled up next to him during the night. Heavens, he hadn't been able to get away from her fast enough! And when he'd returned, the way he'd hunched his back toward her and yanked the sheet up around his shoulders had told her plainly enough that he could hardly wait to have the bed to himself again. How would they ever keep up appearances if they were flung together all day while they acted as tour guides for her parents?

"But don't you find it hard on your marriage, with your wife away so much of the time?" her father was asking, when Gabriella finally pulled herself together enough to return to the dining room with the apricot torte dessert.

It was precisely the kind of question she dreaded, and almost enough to make her flee to the kitchen again.

Max, however, didn't turn a hair. "Gabriella wanted to pursue a career. I didn't see it as my right to interfere with that."

"But you're her husband!" Her father gave the table a gentle but emphatic thump that set the ice in the water goblets to chiming like little bells.

"Her husband, yes, but not her keeper, Zoltan."

"It would not do for me. In my day, being a wife was all the career a woman could want."

Feeling obliged to contribute something to the discussion, Gabriella set the torte on the table and, resting her hand on Max's shoulder in a splendid display of marital unity, said, "Times have changed, Father. And things are different in North America."

"Different, perhaps, but not, I think, better. You belong exactly where you stand right now—at your husband's side."

"It's a long commute from Rome or Tokyo to Vancouver, Zoltan," Max said lightly. "The camera loves Gabriella, and a certain amount of separation comes with the territory when a man finds himself married to a model as much in demand as my wife's become." He turned a disgracefully angelic look Gabriella's way. "Isn't that right, my love?"

"Yes," she murmured. "Absolutely."

"And then there's her age to think about," he went on. "She's not getting any younger and this is definitely a young woman's game. She might as well make the most of it before her looks start to go."

Oh, the rogue! It was all she could do not to push his

face into his dessert! "I'm only just twenty-four, for heaven's sake!"

"Is that what you're telling people these days?" He smiled at her benignly, before switching his attention back to her father. "Ah well, even you must agree that it's the quality of time spent together that counts, Zoltan."

"Those terrible newspapers say you live apart because you cannot live together," her mother put in, finally giving voice to the one area of her marriage Gabriella most dreaded having to explain.

As if he felt the tremor that passed over her, Max covered Gabriella's hand with his and gave it a squeeze. "Which is precisely why they're terrible, Maria. They thrive on sensationalism, not truth."

"Even so, how can there be babies, if...?"

"I'm sure Gabriella will have babies," he said smoothly. "In time."

What he didn't say was that, if she did, they wouldn't be his. He'd made it abundantly clear he wasn't interested in fathering children with her. "I'd throw a party, except there's nothing in any of this to celebrate," he'd said bitterly, when she confessed she'd been mistaken about the pregnancy. "Kids deserve parents committed to something a bit more compelling than the fact that one felt obligated to marry the other. There won't be any more such *mistakes*, Gabriella."

He'd made sure that there weren't. Whenever he came to her bed after that, he brought a condom with him.

"Don't wait too long," her mother said wistfully. "Zoltan and I are no longer young, and I would so love to hold a grandchild in my arms before I die."

Gabriella knew that the quaver in her mother's voice and the pain in her eyes meant she was remembering the son who'd died during the revolution, and it was all she could do not to cry out, *I'll give you a grandchild, Mama, I will! A little boy called Stefan, just like my brother!*

But there was a limit to how far she'd take the duplicity. Being near him again left her convinced there'd never be any other man for her but Max, and she would not make promises she knew she couldn't keep.

"I don't know that I can do this after all," she told him, once her parents, worn out from the long journey, had made an early night of it. "Two weeks of pretending, of telling lies... Max, it's turning out to be so much harder than I thought it would be, and we still have thirteen days to go!"

They were in the kitchen again, and she was putting away the last of the dishes they'd used at dinner. The kitchen seemed to be the place they always did the most talking, perhaps because it was the least intimate room in the penthouse and so the one least likely to stir up pointless longings.

Not that Max suffered from any of *them,* as his next comment proved. "Time was that lying came so easily to you, you never gave it a second thought," he said, standing in the open doorway to the terrace and looking out at the brightly lit city skyline. "Guess you're a bit out of practice, my dear."

For a moment, she stared at him. At the white dress shirt lying smoothly across his big shoulders, at the sun-dark nape of his neck and his thick, black hair, and the long elegant line of his spine.

Just so had she first come across him: from behind, in the garden at her parents' home in Budapest. She'd known before he turned around and she saw his face that he'd be more beautiful than any man she'd ever met. Had recognized, within five minutes of looking into his blue, blue eyes, that she was in love with him and would remain so for the rest of her life.

Silly, girlish notions that had no bearing on the way things were today! Swallowing the tears which seemed never to be far from the surface where he was concerned, she said bitterly, "Perhaps because I no longer need to lie in order to find acceptance from the people around me."

He spared her a brief, backward glance. "Has it been worth it, Gabriella—all the fame and fortune you've won? Have they been worth the price you've paid for them?"

"What price? I had nothing to lose to begin with."

"You had a husband and a marriage, things you once claimed you wanted more than anything else on earth."

"Those I still have."

"In name only."

She dried the last of the hand-washed wineglasses— slender, lovely things, delicately crafted. "That was your choice, Max. I was prepared to stay and try to make our marriage work."

His laugh told her what he thought of that reply. "You were gone within six months. I'd hardly call that hanging in over the long haul!"

"And you did nothing to stop me."

"Would you have stayed, if I'd tried?"

"No," she said, fighting to keep her voice steady because, by then, she was losing the battle with the tears which blurred her vision and turned the wineglass she still held into an iridescent bubble. "Because you didn't want me. You've never wanted me."

He'd always hated it when she cried and more than once had accused her of turning on the waterworks as a means of getting her own way. If he realized she was crying now, he'd say something cruel like, *Save the tears for someone who cares.* Or worse, *No, I never did. Isn't it nice that we at last agree on something?*

Determined not to give him the satisfaction, she swiped at her eyes with a corner of the tea towel and, in doing so, knocked the wineglass out of her hand. It hit the granite counter with a brutal crash.

"Oh!"

The sound of splintering crystal, almost musical compared to her wail of dismay, brought Max spinning around to see what had happened. Bending her head to hide her misery, she began scooping the fragments into a tidy heap and found that the stem of the glass, still intact, had snapped cleanly off the bowl. Such a pity!

"Watch what you're doing!" He crossed the kitchen floor in rapid strides and pulled her hands away from the debris. "For Pete's sake, Gabriella, you're dripping blood all over everything."

Amazed, she stared at the thin line of scarlet beads forming along the side of her finger. How was it possible that she'd sustained such a wound, yet felt no pain? And if one part of her could remain numb to injury, why couldn't another? Why did the raging ache in her heart keep getting worse?

Unable to face the answer, she took what was left of the bowl of the glass and tried placing it on top of the severed stem. "Perhaps if I keep all the pieces, it can be put back together again. I know they do marvelous things these days to repair broken treasures."

For all that she tried to control herself, her words came out on a sob and the infernal tears broke loose and rolled off the end of her nose. Oh, what a mess she must look, and how repelled he must be at the sight of her!

Oddly, though, his voice was full of something other than the contempt she expected. It was warm and rather kind. "I'm afraid it'd take a miracle, honey. This thing's past repair. Let's just sweep the whole mess into the garbage can and forget it."

"But it's one of twelve we received as a wedding gift, Max," she whimpered. "Now the set's incomplete."

"Well, that's a shame, but you ought to know by now there are some things that can't be mended, no matter how much you wish they could be."

"Sort of like us, when you think about it," she said wistfully. "We're supposed to be a couple, but we're not. There's no bond to hold us together."

Dear heaven, where was her pride? She sounded as plaintive as a tragedy queen about to breathe her last!

Of course, he noticed. "Let's not turn a minor accident into a melodrama!" he said, hurriedly putting the safety of the kitchen counter between them as if he feared she might fling herself at his feet and beg him to toss her a crumb of affection.

If nothing else, his unsympathetic about-face snapped her out of the well of self-pity she'd been about to drown in. She grabbed a tissue from the box on the shelf next to the telephone desk, folded it around her finger in a makeshift bandage, then took another and used it to sweep the shards of glass into the waste bin. "You're absolutely right, for once. Some things are broken beyond repair."

Including our marriage, and the sooner I face up to that, the better off I'll be!

He was watching her, his expression inscrutable. "If it were my business to begin with, I'd tell you you look like hell. You sure you're feeling okay?"

It took some effort, but she managed to brush off his concern with an airy, "Now who's making something out of nothing?"

"I'm not talking about your finger," he said, coming

back to where she stood and tilting up her chin so that she had no choice but to return his steady gaze. "It's the rest of you that has me wondering. Do you get enough rest?"

"Since you mention it, as a rule, yes. But the last few weeks, and the last couple of days in particular, have been stressful. Contrary to what you might choose to think, I don't enjoy deceiving my parents."

"Then why not tell them the truth and have done with it?"

"Oh, Max, you already know why!" She sighed and massaged her temples wearily. "You can't have missed how much they've aged in the last two years, especially my father. Divorce goes against everything he and my mother believe in, and it would kill him to learn our marriage is a failure. It would be different if they lived on our doorstep and could see for themselves that life goes on even when a couple breaks up, but they're half a world away geographically, and belong to a different era. They don't understand the modern way of doing things and I don't have it in me to destroy their illusions. What's the harm in letting them think our marriage is strong like theirs?"

"Plenty, if it has you tied up in knots like this."

"It's just a headache. I get them sometimes when I'm under pressure."

Turning her around, he began kneading the tense muscles in her shoulders. The warmth of his touch, the strength of his fingers probing her flesh to seek out and relieve each sore spot, left her sagging. She leaned both hands on the counter. Her neck drooped, unable to support the weight of her head. Her legs turned to jelly.

She was wearing a low-backed dress held up by a halter strap. He pressed his thumbs lightly over each exposed vertebra. His breath a caress at her ear, he asked, "Is this helping?"

His magician's touch was draining her, leaving her weak as a kitten. She could barely summon the energy to say, "More than you can...begin to imagine."

Methodically, his thumbs traveled lower. She heard the subdued purr of her zipper opening. Felt his palms radiating from her spine to encompass her ribs in soothing, ever-widening circles, until his fingertips almost brushed the sides of her breasts.

Soothing? Oh, who was she deceiving this time? Electrifying was what it was. Thrilling. The most sensuous, drugging delight she'd ever known!

She felt his breath in her hair and then, astoundingly, his lips, warm and damp, at her ear. His kiss, soft as a snowflake, deadly as an earthquake, thundered to the inner depths of her soul.

What began as a moan of pure pleasure evolved into a drawn-out murmuring of his name. "M...a...xxx...!"

She should have kept her mouth shut. The sound of her voice jarring the outer silence broke whatever spell he'd been weaving. The kiss ended. Abruptly, he removed his hands, drew up her zipper and stepped away. "Ten minutes in the hot tub would do you more good than this," he said harshly.

Of course, she knew ahead of time that the question was pointless, but she asked it anyway. "Will you join me?"

Already halfway to the front hall, he flung his reply over his shoulder. "No, thanks. I brought work home and should get to it. Hope you sleep better tonight."

How *dare* he offer her a glimpse of paradise, then, when she was almost fainting with longing, snatch it away again? Waspish with disappointment, she snapped,

"There'll be a better chance of that if you wear pajamas to bed."

That stopped his flying exit! "How do you know I didn't last night?" he said.

"Your torso wasn't covered when I woke up this morning—not by the bed linen, and not by anything else."

"Why, shame on you, Gabriella!" he chided. "Were you spying on me while I slept?"

"Spying, my left foot! I'm not blind, Max, and a man your size is pretty hard to miss."

She should have been more specific and said *A man with shoulders the size of yours is hard to miss,* because he turned to her, a grin inching over his face, and she knew exactly what he was referring to when he said, "I'm going to take that as a compliment, my dear."

She refused to blush and she refused to look away. Instead, determined to have the last word for a change *and* pay him back for his earlier remark about her age, she said, "You'd be a lot better off going on a diet. I can't say I paid too much attention, but it looked to me as if you're running to fat."

Considering she had yet to set eyes on a more gorgeously put-together specimen than Max Logan—in *every* respect!—her parting shot was nothing less than a bald-faced lie. And the way his laughter followed her as she fled past him and scuttled up the stairs told her he knew it as well as she did.

Once inside the bedroom, she collapsed into a chair, her heart pitter-pattering like an overwound toy. With care and a lot of luck, she might make it safely through the next thirteen days. But the nights?

Dear Lord, the nights were a different matter altogether!

CHAPTER FOUR

THE next several days passed uneventfully enough. She took her parents sight-seeing and shopping, and was glad when they confessed they'd find traveling further afield too exhausting. In truth, she preferred a less-hectic pace herself and was content to spend quiet hours alone with them.

It was a happy, serene time, full of sunlight and laughter. And most of all, of love. It flowed over and around Gabriella from every quarter—except for the space occasionally occupied by her husband. His little corner exuded pure, malevolent mischief!

Then, on the Thursday, he phoned just as she was cleaning up the kitchen after serving her parents a late breakfast. "Check the society column in today's newspaper," he said shortly, obviously so put out by whatever it contained that he felt disinclined to preface the order with anything as civil as "Good morning." "Your arrival in town hasn't gone unnoticed. Better be prepared for the rest of the media to horn in on the fact. My assistant's already fielding calls at the office."

"Interviews go with the territory in my profession," Gabriella replied breezily. "I've grown quite accustomed to handling them."

"No doubt. But how comfortable are you going to be if someone shoves a microphone in your face and asks if there's any truth to the rumors that our marriage is in trouble? From the way you coped the other night when your mother aired the same question, it's my guess you'll have a tough time coming up with any sort of convincing answer. Where are your mom and dad, by the way? Not listening in, I hope?''

''No, Max,'' she informed him, matching his sarcasm and then some. ''It would never occur to them to eavesdrop on a private conversation. They're far too well bred. If you must know, my father's in the pool, and my mother's being a good wife and watching to make sure he doesn't overdo it. As for your other concern, should a reporter approach me and want details of my relationship with you, I'll say what I always say—that my private life isn't open for discussion.''

''Dear heart,'' he sneered, ''it's already under the public microscope. You show up after months away and there's no loving husband at the airport to meet your flight. Instead, you're caught on camera looking as grim as if you've just been handed a life sentence behind bars. Then you're seen hitting all the high spots around town in the company of two elderly guests, but still no sign of the errant husband in tow. Face it, Gabriella, the situation calls for a little damage control.''

She recognized from the take-charge tone in his voice that he already had a plan in mind. ''And how do you propose we go about it?''

''Lunch,'' he said. ''You, me, and the parents, at my club. This morning's columnist's always hanging around the place looking for gossip, so we might as well hand him his daily quota up front and save him the trouble of having to do any more speculating. I'll send a car to collect you at eleven-thirty.''

The car, as she might have expected, was not a plain taxi as she'd been using, but a long, black limousine with a uniformed driver at the wheel. Except for his raised eyebrows, which might have indicated approval or criti-

cism of such extravagance, her father made no comment.
Her mother, though, was charmed.

"So lovely," she breathed, sinking into the luxurious
leather upholstery, her air of appreciation for fine things
harking back to happier days when being a member of
the Hungarian aristocracy had gone hand in hand with
wealth. "Elegant and dignified, the way life used to be
for us, before."

She didn't need to elaborate. Gabriella had heard that
same qualification from the time she'd been born.
Everything about today was compared to the way things
had been *before the troubles.* Some people had adjusted
to the changes they brought; her parents, especially her
mother, had not. They had lost too much, including a son.

Max was waiting outside when the car drew up under
the canopied entrance to his club. Before the driver had
a chance to do the honors, he opened the door and taking
Gabriella by the hand, ushered her out. Not about to be
thrown into confusion by another of his phony displays
of affection, she gave him a hurried peck on the cheek,
then immediately stepped a safe distance away before in-
quiring, "Have we kept you waiting long?"

"Not at all, my love." It was another sunny day and
he was wearing dark glasses, so she couldn't see the expression in his eyes, but the thread of amusement in his
voice and that ironic endearment told her he'd noticed
how she'd fairly bolted away from him. "I got here only
a couple of minutes ago myself."

He'd reserved a table overlooking the harbor and preor-
dered from the club's excellent wine cellar. But neither
the vintage Pinot Gris nor the cold prawns vinaigrette
quite managed to dim Gabriella's awareness of his knee
pressed too close to hers under the table, or the way he'd
ever so casually manage to nudge her shoulder or brush

his fingers against hers under one pretext after another. *Pass me the rolls, will you, Gabriella? Here, my love, have a little more dressing. What do you think, sweetheart, shall we order strawberries for dessert?*

It was all for show, she knew, and she supposed she ought to be grateful that he was working so hard to maintain the myth of husbandly devotion. But his proximity, close enough that she could feel his heat, see the new beard growth already stippling his jaw, and inhale the scent of his aftershave, was driving her to distraction.

Stop touching me! she wanted to scream. *Stop stealing the air from my lungs and making my heart flop around like a landed fish!*

Of course, she did no such thing. Even if the society columnist seated two tables away hadn't been mentally photographing every nuance and gesture so avidly that it was a wonder he didn't fall off his chair, her parents' unalloyed relief at such an exhibition of marital bliss made it worth what it cost her to suffer in silence. Only later, after Max had insisted on taking the afternoon off to spend a little more time with them, did she realize she hadn't begun to pay nearly dearly enough.

They'd come out of the art gallery and were headed back to where the limousine waited when her mother paused to admire a display of diamond rings in the shop window of a well-known jeweler. "Such lovely things," she sighed, "but not, I think, as beautiful as your wedding band which I notice you are not wearing, Gabriella."

At a loss—for how could she say, *I left it behind when I walked away from my marriage and don't know what my husband did with it?*—Gabriella turned helplessly to Max. "When Gabriella's traveling, we keep it in the safe at home," he said. "That way, there's less chance of it being lost or stolen."

"But she is not traveling now," her father said pointedly. "And it seems to me that a wife should always wear the symbol of her marriage, especially when she is away from her husband, as a reminder of what is most important in her life."

As if the mere idea that Gabriella could easily forget him was too funny for words, Max laughed and pressed a bell set discreetly beside the outer door of the shop. "Since you're taken with the things in the window, Maria, come inside and meet the man who created them. Gio Salvatore's an old acquaintance of mine and I'm sure he'll be delighted to show you other examples of his work."

The atmosphere inside the shop, so hushed it was almost reverent, reminded Gabriella of a church. The sleek glass display cases, lined with opulent black velvet and made all the more dramatic with artfully concealed spotlights, provided a perfect setting for the finely crafted work on show.

Like the decor, Gio Salvatore himself was a man of tasteful restraint. Immaculately turned out in a navy three-piece suit, his platinum-silver hair rivaling that of some of his creations, he emerged from a back room when informed of his visitors, and greeted Max with obvious pleasure.

"I'm honored," he said, gesturing expansively to Gabriella and her parents after the introductions were made. "Please, if there's a piece you would like to examine more closely, you have only to ask."

Max, all benign smiles and easy authority, saw her mother's reluctance and urged her closer to the showcases. "Don't be shy, Maria. If something takes your fancy, try it on."

"No," she said. "I would like to look, that's all."

But her gaze lingered on the lovely pieces and Gabriella

knew she was remembering the things they'd been forced to sell in order to effect basic repairs to their home and country estate. ''The reason,'' her father had explained, when Gabriella at ten had asked why her mama never wore the diamond necklace and pendant earrings shown in the portrait of her hanging over the mantel in the main salon, ''is that they are luxuries we can no longer afford. Although we are members of the old aristocracy and the property we lost for so long has finally been returned to us, we are, like many of our friends, penniless.''

Since she'd found success, Gabriella had tried many times to make their lives easier, but her parents had steadfastly refused to let her give them money. It had taken all her considerable powers of persuasion to make them accept the gift of airline tickets so that they could visit her in Canada—and only then, she suspected, because they believed their traveling years were coming to an end and they couldn't bear to pass up the chance to see how she lived in her adopted country.

''Mama,'' she whispered now, ''it would make me very happy if you would please choose something and let me buy it for you as a souvenir of your visit.''

''What do such fine things matter?'' her mother replied, stroking her hand. ''To know that you and Max are so much in love is worth more to me than all the jewels in the world.''

Had old age left the mother more susceptible to being hoodwinked, or was it that the daughter had become so adept at deceit that she could fool even her own parent? The question shamed Gabriella and left her eyes so hot with unshed tears that she had to turn away.

Like a watchful bodyguard, Max materialized at her side. ''Sweetheart,'' he said with uncommon gentleness, bracing her with an arm around her shoulders and forcibly removing her from her mother's shrewd observation, "there's a piece over here that you have to see. If it weren't that the gold work is a little too much for a neck as slender as yours, it might almost have been especially for you."

Shielding her with his body, he steered her to the other side of the shop and pointed out an emerald-cut aquamarine pendant set in a gold filigree chain studded with small but exquisite diamonds.

He meant to be kind; to divert attention away from her distress and give her the chance to recover herself. But tenderness and compassion were not his habit with her and she was in too fragile a state to accept them with equanimity. The aquamarine flared with light, its edges fractured into prisms of brilliant fire by the tears seeping from her eyes.

"This won't do," he murmured, producing a handkerchief and passing it to her. "You're going to give the game away if you keep on like this."

"My mother thinks we're in love, Max!" she snuffled. "How can I let her remain in ignorance?"

"Perhaps you can't. Perhaps this is too great a deception, even for you. But before you decide to lay out the truth, consider what hearing it will cost her. Are you really prepared to make her pay that high a price, Gabriella?"

She drew in a shuddering breath. "No. Whether that might have been the right thing to do at the beginning is beside the point. We've set out along this path, and it's too late to turn back now. I just didn't know I'd find it so…so…."

Painful being near you. Knowing we're going through the motions only when what I most wish is that the feelings between us were real instead of make-believe.

"Difficult?" he suggested, noticing her hesitation.

"My goodness, Gabriella, can it be that your high-profile success has forced you to develop a conscience? Or is all this breast-beating just another attempt to make a fool of me?"

Thanks to his thoughtfulness, she'd almost managed to bring her emotions under control, but the sudden about-face to his usual self unraveled her so thoroughly that she wanted to slap him. Hard!

She refrained, not because it would have laid bare their mockery of a marriage but because, regardless of whatever mistakes she'd made in the past, she *was* a Siklossy by blood, and she refused to let him reduce her to behaving like a savage. "Oh!" she muttered instead, flexing her fingers convulsively. "Just when I begin to find myself almost liking the man I married, you remind me what a wasted effort it is!"

Surprisingly, he didn't come back with an equally searing reply. If anything, he looked almost subdued. "I guess I asked for that," he said quietly. "My remark was uncalled for and I apologize. It looks as if we're both finding this more of a strain than we bargained for. Why don't I go keep your parents entertained while you compose yourself? When you feel ready to face them, I'll phone for the car to pick you up here and take you home."

"You're not coming with us?"

Don't be foolish, Gabriella! It's better that he doesn't.

"No." He glanced at his watch. "I need to get back to the office. And before I forget, I won't be home for dinner tonight."

"Oh, Max, why not? I was counting on you to be there!"

"Because," he informed her severely, "to accommodate you, I canceled a previous lunch engagement and have had to reschedule it for this evening."

Unreasonably disappointed, she said, "Oh, really? And I suppose the next thing you're going to tell me is that it's business?"

He stared at her and waited a heartbeat before replying coldly, "It's certainly not *your* business, Gabriella."

Something about the way he turned aside her question reminded her of her first night back at the penthouse…

Have you been with another woman, Max? I want to know the truth.

I doubt you could handle it in this instance…

"Why not?" she flared with sudden disquieting fury. "Because you're meeting the woman you as good as admitted you've been seeing while I was away?"

She could no more miss the grimace of distaste that crossed his face at her outburst, than she could suppress the demons of jealousy which she'd allowed to goad her into asking such a question in the first place. "Well, naturally!" he said, his voice and eyes chilly as a midwinter's day. "Our assignations always take place in my office. I usually have my wicked way with her on my desk once everyone else has vacated the premises. Of course, we have to be careful we don't get caught by the night cleaning staff, but that just adds a bit of extra spice to the whole business. Is that what you wanted to hear?"

"No," she said, so mortified she couldn't look at him. "Go to her with my blessing. Stay out all night, if you wish."

He'd be doing her a favor if he did! She'd already come too close to having him break her heart all over again, and they'd been together only a few days. The more reason he gave her to mistrust and despise him, the easier it would be, at the end of their two weeks, to say goodbye to him and walk away whole.

"I doubt I'll go quite that far," he said, barely managing to smother a grin, "but it could be late when I get back so don't wait up for me."

"I wouldn't dream of it. And please don't let me delay you any further. Thank you for a very nice lunch. I hope your...dinner is everything you'd like it to be."

"You're welcome, and thank you. I expect it will."

Rather than endure another farcical display of affection, she turned away from him and, pretending an interest in a sapphire-and-platinum starburst brooch pinned behind the glass of a wall display, glared miserably at his reflection as he stopped to say a few words to her parents, then strode to the door.

Like Gio Salvatore, he wore a beautifully tailored suit, but where the jeweler looked dapper in navy, her husband exuded raw power in charcoal-gray. He was cut out for the ruthless world of business, not domestic bliss, and in all fairness, he'd never led her to believe otherwise.

When she learned that she wasn't pregnant, he hadn't for a moment pretended regret. That he'd even proposed to her in the first place was because he was a man of honor, of ethics. He believed in being held accountable for his mistakes, and he did not willingly renege on a deal—not even one as flimsy as their marriage had turned out to be. How else to explain that he'd done nothing to end it?

That, she acknowledged sadly, would be up to her, and the sooner she went about it, the better, after all. Because leaving herself open to the kind of sordid, gnawing uncertainty currently plaguing her was too undignified to be countenanced.

Rather than face the evening knowing she'd be listening all the while for his key at the door, she took her parents out for an early dinner to a pretty little French restaurant a few blocks away.

Afterward, they strolled along the seawall and got back to the penthouse just after nine. To Gabriella's surprise, Max was already there, sprawled on the sofa in the living room. He'd exchanged his suit for a pair of blue jeans, and his dress shirt for a sports shirt.

Because there were lipstick stains on his collar, perhaps?

His hair wore the rumpled look that comes of having fingers raked through it.

His own—or his dinner date's?

"Hey," he said, springing up and offering his seat to her mother, "I was beginning to wonder if I should be organizing a search party. What happened, did the limo driver take the long way 'round when he brought you home?"

The words were uttered lightly, but his smile seemed forced and if the idea hadn't been completely preposterous, Gabriella would have thought he'd been worried by their absence. "We went out for dinner," she said, dropping her bag on a side table. "I didn't feel like cooking."

"Well, try leaving a note the next time, my love. If I'd known where you were, I'd have joined you."

"You said you were dining out and wouldn't be home until much later," she reminded him sweetly.

"I changed my mind." He came to where she stood and stroked his knuckles along her jaw. "Where'd you go?"

"Pierre's."

"That's some distance away. How'd you get there and back?"

"We walked," she said. "For heaven's sake, Max, if

I were to quiz you like this, you'd waste no time telling me to mind my own business!''

''It's a husband's prerogative to be concerned when his wife goes missing and she's as well known as you are,'' he said sharply. ''The streets aren't as safe at night as they once were, you know.''

Concerned? Suspicious was more like it—and a tiny, mean-spirited part of her rejoiced in the fact. What was sauce for the goose, after all, was sauce for the gander, too!

Her tone equally astringent, she said, ''I was hardly missing, nor was I alone. And you seem to forget I'm used to taking care of myself.''

As if he realized their exchange had strayed from natural curiosity to barely veiled hostility, Max kissed her lightly on the lips and said, ''You're right, and I apologize. You had no way of knowing my plans had changed.''

''As a matter of interest, why did they?''

''The person I'd hoped to meet couldn't make it.''

The person? How about "the other woman", Max? she thought bitterly, irked at the ease with which he turned the tables on her small victory.

Masking her rancor behind a smile so dripping with saccharine sweetness that she almost gagged, she said, ''What a shame! Were you terribly disappointed?''

''Not really. Rather pleased, in fact. You and I spend few enough evenings together as it is, and I was particularly looking forward to tonight because I have something for you.''

He left the room and she heard him cross the hall and enter his study. Shortly after, he returned with a bottle of cognac and two leather jewelry boxes, the smaller of which he presented to her mother. ''These are for you,

Maria. Gio thought you seemed quite taken with them this afternoon, so I hope they're to your liking. But if not, they can be exchanged for something else.''

They were earrings, small and delicate, each with an oval of translucent jade poised like a teardrop above a small diamond—an exquisite gift, expensive without being ostentatious, and her mother's flush of pleasure betrayed how delighted she was to receive them.

''And this,'' he went on, opening the other box and lifting out the aquamarine pendant they'd looked at earlier, ''is for my wife because she is the only woman I know lovely enough to do it justice.''

Gabriella stared at the necklace, knowing everyone was watching her expectantly, and that she was supposed to make some sort of appropriately enthusiastic response. It was, after all, a truly magnificent piece. Instead, horrifyingly, she heard herself ask baldly, ''What's it for?''

As if it were his habit to drop priceless jewels into her lap on a weekly basis, he smiled and said, ''Why, to wear, my love. Put it on so we can see how it looks.''

''No!''

The tiny frown puckering his forehead told her she was stretching his good will past all reason. He'd made a grand gesture, to impress her parents, and now it was her turn to show suitable appreciation of the fact. ''Come on, Gabriella, it won't bite.''

''I'm not wearing…'' She backed away, semi-hypnotized by the pendant twirling and winking at her in the lamplight. ''…the right clothes. A thing like this calls for an evening gown—something rich and sumptuous.''

''It needs only you.''

He stalked her until she found herself pinioned against the arm of the sofa. His fingers brushed the back of her neck, lifted her hair, fastened the clasp of the necklace securely in place. The gold filigree chain nested lightly against her skin; the aquamarine lay heavy and cold at her throat.

He brought his hands to rest on her shoulders, turned her around to face her parents, and solicited another opinion. "What do you think, Zoltan? Will it do?"

"It is very beautiful." Her father was completely won over. There were tears in his eyes. "In the old days, our daughter would have grown up taking such lovely things for granted, but times are not as they once were, and I thank you from the bottom of my heart for restoring her to the kind of life which should have been her birthright."

"In that case, you make me doubly glad I chose it." Max paused long enough to cast a reproachful glance at Gabriella who stood there unable to dredge up so much as a semblance of enthusiasm. "Even if my wife wishes I hadn't."

"It's not that I don't appreciate the thought," she felt compelled to reply. "I just feel rather foolish wearing it when it clearly calls for a special occasion. As it is, I'm afraid it'll spend most of its time in the safe, along with my other jewelry."

Max dug in his shirt pocket and hauled out her wedding band. "That reminds me, let's put this where it belongs before I forget I have it and it winds up in the laundry! Here, my love."

He slid it over her knuckle and, if she'd allowed it, would have raised her hand to his lips and kissed it. She forestalled him, snatching her fingers away as if he'd burned them, and pulling off the ring. "No! I can't wear it!"

It was quite the wrong thing to do, and if her own common sense hadn't told her so the minute it was too late to take back the words, her mother's appalled gasp certainly conveyed the message. ''Gabriella, whatever is the matter? You should be proud to wear your husband's ring!''

''I know,'' she said miserably. ''And I would be, if only…'' *If only it were for the right reasons.* But the truth was, having him put it on her finger on their wedding day had been difficult enough, knowing, as she had, that he was an unwilling groom roped into marriage because she'd thought she was expecting a baby. She could not stomach a repeat performance now when they had not even the excuse of an unplanned pregnancy to hold them together. ''If only,'' she amended, sliding the ring back and forth over her knuckle several times to demonstrate, ''it weren't so loose. But as you can see, it slips off very easily, and I'm afraid I'll lose it.''

Max rolled his eyes. ''What do you expect, when your idea of a square meal is a stick of celery and a grape?''

''Oh, Max, that's an exaggeration, and you know it!''

''Do I?'' Once more, he appealed to her parents. ''You must have noticed how she picks at her food, and you can't have missed the fact that she's dropped at least two dress sizes since you last saw her.''

''But not because I've been dieting,'' she insisted. ''It's all the traveling that's done it. Jet lag and too hectic a schedule.''

That, and eating my heart out over you! Did you ever try packing away a steak, Max, when you're hollow with misery inside and there's a permanent lump in your throat?

''Well, your father made a good point earlier,'' he said. ''You're not traveling now, and before you take off on your next whirlwind tour, I want to see you put back those pounds you've lost.''

''As if you care!'' A slip of the tongue too bitter to be contained, it was out before she could contain it.

''I care,'' he snapped, making no effort to hide his annoyance at her attitude. ''Being seen with a wife who looks like a bone rack isn't my idea of a good time, nor do I think you're setting any sort of example to the ranks of gullible young women around the world whose ideal is to wind up looking just like you!''

''Then don't be seen with me, if it offends you so much! I've grown quite accustomed to being on my own, and you've as good as admitted you never are, so—!''

They were hurling angry words at each other, unmindful of their audience, and who was to say what irreparable damage she might have done with her last remark had Max not suddenly yanked her to him, and stopped her in midflow with a kiss which resonated throughout her body.

Arms hanging limply at her sides, she flopped against him like a rag doll, aware of his eyes glaring into hers and sparking blue flame. His mouth sealed hers so thoroughly, so crushingly, she could barely breathe and when she tried to squirm free, he nipped her lower lip just hard enough to remind her that if a contest of brute strength was what she wanted, she'd better be prepared to come out the loser.

But the really pitiful thing—the shameful, humiliating fact of the matter—was that for all her outrage, her body...and yes, her mind and heart and soul, relished every second! Just as well he had her encased in a steel grip, she thought hazily, or she'd have wound up in a mindless, soggy heap at his feet.

Sensing he'd won this latest round, Max softened the kiss. The nip became a nibble so persuasive that her lips parted and allowed his tongue to trace an apology inside her mouth, to flick and swirl against hers in tormenting reminder of what intimacy was all about.

A flash of heat, so sudden and intense it made her thighs quiver, shot to her lower abdomen and dissolved into liquid yearning. If she could have had one wish, it would have been to freeze the moment and make it last forever. To cast it like a veil over their marriage and disguise all the ugliness which kept her and Max apart.

He labored under no such fanciful delusion. With a disarming show of remorse, he pulled her into a tight hug and, resting his chin on the crown of her head, addressed her parents who sat in paralyzed fascination watching the entire performance. "I guess the secret's out and there's no use pretending it's not, so we might as well come clean. The truth is—"

Appalled that he seemed prepared to reveal their duplicity in all its shabby glory without regard for the fallout sure to follow, Gabriella struggled free. "No, Max, please! Don't do this!"

She might as well have saved her breath. "Sometimes we fight," he explained blithely, hauling her back and pressing her face into his shirtfront to silence her, "and I'm the first to admit I'm usually the one who starts it. But the truth is, I worry that Gabriella's pushing herself too hard with this modeling business. I wish she could spend more time here where she belongs, so that I can take better care of her, but that's just not feasible with her schedule."

"So you love her," her mother crooned. "We understand. And she loves you. And people who love with passion, they fight with passion."

"They make up with passion, too, Maria," he interjected quickly.

Her mother's English might not be perfect, but she understood well enough what he was implying. "So go!" she chuckled, shooing at them as if she were chasing away chickens. "It is time now to make up!"

Keeping Gabriella cinched to his side, Max picked up the bottle of cognac and offered it to her father. "Zoltan, I couldn't quite see you wearing earrings, but I remember you appreciate good brandy, so this is for you. I'm sure you'll forgive us if we leave you to enjoy it in relative peace and quiet."

Brushing aside her father's thanks, he then turned a wicked smile on Gabriella. "Now, what do you say, sweetheart? Ready to take your mom's advice?"

What choice did she have but to return his smile and go along with the suggestion? Fully aware of her parents' watchful gaze, she linked her arm around Max's waist and let him lead her toward the stairs.

CHAPTER FIVE

THE charade came to an end the minute they reached the bedroom. "Well," he said, strolling to the window and casually unbuttoning his shirt while she wilted against the closed door, "for someone supposedly bent on preserving the myth of happy-ever-after, you certainly came close to blowing it! Care to tell me why?"

"I'm not stupid, Max," she said. "I don't know why you came home early tonight, but I do know it had nothing to do with wanting to be with me."

"As a matter of fact, it did. Looking back, I decided I was out of line in the way I handled our rather tense exchange in Gio's."

"So you thought you'd try to bribe me into forgetting about it with this?" Unclasping the pendant, she flung it at him. "No, thanks. I'm not that easily bought off."

He caught the thing and regarded her impassively. "So what do you suggest I do with it?"

Resisting the urge to give him quite graphic instructions, she said, "Give it to someone who'll appreciate it."

"You have a specific 'someone' in mind, or will just anyone do?"

"Oh, stop playing games!" she exploded. "For obscure reasons known only to you, you decided to make a few more brownie points with my parents tonight by playing the doting husband and son-in-law. Well, congratulations! You gave a near-flawless performance and they were definitely impressed. But the curtain's been rung down now and there's no one but me left in the audience, so you can drop the phony act.''

He examined the heap of gold and precious gems cradled in his palm. ''There's nothing phony about this, I assure you. Would you like to see the appraisal certificate that came with it? Or the receipt, perhaps? Would *they* convince you it's the genuine article?''

''I'm not questioning the authenticity of the jewelry. It's your integrity that's on the line here, Max. Pretending we're happily married is one thing, but you take things too far when you show up loaded with expensive gifts, and start quizzing me about where I've been as if you were worried sick about me.''

''You didn't come in until after nine, and there was no sign you'd been home since morning.''

''I wasn't aware I had to report my every move to you or that I was under any sort of curfew.''

''Jeez, Gabriella, will you stop making something out of nothing, and try being reasonable for a change? Your parents are getting on, your dad had to get his doctor's permission to make the trip over here, and you have the kind of high public profile that leaves you vulnerable to every weirdo out there, so naturally I was concerned when I got home to find the place empty.''

''Rubbish! You were trying to justify your own behavior by shifting guilt on to me.''

He stared at her blankly for a moment, then said, ''You know what? You're nuts! You're so caught up in your own fantasy world that you can't tell the difference between it and reality.''

''The first night I was back here, you as good as told me you're seeing someone else, and that's just plain fact, Max. Not my imagination playing tricks on me, and not another of the lies you're so quick to accuse me of manufacturing. When I confronted you about it this afternoon, you wouldn't—or couldn't—simply tell me I was worrying about nothing. So you bought me a trinket to ease your conscience."

He dangled the pendant from his forefinger and let loose with a bellow of laughter. "Some trinket! I know you think I'm made of money, Gabriella, but even I don't throw it around quite that casually."

"Stop trying to change the subject," she fired back. "This isn't about money—it's *never* been about money, for all that you like to think that's why I married you! It's about principles...and...." She fought back the sob rising in her throat. Damn it, she *wouldn't* let him make her cry! She *wouldn't* back down when every instinct told her she was right!

"You're a fine one to preach to me about principles, given the way you went about snagging me in marriage!"

Beside herself, she gave in to the jealousy and doubt eating holes in her heart. "I'm not the one with a lover waiting in the wings, either."

"Oh, for pity's sake!" He smacked the heel of his hand against his forehead and advanced toward her. "Listen carefully, Gabriella, because I'm going to say this as plainly as I know how, and I'm only going to say it once. *There is no other woman*...not anymore."

At his denial, initially so clean and convincing, a huge uprush of hope rose inside her, only to be smashed into oblivion by the squalid little qualification he tacked on at the end.

"But there was," she mourned on a fragile breath, the pain of his admission so acute that her words were barely audible. Only a sadist would withdraw the knife from a person's heart for the pure pleasure of plunging it in more deeply a second time!

"Yes." Recognizing the wound he'd inflicted, he caught her hands in his. "But not in the way you think. When it came right down to breaking my marriage vows…" He lifted his shoulders in a mystified shrug. "I couldn't do it."

She should have taken comfort wherever it was to be found, but the perverse need to punish herself further made her ask, "Are you saying you've never kissed her?"

He hesitated, his eyes scouring her face, his own expression a mixture of regret and amusement. "Oh, I've kissed her," he finally admitted, cupping her face in his hands and bringing his mouth so close to hers that she could almost taste it. "But never like this."

She had thought nothing could equal the upheaval he'd created with his earlier kiss, put on for her parents' benefit. She had thought nothing could ever erase the devastation of hearing him concede he'd turned for solace to someone else. But the way he settled his mouth on hers, unprompted by obligation or duty, swept aside all the previous hurts. All at once, the sincerity of the here and now were all that counted.

"You're a thorn in my side, Gabriella," he murmured, the words grazing her lips. "I would prefer to ignore you…forget I ever met you…but even when you're half a world away, I'm never really free of you."

"And you hate me for that," she whispered without any real conviction.

"You irritate the hell out of me." His mouth drifted to her jaw and down the side of her neck, stitching expert little kisses between each word.

"I know," she sighed, aware in a distant corner of her mind that his hands had strayed down past her waist and were tracing delectable patterns over her hips.

If she had an ounce of moral fiber, she'd put an end to

his seduction. What kind of woman settled for the transient pleasure of the moment when the past was riddled with one betrayal after another, and the future too uncertain to contemplate?

Yet, what right had she to object, when she herself had thrust aside the open front of his shirt and was conducting an uninvited tour of the planes of his chest? How warm and solid he was; how deeply, dearly familiar!

He reached behind her to pull down the zipper on her dress. ''You infuriate me.''

''At least I haven't kissed another man since I married you.'' Reaching up, she punished his transgression by nipping lightly at the smooth, tanned skin of his shoulder.

He let out a faint gasp.

Annoyance? Pleasure? She thought the latter.

''You're never going to let me forget that, are you?'' He'd inched her dress off her shoulders. It slithered the length of her body and fell with a rustling sigh around her ankles. She heard the soft click of her bra being undone. A cool draft of night air whispered over her skin except where his hands warmed her bare breasts. ''You're going to blackmail me with it for the rest of my life.''

''That shouldn't come as any great surprise. You persist in believing I'm a conniving witch out to trick you at every turn.'' Her throat closed over the accusation as he took her nipple in his mouth. Could he tell that each time his tongue circled her flesh, a tiny paroxysm of sensation throbbed deep within her? Did he know she was wet with wanting him?

''But you *did* trick me,'' he said, dropping to his knees and leaving the damp imprint of his kisses against the thin silk of her panties. ''You told me my baby was in *here*.''

She was aching; shuddering all over. Knotting her fingers in his hair, she pressed her knees together to keep herself upright. "I thought it was. My period was late and I panicked."

"You let me think other men had touched you—*here.*"

Sweet heaven, he had cupped his hand over the drenched patch of fabric between her legs! He knew how eager she was for him; how incapable of pretending indifference to his encroachment. His fingers were inching inside her panties. Inside *her,* and moving with such deft purpose, she was about to shatter into a million pieces!

A hoarse cry caught in her throat and she collapsed against him. As if she weighed no more than a feather, he tipped her over his shoulder and rose to his feet. The room swam past in a blur as he strode to the bed and dropped her there, just carelessly enough that she bounced gently on the mattress.

He turned on the bedside lamp and leaned over her, his eyes glittering. "You're not lying now, though, are you, Gabriella? You want to make love, don't you?"

Beast! He already knew the answer, but he was going to make her beg anyway! "I don't really care one way or the other," she said weakly and closed her eyes.

"Look at me when you say that."

Mesmerized, she obeyed. When he saw that he had her unblinking attention, he reached for his belt. The buckle glimmered in the lamplight. He unsnapped the waist of his jeans, and slowly opened the fly. "Do you still not care?"

She bit her lip and refused to answer.

He smiled grimly. "You want to touch me, don't you, my love?"

"No," she whimpered, even as her hand stole out to shape him. He was hard, powerful; throbbing with suppressed energy and life.

"Shall I leave you then, and go take a cold shower?"

"No!" Driven past all reason, she lunged at him and tore frenziedly at the blue jeans. He wore jockey shorts underneath, dazzling white against the dark tan of his thighs. And oh, such thighs they were, tapering from his hips in one long, smooth sweep of muscled flesh!

"Help me!" she implored, struggling with the unyielding denim and quite beside herself. She wouldn't settle for a hurried, halfhearted coupling, not after all those days and nights of unanswered yearning! "You've got me where you want me—naked and vulnerable. I want to see all of you, as well."

Pinning her in a searing, heavy-lidded gaze, he shucked off what remained of his clothes and stalked her across the bed with the unhurried grace of a lion moving in for an easy kill.

When at last he was close enough that his breath ruffled her hair, he growled, "Not quite naked, my love," and stripped off her panties, then pushed her back against the pillows and went about the business of reacquainting himself with her body, touching her first with his hands, and then with his mouth.

He kissed her eyes and her throat; her elbows, her feet, each separate vertebra in her spine. And when every other inch of her had received its benediction and was humming with pleasure, he pushed apart her knees and touched his tongue to her most secret and sensitive flesh.

He'd brought her to climax before, but never so swiftly or so savagely. She tried to resist it, to tame it. But her body had gone too long without him and responded with the avid greed of a starving thing. Racked by spasm after spasm, she clung to him, sobbing his name.

As the tremors faded to a sweet echo, he sank down beside her and went to take her in his arms. But seeing the tears tracking down her face, he rose up again on one elbow and said ruefully, "Heck, Gabriella, it seems no matter how hard I try to please you, all I ever do is make you cry."

She uttered a shaky laugh, and ran her hands over his torso, loving the feel of him, all muscle overlaid by smooth, olive-tinted skin. "You took me by surprise, that's all."

"Keep up what you're doing, and you'll be surprised all over again," he warned her. "You're wandering into dangerous territory, sweetheart, so unless you're prepared to deal with the consequences, better keep your hands to yourself."

"Not a chance," she said, pressing him back against the mattress. "You've had your fun. Now it's my turn."

The hint of complacency in his smile suggested he thought there was little chance she could wreak on him anything approaching the havoc he'd brought to her, but as she inched her way down his chest, she heard the uneven thump of his heart and knew he wasn't nearly as much in control as he'd like her to believe.

"Is this what you meant, when you asked me if I wanted to touch you?" she whispered, closing her fingers possessively around the straining evidence of his arousal.

He inhaled sharply.

Encouraged to boldness, she inquired huskily, "Or is this more what you had in mind?"

At the brush of her lips, a groan escaped him. "Woman," he ground out, "you're playing with fire."

Undeterred, she swept her mouth over him again, branding him with hot, impassioned kisses. Being together with him like this was a gift from the gods she did not intend to waste. The next time he was tempted to stray, she wanted hers to be the touch he'd yearn for, hers the face to haunt him in the night.

He might resent her until the day he died, but like it or not, *she* was his wife, and for all that she'd thought divorce was her only option, she knew now that she would not easily relinquish the role to someone else. Suddenly, *For better or for worse, till death us do part* assumed new and powerful meaning.

"Gabriella…!" Her name emerged on a long, unsteady breath. Gripping her shoulders, he hauled her up beside him again, rolled her onto her back, and knelt astride her. His forehead gleamed with sweat. A pulse raced at the corner of his jaw, keeping pace with the speeding rush of her own heart. His voice rough with passion, he said, "Enough! I want to be inside you when I come."

"Yes," she sighed dreamily, her entire body vibrating with anticipation as he nudged apart her thighs. And then the long, lonely waiting was over. He was where he belonged and for once happy to be there…velvet sheathed in satin…and they were moving together in remembered rhythm. Rediscovering each other. Turning painful past knowledge into beautiful, shimmering new experiences. Holding on to each other as the tempo increased and they tried to outrace the roaring tide gathering force and threatening to tip them, end over end, into extinction.

It was splendor enough, more than she'd dared dream about, and she would not have asked for more. But just as he lost the battle for supremacy and his seed spilled hotly within her, he gave her one last gift—words dredged up from the darkest depths of his soul, tortured and almost indistinguishable.

"Darling!" he muttered feverishly, crushing her to him. "Beloved!"

Impossible words. She could not have heard him correctly.

Lifting her hand, she stroked the hair from his brow. "What did you say, Max?"

He let out an exhausted sigh and rolled to his side, his body still fused with hers. "Hush. It was nothing."

"You called me 'darling.'"

"Uh-uh. 'Devil', more like it."

"And 'beloved.'"

"Let it go, Gabriella." He flopped onto his back and tucked her head into the crook of his shoulder.

"I can't," she cried, bereft of his warmth and the sweet sense of completion that came of having him buried inside her. "What just happened…didn't it mean *anything* to you?"

"What do you think?"

"That it was beautiful. That for the first time ever, neither of us was using the other. Instead, we gave to one another, and in doing so, we truly did *make love*." She stopped and drew in a tormented breath. "Am I wrong?"

He debated the question so long that she found herself biting her lip to keep it from trembling. *Please,* she begged him silently, *please don't turn what we just shared into something cheap and tawdry!*

"You're not wrong," he finally admitted. "The question is, where does that leave us?"

"We're husband and wife, Max. Can't we take it from there and try to make something worthwhile of our marriage?"

"Being legally bound to each other no more makes for marriage than great sex does. Face it, Gabriella, your life isn't with me, it's wherever your work takes you, be it Rome or Paris or Buenos Aires."

"If you asked me to, I would give it all up in a heartbeat."

"In exchange for what? Being unhappy, the way you

were before you made a new life for yourself away from me?''

''I could be very happy with you, if you'd let me,'' she said urgently. ''Will you do that, Max? Will you give us another chance?''

''I'm tempted, I admit.'' He looked at her long and seriously before continuing, ''Will you settle for giving it a trial run on the understanding that, after your parents leave, we'll take an honest look at where we stand and if we find it isn't working out, we'll agree to part without recrimination or blame on either part?''

It will work out! she promised him silently. ''Agreed.''

''Not so fast. You also have to promise me—''

''Anything!'' she cried softly, the fulfillment of all her hopes and dreams hanging by a thread.

''There'll be no more lies. And I'm not just talking about lying to each other. We've got to stop fooling ourselves, Gabriella. Regardless of where it might lead, I want your promise that you'll assess *us* honestly. No skating over the bits you don't like, no pretending that if you ignore them, the problems will go away. Otherwise, we don't have a snowball's chance in hell of repairing what's broken between us.''

Solemnly, she drew a cross over her heart. ''I give you my word. And, Max, one more thing…''

''What now?''

She picked up the necklace from the bedside table where Max had tossed it, and fastened it around her throat again. ''Thank you for this. I love it.''

''Good. Because I pressured Gio into staying late at the shop and taking some of the links out of the chain so it would fit properly.'' He leaned over and switched off the bedside lamp. ''If you behave yourself, I might have him make up something from the left-over diamonds and gold.''

''I don't need anything else,'' she whispered. ''What you've given me just now, here in this room, is worth more to me than all the diamonds and gold in the world.''

He reached for her in the dark. ''Want to know the best part about tonight?'' he said, his voice rough with renewed passion. ''It isn't over yet.''

It was after ten when she opened her eyes the next morning. ''You should have woken me sooner,'' she scolded her mother whom she found snipping dead roses from the climber on the terrace while her father put himself through his usual twenty laps in the pool. ''Imagine letting me sleep most of the morning away when you're already halfway through your time here!''

Her mother uncovered a dish of berries and cream waiting on the patio table. ''Your man said not to disturb you. And he is right. You're worn to skin and bone, my daughter. You need rest and good food. So, sit and eat, and I will make eggs the way you used to like them, with fresh rolls and sweet butter.''

''No eggs, Mama, thank you. Fruit and a roll will be enough, though I'd love a cup of coffee as well, if you'll join me.''

Humming under her breath, her mother bustled inside the penthouse. Overhead, seagulls glided across a calm blue midsummer sky. A rose in a bud vase in the middle of the table glowed deep gold in the sunlight. Down in the bay, a boat drifted slowly under sail, headed for the open sea.

Paradise! Gabriella thought, stretching lazily and savoring every tiny body ache for the reminder it brought of the night just past. She closed her eyes, the better to

review the film unwinding in her mind—of waking somewhere around two in the morning, with the moon casting
long pewter shadows over Max's limbs entwined with
hers; of the sandpaper burn of his beard against her skin,
the thrilling crescendo to their lovemaking, so vivid in
recall that a tremor of sensation spiraled through her
womb. Of the musky scent of afterward, deeply private,
intensely intimate, and the warm, secure feel of her husband's arms folded around her in sleep.

Yes, paradise indeed—or a miracle so impossible that
she found herself wondering if it had all been just a
dream. Would he come home later and look at her from
cold, empty eyes? Would his kiss once again be only a
parody of the real thing?

Suddenly, she needed to hear his voice, to hear him
turn her name into an embrace, the way he had in the
quiet hours before the dawn—*Gabri…ell…a!*

A remote phone lay on the table, preprogrammed with
his office number. It rang twice before a woman answered.
"Willow McHenry," she purred.

"I…um, that is, I thought I'd dialed…" Annoyed to
find herself stumbling over her words, Gabriella sat up
straight and began again. "Is this Max Logan's office?"

"It is."

"Then may I speak to him, please?"

"I'm afraid Mr. Logan's unavailable at the moment.
I'll be happy to relay a message to him."

If he was unavailable, why could she hear his voice
quite plainly in the background? "No," Gabriella said
firmly. "I wish to speak to him in person."

There was a muffled pause, the kind which comes from
a hand being placed over a receiver to disguise the conversation taking place at the other end. Finally, her tone
suggesting that importuning Mr. Logan was no one's pre-

rogative but hers, Willow McHenry came back on the line to inquire, "Who may I say is calling?"

Who? The woman he made love to all last night, that's *who!* "His wife," Gabriella said.

Another pause, lasting perhaps five seconds or more, and so utterly silent this time that there was no question of any conversation taking place at the other end of the line. Gabriella flinched as the phone smacked against some hard surface, then Max's voice came on the line, not as loverlike as she'd have preferred, but not chillingly neutral, either. "Hi, Gabriella. What's up?"

"Well, I am—finally," she said with a laugh. "But I missed saying goodbye to you this morning."

"You were sleeping so soundly, I thought it best not to wake you."

In the background, a door closed sharply.

"I wish you had."

He waited a moment before replying, and there was answering laughter in his voice when he said, "I had a conference call scheduled for eight o'clock and didn't want to risk being late."

"I wouldn't have kept you very long."

"Yes, you would, you insatiable wench. We'd likely still be rolling between the sheets."

She turned liquid with pleasure. "I miss you. Come home early, will you?"

"As soon as I can. I'll take us all out for dinner. Choose some place nice outside town that you think your folks might enjoy seeing, and make a reservation for eight."

Smiling, he hung up the phone.

"Well," Willow said from the other end of the room, "aren't you the dutiful husband all of a sudden!"

He cast her a sideways glance before turning his attention to the contract lying on his desk. "I think we both know that's been my role all along."

"Not quite," she said. "I remember an occasion when you came very close to forgetting you even had a wife."

His hand stilled on the pages he'd been leafing through. "Let's not rake up the past, Willow," he said flatly. "We were both at a low point in our lives, but we managed to get past it without hurting anyone."

"You might have, Max," she said, coming to face him across the desk, "but don't presume to know how I felt."

He didn't like the tone of the conversation; he liked even less the brittle tone in her voice. "We're talking about a couple of kisses one night, eight months ago," he said, staring her straight in the eye. "I thought we'd both moved on since then. But if you find you haven't, or can't, I'll be happy to arrange a transfer to another department, or give you a reference, if you prefer to move to another company."

"No." She flashed him a brilliant smile. "You're quite right, we *have* moved on. I'm involved with someone else and you're...still married."

"Yes," he said. "And the next time my wife phones, put her call through right away. I'm never too busy to talk to her."

"Of course. She has a lovely voice, by the way. Charmingly young and foreign. Naive, almost, which I wouldn't have expected from someone so used to public exposure." She scooped up the letters she'd left for him to sign and made for the door connecting their two offices. "Oh, a couple of things I should mention before I forget. First, that person from the local TV station called again yesterday, wanting to set up an interview with you. What shall I tell him?"

''Anything, as long as I don't have to go in front of the camera. That's my wife's forte, not mine.''

''All right. I'll suggest they line something up with her instead.''

''Sure, as long as she's agreeable.''

''And the Overseas Development Dinner's next Thursday. Since you're almost certain to win an award, shall I order extra tickets for your wife and her parents?''

''It hadn't occurred to me before, but now that you mention it, yes, do. I think they'd enjoy themselves.''

''Fine.'' She bathed him in another smile and was gone.

He remained standing behind the desk, though, uneasiness tugging at his gut—with a dollop of guilt thrown in for good measure.

It had started out innocently enough with Willow: working late, and sharing a take-out dinner while they raced to complete a deal on time; lunch to celebrate final approval on a building site or a five-star rating on the latest hotel; flowers delivered to her at home in recognition of the extra hours she pulled down when he was out of town; a token gift to go with the annual bonus at Christmas; a friendly kiss at the office party.

He should have left it that. But then, there'd been the night at the penthouse, a couple of glasses of wine too many, an ill-advised attempt to start an affair which fizzled before it properly began, and that had been it. As far as he was concerned, their relationship had been strictly confined to business ever since.

If anyone had asked him yesterday, he'd have said with absolute certainty that she felt the same way. She was too smart and attractive to hanker after a married man when there were any number of eligible guys available. And too ambitious to jeopardize a job that paid handsomely and offered the kind of perks that went along with being chief assistant to the company boss.

Today, he wasn't so sure. There'd been something in her voice, something in the way her expression closed up when he'd suggested she might be happier working for someone else. He'd been reminded of a dog prepared to fight to the death defending its territory all the time it was wagging its tail in a show of apparent friendliness.

Scowling, he paced to the window, all too aware of the potential fallout if he didn't handle the situation delicately. Given the turn of events with Gabriella, the ideal solution would be to transfer Willow, preferably to one of the overseas branches. But given today's climate in the work place, he knew well enough he'd leave himself wide open to a suit of sexual harassment if he tried to force the issue. The best he could do was keep their relationship thoroughly professional, and hope like hell that she'd show up one day soon with a ring on her finger, and a letter of resignation in her hand.

The damnable thing was, a week ago he hadn't much cared which way it went. She could accept the status quo, or she could leave. But then, a week ago, he'd had nothing to lose if she stayed. The last thing he'd expected was that his marriage which had seemed doomed from the start, might be worth saving, after all.

CHAPTER SIX

GABRIELLA had made an eight o'clock reservation at a restaurant in White Rock, a residential community famous for its beaches and spectaculars views, some forty-five-minute drive south of the city. The rush-hour traffic was long over by then and he'd normally have made it out there with time to spare. Coming home to find her all rosy from the shower and wearing only a silk camisole and bikini panties, though, threw the schedule seriously off track.

Leaving her parents happily sipping dry sherry downstairs, Max locked the bedroom door behind him and dedicated himself to stripping his wife naked and pulling her back into the shower—this time, with him.

"We'll be late," she said, wrapping her long golden legs around his waist. "Max, they won't hold our...table if we're...ah...!"

Her protest, halfhearted to begin with, died as he parted the sleek folds of her flesh and slid inside her. He'd have preferred to take her at leisure, to track the curls of steam writhing around the tips of her breasts. To watch the flush riding up her neck as he edged her closer to the brink of orgasm. He'd have liked to taste the lush ripeness of her mouth and muffle her little cries of delirium as she convulsed helplessly around him.

But almost immediately, the ache lurking all day in his lower belly tightened excruciatingly, and before he could help himself, he had her cushioned between him and the glass wall of the shower stall, the pulsing urgency gushed free, and he was left drained and gasping.

"That's what comes of being celibate too long," he panted ruefully, dropping his forehead to hers. "Now that you've reminded me what I've been missing all these months, I can't hold out long enough to make it worth your while."

But the unfocused dreaminess in her eyes put the lie to his allegation as surely as the diminishing contractions clenching her body. "Don't say that!" she cried, her breath sweet against his mouth. "It was—*you* are…" Her eyelids drooped fetchingly. "…out of this world!"

Reluctantly, he set her back on her feet and lathered a sponge. "Much more of that kind of ego-stroking and I'll be fueled up and ready to go another round—which wouldn't be such a bad thing if it weren't that you can't afford to miss a meal. Turn around, sweetheart, and I'll scrub your back."

She was as beautiful from behind as she was in front. Her spine ran straight and delicate, bisecting her in perfect symmetry from her tail bone to her nape. Her ribs, too thin still but elegantly fashioned, tapered to the kind of narrow waist which women used to lace themselves into steel corsets to achieve. As for her hips…oh, brother! Dangerous territory and not a good idea to let his thoughts linger there!

"You're done," he said, sounding as if he'd just swallowed a pail of coarse sand.

Eyes and smile alight with mischief, she pivoted to face him and made a grab for the sponge. "I'll be happy to return the favor, if you like."

He slid open the shower door and practically shoved her out of the stall. "Get yourself dressed and downstairs before your folks come looking for us, wenchkin! The sherry decanter must be empty by now.''

It wasn't. Not even close. But her parents had enjoyed the small amount they'd consumed. Either that, or they owed their rosy glow to whatever Gabriella was telling them when Max joined them in the living room, ten minutes later.

''Don't be too forthcoming about the way things seem to be turning around with you and me,'' he warned her quietly, as they waited in the building's main foyer for his car to be brought up from the garage. ''We don't know ourselves how well it's going to work and it wouldn't be fair to raise their hopes needlessly if, at the end of it all, we decide to call the marriage quits.''

She looked a little hurt, which worried him. Sure, they were about as compatible as any couple could be when it came to sex—they always had been, even when things were at their worst. But she had to know they couldn't predicate the future on a truce which had yet to survive the light of two days, let alone two weeks.

''I haven't mentioned a word,'' she said. ''Not that it would make any difference if I had. They're already convinced we're a match made in heaven. I'm just hoping they're right.''

He squeezed her hand. ''It's early days still is all I'm saying.''

''I know.'' Her mouth drooped a bit, then turned up in the smile the rest of the world knew so well. Blinding. Stunning. ''But I'll take my chances. We've been given a second chance, and that's more than I ever expected.''

''You look lovely, you know that?'' He fingered the collar of the little linen jacket she wore. ''I'll be the envy of every other man in the restaurant.''

He wasn't far wrong. From the commotion her arrival

caused, she was obviously recognized. Conversation dribbled to a halt. Heads swivelled to watch as the maître d' did a double take, nearly tripped over backwards bowing her to their table, and just about wet his drawers when she began discussing the menu with him in fluent French.

Hiding his grin behind the wine list, Max said under his breath, "You planning to talk dirty like that to me in bed tonight, dear heart?"

Hidden by the tablecloth, she walked her fingers from his knee and all the way up his inner thigh to the danger zone. "I'll do better than talk," she promised him.

He laughed, not only because her audacity amused him, but because...damn it, she made him happy.

How had it happened? When they'd first married, he'd been so bloody angry that, once his pride had adjusted to her walking out on him, he'd embraced the peace she left behind. What others might have called lonely and boring, he'd viewed as a return to bachelor contentment. Any time he'd found himself inclined to wonder about her—even to miss her—all he'd had to do to snap out of it was think back to the emotional storms and manipulations which were her trademark, and count his blessings at being rid of her.

Yet here she was again, creating a different kind of upheaval, but an upheaval nevertheless, and he felt alive for the first time in over a year. "I'm starting out with oysters on the half shell," he told her, clamping his hand over hers before she got them both thrown out on their ears for lewd behavior in a public place. "I get the feeling I'm going to need them."

Another two days went by before the glow began to wear off. Then, early on the third morning, a Friday, the phone rang.

"Mrs. Logan? It's Willow McHenry, Max's executive assistant."

Even before the woman identified herself, Gabriella recognized her voice. Noticed, too, the possessive way she wrapped her mouth around Max's name.

"I'm calling to arrange a time for your interview."

Gabriella stared at the phone. "I beg your pardon?"

"Your television appearance, Mrs. Logan. Max has already given it the go-ahead in the hopes that it will satisfy the media's preoccupation with your visit. Your being in town is causing such a stir, and he so dislikes being flung in the spotlight, as I expect you know." She allowed a pregnant pause to spin out. "Or perhaps you don't. In any event, this is something he and I have discussed at length—the interview idea, that is. Am I to assume that he forgot to mention it to you?"

"We talked about my arrival not exactly going unnoticed by the press, but—"

She might as well have saved her breath. Willow McHenry tromped right over her reply as if it amounted to yet one more tiny inconvenience in the lives of the rich and powerful, and continued smoothly, "Small wonder if he overlooked it, given how very busy he is, but that's what he pays me to do—take care of the minor details he doesn't have time for."

Willow McHenry, Gabriella decided, came across as a tigress of a woman, formidably competent and immovably certain of her place in the greater order of things. A future CEO in her own right, she was most likely tall and frighteningly attractive, probably wore a lot of black, with plum-red lipstick and nail lacquer for contrast—and was so ultra chic and efficient that lesser mortals cringed in her presence!

Unaware of the impact she'd made, Willow forged

ahead. ''I've suggested to the person who'll be conducting the interview that the taping take place at the penthouse, an idea which she quite likes.''

Finally finding her voice again, Gabriella said, ''I'm not at all sure that I do. My home is private and I prefer to keep it that way.''

Another tiny paused ensued. ''But Max's living room is so elegant—quite beyond anything you'd find in a television studio, and the view from the terrace is breathtaking. If you're concerned about having to prepare for the event, I'll be there ahead of time to run interference and make sure you're inconvenienced as little as possible. All you need to do is look ravishing, which is something you're quite used to and which will, I'm sure, require no effort at all.''

''Thank you—I think.''

The irony was lost on Willow. ''Mrs. Logan, we need to settle on the date. How's your calendar looking for Tuesday?''

''I'll have to check with my husband. My parents are visiting from overseas and we might have other plans.''

''Not for Tuesday you won't. Max is flying to New Mexico on Monday and won't be back until Wednesday. And while we're talking dates, there's the Overseas Development Awards Dinner on Thursday—I've arranged extra tickets for you and your guests, by the way—so how about I pencil you in for ten o'clock Tuesday morning? Will that give you enough time to get yourself dressed and ready?''

It was all Gabriella could do not to come back with, *I'm a model, not a moron, I've been dressing myself since I turned five, and I've yet to show up in mismatched shoes!* ''I think I might be able to manage that,'' she said from between clenched teeth.

''Then it's arranged. I've already run the time past the studio crew and they're available. I'll see you on Tuesday around half-past nine.''

After dinner that evening, Max suggested he and Gabriella take a stroll through the park, just the two of them. ''I'm enjoying your folks' company,'' he said, linking her fingers in his and leading her along a deserted path shaded by Japanese maples, ''but I think it's important for you and me to spend time alone together.''

''We're by ourselves every night in bed.''

''I know!'' He leered at her disarmingly. ''But we just keep covering the same old ground in there! Not that I'm complaining, you understand, but if we're serious about trying to make this marriage work, we need to put it to the test in other areas, as well.'' He swung their joined hands back and forth. ''For instance, I thought you seemed a bit preoccupied at dinner tonight. Is something wrong?''

Should she tell him, or would it be more prudent to push aside the misgivings which had dogged her ever since the conversation with Willow McHenry?

Catching her hesitation, he pulled her to a stop and forced her to look him in the eye. ''Okay, you just answered my question. What's up?''

''I haven't said a word!''

''You don't have to. Something's bugging you and I want to know what it is. Come *on*, Gabriella, this is exactly the sort of thing I'm talking about! You can't go sweeping stuff under the carpet and hope it'll go away, because we both know that's not how marriage works. So spit it out, whatever it is, and let's deal with it.''

''All right. Your assistant phoned me this morning.''

''Yeah?'' Was it her imagination, or did his gaze become a little less direct, a little more guarded? "What did she want?"

"It seems the two of you decided I should be interviewed on television."

"Oh, *that!*" He made a wry face. "I wouldn't put it in quite those words, but she was basically correct."

"Max, why would you give permission for something like that without asking me first?"

"Honey, you're already headline news around here—*World Famous Model Comes Home,* and all that jazz. Because the penthouse isn't listed in the phone book, you've been spared any personal harassment, but the endless calls Willow's had to field at the office on your behalf have really cut into the time she'd allocated for other things."

Gabriella could well imagine how the super-efficient Ms. McHenry would resent that! Still, "I wish you'd discussed it with me before you went ahead. My reasons for being here are private, and I'm not about to air them in public."

Laughing, he slung a casual arm around her shoulder and resumed walking. "Don't tell me you're nervous in front of a camera! If anyone can handle herself, you certainly can."

"It's not that so much as..." She gnawed the inside of her cheek, uncertain of the wisdom of airing her real concern.

"What? Come on, sweetheart, stop looking like Bo Peep about to be attacked by the spider! Tell me what's really troubling you."

How could she say, *We've never met, but I sense your assistant doesn't like me any more than I'm inclined to like her—or the fact that she seems to be very familiar with the layout of our home!*

She couldn't, it was as simple as that. Their truce was

too new, too fragile. So she settled for a safer middle ground. "Okay, it's the way I've been swept into this. I don't mind telling you, I find Ms. McHenry rather overpowering."

"She does come on a bit strong at times, but she means well and she's very efficient. She'll see to it that everything runs like clockwork."

"She's also very...protective of you." Yes! *Protective* was a much wiser choice than *possessive* which was the word she'd have preferred to use. "I got the distinct impression that she resents me. She as good as said my being here was interfering with your work."

"Then she was out of line and I'll speak to her. It won't happen again."

Gabriella flung him a sideways glance. Something—a certain tension threading his voice, and the same rare uneasiness in his manner which she'd seen her first night back when the subject of marital fidelity had come up for discussion—set off warning bells and forced her to confront the suspicion she'd tried desperately hard to ignore. *Willow McHenry was the woman who'd almost made him forget his wedding vows!*

"Is she right, Max?" she asked him quietly. "Do you wish I'd stayed away?"

"Do you think I'd have agreed to try to revive our marriage, if that were the case?"

It was still there, that twinge of disquiet he couldn't quite suppress.

Say "no", and make light of the whole business. Change the subject. Don't give him grounds to accuse you of trying to keep him on a leash like a pet dog, the way he did when you were first married and couldn't bear to be apart from him!

"She sounded very sure of her facts."

"What about what I'm telling you? Shouldn't that count for more?"

"It does," she said, wishing she'd kept her mouth shut. Even if Willow McHenry was the other woman, he'd told Gabriella nothing had really happened beyond kissing. "Of course it does."

Bracing his hands on her shoulders, he held her at arm's length. "I hope so. Because this attempt at a reconciliation is about us—you and me—laying our hearts on the line and daring to take each other on trust. No one else comes into the mix, Gabriella. And if you find yourself questioning that—"

"I'm not," she cried, turning her head to press a kiss to his hand. "I do trust you, Max."

He regarded her soberly. "I hope so," he said.

But the doubts she heard in his voice found an answering echo in her heart. Try as she might, she couldn't shake the feeling that Willow remained a threat, whether or not Max realized it. And because of that, Gabriella's bright hopes no longer shone with untarnished brilliance.

Nor, it appeared, did his. He didn't hold her hand again, and the easy camaraderie they'd known when they started out dwindled into strained silence. He strode back to the penthouse immersed in his own thoughts and seemed almost to have forgotten she was there beside him.

Why? Because he was thinking about Willow whose self-confidence was such that she'd never known a moment's uncertainty in her life? Was he wishing he was with her, instead of his neurotic wife?

The questions nagged at her unmercifully.

She and Max didn't make love that night. They lay side by side, not touching, the unacknowledged rift between them slight and intangible as a moonbeam. He fell asleep before she did. In the glow of city lights infiltrating the bedroom, she could see the steady rise and fall of his chest, the dark blur of his head against the pillows.

He was close enough that she could feel the warmth of his skin, yet so far removed that a million miles of loneliness separated them. It was her fault. She should not have brought the ghosts out into the open. They belonged in the shadows.

Miserably, she curled up on her side away from him, and forced herself to close her eyes and not…*not*…give way to the gremlins of uncertainty gnawing at the edges of her mind. *He had said it was over and he would never deceive her! It was not his style.*

She slept poorly, chased by uneasy dreams. Then, just as the sky began to lighten, she awoke to find his body pressed against hers, hard and ready. Without a word, she turned into his arms and opened herself to him.

They fused with a passion touched by desperation. Time and again he tormented her, withdrawing almost completely and then, when she was ready to weep with need, plunging deep within her, rapidly, fiercely, as if he were seeking to take hold of her soul. "I missed you last night," he told her hoarsely, between thrusts. "Don't let silly unfounded fears come between us like that again."

The woman who rang the doorbell at precisely nine-thirty on the morning of the interview could not possibly be Willow McHenry, Gabriella decided, barely masking her surprise. There were no long red fingernails, no hard unsmiling mouth, no dark hair secured in a sleek French twist.

This woman was shorter than Gabriella by a good six inches, with a sweetly rounded body, warm brown eyes and gleaming light brown hair curling softly around her face. She wore a buttery-yellow linen suit with a skirt which came to just below her knees, and sensibly stylish sandals with a bit of a wedge heel. Her nose was slightly freckled, her mouth rather full and defined by tawny lip gloss, her smile wide and generous. Not a beauty, by any means, but definitely pretty—and still frighteningly capable.

"Good morning, Mrs. Logan, I'm Willow, I see you're ready, that's good," she rattled off, breezing into the penthouse with an armful of creamy-pink roses and a large straw bag extravagantly embroidered with bright orange raffia marigolds.

Gabriella couldn't take her eyes off the bag. She'd expected an alligator briefcase. And very high heels.

"We'll need coffee," Willow declared, making a beeline for the kitchen.

"I'll make some," Gabriella offered, trailing after her in stunned amazement. This woman a marriage wrecker? Absurd! She was too…wholesome.

"No need," Willow warbled. "I came prepared. I'll just arrange the roses before I do anything else."

"I already have flowers—"

"Well, you know what they say. You can never have too many flowers or be too thin, though I'd say you're coming pretty close to disproving the latter! You're so slender, a person could almost snap you in half with her bare hands."

"I'll go find you a vase," Gabriella said, trying not to back away too hastily. Willow McHenry's hands were as capable as the rest of her, and looked more than equal to the task.

"I'll do it. Max made it very clear that you're not to be put to any extra trouble, so please just sit and relax— on the terrace would be best, so that you're not in the way while the camera crew sets up. You look lovely, by the way. Your photos don't begin to do you justice.'' She pulled open the door to a corner cupboard and peered inside, rising up on her toes to gain a better view. ''What happened to the vases which used to be in here?''

''I moved them,'' Gabriella said, a prickle of annoyance riding up her spine. Whose kitchen was it, anyway?

''I see. In that case, if you'd be so kind…?'' Willow's raised eyebrows and upturned palms spoke volumes, but just in case her request wasn't coming across clearly enough, she followed up with, ''Where did you put them, dear?''

''In the storage room.''

''Ah!'' She bustled unerringly across the foyer to the little room under the stairs.

Gabriella watched in numb fascination and reminded herself that Max had almost missed his flight to New Mexico the day before, because he hadn't been able to tear himself away from her. *That* was the important thing, not the proprietary way his assistant had swept in and usurped the role of lady of the house!

''I brought a list of questions you're likely to be asked,'' Willow announced, reappearing with a Waterford rose bowl and tall antique urn. She set them down on the counter and reached for a folder in the straw bag. ''Here they are. Why don't you go look them over and leave me to take care of things in here? As soon as it's brewed, I'll bring you some coffee. Are your parents here, by the way?''

''Yes,'' Gabriella said. ''They're enjoying the morning sun on the terrace.''

''How sweet. You must introduce them to me when I have a moment.''

She reached into the bag again, and brought out a sack of coffee beans, a carton of light cream, and a small round cake tin with a picture of the late Princess Diana on the lid. "Oatmeal cookies," she explained, noticing Gabriella's curious glance. "I baked them myself, just this morning."

You probably spin your own knitting wool and do prize-winning petit point, too! Gabriella thought uncharitably, and hurriedly left the room, more annoyed with herself than the amazing Ms. McHenry.

I'll phone you every night, Max had promised, before he'd dashed through the departure gate at the airport. *Honey, I'm sorry to be taking off like this, but when Willow set up this meeting, she wasn't aware you and your folks would be here, and it was too late to change things by the time I realized the conflict.*

Ha! Gabriella suspected Willow had been fully aware, but what she didn't know was that Max had phoned his wife three times last night, and told her he missed her so much he didn't think he could hold out until Wednesday and was trying to wind up his business a day early so that they didn't have to wait until tomorrow to be together again.

So she had no reason to feel threatened. No reason at all. Let Willow do her worst. When it came right down to it, the only person truly capable of undermining her confidence was Gabriella herself.

Burying a sigh, she wandered into the living room and picked up the photograph of her and Max on their wedding day. She'd worn her grandmother's bridal veil and a dress embroidered with seed pearls. Max had worn a morning suit, and the same grim expression that had transformed his face the day he'd learned she was pregnant...

"You're what?" he'd roared in subdued horror, when she told him the news.

They'd been sitting outside at Gerbaud's, Budapest's

most famous and elegant coffeehouse, and patrons at nearby tables had turned their heads to discover who was causing such an untoward commotion.

Gabriella had cringed, and repeated the news in a whisper. "I'm going to have a...baby."

"And you're saying it's mine?" He'd waved the question aside and regarded her from haunted eyes. "No, don't answer that. Who else's could it be?"

"I'm sorry, Max," she'd said in the same low voice. "I know this wasn't part of your plan."

"Was it part of yours?" he'd flung at her contemptuously.

"Of course not! I had no idea—"

"Right! You just happened to climb into bed with me when you were at your most fertile!"

His chest had risen in a massive sigh. "Well, never let it be said I walked away from my mistakes. If I've fathered a child, I'm prepared to face the consequences."

Those had been his exact words, but the way he'd looked had suggested he'd prefer to face the executioner's block. Nervously, she'd asked, "What do you mean?"

A bleak smile had touched his mouth. "Exactly what you're hoping I mean, my dear," he'd replied. "I'm not waiting for your father to come after me with a shotgun before I do the decent thing. We'll get married as soon as it can be arranged, and if anyone questions the unseemly haste of the arrangement, you can tell them in all honesty that I have to be back in Canada before the end of the month. That way you'll be safely out of sight before you start to show, and no one but you and I need to know the real reason we sprinted to the altar."

"You don't have to do this, Max," she'd said, seeing how much he hated the idea.

"Of course I do, and that's exactly what you've been counting on."

"No. Marrying me was never part of your plan."

"It was part of yours, though, wasn't it?" he'd said scornfully. "The minute you clapped eyes on me, you started casting about for a way to snag me."

"No!" she'd protested, her heart breaking. "Max, I love you!"

"You don't even know me. I could have a prison record as long as your arm and six ex-wives stashed in the closet, for all you care. What matters is that I'm rich and can afford you, and while you'd have preferred it if I'd gone down on my knees and proposed in the good, old-fashioned way, when you realized it wasn't going to happen quite that easily, you decided to help matters along even if it did mean dispensing with your moral rectitude and putting your virginity on the block. Money's a powerful aphrodisiac when you don't have any, isn't it, Gabriella?"

She'd jumped up from her chair, uncaring that people were staring. "How *dare* you insult me!" she'd gasped. "I am a Siklossy and we have never sold ourselves for money!"

"Oh, sit down and stop making a fool of yourself!" he'd said bluntly. "Your family doesn't have a pot to pee in, the old family mansion's crumbling around your ears and needs an injection of cash in the worst way, so when a nice North American millionaire came along ripe for the picking, you did what you had to, to reel him in." He'd slapped a fistful of forints on the table and leaned close. "Well, congratulations, Gabriella! I hope like hell you find it's worth what it's going to cost you."

It had not been, not for the longest time. The six months following had been the most miserable of her life. She'd often wondered if, in fact, there really had been a baby and the sheer stress surrounding the days following their farce of a wedding had caused her to miscarry, even though the specialist Max dragged her to see when the bleeding began determined otherwise.

"Your pregnancy test's negative, and there's no other physical evidence to indicate spontaneous abortion," he'd said. "Given that your cycle is irregular anyway and you've gone this long before without menstruating, it's my guess your doctor made a misdiagnosis in the first place. How soon after your last period did you see him?"

"I...didn't," she'd admitted. "I just assumed...because my husband and I had made love..."

How pathetic her reasoning had sounded; how pitifully inadequate. And yet, it had been the truth, even though she'd never convinced Max of that.

"Irregular cycle?" he'd sneered with blistering anger, afterward. "Missed periods? And it never once occurred to you to mention that small detail to me? You just let me infer you'd seen a doctor and hoped I'd never find out differently? Gee, Gabriella, you're just full of surprises, aren't you? What's next on your devious agenda? Twins left in a basket on the doorstep?"

Small wonder their marriage had turned into such a nightmare. But they'd been handed the chance to turn things around and this time, she wasn't battling on her own. She had Max on her side, and she wouldn't allow anyone or anything to drive them apart.

"Good grief!" Willow McHenry exclaimed, swanning into the room and taking a good, long look at the wedding picture. "Better put that away, Mrs. Logan, before the interviewer sees it and decides there's something, after all, to the rumor that your marriage is in trouble! Poor Max looks as if he's headed for the hangman's noose!" She traced a fingernail polished with clear enamel over his face, then flicked her gaze to his bride. "You look gorgeous though. Positively radiant. Maybe he was just nervous, wondering how he'd ever manage to live up to your expectations."

"Oh, he manages that very well," Gabriella assured her blandly. "In every possible respect. I couldn't ask for a more devoted or attentive husband."

"Really?" Willow bathed her in one of her warmest smiles and patted her arm. "Isn't it nice that you think so!"

CHAPTER SEVEN

GABRIELLA refused to let the remark throw her off stride—even though she was quite convinced that was its primary aim. Willow worked hard to give the impression she was as warm and fuzzy as a doting mother cat, but she knew how to unsheathe her claws and though her attacks were swift and subtle, the scratches she left behind stung.

"Well, it can stay where it is, if you insist," she said, taking the photo from Gabriella and giving the glass a quick polish with the hem of the little apron she'd tied around her waist. The same apron, Gabriella realized with a small sense of shock, which she'd come across, her first day back at the penthouse.

Against her better judgment, she said, "Where did you find that apron, Willow?"

"Right where I left it, dear. In a drawer in the kitchen."

That *did* rock Gabriella's composure! Fortunately, the television crew showed up just then, and the ensuing chaos as they moved furniture, strung cables across the floor, and set lights and cameras in place, distracted her enough that she had no choice but to wait for a more appropriate time to analyze this latest affront to her peace of mind.

Whipping off the little Susie-homemaker apron, Willow donned her suit jacket again and, armed with her clipboard and pencil, reverted to self-assured executive assistant very much on the job. "I'm afraid that's out of the question," she ordained, when the interviewer, Jaclyn, a nice woman in her early forties, suggested they might take a few shots of the penthouse as a lead-in to the main event. "My employer is a very private man and his home is off limits, except for this room and possibly the south-facing terrace. There's nothing else to see on the main floor anyway, except for the dining room and his office, and nothing but two en suite bedrooms upstairs. Nothing out of the ordinary at all."

"Well, I find this room quite *extra*ordinary," Jaclyn said, smiling at Gabriella and indicating the two armchairs positioned before the cameras. "You have wonderful taste, Mrs. Logan, and it's reflected in your choice of decor as much as in the clothes you wear so well."

"Actually, Mr. Logan chose the furnishings in here," Willow supplied helpfully.

"Really?" Dismissing her rather sharply, Jaclyn turned back to Gabriella. "Let's get started, shall we?"

She began straightforwardly enough but though her tone remained sympathetic, inevitably the subject came around to the rumors of a troubled marriage. "You and your husband are apart much of the time," she said tactfully. "How do you respond to the speculation that this has put a severe strain on your relationship?"

"It's true that our careers often take us in different directions, but we both recognize it's the *quality* of the time we spend together that counts, and not necessarily the *quantity*." Fully aware of Willow hovering in the background, Gabriella stroked her finger fondly over the wedding photo on the table beside her, then looked directly into the camera. "But I can say without reservation that my husband and I have never been closer. Regardless of what the tabloids might hint at, we have *never* been happier."

Jaclyn leaned forward in her chair. "I find that quite

remarkable. So often, when a woman achieves the kind of success you've realized, home and family tend to fall by the wayside.''

"Not in my case,'' Gabriella replied emphatically. "I am even more deeply committed to my husband now than I was on the day I married him. Realistically, my career as a model will last, at most, another few years. I intend to make my marriage last a lifetime.''

She punctuated the last remark with a glance at Willow, and only her professional training kept Gabriella from recoiling at the fleeting expression she surprised on the other woman's face. The full and smiling mouth was pinched in a grimace as if its owner was hard-pressed to keep it silent, but most shocking was the unbridled rage blazing from those hitherto friendly brown eyes.

Then, just as swiftly, the genial mask fell into place again and the moment passed. "Congratulations, everybody! I think that went very well,'' Willow announced, resuming charge as the interview came to an end. "Gabriella, thank you for allowing us to make such a mess of your living room, but rest assured I'll see to it that everything's returned to its proper place before I leave.''

Gabriella, though, felt anything but reassured. In her line of work, she'd come across too many women eaten up with jealousy not to recognize it when it was staring her in the face. Willow might like to give the impression she was content to be known only as Ms. McHenry, Max's loyal assistant, but in reality she aspired to much more. Her ultimate goal was to be Mrs. Max Logan, and she wasn't going to let the small matter of a current wife stand in her way. And that, without question, made her Gabriella's enemy!

*   *   *

Something was wrong. He heard it in Gabriella's voice when he phoned to tell her he wouldn't make it back before Wednesday afternoon, after all, and he heard it again when he called from Denver to explain his connecting flight was delayed because of mechanical problems. Her responses were too careful. Too flat. And that made him uneasy as hell, though if truth be told he'd been antsy ever since the previous week's unsettling conversation with Willow.

He'd thought they understood each other; had believed she recognized that incident eight months earlier for what it really had been: the brief and isolated lapse in judgment of a lonely man who came to his senses before any real damage had been done.

Now, he was no longer so sure Willow saw things quite that way. His gut instinct warned him that what he'd long ago dismissed as something that ended before it properly began, she had blown out of all proportion and turned into a major affair. He couldn't put his finger on anything specific; it was more that a lot of little things, though piddling in themselves, assumed disturbing significance when added together.

He wasn't a superstitious man, and he didn't believe in courting trouble. But he was no fool either. He knew better than anyone that if it did occur, ignoring it wouldn't make it disappear. A man who wanted to stay in control of his own life and protect the people and things he cared about, had to take action and neutralize a problem *before* it ran amok.

He and Gabriella had come a long way in the last week, and he wasn't about to stand idly by and watch their marriage go down the tubes through any default on his part. Perhaps he needed to be more proactive in making that crystal clear to the world in general—and to Willow in particular. Conveniently, the next night's awards dinner would provide him with the ideal opportunity to do precisely that.

He hoped she'd be smart enough to get the message, but if she chose to be obtuse, he was perfectly prepared to spell it out for her, one syllable at a time. And if *that* wasn't enough to convince her she was pinning the tail on the wrong donkey, he'd fire her and to hell with the possible repercussions. He wasn't about to be held up to ransom by her, or anyone else.

It was close to midnight when he finally arrived at his own front door. The penthouse was silent and only one lamp in the foyer had been left on. Gabriella was half asleep, and although he'd have liked nothing more than to make love to her, he was pretty bushed himself. So, foregoing the pleasure until they were both in better shape to appreciate it, he crawled into bed, wrapped his arms around her, and fell into the deep and dreamless sleep of a man confident that he had a firm hold on more than just his wife's warm, delicious, sweetly scented body.

When she stepped into the reception area outside the hotel's vast mirrored ballroom on Thursday night, Gabriella decided she could just as well have been attending an opening at one of the world's most recognized fashion houses. Certainly, every designer she'd ever worked with was represented in the gorgeous silks and beaded creations worn by the women around her.

And the jewels! Diamonds that put the fire of the crystal chandeliers to shame; Colombian emeralds, pigeon's blood rubies, sapphires the size of walnuts! Absently, she fingered the aquamarine lying snugly at her throat.

Noticing, Max murmured, "It might not be the showiest piece in the room, but it's hanging around the most beautiful neck.''

She loved the way he leaned into her when he spoke, the movement so slight as to go unnoticed by a casual observer, but possessed of such a subtle intimacy that a tiny explosion of delight vibrated throughout her body. She loved the way he looked, too. There wasn't a man in the room who matched his black-tie elegance.

''It's perfect and I wouldn't change it for the world,'' she said.

His gaze slid to the Swarowski crystal studs in her ears. ''I should have commissioned matching earrings.''

''You had my wedding ring resized so that I can wear it again.'' She brushed a minuscule thread of lint from the satin lapel of his dinner jacket, and let her left hand drift up to caress his jaw, loving the way the light gleamed on the simple gold band as she did so. He'd given it to her after she'd finished dressing that evening, and as he'd slipped it on her finger, she'd promised herself she'd never take it off again, no matter what. ''This means more to me than any number of expensive gifts.''

''Unless you want to cause a scene, quit touching me like that,'' he growled, snagging her wrist. ''It's been almost four days since we made love and I'm feeling deprived.''

''Me, too,'' she told him on a shaken breath, the heat he so easily aroused with a glance, a word, streaking through her. ''I missed you so much when you were away, Max.''

She wanted to tell him she loved him, too, but not until after he'd said it to her. Only then could she be sure he was ready to hear the words he'd steadfastly refused to believe when she'd spoken them to him in the past.

He raised her hand. Kissed the pulse beating at her

inner wrist. Traced a covert, sensual circle in her palm with his thumb, and nodded to where her parents were engaged in animated conversation with the Austrian consul and his wife. "What do you say to us making up for lost time by cutting out of here early? We can send the limo back to collect your folks later."

"I hope I didn't just hear what I thought I heard!" Willow McHenry, demurely resplendent in bronze taffeta, materialized out of the crowd, champagne glass in hand. "You can't possibly leave early, Max. It's out of the question."

Out of the question, Gabriella thought with some amusement, tripped off Willow's tongue with practiced ease any time events threatened to disrupt her well-orchestrated plans. Hopefully, she'd soon apply it to her secret hopes for a more intimate liaison with Max!

During his absence, Gabriella had had plenty of time to mull over Tuesday's events and remained more convinced than ever that her instincts were on target. Even her mother had commented on the proprietary way Willow had taken over. "She thinks I am too old and unimportant to be of any consequence," Maria had said darkly, "but I am still smart enough to recognize a snake when it slithers into my daughter's home. Beware of her, my child. She is dangerous."

The snake had wound itself around Max's other arm. The brief glance he spared it, and the speed with which he disentangled himself made Gabriella glad she'd decided not to undermine their reconciliation by voicing her suspicions to him. He'd said "it"—whatever *it* had been—was over, and if she couldn't take his word over Willow McHenry's, she had no business wearing his ring and passing herself off as his wife now.

"There must be five hundred people here, Willow," he said tersely. "I doubt we'd be missed."

"Of course you'd be missed!" She swung her gaze to include Gabriella and bared her teeth in a smile. "Both of you. It's not often the city scene's brightened by a celebrity of your wife's magnitude, on top of which tonight my boss is a star in his own right, as well." Undeterred by the way he'd shrugged her off, she tucked her hand beneath his elbow and nodded toward the waiters setting plates of smoked salmon on the linen-draped tables in the ballroom. "I think we should find our seats, don't you? It looks as if dinner's about to be served."

Your wife...my boss? Amazing!

Biting her lips to stifle the giggle threatening to erupt, Gabriella marveled at how, one way or another, the woman managed to worm her way into their private universe and turn them from a couple to a trio. "Are you here alone, Willow?" she inquired politely, when she managed to bring herself under control again.

Willow's gaze narrowed, but her smiled gleamed as implacably as ever. "Of course not, dear. Here's my date now. Max, you already know Brent, I believe?"

Max shook the man's hand. "Sure. Nice to see you here, Brent."

"And this," Willow continued with superbly subtle contempt, "is the famous Gabriella Siklossy, Brent."

"Also known as my wife," Max put in blandly, placing a possessive hand at Gabriella's waist and inching her a little closer. "Brent works in the drafting department at Logan Enterprises, sweetheart, and drew up some of the preliminary plans for the Budapest project."

The three of them chatted briefly about the success of the restoration and the charm of her native city in general, and for once Willow was unable to insinuate herself into the conversation.

That she didn't like being relegated to the sidelines was obvious. "It's never been on my travel agenda," she said brusquely when, in an attempt to include her, Gabriella asked if she'd visited eastern Europe.

She immediately reasserted herself, though, when they reached their table. "I think you should sit here, next to the podium, Max," she proclaimed. "That way, you won't have to climb over our laps to get to the microphone."

The little laugh she tacked on to her remark was meant to imply she was joking, of course, but Gabriella was willing to bet Willow would give up six months' salary for the chance to get better acquainted with Max's lap— or any other part of him she could lay hands on. In all honesty, Gabriella could hardly blame her. He was the most gorgeous man in the room, and quite possibly the entire world!

Her tolerance was short-lived though, when the relentless woman tried to relegate her to a seat about as far removed from Max's as it was possible to get, short of moving her to another table. "And you over here, with your mother and father, Gabriella."

Once again, Max intervened. "My wife, her parents, and I will sit together, Willow."

"Oh…!" She shrugged indifferently. "All right, if you say so. But I was rather hoping you'd give the rest of us a chance to rub shoulders with your famous guests. Sort of share in the reflected glory, if you see what I mean."

"Afraid you'll have to make do with admiring them from a distance," he said, his voice cut with steel. "And just for the record, I don't share my wife with anyone."

Although warmed by his words, a thread of uneasiness

wove through Gabriella. Was it her imagination, or was he playing the attentive husband with a little too much dedication tonight? And if so, for whose benefit?

"I don't mind mingling," she told him.

He ushered her to her chair and took a seat next to her. "I do," he said. "I want you by my side, close enough to touch."

She had never felt more secure, never more certain that they belonged together. If only they could have done as he'd suggested and slipped away when the meal was over, how differently the evening might have ended. But a person's whole world could come crashing down on *if only's,* and Gabriella's began to fall apart in the lull between dessert and the presentation of awards.

She had slipped away to the ladies' room and was seated on a stool at the vanity table, touching up her lipstick, when the door opened and Willow came in. Their eyes met in the mirror and although there was a steady stream of traffic in and out, an irrational sense of danger swept over Gabriella, raising the hair on the back of her neck and sending tiny thrills of fear chasing over her skin.

"I thought I might find you in here." All cozy smiles, Willow plopped onto the stool next to hers. "I've been waiting all night to tell you how perfectly divine you look, and I absolutely adore your pendant." As if they were very old, very good friends, she leaned across and scooped the aquamarine onto the pad of her finger in order to examine it more closely. "It's one of Gio's pieces, of course. The craftsmanship and design are unmistakable. Was it a gift from Max?"

"Yes," Gabriella said, trying not to shrink at the touch of that cool, intrusive finger at her throat.

"Well, aren't you lucky! All he ever gave me from there are these." She let go of the pendant, and tilted her head to show off the topaz-and-gold studs in her ears. "Not that I'm complaining, mind you, since the most expensive thing I've ever given him is the pen set he keeps on his desk at the office—oh, no, that's not quite true!" She tapped a reproving forefinger against her pursed lips. "I gave him the marble clock beside his bed, too. But that hardly counts, because it was my fault the one he had before got broken."

Apparently oblivious to the impact of that little gem of information, she turned to the mirror and pushed her fingers through her hair, arranging a curl here, another there, then leaning forward to inspect her teeth, presumably to make sure no debris from the spinach soufflé accompanying the main course had overstayed its welcome.

"How could it have been your fault?" If it hadn't been that she suddenly found herself floundering like a non-swimmer tossed into a bottomless lake, Gabriella would have rejoiced at how unperturbed she managed to sound.

"Hmm?" Another curl was lovingly tucked into place. "Oh, you mean about the clock? I knocked it off the bedside table by accident, one night. I suppose I could have had it repaired, but things like that generally aren't worth what it costs to have them fixed, and it was rather badly smashed, so I decided to buy him a new one instead."

"Not worth fixing? For your information, it had a one-of-a-kind crystal case signed by the artist and—"

"Tell me about it! I was afraid to walk barefoot on the carpet for days afterward."

Don't assume the worst! Gabriella told herself sternly. *Just because she's been in your bedroom doesn't necessarily mean she's been in your bed as well! She's playing some sort of sick mind game and if you want to emerge the winner, you'll walk away from her. Now! Only a devil for punishment would leave herself open to further injury by asking her what she was doing upstairs in your home to begin with.*

So true! But sometimes, the only way to put an end to the doubts was to drag them out into the clear light of day and confront them. How else to lay them to rest and go forward with one's life? No matter what the outcome, anything was preferable to leaving them to fester like some insidious disease.

Replacing the cap on her lipstick, she took a tissue from the box on the vanity table and blotted her lips. "What were you doing in our bedroom, Willow?" she asked, proud of the cool detachment in her voice. She was the only one who knew she was shaking inside. With fear, with pain, with anger.

A smile so slight it was almost a smirk crossed Willow's face. "Among other things, I was sleeping in there, dear."

Among other things? The witch! "With Max's permission?"

Willow glanced at her, eyebrows raised in astonishment. "Don't look so shocked, Gabriella. Certainly with Max's permission! What did you think? That I just wandered in there uninvited and made myself at home?" She sighed, and a faraway look came into her eyes before she let them drift closed. "That mattress was pure heaven, just as Max promised!"

Perhaps if she hadn't been blindsided by shock, Gabriella might have managed to handle the situation with more poise. She was, after all, a woman of the world, and men cheating on their wives was hardly a novel concept. Some might even go so far as to say that, in Max's case, it was justified; that she'd driven him to it by walking out on him and leaving him to his own devices too long. She might even have believed it herself and been able to forgive him—*if he hadn't sworn to her that he'd remained faithful.*

It was this last betrayal of trust that unraveled her and had her leaping up from the stool so violently that it tipped over. She didn't care that two other women who'd been chatting together on a love seat in the corner eyed her suspiciously and practically tripped over each other in their eagerness to leave before the catfight began. "You're lying! You've never set foot in my bedroom!"

Oh, how shrill she sounded. How pathetically hysterical.

"I'm afraid I have, dear," Willow said, calmly collecting her bag and standing up also. "And in your lovely luxurious soaker tub, too. My stars, it's almost as comfortable as the mattress and vastly preferable to the shower! And I'll never forget the view from the bed on a clear night. There's nothing quite like being all warm and cozy under the covers and watching the moon rise over the sea, don't you agree?"

Gabriella simply stared at her, too speechless with dismay to muster a reply. Instead, she stood frozen with incredulity as Willow patted her cheek and admonished kindly, "Pull yourself together, dear. It's high time we got back to our table and you don't want some photographer capturing you looking like this and splashing your picture all over tomorrow morning's paper, now do you?"

That soft little hand, the phony, concerned smile, the anxious query in the brown eyes which weren't anxious at all, but completely empty and without soul—the combination was more than Gabriella could bear. *"Don't touch me!"* she whispered, springing back with a shudder. *"Don't ever come near me again."*

"Well, if you prefer to spend the rest of the night sulking in here, that's your business." Willow shrugged. "But don't worry, I'm certainly not going to insist on staying with you and holding your hand through yet another emotional crisis. No wonder poor Max got tired of trying to keep you happy. I can see now why he felt he was wasting his time.''

She swept out and let the door swish closed behind her. Alone in the blessed silence, Gabriella set the stool upright again and collapsed on its padded seat. *So, finally, the gloves were off!*

She supposed she ought to be relieved. But she felt nothing. Was so numb, in fact, that she wondered briefly if she was trapped in some horrible dream brought on by too much champagne. Except she'd drunk barely two glasses all night, and the tears glazing her cheeks were hot and wet and all too real.

A few minutes later, the door swung open again. Too distraught to face anyone, Gabriella fled around the corner and into the nearest toilet stall. Footsteps followed and stopped on the other side of the cool marble wall behind which she hid. ''Gabriella,'' her mother said softly. ''I've come to help.''

It was perhaps the one voice in the entire world capable of melting the ice encasing her heart; the only voice that had always known how to heal the hurts. And oh, how she was hurting, now that the numbness was wearing off! So much so that her face was contorted with the pain, and great ugly noises were coming from her mouth.

''Open the door, my darling,'' her mother coaxed.

And she did. Because her mother would love her no matter how she looked or sounded. She didn't have to pretend to be brave or impervious or invincible, and she didn't have to be perfect. All she'd ever had to do for her mother to love her was be herself.

''Oh, Mama!'' she wept, sliding back the bolt and falling into her mother's arms. ''I think I'm going to die!''

''Rubbish!'' her mother said. ''You have too much to

live for. Wash your face, then come and sit on that little couch where all the mirrors are, and tell me what's gone so terribly wrong in the last half hour that you're hiding in here like a refugee. Your poor husband's beside himself with worry. I believe if I hadn't come myself to investigate, he *would* have.''

Oh, how tempted she was to unburden herself! How she wished she could paint a truthful picture of her troubled marriage and solicit her mother's advice, lean on her wisdom! Yet what right had she to weigh down a seventy-year-old woman with such knowledge, then expect her to return with an easy mind to a home on the other side of the world?

No, her mother deserved better. Both her parents did. It was for their sake that she'd entered into the charade of happy wife in the first place, and she did not have the right to shatter the image now. With only two more days left in their holiday, she had an obligation to preserve the myth, no matter how painful or difficult she might find it.

Clamping her fingers to her mouth to stop its trembling, she took a deep breath. ''You're right, Mama,'' she admitted shakily. ''Sometimes, I say the first thing that comes into my head without any thought for whether or not it makes sense. Of course I'm not dying. But for a little while, it felt as if I might.''

''Did that woman say or do something to upset you, darling? She's the one who told me I ought to come looking for you.''

Gabriella forced a smile to her lips and shook her head. ''It was something I ate. Suddenly, I felt...'' The memory of Willow's self-satisfied smirk rose up in her mind, and a tremor of distaste ran over her, revolting as insect feet. ''...very unwell. But I'm better now.''

Her mother watched her a moment, her eyes so full of love and compassion that Gabriella's heart broke all over again. "Yes," she said. "I think you are. Or if not, then you will be. Comb your pretty hair, my darling, and pinch your cheeks to make them rosy again. Max has won a prestigious award for his work preserving old buildings, and you should be at his side helping him celebrate his success."

She could not face him again, not tonight, not after what she'd learned. And yet, if she did not, wouldn't she just be playing into Willow McHenry's merciless little hands?

"I will," she said. "I just need a moment to myself. Go back to the table, Mama, and tell him I'll be there soon."

She waited until she was alone before daring to look in the mirror again. She was not a pretty sight. Her face was blotchy, her eyes red-rimmed. As for her famous smile, she doubted she'd ever be able to produce it again. If he could see her now, her agent would probably ask to be released from his contract, certain her career was over.

But she hadn't climbed to the top of her profession without learning a few tricks on the way. Cold water was a model's best friend; never being caught without basic essentials the one unbreakable law which ruled her life. A little concealer under the eyes, a touch of pressed powder to nose and cheeks, a stroke of mascara on the lashes, and long, soothing sweeps of the miniature hair brush she'd tucked in her bag, worked a minor miracle. Add a spine of steel, and the makeover was complete.

Smoothing the long full skirt of her dress over her hips, she stepped back and flung a last challenging glance at her image. "Curtain time, Gabriella," she announced softly, then, head held high, she turned to the door and prepared to face her nemesis.

CHAPTER EIGHT

SHE found Max impatiently pacing the hallway outside. "What the devil took you so long, sweetheart? I was beginning to think you'd moved in there permanently."

"Don't think I wasn't tempted," she shot back, ignoring his proffered hand and sailing past him under her own steam into the ballroom.

The shimmering light from the chandeliers had been dimmed so that only the glow of candles was reflected in the mirrored walls, and those people who weren't chatting over after-dinner drinks were dancing to a small orchestra. But what should have been a dream setting had turned into a nightmare for Gabriella.

Max caught up with her before she'd taken more than half a dozen steps. "Ahem! Want to talk about whatever's got you so steamed?"

"Not right at this moment, no." She smiled and nodded at the Austrian consul and his wife as they pirouetted past. "Congratulations, by the way. I hear you won an award."

"Screw the award, Gabriella!" Max snapped, grabbing her by the arm and swinging her around to face him just as she was about to plunge through the crowd to their table. "And while you're at it, screw the frozen attitude, too! Something's up and I want to know what it is."

She steeled herself to meet his gaze. Until that night, she'd never been able to look into his candid blue eyes without her heart doing a little flip-flop somersault. But that was before she'd been given reason to suspect he was, above all else, a consummate liar. Now, she was afraid she'd either slap his face or burst into tears.

"This is neither the time nor the place, Max. It can wait."

He flung an exasperated glare at the people swirling past them. "Fine. If you won't talk, we'll dance. Because I'm damned if you're going to treat me as if I'm not even here!"

"I don't want to dance with you."

"Prove it." He pulled her against him, locked one arm around her waist, and positioned his hand in the small of her back with sufficient pressure to mold her hips to his. Disguised by the folds of her skirt, he forced his knee between both of hers, leaving her with the choice of moving with him as he began a sultry waltz, or remaining stationary and having him rub up against her in a way that was downright indecent.

"I am not enjoying this," she informed him starchily.

"Oh, yes, you are," he said, bringing their joined hands to rest against his chest, and brushing his knuckles over her breasts until she thought her nipples would self-destruct. "I've got you so hot and bothered, you can barely stand up."

He wasn't always a liar. Sometimes, he homed in on the truth all too well. If she didn't sit down soon, she'd fall down. Her legs were trembling and the ache between her thighs had left her moist with heated longing. "Don't be ridiculous!" she said.

He laughed and nuzzled his mouth to her ear. And what he was doing with his hips didn't bear thinking about! "You forget how well I know your beautiful body, my love. I recognize what it's telling me."

"You're the one with the erection, not me," she said boldly. "You should be ashamed of yourself."

"Why? Because I find dancing with my wife such a turn-on?"

"I wish they'd turn on the overhead lights," she fumed. "I bet you wouldn't be quite so cocky then!"

For once, she actually managed to leave him at a loss for words. He stopped dead in the middle of the floor, his arms fell to his sides, and if it weren't that she was so hurt and bewildered by the confrontation with Willow, she'd have laughed at the conflicting expressions chasing over his face.

He recovered quickly though, and bathed her in a smile so dazzling and engaging, it tore holes in her already battered heart. "Was that a deliberate double entendre, or merely your way of showing off how well versed you've become in colloquialisms?"

A furious blush engulfed her then, as the import of what she'd said sank home. "Trust you to put the worst possible connotation on every little word that comes out of my mouth! But then, what else should I expect from a man with the morals of a goat!"

Her eyes were brimming with tears, and she didn't care who saw them. He did, though. "Hey," he said, drawing her back into his arms. "What have morals got to do with anything? You know I'm just teasing you, so what's really going on here, Gabriella?"

He wore such a look of concern, invested such a wealth of tenderness in his question, that she was sorely tempted to lean into his embrace and spill out everything bottled up inside her. But just then the music stopped and before she could speak, another voice intruded—one she'd come to despise for the venom underlying the syrup that coated every word.

"Oh, *there* you are, dear!" Willow crooned, feigning solicitude. "I was just on my way back to the ladies' room to find out if you were feeling better, but I can see I was worrying needlessly.''

''What's going on?'' Gabriella glared at Max. ''Why don't you ask *her?* She's the one with all the answers.''

He stepped back a pace and looked from her to Willow, his eyes very cagey all of a sudden, but his face otherwise wiped clean of all expression. ''Because I'm asking you, and I'm getting tired of waiting for an answer that makes sense.''

''I'm afraid,'' she said, tossing her head contemptuously, ''that what I have to say isn't something you really want to hear.''

''Gabriella, stop this!''

Once upon a time, she'd have heeded that imperious command. She'd have walked through fire, if he'd ordered her to do so. But those days were over. Ignoring him, she plowed through the crush of bodies to the double doors that opened onto the curving balcony overlooking the main lobby of the hotel, and down the escalator to the back entrance where a doorman was hailing taxis for departing guests.

The evening had long ago lost whatever charm it might once have held for her, and all she wanted now was for it to be over.

''Let her go, Max.'' Willow grabbed a pit bull hold on his arm when he tried to follow Gabriella. ''There's nothing you can do.''

''The hell there isn't!'' he snapped, shaking her off. ''What have you said to my wife, that she looks ready to take a chain saw to both of us?''

''Nothing.'' She gazed at him, all wide-eyed innocence. ''Nothing but the truth.''

He stopped dead in his tracks at that, knowing with

sinking certainty that it had been a truth custom-designed to suit Willow's purposes and undermine all his efforts to shore up his sagging marriage. A cold sweat prickled unpleasantly over his skin. "Whose truth, Willow?" he inquired, closing in on her menacingly. "Yours?"

"Really, Max!" She raised her hands and placed both palms flat against his chest. "You're making a scene. Calm down!"

"I'm not in the mood to calm down. I'm going after my wife, and when I find her, I'm…"

Going to wring her neck! Then I'm coming back to wring yours!

Choking back the threat, he pushed past her and cut a swath through the packed room, following the direction Gabriella had taken. Leaning over the low glass wall of the mezzanine, he scanned the area below, searching for a glimpse of her and spotted her almost immediately. With her looks and in that eye-catching dress, she was hard to miss.

She stood at the concierge's desk, scribbling something on a piece of paper. Not ten yards away, revolving glass doors opened onto the porticoed parking area where a fleet of limos and taxis waited. Another minute, and she'd be gone.

Luckily, the mezzanine was relatively deserted. He made it down the escalator in record time and practically sprinted across the main lobby, coming up behind her just as she handed the note to the concierge.

"Please have this message delivered to Mr. and Mrs. Zoltan Siklossy at table six in the Crystal Ballroom," she instructed him.

"That won't be necessary," Max said, intercepting the folded slip of paper and crumpling it into a ball.

At the sound of his voice, she swung around, practically

spitting with fury. Looked so much like an exotic cat about to attack, in fact, that if he hadn't been so royally ticked off himself, he'd have applauded. Her huge aquamarine eyes had narrowed to slits, her teeth were bared in a grimace, her silky blond hair flew around her head like a mane.

And still she managed to look stupendous. Tall and proud and aristocratic, with the bottle-green satin of her strapless dress glowing against her honey-gold skin and swirling rich and full around her long, magnificent legs.

Then she spoke, bursting into wild, impassioned Hungarian, which was just as well because he didn't need an interpreter to tell him that she'd probably have been arrested if she'd resorted to English.

"Settle down," he ordered.

He'd have been better off keeping his mouth shut and exercising muscle instead, because all he succeeded in doing was stoking her rage to greater heights. Talk about putting on a show! Her performance held the concierge and two bellhops paralyzed with fascination.

Well, they might be enjoying it, but he'd had his fill of melodrama for one night. "Gabriella!" he thundered.

Her mouth remained open but the torrent of noise stopped. Knowing it was a temporary cease-fire only, he wasted no time on persuasion or diplomacy.

"We will take this some place private," he informed her. "You might not care that you're making a fool of yourself, but I do."

"I refuse to remain here with the two of you!"

Two? He'd have thought she was hallucinating on top of everything else if a quick glance over his shoulder hadn't revealed Willow bringing up the rear. *Just peachy!*

Dismissing her with a glare, he turned back to his wife. "You'll damn well do as you're told, for once," he advised her. Then, fishing a fifty-dollar bill out of his wallet, he snapped his fingers to bring the concierge out of his trance. "Find us a room where we can be alone."

"At once, sir." Palming the tip, the man hustled them into the small office behind his desk. Lit by a single bulb and equipped only with a wooden table, a couple of chairs and a spare coatrack, it hardly matched the elegance of the public rooms, but it served the purpose.

"Okay." Fists on his hips, Max eyeballed his wife. "Start talking, Gabriella, before I really lose patience."

"And make sure you stick to the facts!"

He whirled around, realizing too late that Willow had followed them into the office. "I don't recall inviting you to join the party."

The way she leaned against the door made it clear the only way she was leaving was if he threw her out bodily. "I have the right to defend myself against this woman's insane accusations."

Gabriella let out a hiss and lunged forward. She was taller than Willow by a good five inches, and though there wasn't much meat on her bones, what she did have was toned to perfection. Willow would end up picking her teeth out of the carpet if it came to a wrestling match and loath though he was to defend her, Max felt obligated to intervene on her behalf.

"Gabriella, for crying out loud!" Not sure of the protocol for breaking up a catfight, he grabbed her around the waist and swung her off her feet.

Her high heel caught him a sharp blow on the shin, one flailing fist connected with his jaw, an elbow jabbed him in the ribs. And as if that wasn't punishment enough, she let fly with another Hungarian tongue-lashing.

Alarmed, Willow shrank against the door and he couldn't say he blamed her. Given a choice, he'd opt for a football scrimmage any day of the week over trying to contain a woman on the warpath! "Listen, Gabriella," he panted in her ear, pinning her arms and hauling her against him so that her shoulders were sandwiched to his chest, "keep this up, and someone's going to get hurt. I'd as soon avoid that, and if you stop to think about it, I think you'll agree with me."

"Precisely," Willow chimed in. "Lay a hand on me, Gabriella Siklossy, and I'll slap you with assault charges so fast, you won't know what hit you. Just think what *that*'ll do for your public image!"

"Peasant!" Gabriella spat.

"Put a lid on it, both of you, and start acting your age!" he bellowed. "I've had it up to here with your histrionics! I don't know what the devil's gone down between the two of you tonight, and I'm beginning not to care."

Wrong thing to say! Gabriella wriggled around and tried her damnedest to knee him in his most delicate parts. "You've never cared!" she cried. "You announce at dinner that you don't share your wife, but you expect her to share you! If I weren't here now, you'd probably throw that…that *creature* down on the table and have sex with her. But then, it wouldn't be nearly as comfortable or private as our bed, would it, and she couldn't wash the smell of you off her body in our bathtub afterward, could she?"

"You want to tell me what the hell she's talking about?" he asked Willow.

Apparently not sure he had the situation fully under control, she pushed away from the door but kept a wary eye on Gabriella. "It's really very simple. I ran into your wife in the ladies' room. We compared jewelry and in the course of making pleasant conversation, I happened to mention how much I'd enjoyed living in the penthouse.

She became totally unhinged and went so far as to call me a liar in front of an audience. I'd appreciate it if you'd set her straight on the matter.''

"Gabriella?" He relaxed his hold slightly. "Is that all there was to it?"

"It's not *enough?*" she exclaimed, vibrating with outrage. "First, you buy her expensive earrings, then you move her into my home?"

"No, it's not quite enough," he said, "but it'll do for now."

"You don't *deny* it?"

"No," he said. "Basically, she told you the truth. Too bad it never occurred to you there might be more to the story."

She squirmed to face him. "Then defend yourself! Show me that I can trust your word over hers!"

"Why? What difference would it make? You've already judged me and found me guilty."

"Max, *please!*" The anger was seeping out of her like water running down a drain. But instead of feeling vindicated, he knew only a sense of defeat. Of resignation.

"You see?" Willow said smugly, reading his expression. "There's absolutely no pleasing her, no matter how hard you try."

"And what would it take to please you, Willow?" he asked.

"Well, an apology from her, for a start."

"I'll see that you get it."

"Never!" Gabriella exclaimed haughtily. "I will not apologize to the woman who has done her best to steal my husband."

He pushed her down on one of the chairs and leaned over her. "Yes, Gabriella, you *will* apologize because, strictly speaking, every word she told you is the truth.

And when you have, I'll fill in all the important little bits she somehow forgot to mention, and you'll see you have no reason to believe I've ever betrayed you. Perhaps then, you'll feel like apologizing to me, too.''

''Max…!'' Her hands fluttered helplessly, then fell into her lap. She stared up at him, her lovely eyes wide with distress. ''If I've misunderstood, please tell me how!''

''The apology comes first, Gabriella.''

She drew in a long, deep breath and for a moment he thought her pride might get in the way and she'd tell them both to go to hell. Then she slowly rose to her feet, straightened her impeccable spine, and pinned Willow in that compelling green gaze. ''I'm sorry if I have accused you unjustly, and I apologize.''

Just that. No beating around the bush with excuses, just a straightforward admission uttered with all the dignity and grace of a true aristocrat. He hoped he could carry through with what he had to say, with half her class.

''Okay,'' he began. ''First, the earrings were in recognition of the extra hours Willow put in to help save a project that would have gone down the tubes otherwise. Instead, it paid off handsomely, and I acknowledged my gratitude in similar ways to everyone on my staff who gave up evenings and weekends to get the job done. The women got earrings, the men watches.''

''Well, if I'd known that, I'd—''

''Second, she had to vacate her leaky condo for a month while it was being repaired, so I offered her the use of the penthouse. If it matters at all, I happened to be in Cairo the entire time she stayed.''

Gabriella moistened her lips with the tip of her tongue. ''I see.''

''Yes,'' he said wearily, ''I'm sure you do, now. The

pity of it is, you didn't see fit to come to me for the answers in the first place.''

''How was I to know there was more to her story?''

''Because you know me, Gabriella. At least, I thought you did. And I thought we'd agreed we'd be up front with each other about any concerns or questions we might have. Apparently, I was wrong on both counts.''

He turned again to Willow. ''Is there anything else I can do for you?''

''No, Max. All is forgiven.''

''Not quite,'' he said. ''I'd like your resignation on my desk first thing tomorrow.''

Aghast, she stared at him. *''Why?''*

He'd have felt sorry for her if he'd had a drop of pity left in him. But he was so choked, it was all he could do to be civil. ''Because there's a world of difference in the way we interpret the truth, Willow.''

''I won't do it,'' she said, her face pale with disbelief.

''Then I'll fire you.''

''You can't!''

''Watch me!'' he said harshly. ''Not only will I fire you, I'll sue you for sexual harassment.''

''*You*'ll sue *me?*'' She laughed. ''I think not! You seem to have forgotten about a certain night when you lured me to the penthouse and poured wine down my throat—''

''And kissed you. I haven't forgotten.''

Jeez, but he was a fool! He'd seen this coming for weeks but, in the end, done nothing to defuse it. So much for his belief in confronting trouble head-on!

''Then you might want to reconsider asking me to resign.''

''Before you think about trying to blackmail me, Willow, let me remind you that the incident to which you refer took place nearly nine months ago, that you arrived at my front door uninvited, brought the wine in question, and showed yourself more than willing to engage in an affair with me, even though you knew I was married. You even went so far as to follow up with a letter stating as much.''

''You received no such letter from me!''

''No, I didn't. But you did write it, and were careless enough to leave a copy of it on your desk. And I'm perfectly prepared to produce it as evidence, if I have to.''

He was bluffing, of course. He'd shredded the letter months ago. But she didn't have to know that.

''So this is what it comes down to, is it? You'll fire me to placate the woman who walked out on you and left me to pick up the pieces?''

''You leave me little choice.''

He thought he knew all there was to know about her. He'd seen her at her most efficient, her most sympathetic, her most charming, and at her most vulnerable. But he'd never seen the controlled rage that crept over her features then. ''This is my reward for all those times I listened while you poured your heart out about the mistakes you made with her? For the times I picked up your dry cleaning, made sure your passport was renewed on time, filled in as your hostess?''

Her voice quavered; her big brown eyes filled with tears. ''I remembered your birthday. I made fruitcake for you at Christmas, and fudge. I even sewed a button on your jacket once! And not one of those things was part of my job description.''

''That's not to say I didn't appreciate your efforts.''

''I don't want your appreciation!'' she wailed. ''I want *you*, and I thought, in time, you'd see how much better off you'd be with someone like me.'' She pointed a distraught finger at Gabriella. ''I might not be beautiful like *her,* but I'd look after you. You'd never come home to an empty house. You'd never have to go out to get a decent meal. I'd be there, whenever you needed me. I'd *never* leave you the way she did. I wouldn't steal the limelight every time we went out in public. I'd give you babies and make you proud and..."

The words dissolved into a sob.

"The only flaw in all that, Willow," he said gently, "is that I never saw you in any role other than my executive assistant. I admire and respect you for what you brought to the job, but that's as far as it goes."

The tears rolled unchecked down her cheeks. "It could have been more, if she'd stayed away!"

"No. And that isn't going to change, regardless of where my wife chooses to live."

"Then I guess there's nothing more to say." With a mighty effort, she wrenched herself under control and smeared the back of her hand across her wet cheeks.

"I'll have Brent paged and get him to take you home," he said, because it was the kindest way to put an end to a scene which had already dragged on too long.

"I'm sure he'll be delighted to oblige. You're the boss, after all, and what you say goes, doesn't it?" she said sullenly. "I suppose you want the earrings back, as well. Well, why not? You've taken away everything else I ever cared about."

"Keep the earrings, Willow. You earned them."

"I'd rather have earned your love."

Love? The word lingered like bad wine on his palate in the silence she left behind. If lying and manipulating amounted to love, he wanted nothing to do with it.

After a moment, Gabriella came to where he slumped against the table and slipped her hand into his. "Oh,

Max," she murmured, "I feel so sorry for her! And it's all my fault! If I'd listened to you—"

Pointedly, he freed his hand and checked his watch. "Look at that—after midnight already. The do upstairs must be winding down. Go get your parents while I line up our limo."

He must have sounded as peeved as he felt because she looked at him anxiously. "But you and I will talk later?"

"Enough's been said, for one night, Gabriella."

For a lifetime, come to that. Because, as the old saying went, the more things changed, the more they stayed the same.

Impassively, he watched her leave. It was the one thing he could always count on her doing well.

Max barely said a word on the way home but her parents were very tired and seemed not to notice. They declined her offer of hot chocolate, and went straight upstairs as soon as they reached the penthouse.

Alone in the big living room, Gabriella faced her husband, tension arcing between them like invisible lightning. "Is there anything I can get for you, Max?"

"No." He ripped loose his bow tie. "Go to bed, Gabriella. If I want something, I'll get it myself."

"You're not coming up with me?"

He looked her over from head to toe with such slow and scrupulous attention to every detail of her appearance that even she, used as she was to being in the public eye, found herself twitching nervously.

"No," he finally said again. "You're a very desirable woman and despite everything that's gone down tonight, I'm not sure I trust myself not to make love to you."

She shrugged and drummed up a smile to cover the

ominous uncertainty sweeping over her. "Would that be so very terrible?"

"It would be disastrous," he said harshly. "I'm realistic enough to recognize a lost cause when it's staring me in the face. You and I are not going to work out, Gabriella, much though we might wish we could."

His words struck a dull, thudding pain to her solar plexus. "You're giving up on us, because of what happened at the hotel?"

"Name one good reason why I shouldn't."

"I love you!" she cried, reaching for him. "Enough to fight for you, which I surely proved tonight."

"Wrong," he said. "All you proved is that when it comes down to the crunch, we play by different rules."

"We were happy until Willow came between us with her half-truths!"

He went to stand at the open doors leading to the roof garden, and took a deep breath as if to cleanse his lungs of the air she breathed. "Willow is not the problem, Gabriella," he said flatly, staring out at the bright city lights. "*We* are. The only way she was able to come between us tonight was because we let her. And the only thing we proved tonight is that our marriage is too fragile to withstand any sort of outside pressure."

"How can you say that? We won."

"That might be your idea of a victory, Gabriella, but it's not mine. I'd rather have no marriage than one so flawed that I never know from one day to the next if it's going to fall apart because of some imagined sin on my part."

She'd remained standing by the sofa, but anger sent her rushing over to grab him by the sleeve and haul him around to face her. "You listen to me, Max Logan! I'd find your holier-than-thou attitude a bit easier to swallow if you weren't every bit as much to blame as I am for the state our marriage is in. You never miss a chance to throw it in my face that I've deceived you in the past, but I notice *you*'re not above resorting to blatant lies when it suits your purpose.''

''I have never knowingly lied to you.''

He bore no resemblance at all to the man who'd seduced her with such tender passion just a few days before. His tone, his expression, even the arm she clutched, were iron-hard, and brought back such vivid reminders of the weeks following their marriage that the old Gabriella would have crumbled in the face of it. But that pale, intimidated creature had had so little left to lose that fighting to hold on to it had been a lost cause from the start.

Today's woman, though, had seen a glimpse of paradise and wasn't about to forfeit it willingly. ''You did!'' she said heatedly. ''You told me the apron I found in the kitchen had been left behind by a housekeeper when you knew it really belonged to Willow.''

''If that's the case, this is the first I knew of it and I made an honest *mistake,* which is a whole hell of a lot different from telling an outright lie. But the fact that you'd allow so insignificant an item to be instrumental in eroding what little trust you have in me merely proves my point.''

''It need never have been an issue, if you'd been up front with me in the first place and told me Willow lived here for a month. But you couldn't bring yourself to do that, could you?'' She let go of his sleeve with fastidious distaste. ''And you want to know why? Because you do such a good job of deceiving *yourself,* and I am disappointed beyond words to discover you could be such a coward.''

His face flushed dull red, his eyes sparked blue fury.

"Don't push your luck, Gabriella. I'd flatten any man who dared call me that."

"Sorry if the truth hurts, but that hardly changes it. If you'd dared to face up to what Willow has really been after for months now, things would never have come to such a pitiful pass tonight."

He shrugged. "Pitiful's the word, all right, if a pair of earrings or an apron can bring about this much damage!"

"I'm not talking about material things like jewelry, or having some other woman make herself at home here. For heaven's sake, you're not a stupid man, even if you sometimes act that way. At some level, you must have known that her feelings for you crossed the line from professional to personal a long time ago."

"Not necessarily. I don't go around assuming every woman I clap eyes on has the hots for me."

"Oh, spare me, Max! You kissed her and from all accounts, she kissed you back. Are you trying to tell me you thought she was being *motherly?*"

Even before he replied, she knew she'd scored a point from the way his lips thinned into a severe line. "At the time, she agreed with me that it was a mistake best forgotten."

Gabriella shook her head despairingly. "How is it that you are so ready to believe what another woman tells you despite evidence that's she either lying or deluding herself, yet you refuse to accept that I mean it from the bottom of my heart and soul when I say I love you, and everything I've ever done, ill-conceived or otherwise, proves it?"

"You call walking out on me after only six months of marriage proof that you...care about me?"

"It's because I cared that I left. I couldn't stand watching us destroy each other. And how come a man who claims he isn't a coward can't bring himself to say the word 'love'?''

"Because I don't believe in tossing it around as a Band-Aid solution every time something goes wrong in a relationship. It takes more than that to hold a couple together.''

"Yes, it does," she said. "But love also goes a long way toward keeping a marriage intact when the going gets rough.''

"Then I guess that explains why ours is such a mess.''

He tossed the words at her almost glibly, but she wasn't about to let him get away with that. "It might not be in such bad shape if you were as quick to recognize your own weaknesses as you are mine.''

"And how do you figure that?''

"You make much of my not being able to trust you, but the fact is, you're afraid to trust yourself.''

"I am not!''

"Yes, you are," she said defiantly. "You're afraid to look into your own heart.''

"Bull!''

"Really? Then answer me this.'' She cupped his jaw and forced him to meet her gaze. "Have you ever, for a single moment, loved me?''

His glance veered away, past her and out to the dark waters of the strait. And she knew, if he could, he'd have disappeared into them and never surfaced again. Anything to avoid having to deal with a subject she'd never laid bare to him before because she hadn't wanted to put him on the spot, and she supposed, if she were honest, because she'd been afraid to hear how he might respond.

But the way she saw it, they were at such a low point

that she might as well face all her demons and have done with.

"Well?" she said. "I've put my pride on the line and asked the question, Max. Do you have the guts to answer it honestly?"

CHAPTER NINE

THE strain of maintaining appearances for those last hours of her parents' visit was worse than all that in the days which had gone before. Not that anyone made specific reference to the previous night's closing act at the hotel; in fact, the morning routine they'd established began as usual. After Max left for the office, Gabriella served oven-warm brioches with fruit preserves, then her father took a swim in the pool while she and her mother lingered over coffee.

They were barely settled under the terrace umbrella, though, when Maria observed, ''You have dark circles under your eyes, darling. Did you not sleep well?''

''Not particularly.'' Gabriella pushed her fingers through her hair dispiritedly. ''I miss you already, Mama. The time's gone by so quickly and we haven't taken you to half the places we'd planned to show you. You've spent most of your time here in the penthouse.''

''But we've seen how you live. When I'm home again, I'll be able to picture you here with your husband, and I'll remember the happy times we've shared with you.''

''Happy? Oh, Mama!'' She'd promised herself she wouldn't cry, but trying to hold back the tears was as impossible as trying to get Max to say he loved her. ''You could hardly have helped hearing us after you'd gone to bed last night. The French doors were wide open, and I think half the people in this city probably must have heard.''

''So?''

"So you know that Max and I are anything but happy!"

"I know that two people can fight as fiercely as they love. I know, too, that sometimes the love can become poisoned and seem more like hate."

"And this doesn't upset you?"

Her mother took a sip of coffee before replying, "It would upset me more if I saw only apathy between you and your husband. Passion doesn't kill a marriage, my daughter. Only indifference can do that."

How true! Max's dismissal of her question, his bruising detachment when at last he'd joined her in bed, had spelled out quite clearly that, as far as he was concerned, their marriage was dead. The poison, as her mother put it, had been left too long to do its treacherous work.

Her mother stroked her hand lovingly. "You'll make up, as soon as we're gone, Gabriella. It puts a strain on any marriage always to have to be on one's best behavior in front of guests."

"It's more than that, Mama. I'm afraid the truth is that Max and I are too used to living apart. We don't know how to be a real couple anymore."

"Then stay at home. Remind him all over again how it is to come home at night to find his wife waiting."

But sound though the advice was, and much though Gabriella would have loved to follow it, it came too late.

"I suppose you'll be leaving right after your parents are gone?" Max had said to her, just that morning.

She'd been in bed still when he'd come out of the bathroom wearing only a pair of white briefs. His hair, still damp from the shower, lay flatter than usual against his well-shaped head. His jaw was smooth as silk, his eyes a stunning blue against his sun-dark skin.

He strode past the foot of the bed to fling open the long windows and as he passed, she picked up on a faint trace of his aftershave: Davidoff's Cool Water—a fitting choice for a man who was, above all, coolly contained on the outside regardless of whatever demons haunted him within.

"I might as well," she'd replied, covertly watching as he crossed the room again to the tray on his valet where he kept his wallet and other small personal items. He looked utterly beautiful, utterly masculine. And utterly remote. "I've got a ten week overseas assignment coming up, starting in Tokyo next Wednesday, and I like to leave myself a couple of days to catch up with the time change."

"Sounds like a brutal schedule."

"I'll be at my usual hotel in Paris by the end of September, but if you need to get in touch with me before then, my agent—"

"I know how to reach you, should something come up. What I was going to say is, if you want to hang out here an extra day to catch your breath, you're welcome to do so."

"Thank you, but there's nothing to be gained in my staying. I'll put everything back the way I found it and be out of your hair by Monday at the latest."

He picked up his watch, the same stainless-steel Rolex he'd worn since before he met her. For all his millions, he was not an ostentatious man and though he was often generous to a fault with others, his personal tastes ran along rather austere lines.

His next words illustrated the point with chilling accuracy. "I was going to talk to you about that," he'd said, snapping the bracelet closed around his wrist. "You ought to arrange to have all that stuff you left behind the first time you took off shipped to your place in Rome. It's yours anyway, and you probably have more use for it than

I ever will. In fact, I don't know why you haven't claimed it before now.''

She could have told him the reason, if she'd thought he was the least bit interested in hearing her say, *Because I secretly hoped we'd find our way back to each other, and enjoy it together.*

But he'd laid to rest any chance of that happening when he'd turned away from her question the night before. *I fail to see where love comes into the picture,* he'd replied, and the emotional distance he'd put between them since bore out the sincerity of his belief.

''I'll arrange to have it removed as soon as possible,'' she said, and turned her face away before he saw the misery she knew must be obvious even to the most casual observer.

I will remember this moment for the rest of my life, she'd thought, closing her eyes but unable to shut out the picture emblazoned in her mind of the sun spearing the room to burnish his shoulders, and highlight his profile in such a way that his lashes formed dusky shadows on his cheeks.

Sublimely indifferent to her misery, he'd strolled into his dressing room—a respite she gravely needed—and returned a couple of minutes later wearing dark gray trousers and a white dress shirt. ''Would you like to take your folks out for their last night here?'' he asked, sliding a burgundy-and-blue silk tie under the shirt collar. ''I'll be happy to reserve a table somewhere.''

''No,'' she said hurriedly. She'd had enough of being in the public eye for one week, on top of which she'd seen how her parents' energy, particularly her father's, faded by the end of the day. ''I'm sure they'd prefer to spend a quiet evening here with just us before they undertake the long journey home tomorrow, but I'll understand if you'd find that too difficult and prefer to stay away.''

He'd fixed her in a somber gaze. ''I have no quarrel with your parents, Gabriella. I like and respect them both, and I'm no more interested in upsetting them than you are. If a quiet evening with just the four of us is what you think they'd like, that's what they'll get.''

''Thank you.''

Her mouth had been trembling so hard, she'd barely been able to articulate the words. Noticing, he'd given the Windsor knot in his tie a final inspection, then hooked his hands on his hips and blown out a breath. ''I like you, too, you know, and for what it's worth, I'm disappointed we weren't able to work things out.''

''Gabriella?'' With a start, she realized her mother was observing her with all the wisdom that came of having weathered seventy-odd years of more turmoil and heartache than any one person should be asked to bear.

''How do you do it, Mama?'' she asked, struggling to keep her emotions under control. ''How is it that you've never lost faith in yourself? How have you managed to get up and face another day, when so often you must have thought you had nothing left worth living for?''

''Never lost faith?'' Her mother smiled. ''Oh, my darling, if you only knew how many times I was ready to give up! When your brother was killed, I wished I had died with him. I blamed your father for not having taken us to a safer place until the troubles were over. But he wouldn't desert his country and when it came right down to it, I couldn't desert him. I loved him too much, just as you love your Max. And in the end, I was rewarded. I was blessed with you—a beautiful daughter when I thought my child-bearing years were behind me. It's true that good things come to those who wait, Gabriella. The secret lies in not giving up the fight, and trusting in the healing power of love.''

She spoke with such calm assurance that Gabriella was almost persuaded to believe her. A whole weekend alone with Max stretched ahead: two full days and two long nights. Only a week or so ago, when they'd finally dared let down their defenses, they'd found their way back to each other in less than an hour. Surely, if she put her whole heart and soul into it, she could pull off another such miracle?

But not without Max's cooperation and that, she discovered, was not forthcoming.

''I hoped I'd be able to take the morning off and drive you to the airport tomorrow,'' he told her parents, that night at dinner, ''but I just got word that clients I've been expecting are flying in from Geneva tonight and it looks as if I'm going to be completely tied up with them for the next couple of days.''

''We can order a taxi,'' Gabriella said, doing her best to swallow this latest blow to her hopes.

''No need. You can take my car instead. It'll be more convenient, especially with all the errands you have to run between now and Monday.''

Good grief, he could hardly wait to be rid of her! ''But if you're entertaining clients,'' she said, ''surely you'll need it yourself?''

''No.'' Impervious to the pain his words inflicted, he calmly helped himself to more salad. ''I've chartered a helicopter to fly us to Whistler for a few days of golf.''

''When do you plan to leave?'' she asked him, after they were in bed.

He yawned and stretched, then clasped his hands behind his head and closed his eyes. ''Tomorrow, as soon as the morning meetings are over.''

So much for a weekend of miracles! "Does that mean I won't see you again after tonight?"

"Not if you take off on Monday as planned."

"And if I don't?"

His eyes opened a crack. "I thought you had to be in Tokyo by Wednesday?"

"There's a lot to do here, between now and then. I could always wait an extra day."

"Why, Gabriella?" he said, slewing a weary glance her way. "What would be the point?"

Stung, she said tartly, "I know you're glad this entire charade is into its final act, but you might at least try to pretend a little regret that it's not ending as well as we'd hoped!"

"Regret, like guilt, is a waste of energy."

She wanted to shake him! "How can you lie there so passively with our marriage in its final death throes, and not feel *something?*"

His chest rose in a massive sigh. "What do you want me to say? We gave it our best shot and still managed to screw up big-time, and I refuse to keep on doing it—to me or to you. I feel like a big enough fool, as it is."

"No more than I do!" she retorted, deeply angered by his attitude. "I must have been crazy to believe you ever intended to make a serious effort to reconcile. Why would you, when you have Willow waiting to fill my shoes? She's obviously so much better suited to the job of catering to your needs than I ever was."

"Crazy?" he echoed mockingly. "Add *jealous* and *suspicious* to the list, and you're finally coming close to discovering what I've suspected all along—you're the over-the-top star in your own tragic soap opera!"

"Am I, Max? Or is it more that I'm coming too close to the truth for your comfort? Because the fact remains that you shut me out when I tried to be a wife to you, but you let her in.''

''You didn't stick around long enough to learn the first thing about being a wife! We never took the time to get to know each other at the start, to find out what, if anything, we shared in common—besides good sex, that is—and we're still making the same mistake now. And whether you believe it or not, at least I know Willow well enough to recognize she's not what I want. Whereas with you—!''

Frustrated, he jerked half upright, yanked his pillow from behind his head and dealt it a savage punch, then stuffed it under his shoulder and angled himself away from her.

''What about me?'' Furious herself, she glared at his back. ''Come on, Max, you're so fixated on spitting out the truth at all costs, so speak your piece. After all, it might be your last chance ever to tell me exactly what you think of me!''

''Never mind,'' he said, gazing stubbornly at the window. ''I won't be part of this anymore. I'm tired of trying to separate fact from fiction, truth from fantasy. And I'm tired of rehashing history. This isn't yesterday, or two years ago. This is now—and it's about us. About how we haven't learned a damned thing from past mistakes, and just keep repeating them. And I take full responsibility for it. If I'd followed my instincts and turfed you out of my room that first night, we wouldn't be in this mess now.''

''How noble of you—and how hypocritical!''

She sensed rather than saw the indignation sweep over him. ''What the devil's *that* supposed to mean?''

''Your instinct was to take what I was so willing to give, and no questions asked! You welcomed me with open arms.''

He bolted up from the bed. "You took me by surprise!"

"And you simply *took* me! Very willingly, I might add."

"You're a lovely, passionate woman, Gabriella, and hard to resist when you put your mind to it," he said, slumping back against the pillows. "I've never denied that, anymore than I have that, physically at least, we're ideally suited. Too bad that's *all* we have going for us, because by itself it's not enough to float a successful marriage, and any doubts we might have entertained on that score have been laid to rest with a vengeance in the last twenty-four hours."

"Really?" she taunted him. "I think it has more to do with the fact that there might be a great deal more to our relationship than you're willing to admit, because that would involve your looking honestly into your heart, and you're afraid of what you might find. And you know what? That sets me free to go forward without you."

"I see." He half turned and regarded her coldly. "And the point of your little homily is?"

She swallowed the tears that suddenly threatened because he was right: regret was useless, and guilt a burden she didn't deserve. She'd done penance enough for past sins. "That I'm accepting failure—mine *and* yours!— and I'm ready to close the book on us. I'll begin divorce proceedings as soon as possible. You'll never have to see me again after tomorrow morning."

If she'd hoped that might shock him into realizing he was throwing away something precious, he quickly disabused her of the idea. "At least you have the decency to be up front about leaving this time, instead of leaving a note."

"Yes," she said. "I'm no longer that insecure, homesick little bride trying to adjust to a new life in a new country and desperate to win her husband's approval at any cost. I've grown up, Max, and I think it's time you did the same.''

''Huh?''

If she hadn't been too emotionally battered to feel anything but a blessed numbness, she'd have found his thunderstruck expression comical. "You heard," she said. "Instead of lecturing me about letting go of the past, try practicing what you preach. Stop hanging on to old resentments and using them to justify your present choices. Maybe if you can learn to do that, you'll find sharing your life with someone isn't such a burdensome undertaking, after all.'' She pulled the sheet up to her chin and edged closer to her side of the bed to give him as wide a berth as possible. "Who knows? You might even learn to be truly happy one day.''

"You speak from personal experience, no doubt!''

She flinched at the biting sarcasm. "Not yet, but I'm not giving up. I'm willing to try again, and the next time, I'll choose more wisely and get it right.''

"I wish you luck.''

"Luck doesn't enter into it. I've done my best to right all the wrongs that caused so much trouble and damage to our marriage, and whether or not you believe it, I've learned from the experience.''

"Have you really, Gabriella?'' he sneered. "And what is it, exactly, that you've learned?''

She gazed at the reflection of the pool shimmering on the ceiling and thought a moment before saying calmly, "Mostly that it takes two to make a couple. One person can't do it on her own, no matter how hard she tries. In our case, I want to be happily married, but you don't. So, I'm cutting my losses and moving on in the hope that, someday, I'll find a man willing to share more than just his bed with me.''

Brave words spoken with commendable assurance, but *so* difficult to abide by the next morning as she stood in the penthouse foyer, watching as Max made his farewells to her parents and knowing that, when he finally turned to her, it would be for another last goodbye.

He took her hands and for a long aching moment, looked into her eyes. ''Well,'' he said, his voice a little rough, perhaps even a little uncertain, as though the words were hard come by, ''don't let them work you too hard and stay safe, okay?''

''Okay.'' She must have seemed composed enough on the outside, because neither her mother nor her father appeared to notice anything amiss, but inside she was dying—*dying!*—an inch at a time, in slow and torturous agony.

''And start taking better care of yourself.'' His thumbs traced warm little circles over the backs of her hands. He bent his head, pressed a kiss to her forehead, smudged another to the corner of her mouth. ''Make sure you eat properly. I hate to see you looking so thin.''

For him to be killing her with kindness now was insupportable and she knew a swift and fervent urge to punish him. Before she lost courage, she threaded her fingers through his thick, black hair and kissed him back, a deliberately slow, intimate kiss full on the lips. One which dared him to rebuff her.

She angled her face so that her lashes fluttered against his cheek, and let her eyes drift closed. She drank in the scent of him; the taste and texture of his beautiful, sexy mouth. She imprinted her body against his one last time, and had the small satisfaction of hearing the sharply in-drawn breath he wasn't able to suppress.

"Be good to yourself," she whispered when at last she pulled away. Then, unable to bear seeing him leave, she turned and ran up the stairs. Once inside their bedroom, she leaned against the closed door and let the tears run free in silent, shuddering sobs.

Four hours later, she was weeping again, this time as she watched her parents pass through the security gates at the airport. As she had several times in the previous two years, she would visit them whenever her work took her close to her native home, but right at that moment, she felt as if she was being abandoned by the only people left in the world who cared whether she lived or died.

As if he knew it, too, her father had almost broken down when it came to their parting. "Remember we love you and that, however much other circumstances might change, you will always be our daughter," he'd muttered, enveloping her in a bone-crushing hug. "Remember, too, that we are only a phone call away any time that you need us."

Reliving the words in her mind as she drove out of the airport and merged with the heavy traffic heading toward downtown Vancouver, she thought it unlikely that he'd been taken in for a moment by the lengths to which she'd gone to portray a happily married woman. Instead, he'd simply played the game, along with everyone else.

Would he accept news of her divorce with equal for-bearance? she wondered. Would her mother? Or would they be disappointed to learn she lacked the tenacity with which they'd clung to their ideals and dreams?

Perhaps if she'd been less involved in her thoughts and more tuned in to her surroundings, she'd have seen the commotion taking place outside the convenience store a few yards away from where she'd stopped for a red light. She'd have realized the danger before it was too late, and taken the simple precaution of hitting the automatic door and window lock buttons on the console.

But by the time the car's front passenger door was suddenly wrenched open and a body hurled itself inside, it was too late to do anything but stare in horrified fascination, first at the long, vicious blade of the knife resting in uncomfortable proximity to her neck, then at the sullen face of the young thug huddled next to her.

"Out!" he snarled, both his tone and the gesture which went with it indicating she was expected to vacate Max's sleek, expensive imported sedan and leave it to tender mercies of her uninvited passenger.

A distant part of her mind told her she would be wise to obey; that even a life as miserable as hers was more valuable than a mere car. But the emotional paralysis which had gripped her ever since she'd realized her marriage was over left her curiously indifferent to anything but the fact that, even though he didn't love her, his car was one thing Max did prize highly.

So, "I'm afraid I can't possibly do that," she said. "It isn't my car and my husband is already annoyed enough with me that I shudder to think how he'd react if I simply turned it over to the first person who asked."

The youth—for certainly he couldn't have been more than fifteen or sixteen—cast a hunted look over his shoulder. Following his glance, Gabriella saw a small crowd converging on the car. She heard the distant wail of sirens coming closer.

So did the boy. "Start burning rubber, lady!" he snarled. "I'm in one hell of a hurry."

"Certainly. Where would you like me to take you?"

Amazed, she realized that although her hands were shaking, she'd voiced the question with all the aplomb of a duchess offering afternoon tea to a titled guest.

Her uncouth passenger seemed equally taken aback, though only briefly. Mouthing an obscenity, he brought the cold steel terrifyingly close to her throat and grasped a rough fistful of her hair. "You want to see your old man again, hang a right at the intersection and head for the freeway. And save trying to be funny. In case you haven't noticed, I'm not laughing."

Still in a trance, she shifted gear and followed his instructions to the letter. Tires squealing, the big car surged forward just as flashing lights appeared in the distance.

CHAPTER TEN

KEEPING his attention where it belonged—namely on the three overseas clients currently poring over spreadsheets and tossing around figures which ran into millions—was difficult when the only movie playing in Max's head was Gabriella.

Saying goodbye had been a lot tougher than he'd anticipated. At the last, he'd been swamped with doubts. The uncomplicated future he'd thought he wanted shone less brightly. No matter how he added them up, those things he'd always considered important suddenly weren't enough to hold the fabric of his life together.

The idea that he might be losing his taste for business was shocking enough, but the real eye-opener was, he didn't much care. For years, he'd been driven by ambition, thrived on success, treasured the freedom which allowed him to go wherever and whenever the greatest challenge presented itself.

But how many awards did a man need before he knew he'd climbed to the top? How many rivals did he outbid before his competitive spirit lost its edge?

As for the highly touted freedom—what the hell did *that* amount to if, at the end of it all, the only thing he had to come home to was a penthouse so devoid of life that it too often felt more like a tomb than a home, and the only person who even cared whether he lived or died was the assistant who planned his itineraries and penciled in his appointments?

Which brought him to his other big problem. Willow.

Distracted, he rolled back his chair and went to the cloth-draped table at the far end of the boardroom where coffee and pastries were laid out.

I should have insisted she pack up and have done with, instead of agreeing to let her work out her month's notice, he thought irritably, pausing before a highly polished coffee urn—silver, probably, but it didn't make the stuff inside taste any better, so who the devil cared! *She'll be underfoot every time I turn around, trying to make herself indispensable and prove I can't do without her.*

As though on cue, she appeared at the door and with ostentatious stealth made her way to where he stooped over the table, stirring cream into his coffee.

"Sorry to intrude," she whispered, her breath leaving an unpleasantly damp cloud over his ear, "but you have a visitor."

"Not now," he snapped in a low voice. Cripes, had she lost her mind, interrupting negotiations at such a critical stage? Just because he was somewhat disenchanted with business at the moment didn't mean he was ready to watch the last six months' work get flushed down the drain!

"This can't wait, Max. There's a police officer outside, a Detective Janssen, and he's very insistent on speaking to you in person."

"Police?" He snapped his mouth closed on the word and cast a furtive glance around, glad to see he hadn't been overheard and that the clients were still engrossed in the graphs and blueprints spread out in front of them.

Sensing something untoward must be afoot though, his vice president joined him at the coffee table. "What's up?"

"Seems I've got the police breathing down my neck on some matter." Max shrugged, more annoyed than disturbed. "Hold down the fort while I check it out, okay? We've pretty much covered the main points here anyway, so run the video on the Indonesian project if I'm not back before you wrap up, and I'll join you for lunch in the executive dining room."

Making his excuses to the clients, he then followed Willow out of the room. "If this is about an overdue parking ticket, someone's head's going to roll!" he warned her, striding down the hall to his office.

"If it were that minor, I wouldn't have interrupted the meeting," she said reproachfully. "But I got the impression it was something rather more serious than a traffic infraction."

Eyeing the plainclothes officer waiting by his desk, Max decided she was probably right. "Sorry to be the bearer of bad news," Detective Janssen began, once the introductions were out of the way, "but there's been an incident involving an automobile registered in your name."

Gabriella had taken his car to the airport! The first tendrils of fear spiraled through Max's bloodstream. "Incident?" he repeated hollowly. "Or accident?"

"Your car was stolen, Mr. Logan, and used as the getaway vehicle in a botched attempt at armed robbery."

Reaction set in, leaving him light-headed with relief. Gabriella was famously careless about locking up when she parked the car. Couldn't even recall where she'd left it, half the time. Once, she'd come out of a shop on south Granville and spent an hour looking for it before discovering it had been towed away because she'd left it in a restricted zone. Remembering, Max almost smiled. "Is that all?"

Janssen regarded him gravely. "Not quite, I'm afraid. Did you loan your car to anyone this morning?"

"Yes. My wife used it to take her parents to the airport." He did laugh then. "I hope you're not implying she tried to stick up a bank!"

"On the contrary. Whoever was driving your car this morning was taken hostage in the incident."

The blood roared in Max's ears. Unthinkingly, he grabbed a fistful of the man's shirtfront and shook him like a dog with a rabbit in its jaws. "What do you mean, she was taken hostage? What the devil are you trying to tell me?"

The detective calmly pried himself loose and straightened his tie. "According to witnesses, she appeared to argue with the suspect, even though he threatened her with a knife. It's likely he wanted the car and she refused to give it up."

"She did what?" Max dropped into his chair, his heart free-falling in horrific slow motion.

"She refused to turn over the keys. So he took her with him. She was last seen driving south over the Oak Street Bridge, with him holding the knife to her throat."

All at once, Max felt as if he were swimming in thick, gluey oil; as if the whole, ugly world were closing in and squeezing the life out of him.

Just that morning, she'd kissed him. He'd tasted her incredible mouth, felt her long, lithe body pressed up against his, looked into her shimmering green eyes. And told himself he was well rid of her, when what he should have done was tell her that she was right. He *was* a coward! He didn't have the guts to face up to his feelings for her.

And now some half-crazed thug on the run had her— and just what he planned to do with her when she'd outlived her usefulness made Max's blood run cold.

"I realize this is shocking news, Mr. Logan," Janssen

said sympathetically, "but if it's any comfort, we have roadblocks set up. They won't get far. And with her behind the wheel instead of him, the odds are that excessive speed won't be a factor."

That was supposed to comfort him, when a maniac was holding a knife to her lovely throat? "I'm hardly concerned about a speeding ticket right now," he ground out hoarsely.

"Naturally not. What I meant to say is that safety—"

But whatever slim comfort the detective had been about to dish up next was interrupted by the chirping of his cell phone. Pacing to the window, he unclipped the instrument from his belt and answered.

The few words he spoke were too low to be overheard but the conversation was mercifully brief and when he turned again to Max, his face looked a little less somber. "Good news. The car's been found and the suspect apprehended."

Max could barely bring himself to ask, "And my wife?"

"She's being brought in also."

"*In?*" he barked. "In *where?* To a hospital? A morgue?"

"To police headquarters, Mr. Logan. She appears not to have been harmed. If you like, I can take you down there to be with her while she's questioned."

"Oh, I'd like," he said grimly. In fact, there were a number of things he'd like, and right at the top of his list was a raging need to see for himself that she hadn't been hurt. Then he'd like to spank her delectable backside for being such an idiot!

Yet when he was led into the room where she waited, he sagged in the doorway and simply feasted his eyes on the sight of her perched on a bench next to a police-woman, and sipping tea out of a paper cup.

When she saw him, she put the tea aside and slowly stood up, looking for all the world like a kid about to be punished for stealing from the cookie jar. ''I'm very sorry, Max,'' she said, all big stricken eyes and quivering mouth. ''I'm afraid your car's a bit the worse for wear but I'll pay for the repairs.''

''You'd better believe it,'' he said thickly, covering the distance between them and sweeping her into his arms. ''I'm going to take every last cent out of your beautiful hide!''

Then, to his eternal shame and embarrassment, he started bawling like a kid. Fat, sloppy tears dripped into her hair. And as if that wasn't humiliation enough, great jarring sobs took him by surprise and tore through him.

He wished he could fall between the cracks in the floor! He couldn't remember the last time he'd cried, but he thought it was when he was about four and found a dead squirrel in the driveway of his parents' house.

He hadn't cried at his mother's funeral fifteen years later, or when his father drank himself to death within six months of her passing, because grown men didn't cry. They coped at all costs. They kept their feelings bottled up inside and went toe-to-toe with the whole world before they'd allow anything to break them.

''Jeez, Gabriella, the things you do to me,'' he muttered, struggling to get a grip on his emotions.

''I'm sorry,'' she said again, and he realized she was sobbing into his shirtfront. And shaking like a leaf.

Blinking furiously, he fished a handkerchief out of his breast pocket, blew his nose, and wrapped his arms more firmly around her. Seeming to decide she was superfluous to the reunion, the policewoman let the door click shut behind her as she left the room.

Grateful for the privacy, Max led Gabriella to the bench and pulled her down on his lap. "It's over, sweetheart," he murmured unsteadily. "I'm here, and you're safe."

She hiccuped softly and buried her face against his chest, and for a while there was no need for words. It was enough that they were together. Enough that he could run his hand up and down her spine and know she was in one piece. Enough that he could feel the pulse beating beneath her jaw, and feel her rib cage expand with every breath.

Eventually she grew calmer and lifted her head to shoot an embarrassed glance his way. "I must look a mess!"

"You look like something the cat dragged in, and you're the most beautiful sight in the world," he murmured, his gaze scouring her face. Then he saw the angry red welt on the side of her neck; touched it with the tip of his finger and saw her wince. "And I'm going to kill the bastard who did this to you."

"Oh, Max, he's just a boy and he was so frightened."

"Was he really! Well, I was bloody terrified!"

"He made a mistake, and I know what that's like. You start out with something small and before you know it, things have snowballed out of control, and it's too late to put a stop to them."

He rolled his eyes in disbelief. "You'll be telling me next you feel sorry for the little creep."

"I do." She touched her forehead to his. "When I first met you, all I wanted was to kiss you. But the better I got to know you, the less I was satisfied with just that, so I tried to seduce you, and we both know where that led."

"The two situations hardly compare."

"Don't they?" She reared back a little and inspected

him soberly. "Didn't you feel you'd been taken hostage by me and coerced into a situation you didn't want?"

"For crying out loud, Gabriella…!" He leaned his head against the wall and clapped a hand to his brow. "Listen to me. This kid is ruthless enough to wield a knife, rob a store, and take a helpless woman prisoner. In my book, that makes him a criminal. A menace to decent society. And I'm going to have them throw the book at him for what he's put you through this morning!"

She drew her thumb over his mouth. "The way you're carrying on, anyone would think you cared about me."

"Jeez, woman, I *love* you!"

She stared at him, her eyes wide green pools of shock, while the words bounced off the stark walls of the room and ricocheted back to haunt him. "What did you say?"

Pretty shaken up himself, he stared right back. Having this conversation take place in an interrogation room at the local cop shop hardly fit his idea of romantic ambience, but the moment was right, and he'd put off baring his soul long enough. "I love you," he repeated sheepishly.

He kind of thought she'd tell him she loved him, too. After all, she'd been implying it long enough! Instead, she slid off his lap and put a safe six feet of space between them. "No, you don't. Not really. You're just grateful and relieved that I'm not hurt."

"Oh, I'm a lot more than just that!" He shoved himself off the bench and stalked her across the room. "I came close to losing you this morning, and I'm not talking about us going our separate ways or leading separate lives. Out of the blue, I was confronted by the very real possibility that you could have been killed—that there'd be no going back to try again, no making up and starting over.

No occasional long-distance phone calls just to touch base. No more you.''

He swallowed, afraid his emotions were going to seize up and make an ass of him again. "I couldn't handle it, Gabriella. It's as simple as that. So maybe you're right, and I don't love you. But if that's the case, then please explain to me why I didn't want to wake up tomorrow knowing you might not be part of my world anymore. Tell me why I felt as if someone had blown a hole clean through my heart.''

Detective Janssen poked his head around the door and spared her having to answer. "If you feel up to it, Mrs. Logan, we'd like to get a statement from you.''

"Of course.'' She swayed across the room with that inbred elegance that had captivated Max from the first. "Go back to work, Max,'' she said, over her shoulder. "I'll be fine by myself.''

"Like hell, you will!'' He caught up with her in three strides flat. "I'm staying here to take you home when you're done, and that is *not* something that's up for discussion.''

Max had closed the wooden shutters over the windows, leaving the bedroom full of pale, filtered light. The pillow beneath her head was cool and smooth, the light quilt covering her, soft and clean.

The boy's hand had been filthy, his nails bitten down to the quicks.

"Try to sleep,'' Max had said, stroking the hair off her face and dropping a kiss on her forehead. "We'll talk later, have a quiet dinner together. I'll order something in, open a bottle of wine. But right now, you need to get some rest.''

"Stupid, rich cow,'' the boy had spat, when she'd tried

to persuade him to give himself up. "What do you know about living on the street? When was the last time you picked through a back alley Dumpster to find something to fill your belly?"

"Take her home," the kind detective had said, after she'd given her statement. "She's in shock, but otherwise okay. We don't need to keep her here."

Max had led her out into the warm blue afternoon, one arm firmly around her waist. A shiny new Lincoln Continental stood in the parking lot. Opening the door, he poured her into the front seat. Even went so far as to buckle her into her belt, as if he really did care about keeping her safe.

"Where did you get the car?" she'd asked listlessly.

"I leased it. Made a call while you were busy with Janssen and arranged to have it waiting for us after you'd given your statement."

"Some ride you got here," the boy had said enviously, running his hand over the car's rich leather upholstery. "Bet you just take it all for granted, though. Anything you want, your old man goes out and slaps down the money, and it's yours. Easy come, easy go, right down the line."

"You don't have to take me to the penthouse," she'd told Max, knowing how he probably hated the idea now that the whole horrible business with the police was over, and he'd seen for himself that she was okay. "I can stay in a hotel."

He'd stopped with his hand on the ignition key and stared at her. "If that's meant to be funny, sweetheart, you should know I'm in no mood to be entertained."

"Oh, what a coincidence!" she'd gasped, involuntary peals of laughter streaming from her mouth and filling the plush interior of the car with ripple after ripple of merriment. "That's more or less what that poor young boy said when I asked him where he wanted me to take him."

"As far away as I can get from this lousy place."

"But what about your mother? Won't she be worried? Won't she wonder where you are?"

He'd let out an embittered croak of amusement and wiped the back of his hand across his mouth. His wrist was as slender as a girl's. "As long as she gets her daily fix, my old lady don't give a rat's ass about me or anyone else."

"What were you thinking of, all the time he held you at knifepoint?" Max had asked, during the drive back to the penthouse.

"That I was going to die and wouldn't have to divorce you, after all. I'd be your late wife, instead of your ex—a much more respectable way to end things."

She'd meant to sound carelessly sophisticated, to be the woman she so often portrayed in her work—untouched, remote, in control—but try though she might to keep her cool exterior firmly in place, inside she'd come unspooled. Tears had plopped off the end of her nose; her voice had quavered like a child's. A deep, aching pit had opened up where her stomach used to be.

"It's going to be all right, sweetheart," Max had consoled her, folding her hand in his. "I'll look after you. No one's ever again going to hurt you or frighten you like that."

"Put away the knife," she'd urged the boy, when the roadblock had loomed up ahead and flashing lights from a trio of police cars had closed in behind. "Explain you haven't eaten in days, that you have no place to live, that you were desperate. Maybe they'll understand and get you the help you need."

"You're a freakin' fool, you know that?" the boy had

jeered, but his eyes had been wide with fear. "Cops don't understand, and the only one who's going to help me is me. Hit the brakes. I'm bailing out."

When she hadn't immediately responded, his voice had risen to a scream. "Stop the freakin' car, I said!"

She'd slammed both feet on the brake pedal. Felt the heavy car fishtail perilously out of control, then rock terrifyingly from side to side before spinning like a donut across two lanes toward a two-foot-high cement divider separating her from oncoming traffic.

She'd wrestled with the steering wheel, heard the endless squeal of tires, smelled the trail of smoking rubber on the pavement, seen the roadblock rearing up, huge and deadly and then, at the last moment before impact, the passenger door flying open and the boy's fragile body, curled up and catapulting into space, then rolling like a ball into the deep ditch.

And she'd screamed until her throat stung. In terror for his life, and for her own...!

"Gabriella, wake up!" Max's urgent voice penetrated the horror. His strong arms lifted the tangle of quilt from around her legs. His hands—those magical, wonderful hands which knew so well how to thrill her with pleasure—wiped away the sweat pouring down her face. "You were dreaming, honey."

"The boy!" she whimpered, that final scene still vivid in her mind. "They took him away in an ambulance!"

"Janssen phoned while you were sleeping. Apart from a few cuts and bruises, none of them serious, the kid's going to be fine. Well enough to be arraigned first thing Monday morning." He plumped up the pillows and helped her to sit up. "Sweetheart, forget about him and start worrying about yourself. From what I've heard, you're going to be pretty sore tomorrow. If you'd rammed head-on into that roadblock, you'd be lying in a hospital bed now. Luckily, the car scraped by with only a glancing blow on the passenger side.''

"Can it be fixed—the car, I mean?"

"Who gives a rip, one way or the other? It's replaceable. You're not.'' He pinched the bridge of his nose and briefly closed his eyes as if a thousand tiny hammers were pounding in his skull. ''How are *you* feeling?''

She rotated her shoulders cautiously. ''I have to admit, I'm feeling a bit stiff.''

"Hardly surprising, but I happen to have the perfect remedy.'' He glanced at the bedside clock Willow had made such a point of mentioning she'd bought for him. Funny how, in light of the morning's events, everything *she*'d said and done seemed unimportant. ''I'll give you five minutes to get yourself into the hot tub.''

"I've already packed my swimsuit,'' Gabriella said.

"Then make do with your birthday suit. And don't look so fearful. I'm not such a lowlife that I'm going to ravish you in your weakened state.''

Well, of course he wouldn't! And she was ridiculous to be so bashful, when he already knew every inch of her body better than she did herself.

Still, she hesitated. The fact was, the balance of their relationship had shifted in the last few hours. Their roles weren't the same as they'd been that morning, or at any other time in their marriage. Real danger had entered the picture, acute enough that he'd told her, impulsively she was sure, that he loved her.

She'd always thought him too proud to succumb to anything as human as fear. That he wasn't didn't at all lessen him in her eyes; if anything it enhanced his appeal. But it also changed him. Suddenly, he was no longer the man she thought she knew.

Watching her and probably reading the doubts chasing through her mind, Max clicked his tongue impatiently and disappeared into the bathroom, returning a moment later with his thick terry-cloth robe slung over his arm. "Here. If modesty's an issue all of a sudden, wear this until you get down to the pool deck. I promise not to peek."

The prospect of having her aching body massaged by pulsing jets of hot water was tempting, no doubt about it. Certainly, she had no wish to remain in bed, prey to another nightmare rerun of the morning. "All right, you win."

He regarded her unsmilingly. "I usually do, sweetheart. Better learn to live with it!"

He'd ordered dinner—her favorite salad, and lobster in tarragon cream sauce with roasted endive, which she also loved—from a restaurant a couple of blocks away. It waited in the kitchen, packed in thermal containers to keep it at perfect serving temperature, along with a cheese board and a tray of petits fours.

Initially, he'd thought of doing the whole affair up in style in the formal dining room, but in the end had decided on something more intimate. He hadn't wanted her parked at one end of the long polished table, with him at the other. He wanted her close enough to touch. Wanted to be able to thread his fingers through her hair, and stroke his hand up her long, elegant leg. Wanted to hold her and kiss her, and tell her that when he'd said that morning that he loved her, he'd meant it.

So, while she showered and dressed, he started a fire in the living room to ward off the chill of the breeze floating in from the sea, and covered the coffee table with one of the antique hand-embroidered cloths she'd brought with her from Hungary. He hauled out the sterling-silver cutlery, and the Herend china so dear to her heart. Chilled a bottle of champagne and two wafer-thin flutes in a silver ice bucket. Slipped a couple of smoochy blues discs into the CD player and turned the volume low.

Then, as an afterthought, he cut a rose from the climber on the terrace and plunked it in a little crystal vase between the two candles burning on the table.

Still, she didn't appear.

What the devil could be keeping her?

Nervously, he paced the floor. Something about her had changed since the morning's incident, and he didn't just mean that she'd been shaken up. She'd withdrawn from everything around her, especially him.

If he didn't know better, he'd think she was afraid of him. And for the life of him he couldn't figure out why. What he *did* know was that he didn't like the way the foundation of their marriage seemed to be shifting under his feet yet again, just when he thought it had finally settled on solid ground.

Footsteps crossing from the stairs to the living room had him spinning around to find her standing haloed in the light from the foyer, and if he'd thought her beautiful before, he found her breathtaking now.

Her hair hung loose in a smooth pale curve that hid the ugly welt on her neck. Her skin glowed as if it were lit from inside with golden fire. The outfit she'd put on, a silky one-piece jumpsuit thing the color of a Rocky Mountain glacier, clung to her with enviable familiarity. She wore sandals webbed with leather straps so fine they resembled lace. Her jewelry consisted of little gold hoops at her ears and her wedding ring.

He hoped the latter boded well for the future.

"Have I kept you waiting?"

"If you have," he said, wondering why he had a lump

the size of a golf ball in his throat, and hoping like blazes he wasn't going to break down again, "it was worth every second."

She glided toward him, preceded by the merest hint of perfume, and allowed him to take her hands. He wanted to kiss her in the worst way, to crush her in his arms and never let her go.

But it as was if she'd surrounded herself with an invisible shield, one which dared him to try to get past, and he had to settle for giving her a peck on the cheek, then letting her go.

Stymied, he filled the champagne flutes. "Here's to us, Gabriella."

She inclined her head and touched the rim of her glass to his, but offered no answering toast, nor even a smile. Instead, she looked at his housekeeping efforts and said, "You've gone to a lot of trouble."

"You're worth it. I'm just sorry it took me this long to realize it."

Her gaze skittered away and settled on the fire.

Feeling slightly sick to his stomach, he said, "Honey, talk to me, please! Tell me what's put that introspective look in your eye."

Her shoulders tilted in a tiny shrug. "I'm wondering why you're here when I know you should be entertaining important clients."

"You're my wife, Gabriella. Where else would I be at a time like this?"

"I was your wife this morning, too, but that didn't stop you from planning to spend the weekend at Whistler."

He drew in a long breath and took a turn about the room before answering, "Maybe it's because I thought, given everything you've been through, that tonight you might need me more than my clients do. Or maybe it's that I've finally got my priorities in the proper order.''

"I don't believe priorities change that quickly. I think you're overreacting to an unfortunate incident and that you'll wake up tomorrow wishing you hadn't behaved quite so impulsively. I think," she finished carefully, "that we might both live to regret your decision to abandon your overseas guests in my favor."

"Are you saying you'd rather I'd left you here alone?"

"If I were wise, I would." For the first time, she looked directly at him and he saw that her eyes were heavy with unshed tears. "We said our final goodbyes this morning, Max, and I don't know that I can weather having to go through doing that again."

"What if I'm asking you to forget what we said and did this morning, and start out over again with a clean slate?"

She sighed so deeply, her entire body quivered. "And what if, next week, or next month or next year, you change your mind? Again."

He stretched out his hand and cupped her face. "I love you, do you hear? Until this morning, I couldn't bring myself to admit that, and I wouldn't be repeating the words now if I didn't know them to be true."

"Oh, I'd like to believe you!" she cried. "Heaven knows, I've waited long enough to hear you say them."

"So what's the problem?"

She shook her head, looking almost dazed. "It's…too sudden. Too much to take in all at once. I'm all at sixes and sevens inside." She stepped away from him and spread out her hands as if she were warding off an attack. "I need to be strong enough not to keep settling for less than the absolute best in our marriage. It would be so easy to give in to my feelings, to accept what you're telling me and forget all the deceit and mistrust that's gone before. But I know in my heart that that would be a mistake.''

Once he'd set his sights on a specific goal, he went after it with single-minded concentration and could no more fathom her waffling at this stage of their relationship than he pretended to understand the vagaries of the fashion industry.

''I keep hearing what you don't want, Gabriella,'' he said testily, ''but I wish you'd spell out exactly what it is you'd like to see happen with us, because I'm at a loss to figure it out.''

She brushed her fingertips under her eyes and made an obvious effort to put her thoughts into some sort of rational order. ''This morning, you asked me why I didn't just let that child take the car, and I said—''

Some child! he was tempted to snap, but decided he'd be better off sticking to the real issue. ''I know what you said. I assumed it was shock that had you talking such tripe.''

''Not entirely. The thing is, Max, I really wasn't all that afraid when I realized the danger I was in—no more than usual, that is. Because I'm afraid all the time, and have been ever since I married you. And I'm tired of it.''

''You're comparing being married to me with being held at knifepoint?'' He rolled his eyes disbelievingly. ''That's absurd!''

''No, it isn't. I want to be free to love you unreservedly and be confident you're giving the same back to me. I need to know that if I make a mistake, you'll forgive me. I want to be able to open a letter from you and not be terrified you're writing to tell me you've met someone else and want a divorce. When I hear your voice on the phone, I want to be filled with joy and excitement, instead of dread.''

''Hell, Gabriella, if you're asking for a guarantee that we're never going to disagree again, or make any more mistakes, I can't give you one. Marriage doesn't come with that kind of warranty.''

''I know,'' she said. ''But love does. At least, it should, if it's the kind that's going to last.''

He eyed her suspiciously. ''Exactly what are you getting at?''

''I want you to leave for Whistler in the morning and be with your clients. And I'm going to fly to Tokyo on Monday as planned, and from there to Sydney, Milan, Paris, and every other city on my schedule.''

''And then what?''

''I'm not looking any further ahead than that.''

She was making no damned sense and he could have shaken her! Even more, he wanted to put an end to all this *talk* about love, and *show* her what it was all about with actions that spoke more potently than words. ''Are you saying we might be through?''

''I hope we're not. I hope what we've found is strong enough to withstand time and distance, but I know the only way I can be sure is to put it to the test.''

The anger came surging out of nowhere, taking him by surprise almost as much as it did her. ''And this is your idea of a solution? To walk out on me again? Well, forget it, Gabriella! Either you stay and we work things out together, or we call it quits once and for all.''

''That's blackmail, Max, and you know it,'' she told him calmly.

''Call it what the devil you like,'' he seethed. ''Those are my terms. Take them or leave them, because I won't be left here twisting in the wind while you go gallivanting around the world in search of the Holy Grail of matrimony!''

''Is that your final word on the subject?''

''It is.''

She looked at him long and solemnly, and it seemed an eternity before she replied, ''And you wonder why I'm afraid of you!''

Then she left the room, climbed the stairs, and very quietly closed the door to the master suite. It didn't take a rocket scientist to figure out she wasn't coming out again, or that he wasn't welcome to join her.

It was back to the guest room for him. The only difference was, this time she was the one who made that decision.

CHAPTER ELEVEN

PARIS in late September was lovely that year. Mellow and golden, with the sky behind Notre Dame cathedral a deep restful blue, and the trees along the Champs-Élysées just beginning to turn.

The hotel in Arrondissement 8, where she always stayed, remained as elegantly charming as ever. Her fashion shoots at the various couturier establishments had been a smashing success; a recently completed television interview well received.

Every day, she walked through the Tuileries gardens, or along the banks of the Seine. She took her morning café au lait at her favorite sidewalk bistro, dined often with associates and friends at one or other of the many legendary restaurants in the city. And as she had every night since she'd left him, she came back to her hotel, praying that Max might have called.

It had not happened once in the two months since she'd left, and she was afraid it never would. Still, as she turned on to Avenue George V late on the fourth Tuesday since her return to Paris, and entered the lovely Art Deco vestibule of her hotel, her hopes lifted, only to be dashed when the night clerk, anticipating her question, shook his head sympathetically. "I'm sorry, *madame*. There are no messages."

Dejectedly, she crossed to the elevator and as the ornate brass doors rolled closed behind her and the car began its slow ascent, she leaned her head against the marble wall and wondered for the hundredth time if she'd made the right decision. Should she have stayed in Vancouver? Or would submitting to Max's ultimatum merely have compounded the doubts already besetting her?

The answer was plain enough. If he could let her go so easily, how real was his professed love?

The elevator whispered to a stop on the fifth floor. Listlessly, she stepped out and made her way down the hall to her suite. It was after ten already. The Do Not Disturb sign hung on the door, which meant the maid had already stopped by.

Indeed, she'd left a lamp burning in the tiny entrance hall and even replaced that morning's still-fresh flower arrangement with a huge bouquet of yellow roses sprinkled with starlike baby's breath. Their heady scent filled the small suite.

Gabriella dropped her handbag by the door, kicked off her shoes and wiggled her toes in the thick carpet with a sigh of pleasure. A model's feet took more than their fair share of punishment in the course of a working day. Her shoulders, too. The muscles at the back of her neck felt as if they'd been stitched in place with piano wire.

She would take a long, relaxing bath, maybe order a nightcap of hot milk from room service, spike it with cognac from the bar in the little sitting room—and hope the combination would be enough to induce a sleep deep enough that Max wouldn't find his way into her dreams.

Slipping out of her linen jacket and unbuttoning her blouse, she turned toward the bedroom. At the bureau, she stopped to step out of her skirt, and balanced first on one leg, then the other, to peel off her silk stockings. Finally, clad only in a peach satin camisole and panties, she went to unlatch the tall, narrow windows and let in the sweet night air.

Just as she turned the handle and pushed open the first

pane, the bedside lamp clicked on. "Not that I don't appreciate the striptease, my love, but I can't say I care to have half of Paris horning in on it, too."

The words, laced with amusement, floated from the other end of the room and surely, if there hadn't been a waist-high wrought-iron grille between her and the outside, she'd have pitched forward and fallen five floors to her death on the avenue below.

Clutching the velvet drapery, she fought to control the wild fluttering of her heart. "Well, I'm not quite finished yet," she said breathlessly. "I'm saving the best part for last and intend it to be a very private viewing."

She dared to turn then, and meet his gaze. He lay stretched out on the bed, feet crossed at the ankles, hands linked behind his head. He needed a shave, his clothes were travel-wrinkled, his hair a mess, and he looked so utterly gorgeous that she went weak at the knees.

"Hello, Max," she said.

"Hi, sweetheart."

There weren't sparks flying through the air, but there should have been. The atmosphere was so rarefied her lungs could barely function.

She wished she could think of something memorable to say, something she and Max would look back on in their dotage and laugh about. She wished she could find the courage to run to him; to feel his arms close around her and know that, this time, she'd finally come home to stay, even though she was half a world away from Vancouver.

Instead, she simply stared—at his beautiful, sexy mouth, his serious, summer-blue eyes, his wonderful, unforgettable face. And because she was a dolt who never could keep herself together where he was concerned, she did what she always did when the feelings grew too intense to bear. She started to cry.

For once, it was the right thing to do. He leaped off the bed and was at her side in a single bound. "You dope!" he growled. "I'm never letting you out of my sight again. Do you always just walk into your hotel room and start undressing, without first checking to make sure the place is secure?"

"Don't yell at me!" she sobbed.

"Why not? It's what I seem to do best."

But he wasn't yelling, not at all. His voice was flowing over her like warm honey laced with deep, dark chocolate. His hands were stroking over her skin and leaving trails of tenderness in their wake. He was murmuring magical healing words; calling her his darling, his very own beloved. And telling her he'd missed her so badly he'd damn near gone mad.

"I'm such an ass," he said. "A permanent work-in-progress. I don't know how you're ever going to train me to behave. But I hope you'll at least give it a try. Because I need you, my Gabriella, and I'm sorry if it's too soon for you to hear this, but I just don't think I can go another day without you."

"I thought you'd given up on us," she said, still sniffling like a baby. "I really didn't think—"

"On me, perhaps, but never on you. I've gone through a living hell these last two months but it was worth it if, at the end of it all, we're together again. It took me a long time to face up to the fact that each time you left me, I drove you to it, and even longer for me to admit how badly I missed you, or how empty my life was without you in it. So I decided that instead of hoping you'd have the good sense to come back to me, I'd do better by coming to you for a change and throwing myself on your mercy.''

He looked at her searchingly. ''Have I left it too late, Gabriella? Is the kind of glamorous life you lead here more appealing than being plain Mrs. Max Logan? Do I have to follow you all over the world in order to stay close to you?''

''There was a time when you'd have run anywhere in the world, just to get away from me,'' she reminded him. ''Have you forgotten what an unwilling bridegroom you were?''

''No. But I know now that we'd have ended up at the altar sooner or later. It just came sooner than I was ready to accept it, that's all. But I'm ready now, Gabriella, and not so proud or stubborn that I won't get down on my knees and beg for another chance, if that's what it'll take.''

''If you'd kiss me,'' she said, melting against him, ''I think I might be persuaded to dispense with the groveling and settle in favor of being plain Mrs. Max Logan.''

He didn't need a second invitation. His lips closed over hers with such sureness and passion that all the dark, terrible doubts she'd entertained over the last two months— the last two years—finally sank into oblivion.

It seemed the most natural thing in the world for him to take her to bed in that elegant Parisian hotel room. For them to renew their vows to one another in the most romantic city in the world. For him to bring her to the edge of insanity and tell her he loved her as they fell together into that deep, thrilling chasm of release.

But the truly remarkable thing was that they could just as well have been in a hut in the Himalayas, or a tent in the Sahara, because what made it unique and glorious was the trust they'd forged from all the tears and misery—not just in the moment but in tomorrow and all the long, lovely years that stretched ahead.

Miranda Lee is Australian, living near Sydney. Born and raised in the bush, she was boarding-school educated and briefly pursued a career in classical music, before moving to Sydney and embracing the world of computers. Happily married, with three daughters, she began writing when family commitments kept her at home. She likes to create stories that are believable, modern, fast-paced and sexy. Her interests include meaty sagas, doing word puzzles, gambling and going to the movies.

**Look out for Miranda Lee's next sexy story:
HIS BRIDE FOR ONE NIGHT
On sale March 2005, in Modern Romance™!**

MARRIAGE AT
A PRICE
by
Miranda Lee

CHAPTER ONE

COURTNEY knew, the moment she saw William Sinclair's face, that her mother's accountant had *really* bad news. He'd hedged over the phone when she'd asked him if Crosswinds was in financial trouble, saying he just needed to have a little chat with her, face to face.

Courtney hadn't been fooled by that. Her mother's cost-cutting measures these past couple of years had been obvious to everyone. Staff was down to a minimum. The fences had not been painted. Other repairs had been left undone. The place had begun to look shabby. Which wasn't exactly good for business.

If Crosswinds was to compete against the lavish and very modern thoroughbred studs now gracing the Upper Hunter Valley, then it needed to look its very best.

When she'd pointed this out to her mother earlier in the year, Hilary hadn't agreed. 'What we need, daughter, is a new stallion. Not fancy stables.'

Which was also true. Four years earlier, when the stud had been doing very well, her mother had imported a classy Irish stayer named Four-Leaf Clover.

Unfortunately, the horse had contracted a virus and had died shortly after standing his first season at stud. His only crop of foals hadn't been much to look at as year-lings, bringing such poor bidding at auction that Hilary had stubbornly kept most of them rather than let them go for less than they'd cost to breed.

With Four-Leaf Clover gone, and their remaining two sires both getting older, Crosswinds had a real hole in its breeding program. But there hadn't been the money to buy a replacement till this year.

'I'll still have to look for a bargain,' her mother had told her. 'I haven't got much spare cash.'

Her mum had been cock-a-hoop when she'd arrived home with Goldplated in May, especially with the price she'd negotiated. Though no price was a real bargain, Courtney realised ruefully as she walked into the accountant's office, if the money to buy the darned horse had been borrowed.

William Sinclair rose as she entered, being the old-fashioned gentleman that he was. 'Good morning, Courtney,' he greeted. 'Do sit down.' And he waved her to the single chair facing his large, but *large*, ancient desk.

Courtney took off her Akubra hat and sat down, making herself as comfortable as she could in the stiff-backed seat. A fruitless exercise. Tension had already knotted the muscles between her shoulder blades.

The accountant dropped his eyes to the papers in front of him, then started shuffling them around.

Courtney's agitation rose. She wasn't in the mood for any further procrastination.

'Just give it to me straight, Bill,' she began bluntly, and his eyes lifted, his expression faintly disapproving. He'd never liked her calling him Bill. But that was rather irrelevant at the moment. 'No bulldust now. No waffle. I'm my mother's daughter. I can take it.'

William shook his head at the young woman sitting before him. Yes, she was indeed her mother's daughter, he thought wearily.

Not in looks. Lord, no. Hilary Cross had been as plain as a pikestaff. Her daughter had clearly taken after her father, that unknown, unspoken-of male who had miraculously impregnated the forty-five-year-old spinster owner of Crosswinds over a quarter of a century ago, then disappeared off the face of the earth.

Gossip claimed he'd been a gypsy, and Courtney's looks seemed to confirm that, with her long black curly hair, dark brown eyes and rich olive skin. A striking-looking girl, in William's opinion.

Her personality and ways, however, were pure Hilary. Just look at the way she was sitting, for heaven's sake, with her right ankle hooked up over her left knee. That was how *men* sat, not young ladies. And then there was the matter of her dress, 'dress' being the pertinent word. Because she never wore one! William had never seen her in anything but blue jeans and a checked shirt. Yet she had a very good figure.

As for that glorious hair of hers. It was always bundled up into a rough pony-tail, then shoved under a dusty brown stockman's hat. Lipstick never graced her deliciously full mouth. And the only scent he ever smelt on her was leather and horses!

But it was her manner that rankled William the most. Not quite as aggressive and opinionated as her mother, she was still far too tactless with people. And bold in her attitude all round. Bold as brass!

Of course, it wasn't her fault. Hilary had raised Courtney as though she were a boy, letting her run wild from the time she was a tiny tot. He could still remember the day he'd driven out to Crosswinds, when Courtney had been about eleven or twelve. She'd met him at the gate, riding a big black colt with a crazed look in its eye and wide, snorting nostrils. Far too much horse for a man, let alone a wisp of a girl.

'Race you up to the house,' she'd shouted from where the horse had been dancing around in circles, obviously eager to get going. 'Last one there is a rotten egg!' And, nudging the huge beast in the flanks with her heels, she'd taken off at a gallop, hooping and hollering like some bush jockey on picnic day.

Though appalled at her unladylike antics, he'd still gunned the engine and had chased after the minx, certain in the knowledge that any car could easily outrun even the fastest racehorse in the long curving uphill driveway.

And what had she done? Jumped the darned fence and gone straight across the paddocks, scattering mares and foals as she'd leapt fence after fence like the mad daredevil she was. She'd been there waiting for him when he'd finally rounded the circular gravel driveway in front of the house, her dark eyes sparkling at him.

'You'll have to drive faster than that next time, Bill,' she'd teased. 'Or get yourself a sports car!'

It was the first time she'd called him Bill. Before that, he'd at least been Mr Sinclair.

When he'd spotted Hilary standing on the veranda of the house, glaring down at her daughter, he'd experienced some satisfaction that the brazen creature would be suitably chastised for her cheek and foolhardiness.

But what had Hilary done?

Chided the girl for losing her hat!

'Do you want to end up with skin cancer?' she'd snapped. 'Go back and find it and put the thing on, girl.' At which, the bold hussy had whirled her horse and, with another hoop and holler, set off exactly the way she'd come, jumping fence after fence.

When William had dared make some critical comment himself about the girl's recklessness, Hilary had levelled a steely gaze his way.

'Would you have said that if she'd been a boy?' she'd challenged. 'No! You'd have praised a boy's horsemanship, marvelled at his nerve, been impressed by his courage. My daughter needs those qualities in even greater quantities than any boy if she is to take over from me when I'm gone. The world of horse-breeding is a man's world, William. Courtney needs a loose rein to become the sort of woman who can survive in such a world. There's no room for sissies around here. As my heir, she will need more than a man's name. She will need a man's spirit. A man's strength. A man's ego. I aim to make sure she acquires all three.'

And you did a good job, Hilary, William thought now. The girl certainly has courage. And character, for want of a better word. But will she have enough to get out of the spot you left her in?

William gave it to Courtney straight, as requested.

Courtney listened to the very *very* bad news. Not only had her mum borrowed to buy Goldplated, as she'd feared, but to buy Four-Leaf Clover as well. And that horse had cost a small fortune! Worse, it turned out Four-Leaf Clover had not been insured, so when he'd died, the loss had been total and none of the original loan repaid.

'Your mother didn't believe in insuring anything against death,' the accountant informed Courtney, 'and I could never persuade her otherwise. As you know, she carried no life insurance herself.'

Courtney nodded. 'Yes, I know,' she said, a lump forming in her throat as the reality of her mother's death washed over her again.

Hilary's heart attack had come as such a shock to everyone, despite her being seventy last birthday. She'd always seemed so strong...

Courtney frowned. Had this escalating debt been a contributing factor in her mother's coronary? Had she been worried sick about the loan?

She'd never said a word. But then, she wouldn't have. She'd have been too proud to admit to being so foolish.

Thinking of her mother again brought a lump to Courtney's throat and a stinging to her eyes. She coughed, blinked, then gathered herself. Her mother had always hated her to cry. *Tears achieve nothing, girl. Get out and do something to fix whatever's bothering you. Don't sit there blubbering and feeling sorry for yourself!*

'Exactly how much money do I owe?' she asked brusquely.

The way Bill cleared *his* throat before answering was not a good sign. 'Er…three million dollars, give or take a thousand or two.'

Three *million*!

Courtney struggled to hide her shock. And, somehow, she managed.

'Never let the bastards know what you're thinking and feeling,' Hilary had told her more than once. 'Let your guard down, and they'll take advantage of you.'

The bastards, Courtney knew, were all men. And whilst she had not grown up to be the rabid man-hater her mother had been, she was learning to appreciate, first-hand, where her mother had been coming from when she'd lectured her daughter over the predatory nature of the male sex.

The month since the funeral had been an education, all right. She couldn't count the men who'd come out of the woodwork since she'd inherited Crosswinds, smarmily flattering her and asking if there was any way they could help, now that she was all alone in the world, *poor little thing*.

Courtney's thoughts turned wry. They wouldn't come sniffing around if they knew this poor little thing was three million dollars in debt!

Pity she couldn't tell them.

Pride, however, would keep her silent on the subject. Pride and loyalty to her mother. Hilary had spent a lifetime earning the respect of her peers in the horse-breeding world. No way would she let them laugh at her now, especially the men.

But what on earth was she going to do?

'I know it's a lot of money,' Bill said gently. 'I did try to advise your mother not to borrow any more, but she simply wouldn't listen to me.'

Courtney nodded. She understood exactly how stubborn her mother had been, and was determined not to do the same. Bill might be getting on in years but he was an intelligent man, with an old-fashioned integrity she both admired and respected. He would never try to take advantage of her, or give her bad advice. He wasn't one of the bastards. Courtney liked him enormously.

'Is the bank calling in the loan, Bill? Is that it?'

'No. They've been amazingly patient, and suspiciously generous in lending your mother more money, possibly because she had such excellent collateral against any loan. They can't lose, no matter what. Let's face it, Courtney, Crosswinds is worth a lot more than three million.'

Courtney felt the first stirrings of real alarm. 'Are you saying Crosswinds is at risk here? That one day I might have to sell up?'

'If things keep going the way they're going, and you don't try to stem the rising tide of this loan, then I'm afraid such an occurrence will be inevitable. The bank will do it for you.'

Courtney just sat there, staring at him.

How could she bear to live without Crosswinds? The

house. The horses. The land. It was all she knew and loved. It was her lifeblood. She would die without it.

Real pity for the girl swept through William. He hated having to do this so soon after her mother's death, but such things couldn't wait. A loan as large as this grew every day, especially now that interest rates were on the rise again. That loan was like the sword of Damocles, swaying over Courtney's head.

'If you want my opinion,' he said firmly, 'then you should sell some of the horses. And quickly. You have some very valuable brood mares at Crosswinds.'

A scathing look crossed the girl's face.

'Sell the brood mares? Are you mad? Do you know how long it took my mother and her family before her to breed up such stock? The brood mares are the backbone of Crosswinds. They are *in*valuable. I'd sell myself before I sold a single one of them!'

William smothered a sigh. Oh, yes. She was a chip off the old block all right. That was exactly what Hilary had said when he'd suggested the same thing a few days before her heart attack, right down to the bit about selling herself first.

He'd refrained from telling Hilary she was hardly a saleable commodity.

But her daughter was a different matter. As William's male gaze roved over the girl before him, a startling picture popped into his mind, that of a bound and naked Courtney standing proudly on some white slave trader's auction block, her magnificent black hair spread out over her bared shoulders, her beautiful brown eyes blazing defiance at the lust-filled bidders leering up at her.

What a price she would command! He could well imagine some billionaire sheikh paying a king's ransom to install Courtney Cross in his harem.

Did such things happen these days? he speculated. Possibly. But not here, in Australia.

Still, it did give William the germ of an idea…

Courtney got hold of her temper with difficulty. But, truly, Bill didn't know what he was talking about. He might know money, but he knew nothing about horses.

'How long do you think I've got?' she demanded to know. 'How long before the bank starts jumping up and down? One year? Two? Dare I hope for three?'

William suspected the bank in question might carry such a mortgage indefinitely—till it would take more than a miracle for Courtney to extricate herself from debt. In the end, they'd foreclose, and Crosswinds would be sold off, including Courtney's precious brood mares. The trouble was, in such a fire sale, nothing brought its true value. If Courtney wasn't careful, she'd not only lose Crosswinds, but there wouldn't be anything left over for her to live on. She'd be penniless.

He had to force the girl to do something *now*, or all might be lost in the future.

'It'll be the first of August this Saturday,' he said. 'I'd say you might have till the end of the year.'

'But that isn't enough time!' she protested. 'You'll have to talk to the bank, Bill, explain to them that in another couple of years I'm going to have a fantastic lot of yearlings to sell. Mum might have been foolish in some things but she was a great judge of horseflesh. Goldplated is going to be a success. I just know it. Within three years, Crosswinds will have money to burn.'

William sighed. He'd heard that one before. From Hilary. Over the years, he'd learnt that there was no such thing as a sure thing regarding racehorses, either on the track or in breeding.

'Courtney,' he said sternly, 'you must find a way to pay back that loan. And soon.'

'Well, don't go telling me to sell my horses again,' she threw at him, her face set into a mutinous expression, 'because I'm not going to. And that's final! There has to be some other way.'

'I can think of only two other solutions to your problem. Although, come to think of it, only one is viable,' he added drily.

What multi-millionaire would want to actually marry this difficult, stubborn, bossy girl? Beauty alone would not cut it, especially her kind of beauty which was of the wild and natural kind. Wealthy men wanted glamorous, well-groomed wives who stroked their egos and hosted perfect dinner parties, not independent, prickly creatures with an attitude, as well as a money problem.

'What?' Courtney's right foot hit the ground as she hunched forward on the chair, all ears. 'Tell me.'

'You'll have to find yourself a business partner, someone who'll pay cash for a share in Crosswinds.'

Pulling a face, Courtney straightened up in the chair. 'Nope. That won't work, Bill. No horseman would buy a share in Crosswinds and keep his hands off the running of the place. Mum would turn in her grave. And I wouldn't like it, either.'

'I wasn't talking about a horseman,' William explained. 'I was talking about a professional businessman. A city man. He would be a silent partner.'

'Oh, well, now that's the kind of partner I could just about tolerate. So how would I go about finding such a stooge?'

William winced at the word 'stooge'. But it probably described any potential partner of Courtney's to a tee.

'I was thinking that you could ask Lois's help. She's

a clever woman, not just at training horses but in public relations. She's a whiz at getting money out of people for her racing syndicates. She also has some very wealthy clients and a wide range of contacts in the business world. I would think Lois knows quite a few likely candidates with more money than sense.'

William saw the girl's nostrils flare indignantly. 'Are you saying that a man would have to be stupid to go into partnership with me?'

His smile was wry. 'Not you personally. But a wise old accountant once told me never to invest money into anything that had to be fed or watered.'

Courtney sighed. 'You're right. Breeding racehorses *is* a risky investment. This businessman is going to have to be one hell of a rich businessman.'

'Businessmen who get mixed up with racehorses in any aspect usually are, aren't they?'

'True, Bill. True. Look, I can't say I fancy taking a partner, even a silent one, but what must be must be. Better than selling any of the horses. I'll give Lois a ring as soon as I get home. I could hitch a ride down in the horse float this Friday. I'm sending down a couple of young horses she's agreed to syndicate out and train for me. Darned good types, too, but obviously Crosswinds can't afford to pay for them to be trained right now.'

'I'm afraid not,' William confirmed, relieved that Courtney was taking it all so well. Still, he wouldn't have expected Hilary's daughter to fall apart.

'I can't stay away too long, you know. Come this weekend, foals will start arriving.'

'You have staff to handle that. Finding a partner is more important, Courtney.'

'Mmm. Before I go, what about insurance? I don't want to make the same mistake Mum did.'

'I insured everything after your mother died,' William confessed. 'I didn't want to bother you at the time for permission. I hope you don't mind.'

Courtney smiled as she rose to her feet, extending her hand across the desk. 'Not at all. Thanks, Bill. I don't know what I'd do without you.'

He flinched at the steely strength in her handshake. No wonder the horses she rode did as they were told.

'There's no trouble with our general running expenses, is there?' she asked.

'No. Cash input is matching output at the moment. Of course, the place could do with some money spent on it. It's beginning to look run down. So if you and Lois are going to sting some city fool for three million, you might as well try for four, and be done with it.'

She grinned at him. 'Bill! You shock me.'

'I doubt that very much,' he remarked drily. 'By the way, if Lois can't come up with anyone suitable, I suggest you approach a financial consultancy which specialises in handling country-based investments. But that's a last resort. Middlemen always want their cut. A personal contact deal would be much better all round.'

'I agree. If I have to have a partner, then I'd like to have some control over who it is. Now, I'd better get moving. Friday will be here before I know it.'

'Good luck, Courtney.'

'See you, Bill.'

She spun on the heels of her elastic-sided boots and had taken three strides towards the door when she stopped and threw a puzzled glance back over her shoulder at him. 'What was the other one?' she asked.

'What other one?'

'The other solution to my money problems.'

'Oh, that. It was a stupid idea. Not worth mentioning.'

She turned right round again with that stubborn set to her face he knew so well. 'I'd still like to know.'

William let out a resigned sigh. 'I was thinking of what impoverished aristocratic women used to do in the old days when their castles were crumbling around them.'

'What's that?'

'They married for money.'

Courtney crowed with laughter. 'You're right, Bill. That is the stupidest idea I've ever heard of. I think the world has moved on since the days when young ladies went round sacrificing themselves in marriage to aging pot-bellied counts, simply to save the family jewels.'

Actually, William wasn't too sure of that.

'If and when I marry,' Courtney announced as she planted the dusty Akubra hat firmly on her head, 'it won't be for money.'

'Ah-h-h.' William smiled his approval. 'For love, eh, girl?'

'Don't be ridiculous, Bill. Love won't have anything to do with it. It'll be strictly for the sex.' And, smiling a truly wicked smile, she whirled and strode from the room.

CHAPTER TWO

'EVERYONE'S very dressed up,' Courtney said, glancing around at the crowd of racegoers.

All the men were in suits and ties, and most of the women were wearing hats. Lois herself was in a rather flamboyant floral suit and matching hat which might have looked over-the-top on anyone less slender and vivacious. But she carried the outfit off with great panache, looking a lot younger than the forty she admitted to.

'I did warn you, darling,' Lois replied. 'Randwick is a far cry from a country racetrack.'

'You can say that again. Thanks heaps for lending me these clothes, Lois. Sorry I was stubborn about it.'

Lois rolled her eyes. She'd had the devil of a time persuading the girl out of the jeans and checked shirt she'd been wearing this morning, and into the stylish black pants and matching cropped jacket she now had on. This minor miracle had only been achieved by her firmly telling Courtney that the members' section at Randwick had a dress code that definitely didn't allow jeans.

As for that revolting checked shirt... Lois shuddered at the memory.

Lois had learnt many years ago that, in the city, appearance was everything. Just because you were a horse trainer it didn't mean you had to look like one. Lois spent an absolute fortune on her vibrant but stylish clothes, and the expenditure was worth every penny. The press photographers snapped her all the time, and the media were

18

always seeking her opinion on the chances of her horses, possibly because she looked better on TV than most of the male trainers. She talked better, too. And smiled a lot. Lois believed that acting bright and always sounding positive brought her more coverage and more clients than the actual success of her horses.

'You look fantastic in black,' she complimented Courtney. 'Much better than I ever did.' Actually, black hadn't been her colour since she'd had her hair blonded last year. It looked great on Hilary's daughter, however, with her olive skin, black hair and almost black eyes. If the girl had agreed to some red lipstick and to leaving that gorgeous hair of hers down, she'd have been simply stunning. But, when Lois had suggested both this morning, Courtney had bluntly stated that she looked like a clown in make-up and simply couldn't stand her hair around her face.

Lois had argued her case but the girl was adamant. Clearly, she was as opinionated and strong-willed as her mother. Lois had put her foot down, however, when Courtney had gone to scoop her gorgeous black curls back up into that awful rubber band, and had insisted that if her hair had to be off her face, it should be anchored more attractively at the nape of her neck with a gold clip.

Courtney had finally shrugged and given in, as though it didn't really matter either way. Lois could only conclude that Hilary's daughter had no idea of the uniquely exotic beauty she possessed, and which would have more than one wealthy man slavering at her feet if only she knew what to do with it.

Still, what could one expect? Teaching her daughter to make the most of her striking looks would not have been high on Hilary's agenda. Such a stupid, warped old woman. Why hate men when they ran the world?

Tonight, over dinner, she would try to explain to Courtney that when a woman did business in a man's world, she did it as much with her body as her brain. If Courtney wanted to save Crosswinds, then she would hopefully listen to reason.

If not, then it would be up to herself to rescue the darned place single-handed, Lois decided pragmatically. No way was she going to sit back and let that wonderful old property pass into other hands. Crosswinds had the best staying brood mares in Australia. All they needed was the right sire, and a whole crop of champion colts and fillies would be in the making. And she would be right there, willing and eager to train every single one of the little darlings!

Courtney wasn't enjoying her trip to the races as much as she'd thought she would. Her mind was still on Crosswinds and her money problems.

'Do you think we might meet someone here today, Lois?' she asked tautly.

'Someone to bail Crosswinds out, you mean?'

'Yes.'

'Possibly. Though this isn't all that major a race meeting. Not too many of the seriously rich here today. Look, darling, take my advice and don't go worrying about Crosswinds this afternoon. Just relax and enjoy yourself. Tonight, after dinner, I'll sit down and make a list of likely candidates, then tomorrow I'll ring around and issue some invitations.'

'What kind of invitations?'

'Dinner. Drinks. Whatever suits each man in question.'

'You don't know any suitably rich women?' Rich women liked racehorses too, Courtney had been thinking. And there would be less chance of a woman partner wanting to interfere with the management of Crosswinds. She just didn't trust a man not to try to poke his bib in.

Lois looked just a tad exasperated. 'Lord, darling, no woman is going to want to be *your* partner. You're far too good-looking. No, no, no, some filthy rich old bloke is our best bet. Trust me. By the end of the week, we'll come up with just the right person. I have every confid— Oh, good God, it's Jack Falconer. And he said he definitely wasn't going to be here today!'

Courtney followed the direction of Lois's disgruntled gaze and encountered a man standing at the railing of the saddling enclosure, alternately studying the race book in his hands, then the horses being led around the parade ring. A pair of expensive-looking binoculars were hooked around his neck. He was tall, with a strongly masculine profile and close-cropped dark hair.

Courtney's eyebrows lifted. She'd always fancied macho-looking men, and this one was certainly that, despite his sleek, city-smooth clothes. He was somewhere in his early thirties, she guessed. Though she couldn't be certain from this distance. He could have been older.

His being older wouldn't have made him any less attractive to Courtney. She liked older men.

'Who's Jack Falconer?' she asked, intrigued by Lois's reaction to seeing him.

'What? Oh...one of my owners.'

'Rich?'

'Used to be. Not so rich any more.'

'What happened?'

'He chose the *wrong* business partner. The mongrel embezzled a good chunk of their clients' money and did a flit to Paraguay or Bolivia, or wherever. Jack nobly made restitution himself, though legally he didn't have to, and it almost sent him to the wall. He lost just about everything, including his live-in lady. The rotten cow dumped him and married a politician old enough to be her father. Rolling in dough, of course. Jack pretended he wasn't shattered but he clearly was. He was besotted with his darling Katrina. He only bought a share in a racehorse in the first place because she loved coming to the races and mingling with the rich and famous.'

'She sounds awful. Whatever did he see in her?'

Lois laughed. 'When you see her, you'll know the answer to that. And you'll see her today. Her new hubby is presenting the trophy in the main race of the day. That's why I was so taken aback to see Jack here. Because his... Oh, darn, he's spotted me. I'll fill you in later.'

Lois plastered a high-voltage beam on her face and stepped off the veranda of the members' stand into the warm winter sunshine. Courtney followed, more intrigued than ever by the man walking towards Lois. Full frontal and up closer, he was even more attractive, with the sort of deep-set blue eyes that Courtney adored.

No grey in his dark brown hair that she could see, so her guess of early thirties remained. As did her initial impression that he was really built. With his suit jacket flapping open and his tie blown back over his right shoulder, there was no hiding the way his broad chest was stretching the material of his pale blue shirt.

Yet there was no question of fat, or flab. That telling area around his waistline against which his binoculars kept bouncing as he walked showed no hint of a soft underbelly, or of being held in. His stomach looked flat and rock-hard, just the way Courtney liked them.

He was even taller than she'd first thought on seeing him standing alone in the distance. Six four at least. A big man all round.

Courtney adored big men.

The three of them met on the grass, with Courtney hanging back slightly. All the better to observe him from...

'Jack, darling...' Lois presented her cheek to him for a kiss. 'How lovely to see you.'

'Hello, Lois.' He smiled with a slightly crooked smile as he bent to give her a peck. 'You're looking lovely today. There again, you always look lovely.'

'You're such a flatterer,' she said coyly, and Courtney tried not to laugh. But the woman was a riot. As rough as guts around the stables, but here, at the races, butter wouldn't melt in her mouth.

'Now, what are you doing here, Jack?' Lois went on sweetly. 'When I contacted you this week, you said you definitely wouldn't be. What changed your mind? The glorious weather?'

He seemed drily amused by her none too subtle probing. 'No, after we talked I remembered you always said that the first time you put Big Brutus over a bit of distance, he'd win.'

'He will too,' Lois replied. 'I'm very confident.'

Recognition of the horse's name dragged Courtney's attention away from ogling Jack Falconer. Big Brutus was one of Four-Leaf Clover's first crop and the ugliest colt her mother had ever bred. Hence his name. He'd been one of the yearlings she'd refused to sell for peanuts, subsequently leasing him to Lois. He'd been a total dud at two years old, not much better at three, and had turned four this very day, still with only a few minor placings.

But he was bred to stay all day.

Courtney scrambled through her race book to find the

race Big Brutus was entered in. There it was. A handicap over twenty-four-hundred metres, with prize money of...

'Wow!' she exclaimed. 'First place pays a hundred thousand smackeroos. My cut would be what, Lois?'

Those piercing blue eyes swung her way. 'I beg your pardon? God, don't tell me you're Big Brutus's jockey. Tell me she's not the jockey, Lois.'

'She's not the jockey,' Lois said with a wry smile on her face. 'But if she was, you'd have one of the best riders in the country on your horse.'

'That may be, but I've never had much luck betting on female jockeys.'

Courtney bristled in defence of her sex. And irritation at herself for once again being attracted to a male chauvinist. Would she never find a man who looked as she liked them to look, yet believed God created man and woman equal?

'When a race is lost,' she said frostily, 'it's mostly the horse's fault. Or the trainer's. Or the owner's. Not the jockey, be she female or otherwise.'

'I don't see how it can be the owner's fault,' he argued back.

'Some owners insist on seeing their horses run in races far above their talents. And other owners insist their horses not run up to their ability at all!'

'Courtney,' Lois whispered under her breath.

'No, no, let her finish,' Jack insisted. 'Do go on, Ms...er...?'

'Cross,' she announced.

'Yes, I can see that,' he said, smiling.

Courtney would have liked to wipe that smirk off his face with more than her tongue. But she hadn't physically brawled with a member of the opposite sex since she was thirteen, and didn't think the lawns at Royal Randwick Racecourse was the place to begin again.

'Aside from the horse having a lousy trainer or a crooked owner,' she continued tartly, 'the main reason female jockeys don't ride all that many winners is that they are rarely offered the best rides in races, and when they are their male counterparts make sure none of the breaks go their way. It's a sad fact of life that the male sex do not appreciate women taking them on in fields they've always considered their own private turf.'

'Possibly. But you must concede that pound for pound male jockeys are stronger. Take you, for instance. If you were a jockey, quite a few pounds of your riding weight would be wasted on your very nice but less than useful breasts. Strength-wise, that is,' he added ruefully.

'Actually, no, that's not the case,' she countered without batting an eye. It wasn't the first time Courtney had heard that old argument. It had whiskers on it. 'If I were riding professionally, I'd have to strip off at least twenty pounds and my boobs would shrink from their present cup C to a flat-chested double A. Add five hundred push-ups a day, and I'd be every bit as strong as any male jockey. Being female is not the point here. It's a matter of talent and opportunity. A woman jockey can have all the talent in the world, but rarely gets the opportunities.'

He smiled. 'I give up. You win.'

'Thank you,' she said crisply, but didn't smile back. She was still smarting inside for finding him so attractive, and wasn't about to be won over by one smarmy little smile.

Getting the message that he was on the outer, he turned to Lois. 'So explain the mystery to me, Lois? Why is Ms Cross, here, entitled to a share of Big Brutus's prize money?'

'Courtney's mother bred Big Brutus. I leased him as a yearling, then syndicated him out to you and your partner.'

'Oh, I see. Sorry,' he directed at Courtney with another winning smile. 'And sorry about the jockey bit. I was only stirring. I don't know about your riding talents, but your debating skills are excellent. You wouldn't be a budding lady-lawyer by any chance?'

His charm was undeniable, and Courtney struggled to stay angry with him.

'Courtney is a horse breeder, too,' Lois answered for her. 'The Crosses have been breeding thoroughbreds for generations.'

'You don't look like a horse breeder,' he said, and those sexy blue eyes raked over her from top to toe.

Courtney's heart lurched upwards, then did a swallow dive down into her stomach.

Wow, she thought a bit dazedly. This guy is dynamite.

'Since Lois isn't going to introduce me properly,' he said, 'then I will. Jack Falconer...' And he held out his hand.

It was a big hand, naturally. He was a big man.

Reaching out, she slid her own relatively small hand against his huge palm, curling her thumb around half of his and squeezing firmly.

'Courtney Cross,' she replied, steadfastly ignoring her madly galloping heart.

'Delighted.' And he squeezed even more firmly back.

She felt it all the way down to her toes.

Courtney simply could not understand how any woman with an active libido could prefer some aging politician to this gorgeous hunk of male flesh.

The only possible answer was money.

Okay, so he'd fallen on hard times. But not through any fault of his own, according to Lois.

Courtney wondered how he could afford Big Brutus's training fees. Lois didn't come cheap.

'And what is it you do for a crust, Jack?' she asked, not subscribing to the theory that you never asked personal questions on first acquaintance. How else were you going to find out what you wanted to know?

'I used to be a financial consultant,' he said happily enough. 'Or an investment broker, if you prefer that label. At the moment, I'm a gentleman of leisure.'

'You mean you're unemployed.'

'Courtney!' Lois broke in. 'For heaven's sake.'

'It's perfectly all right, Lois,' Jack said. 'I don't mind. If by unemployed you mean I don't work for wages, then you're absolutely right. I am unemployed in that sense. But I'm not broke. And I'm not on the dole. Currently, I am a man of independent means.'

Which meant he was looking for work and living on his savings.

'Would you two excuse me for a few minutes?' Lois interrupted. 'I've just spotted the owners of my horse in the second race. Jack, darling, look after Courtney for me, will you? Take her inside, up into the bar overlooking the track. Get her a drink. I'll find you when I'm finished down here.'

Courtney was not displeased at being left alone with the dishy Jack. But, as Lois walked off, he looked momentarily disconcerted.

'You don't mind, do you?' she said straight away.

His eyes cleared of the cloud that had momentarily muddied them to a bleak grey. 'Why should I mind?'

'Maybe you want to go place a bet on the first race,'

she said. 'Or maybe you have other friends here that you feel you should be getting back to.'

'No. Not at all.'

'What about the other part-owner of Big Brutus?'

'He's in Bolivia. I now own all of Big Brutus.'

'Oh! I didn't realise Lois meant that partner. I wasn't listening properly.' She'd been too busy ogling Jack. 'Owning a racehorse all by yourself is very expensive, you know. Can you afford it?'

'I will be able to, after today. Lois is confident Big Brutus is going to win.'

'Lois is always confident her horses are going to win, especially when there's a cup or a prize at stake.'

Jack smiled a lazy smile. 'She is, isn't she?'

'Still, often enough she's right. She does love those trophies. My mother thought her quite wonderful.'

'*Thought?*'

Courtney swallowed. 'My mum passed away recently.' It still hurt, but the urge to cry whenever she thought about, or talked of her mother was gradually lessening. In a dozen years or so, she might actually get over losing her mentor, and champion.

'I'm sorry,' Jack said gently. 'Had she been ill? She couldn't have been very old. Unless you're the youngest in the family.'

'Actually, she was quite old. Seventy. I was her only child, born when she was forty-five.'

'Goodness. And your father?'

'My father is not a part of my life,' she said with an indifferent shrug. 'I never knew him, you see, and Mum rarely spoke of him, except in general and not very flattering terms. But gossip put him a good deal younger than her. A gypsy seducer, I gleaned from my classmates at school. And others over the years.'

'Ah. Good old gossip. It never lets the truth get in the way of a good story. He was possibly a very nice man.'

Somehow, Courtney doubted that. A very nice man would not have made her mother so bitter. But his absence had never hurt *her*. She'd rather relished the freedom of not having some male hand controlling her upbringing. People said her mother had let her run wild. That wasn't entirely true. The wildness, Courtney believed, she'd been born with.

'But let's not dwell on sadness,' Jack said, hooking his right arm through her left. 'Let's go and have that drink Lois suggested.'

'Yes, let's,' Courtney agreed, delighted to have the company of this very stimulating man.

The table he steered her to in the upstairs bar had a perfect view of the track. She could see the horses trotting out for the first race. But she didn't watch them for long. Her eyes were all on Jack as he went over to get the drinks himself rather than wait to be served at the table.

'Will you be going back into the investment business again?' was her first question when he returned with two glasses of champagne.

'Possibly.'

'I might be in need of an investment broker soon,' she said.

'Why would that be?' Jack asked, frowning.

'To find me a silent partner. For my stud farm. Not that I like the idea. Unfortunately, it's a necessity.'

'You have a money problem?'

Courtney rolled her eyes. 'Do I have a money problem?'

'Tell me about it.'

Courtney could see no reason why she shouldn't tell him. If Lois didn't come through with someone, she just might give him a call. Besides, she fancied him rotten and there was interest in his eyes.

So she told him. Everything. All her mother's mistakes and misfortunes over the last few years. Even the amount of money she now owed and needed to find.

'Lois thinks she'll find some suitably mega-rich businessman from amongst her wealthy racing contacts,' she finished up. 'And she probably will, knowing Lois. But I'm not so sure it's a good idea to take on a partner who's mad about racing and who might develop some private fantasies about becoming a hands-on breeder himself. I'd prefer someone who just looks on this as a financial deal.'

'Fair enough. Have you told Lois that?'

'I've only just starting thinking that way. It's difficult to think straight when you're desperate.'

'Never be desperate, Courtney. Being desperate is the way to disaster. People know when you're desperate and take advantage of you. Always be cool. Never show fear. I'm sure you'd be very good at that.'

Courtney was impressed. It was the sort of advice her mother would have given her.

'You're right,' she said. 'There's no need to panic. The bank hasn't actually foreclosed as yet. So what do you suggest I do?' she asked.

'Take your time in finding just the right person. If the bank hasn't sent out any warning or threatening letters, then desperation hour has not yet arrived. Don't rush into anything. Scout around. I could give you the names of some very good investment brokerages here in Sydney. Ring them up and go see them.'

'How long will that take?'

'How long have you got?'

'I really have to get back to Crosswinds as quickly as I can. It's foaling time and I'm short-staffed. My accountant says this is more important, but he just doesn't understand.'

'It would take at least a week to line up appointments and do the rounds,' Jack said.

'Would you help me? I mean…a personal introduction would be much better than my just ringing up these people out of the blue.'

He seemed a little taken aback by her request.

'You did say you were a gentleman of leisure,' Courtney pointed out with a decidedly flirtatious smile.

He smiled back, if a little ruefully. 'You have a hide, Ms Cross. Has anyone ever told you that?'

'Several people, actually.'

'I'm not surprised. But, okay, I guess I could do worse things with my time than squire a beautiful young woman around town. Have you been down to Sydney before? Or is this your first visit?'

'Lord, no, I've been lots of times over the years. And frankly I'm always happy to get home to Crosswinds.'

'You don't like the city?'

'Can't say that I do. What you see is not always what you get.'

'So young to be a cynic.'

'Is there a right age to see through hypocrisy?'

'I guess not…' He looked thoughtfully down into his champagne for a few moments before glancing back up. He opened his mouth to say something, but closed it again with no words coming out. His blue eyes grew arctic-cold, then colder still, his gaze fixed on something beyond Courtney's shoulder.

Female intuition warned her that only one person could cause this reaction. The treacherous Katrina. The woman who'd ditched him and married another man; the woman Lois said he was still besotted with.

But that didn't look like love glittering in Jack's chilling blue eyes. It was more like hate. Hate, and the need for vengeance.

CHAPTER THREE

WHAT kind of woman, Courtney puzzled as she sat there, could inspire such strong emotions in a man like Jack Falconer?

If Courtney had been alone, she'd have simply spun round in her chair and taken a good, long, hard look. But this situation called for a bit more subtlety, despite the fact that subtlety was not her strong suit.

She improvised. 'I need to go to the loo. I won't be long.' Standing up, she turned and pretended to search the room for the ladies' whilst zeroing in on the direction of Jack's piercing gaze.

And there she was, standing by the bar, clinging to the arm of a white-haired gentleman whose suit jacket was struggling to remain done up over his portly stomach.

Courtney had no doubts it was Katrina.

Lois had said she would understand Jack's infatuation once Courtney saw her. And she did.

Katrina would have given any supermodel in the world a run for her money. She had everything they had, and possibly more. The height. The figure. The face. The hair. Definitely the clothes.

She was wearing a superbly cut calf-length cream woollen dress which hugged her stream-lined body, revealing every flowing but delectable curve. Her hair, which was a similar cream colour, was worn up in a rather severe French pleat which served to emphasise the perfection of her classically beautiful face. Gold and diamond earrings winked in her lobes. Her neck was bare, perhaps because she didn't want to distract any man's eyes from its elegant length, and the impressive cleavage the dress's deep V-neckline put on display.

Courtney couldn't see the colour of her eyes from that distance but she could certainly see the colour of her mouth. A rich blood-red.

Jack's blood, she thought angrily.

Seeing the man Katrina had chosen over Jack, however, confirmed Courtney's guess that this was all a matter of money. Katrina had obviously wanted to marry money, and Jack no longer had enough. What a cold-hearted money-grubbing bitch!

'The ladies' room is over there,' Jack said, misinterpreting her lengthy hesitation.

Courtney whirled back to face him. He'd sounded totally composed, but his eyes betrayed emotions best not explored. 'Where?'

He pointed to a far corner.

Courtney quickly assessed that there were two routes she could use to make her way there. One went straight between the tables, the other skirted the bar. Courtney went between the tables on her way there, and skirted the bar on her way back. Superbitch was still there, sipping a cocktail and hanging on hubby's every word.

'Hi, Katrina,' Courtney said breezily as she passed, but without stopping. Long enough, however, to see the cow's green eyes—they would be green, wouldn't they?—lift in surprise, then trail after her.

Courtney threw Jack a blinder of a smile as she walked towards him, and he automatically smiled back, as she had known he would. 'You were quick,' he said once she'd sat down again.

'Didn't have to touch up my make-up,' she said truthfully. 'Or my hair.'

He gave her face and hair a long, thoughtful look. 'You don't need to. You look great.'

'Thanks. You look great too.'

His laughter was real, and his eyes warm with genuine amusement. 'You are a very unique girl, do you know that?'

'Yep.'

He laughed again. 'Didn't your mother ever teach you modesty?'

'Lord, no. She taught me to say what I thought and do what I pleased.'

Jack's straight dark brows shot upwards. 'A very unusual mother, from the sounds of things.'

'She was.'

'You must tell me more about her. And about yourself. But first, I think another drink is—'

When he broke off, his eyes freezing once more, Courtney knew the reason why. She'd bargained on Katrina watching where she went, then not being able to resist coming over. It was one thing to dump a man. Quite another to find him seemingly happy in the company of another woman. And a much younger woman, at that.

If there was one thing guaranteed to get up the nose of a thirty-something female, it was seeing *her* ex with a younger woman.

And Courtney wanted to get up Katrina's oh, so perfect nose to the nth degree.

'Jack,' came a softly purring voice which could belong to none other but the scheming cow herself. 'I didn't expect to see you here today.'

She drifted into Courtney's view. Hubby, however, was nowhere in sight.

Jack smiled a smile that sent shivers running down

Courtney's spine. Here was a man who would not forgive easily. Or forget. It occurred to her that Jack's embezzling partner would be wise to stay exiled for ever in his South American hide-away.

'Why ever not, Katrina?' Jack drawled, leaning his broad shoulders back against his chair. 'Big Brutus is going to win today and I'm going to be there to accept the trophy. Along with Courtney, here.'

Glittering green eyes swung her way. 'I'm sorry,' Katrina said with lemony sweetness. 'You said hello to me, but I can't seem to place you.'

'Oh, you don't actually know me,' Courtney trilled back. 'But I feel like I know you. Jack has told me *so* much about you.'

'Really,' Katrina said coldly.

'We didn't want to have any secrets between us, did we, Jack?' Courtney smiled over at Jack, who thankfully wasn't looking too poleaxed by her bold charade.

'How nice,' his ex managed to grate out between her dazzlingly white but grindingly clenched teeth. 'So how long have you two been going out together?'

'Gosh, I'm not sure,' Courtney jumped in again. 'I haven't been counting. How long has it been, darling?' By now, she hoped and prayed Jack would back up her story.

'Lord knows, sweetheart,' he returned, his eyes amused on her. 'I haven't been counting, either. All I know is it's been one remarkable experience.'

Courtney could practically *feel* the woman's hostility. If she gripped her purse any tighter, her scarlet fingernails would sink holes in the leather.

'She's a little young for you, don't you think, Jack?' Katrina sniped.

Jack's expression was superbly indifferent to the

woman's barb. What a man, Courtney thought. City-smooth and city-smart. But with such adorably macho looks. A most unusual combination.

'I would have thought she's just the right age,' he replied coolly. 'Can't say the same for old George, however. He's only got a few good years left in him, I would imagine. Look, I'd love to chat, Katrina, but the horses are in the barrier. We're sure to run into each other later, after Big Brutus wins his race, since George is going to present the trophy.'

With that, Jack picked up his binoculars from the table and focused them on the race that had just jumped. Katrina glared pure hate at Courtney, then stalked off.

'She's gone,' Courtney whispered, smiling satisfaction to herself.

'I'm not sure if I should be angry with you, or grateful,' Jack muttered drily, but without shifting his eyes away from the binoculars.

'Grateful would be the more sensible option.'

'I presume Lois told you about Katrina.'

'Only the bare facts. I asked her if you were rich and she told me of your own recent money troubles, which led on to her mentioning Katrina's defection to George.'

'Ah... I see... Yes... That explains everything.'

He fell silent then, seemingly intent on the race. It was only a sprint and the runners were already approaching the turn into the straight, with three of them vying for the lead and another pair hot on their heels. It looked like being an exciting finish.

Yet, for the first time during the running of a horse race, Courtney found her mind wandering away from the action.

A couple of things had begun puzzling her. She could understand why Jack hadn't quite got over Katrina yet.

After all, *he* was the one who'd been dumped. And the woman was simply stunning to look at. Courtney suspected she was hot stuff in bed as well.

But Katrina's jealousy on seeing Jack with another female seemed over the top. What on earth had she expected? That a man like him would never turn his eye elsewhere? Had she imagined for a moment that she was irreplaceable in Jack's life, that her betrayal would turn him into an embittered celibate?

The idea was laughable. The woman had to have a screw loose.

Unfortunately, it *did* seem as if Jack hadn't turned his eye elsewhere as yet. He'd come here today alone, hadn't he? She was just a pretend girlfriend.

'You're far better off without her, you know,' she announced with pragmatic logic just as the horses flashed past the post. 'If she didn't love you poor, then she didn't love you at all, did she?'

Jack lowered his binoculars and gave her a long, hard look. 'I know you meant well in doing what you just did, Courtney. And in a way I'm grateful to you. But you really don't know what you're talking about where Katrina and I are concerned. Neither does Lois. She…oh, oh, talk of the devil. Lois is about to descend upon us. Now, for pity's sake, don't relay to her anything that just happened. And you can drop the besotted girlfriend bit. Katrina and co have left the bar.'

Courtney pulled a face. 'Pity. I was rather enjoying myself. What about when Big Brutus wins? Shouldn't I revive the role, at least for the presentation?'

'Let's wait till the horse actually wins, shall we?' Jack stated drily. 'Hi, there, Lois. Time for a glass of champers?'

CHAPTER FOUR

'SO WHAT *do* you think, Courtney?' Jack asked ten minutes before the main race. 'Will Big Brutus win, or not?'

They were standing by the parade ring, watching the grooms leading their charges around in circles. Lois was standing in the grassed centre, giving her hoop last-minute instructions and suddenly looking very much the professional horsetrainer she was.

'Come on,' Jack persisted. 'You're the horse expert here. Give me your expert advice.'

Courtney had to admit she was impressed by Big Brutus's appearance this time in. He was beginning to look like the classy thoroughbred his breeding indicated, most of his earlier ugly angles filled in with hard muscle.

And there was that superior look in his eye which often denoted a good racehorse. Her mother had always had faith in Big Brutus and her mother had been no mean judge of horseflesh.

'He certainly looks the goods today,' she said. 'Worth a bet at the odds.' He was twelve to one.

'Mmm.' Jack reached for his wallet. 'Each way?'

'Betting each way is for little old ladies,' she scorned. 'Better to put your money straight out on two horses than wimp out on one.'

'Heaven help any man who looked a wimp in front of you!' he returned, smiling wryly. 'Straight out it will be, then. Stay where you are. I'll be back shortly.'

Courtney watched him counting out a lot of notes as

39

he hurried off. She hoped he wasn't going to put too much money on Big Brutus's nose. He probably couldn't afford it. Besides, her record of tipping winners wasn't all that great. Too biased, most of the time.

Strangely, she wasn't much of a gambler herself. Her thrill whenever a Crosswinds-bred horse raced was just as great with or without a bet on it. She didn't need any extra adrenaline charge. Her excitement level was already at its zenith, just watching one of their horses run around. To see it win was the ultimate joy.

Her heart contracted at this last thought. If only her mum could have been here today. She loved it when one of her horses won.

Though in this instance it was a case of *if*, not *when*.

'If you're watching from up there, Mum,' she murmured under her breath with an upward glance into the clear blue sky, 'then ask the Lord for a little help. No, a *lot* of help. This is Big Brutus here. As you know, the best he's finished so far is second. In a maiden!'

The reality of Big Brutus's past form hit home and Courtney sighed. Lois really shouldn't build people's hopes up.

By the time Jack returned to lead her up into the stand to watch the race, Big Brutus' price had tumbled to an alarming six to one.

'My God, how much money did you put on?' she questioned as they squeezed into a spot in the stands not too far from the winning post.

'Nothing I can't afford,' he returned calmly.

'Yeah, right. And if Big Brutus doesn't win? I'll bet come Monday you'll be heading for the dole queue.'

'But you said he *would* win.'

'I said no such thing!' she protested. 'I said he looked well. If you want to lose the rest of your savings on a stupid horse race, then that's your problem. I didn't twist your arm.'

'True,' he said with a smile.

He wouldn't be looking so cool when Big Brutus ran down the track, Courtney thought angrily. Men! Egotistical fools, the lot of them!

Despite her dismissal of any personal responsibility for Jack's bet, Courtney's stomach began churning and chundering like an old washing machine stuck on the spin cycle.

'They're off!' she shouted simultaneously with the course commentator, every muscle in her body tightening.

It wasn't a big field. Only ten starters. But when Big Brutus settled down at the tail soon after the start, Courtney had to stifle a groan of dismay. As much as she kept telling herself this was Randwick, where horses could come from behind once they topped the rise into the straight, Big Brutus's record in races up till now didn't help. He was a good stayer, all right. He usually *stayed* at the back of the field.

By the time they reached the back straight, with half the race already over, Big Brutus was still running last. Admittedly, the front runners were setting a brisk pace, which meant they might tire, and Big Brutus *did* look as if he was just jogging.

'Get a move on, you ugly old brute!' she burst out at long last.

'You talking about the horse or the jockey?' Jack quipped drily out of the side of his mouth.

She threw him a vicious glance, warning him that any smart alec chit-chat was not a good idea at this stage of proceedings. But he wasn't looking at her. His eyes were glued to his binoculars.

'Move him up closer,' Courtney urged loudly from the stand, cupping her hands around her mouth as though by some miracle this action would funnel the advice half a mile away.

'Now, that's definitely advice for the jockey,' Jack muttered, bringing an exasperated sigh from Courtney.

'It's *your* money going down the gurgler,' she pointed out tartly, whereupon Jack dropped his binoculars and started shouting advice as well.

They both fell deathly silent, however, when the field swung into the straight and a still trailing Big Brutus was pulled out into the centre of the track to make his run. His long legs lengthened stride and he began to gobble up his opposition. With a furlong to go, he swept past the tiring front runners.

'The ugly old brute is going to win,' Jack said with awe in his voice. 'Lois was right!'

The reality of his words snapped Courtney out of her own frozen state of shock, and she started jumping up and down. 'Go, boy, go!' she chanted like a demented rock groupie. 'Go! Go! Go!'

Big Brutus went all right, leading the field by ten lengths, stretching out his neck at the winning post as all really good racehorses do. An ecstatic Courtney threw her arms around Jack. 'He won!' she cried. 'He won!'

'He sure did,' Jack said, grinning and making no attempt to disengage her.

'You must have won a good bit,' she said, so pleased for him.

'More than a good bit. The *bookie* is going to be the one heading for the dole queue after he pays me out, I can assure you.'

'Fantastic! Lois, did you hear that? Jack won a stack on Big Brutus.'

Lois didn't hear a thing. She was too busy hugging everyone within hugging distance. It suddenly crossed Courtney's mind that Katrina was probably watching all this hoo-ha from somewhere in the crowded stand. With that thought in mind, she launched herself up on tiptoe and kissed Jack full on the mouth.

For a second or two, she thought he was going to spoil everything and push her way.

But he didn't do any such thing. He did just the opposite. He yanked her hard against him and kissed her back, kissed her with an incredibly explosive passion, kissed her till everything in her head was scattered to the four winds and there was nothing but his lips grinding against hers, his tongue deep in her mouth, and his hands burning hot through her clothes.

And then...*then* he pushed her away.

She gasped and stared up at him with startled eyes. He laughed softly, gathering her close again. She didn't resist. She *couldn't* resist.

Amazing...

'Be careful what you start wanting, Courtney Cross,' he whispered into her ear. 'Or you just might get it.'

Lois's tapping Jack on the shoulder had him drawing back once more.

'Hate to interrupt, folks,' she said, giving a flushed Courtney a raised-eye glance. 'But it's time to go lead Big Brutus in. Would you like to do the honours, Courtney?'

Courtney snapped out of her highly uncharacteristic fluster to congratulate Lois on her brilliant training of Big Brutus, grateful for the opportunity to turn her mind from Jack's kiss. She'd been dangerously turned on there for a while. And he'd known it.

Courtney never liked a man to think he had her at a

disadvantage. She liked to call the shots in every aspect of her life. And that included her sex life.

'You do realise you're leading in a Melbourne Cup contender,' Lois remarked happily as the three of them made their way downstairs.

The Melbourne Cup! Courtney had to admire Lois's optimism. Admittedly, after today, she respected the woman's judgement a good deal more. But Australia's premier staying race over two miles was a big step up from today's mediocre-class handicap.

'You've actually entered him?' Courtney asked, knowing that was not a cheap exercise in itself.

'Your mother did.'

'My God, wasn't that just like her?'

'Your mother knew what she was doing, Courtney. The horse has got a good chance. It's a handicap race, remember? Big Brutus will get in with a very light weight. Of course, he'll have to win one of the qualifying lead-up races to ensure him of a start. But he'll do that easily, after today.'

'Lord, don't say things like that in front of Jack!' Courtney exclaimed. 'Or he'll make Big Brutus favourite next time! He might even be tempted to take some of those ridiculous odds they give Melbourne Cup entries months in advance.'

It was three months till the big race itself took place, on the first Tuesday in November. A veritable lifetime in horse racing. A million things could happen to stop them even taking their place at the start!

And then there was the race itself. Twenty top stayers from all over the world vying for the biggest prize money on the Australian racing calendar, every owner trying, every jockey riding more recklessly and ruthlessly than usual.

'Tell Jack not to waste his winnings, Lois,' Courtney advised firmly. 'Tell him to wait and see how things pan out.'

'As long as Jack's paying Big Brutus's training fees,' Lois said, 'I'll be telling him the truth as I see it. Big Brutus has a good chance in the Cup, Jack. Make no mistake about that. And I'll get him to the post. Make no mistake about that, either. Your money could do worse than to ride round on such a noble animal's back.'

Courtney rolled her eyes at Jack, who tactfully smothered his laughter.

They'd barely made it downstairs and out onto the grass when a tall, balding chap with a microphone grabbed Lois for an on-the-spot television interview.

Courtney hurried over to lead Big Brutus back into the number one gate, patting his sweaty neck and telling him what a good horse he was before remembering to congratulate the jockey on his brilliantly patient ride.

'Just followed instructions,' the jockey said. 'Frankly, you could have knocked me over with a feather when he took off like he did. Never done that before. Still, now that he's hit his straps, I think the big boy will go on to better things. I'd be very happy to have the ride on him again, no matter what race he starts in.'

'What was the jockey saying to you?' Jack asked on her eventually returning to his side.

'He wants to ride Big Brutus, no matter what race he's entered in.'

'And what do *you* think?'

'I think you kiss very well.' Couldn't leave him thinking he'd really rattled her.

He shook his head, laughing. 'You're incorrigible, do you know that?'

'Agnes tells me as much, practically every day.'

'Who's Agnes?'

'She's the housekeeper at Crosswinds. She's also the woman who delivered me. Mum hired her when she was pregnant because of Agnes's midwifery skills. She didn't want any man attending to her, you see. Agnes helped raise me, too. But she gave up when I was around seven. They say that's the age of reason. Agnes claims seven was the age of my becoming *un*reasonable.'

'Perceptive woman, this Agnes.'

'Really!'

'Well, you do suffer from a serious lack of discipline and self-control. One day someone is going to have to take you in hand.'

'Mmm. Sounds kinky. Would you like to volunteer?'

'I thought I already warned you about being provocative.'

'Hey, it was your tongue halfway down my throat,' she tossed at him, 'not the other way around.'

'And weren't you loving it?'

'Is that a crime?'

'No. It's a bloody temptation,' he growled.

'Stop scowling,' she ordered. 'Superbitch is making her way out for the presentation.'

'*Super*bitch?' He practically choked.

'Yeah.' Courtney grinned up at him. 'Good name for her, isn't it?'

He chuckled darkly. 'You could say that. But you could also say that a certain Ms Courtney Cross runs a close second in the Superbitch stakes.'

Courtney fluttered her eyelashes up at him in mock coyness. 'Who? Li'l ole me? I'm just a poor country girl, trying to keep my head in the company of one very handsome city slicker.'

'Who do you think you're kidding, sweetheart? You

could eat this city slicker for breakfast, then spit me out
by lunch-time before getting on your horse and riding out
of town without a backward glance.'

'You think so?'

'Honey, I know so. I've always been attracted to
strong-willed, independent women with more hide than
an elephant, so don't come any of that soft-soap rubbish
with me. It won't wash. Now, put on your best Supersiren
smile, if you must, and we'll go face Superbitch together.'

So saying, Jack slid an uncompromisingly steely arm
around her waist and steered her over to where prepara-
tions for the presentation had been carried out on the
lawn in front of the members' stand. There was a table
which held three magnificent silver and crystal trophies,
one large one for the owners, and two smaller replicas
for the trainer and jockey, plus a microphone on a stand
waiting to service the various speakers.

Oddly, acting the part of Jack's girlfriend during the
ceremony didn't amuse Courtney as much this time. She
was far too aware of that firm arm around her waist, and
the way it kept her glued to his side. It was one thing to
admire Jack's macho body from a distance, quite another
to feel various muscular parts of it hard up against her,
and around her.

There was his long, strong thigh for starters. And the
long, strong side of his chest. But mostly that long, strong
arm, with its long, strong fingers, whose fingertips began
tapping on her hip halfway through the sponsor's speech.

Each tap sent tiny sparks of electricity dancing all
through her body, heating her blood and heightening her
concern over the ease with which Jack could turn her on.
He wasn't even kissing her this time. Just touching her.

No man had ever made her feel what Jack was making her feel, and she wasn't sure if she liked it, or not.

If Katrina hadn't been watching them so closely, she might have pulled away from him and put an end to this highly unusual state of affairs. But awareness of those jealous green eyes fixed on them both had her staying right where she was and smiling adoringly up at him whenever he smiled adoringly down at her.

But once the presentation ceremony was over she excused herself and made a dash for the nearest powder room. She desperately needed a few minutes alone to gather herself. And to think.

She took her time in the cubicle, and was taken aback when she emerged to find Katrina leaning against the vanities, obviously waiting for her. The powder room was strangely empty apart from themselves, yet when she'd first come in the place had been quite crowded.

'I just wanted you to know a few facts of life, little Miss Smug,' Katrina said with cold fury in her voice. 'Jack Falconer does not love you. He'll never love you. So when you're lying in his arms and mooning over how great he is in bed, just remember that it's me he's thinking of when he makes love to you. Not you, honey. Me. Katrina. The love of his life.'

Courtney stared at her. The woman was either a complete nutter or she was telling the truth. Unfortunately, her words had a ring of truth about them.

Courtney did the only thing she could do under the circumstances. She went on the attack.

'Hel-lo? And what planet are *you* from, Ms Seriously Deluded?' she shot back. 'Love of his life? Huh! That's a laugh. Jack has nothing but contempt for you. You're history. So get the hell out of here and go back to your geriatric husband. And when you're lying in his tired old arms tonight, know that Jack *won't* be thinking about you. No man thinks of anyone but me when I make love to them, honey. *I* make sure of that.'

Those already glacial green eyes narrowed to icy slits. 'I'm not the one who's seriously deluded around here. No doubt Jack has fed you a tissue of lies to suit his own agenda. But, believe me, Jack is still mad about me. You're just a stand-in, a cypher, a second-rate substitute. I could get him back just like *that*...' she snapped her fingers '...whenever I want.'

'Prove it,' an increasingly angry Courtney challenged. 'Go out there and get him back. Right now. I dare you to try.'

'Very well. I presume you're seeing Jack tonight, since you're so inseparable?'

Oops. She would call her bluff, wouldn't she? 'Of course,' Courtney snapped.

'He'll make some excuse not to see you.'

'Why?'

'Because he'll be with me.'

'I don't believe you.'

'You will.' Her smile was pure malice as she spun on her high heels, clicked open the lock on the door, wrenched the door open and left, stepping over the 'Room Being Cleaned' sign she'd obviously placed outside the door to keep people away.

A strangely shaken Courtney stayed in the powder room, washing her hands for longer than necessary, her mind revolving. Her well-honed survival instinct warned her to cut and run where Jack Falconer was concerned, to have no more to do with him. He was trouble. Big trouble. And she needed big trouble in her life just now like she needed a hole in the head.

At the same time, she simply couldn't bear to let that

ghastly creature get away with calling her names. To label her a stand-in and a cypher was bad enough. But second-rate?

There was nothing second-rate about her abilities in bed! Men had lost their heads over her in that regard.

This last thought brought Courtney back to the crux of her earlier worries, which were that maybe this time *she* might be the one who lost her head.

Her mother had always warned about the power that lay within some special men, the power to turn normally intelligent, independent females into simpering idiots and mindless sex slaves.

Courtney appreciated the warning, not just because of the way her own father had effortlessly seduced her strong-willed man-hating mother, but because of the evidence of her own eyes over the years. She'd seen the most hard-nosed tomboy stable girl reduced to mush when a certain type of guy came along. And she'd known quite a few level-headed girls fall pregnant to highly unsuitable charmers.

Why?

They all claimed they'd fallen in love, as if that excused everything. At least her mother hadn't used that excuse. She'd known exactly what had propelled her into her gypsy lover's bed. Courtney didn't believe love had anything to do with those other girls' stupid behaviour, either. It was not love that made them lose all common sense, but a serious case of uncontrollable lust.

Now, *ordinary* oestrogen-based female lust, Courtney was well-acquainted with. Uncontrollable lust, however, was another matter, and not something Courtney thought she would ever encounter, or entertain. Jack was wrong about her having no discipline and self-control. She had a lot of self-control, and exercised it ruthlessly when it came to her sex life. Her relationships with men—such as they were—never got out of hand.

But she'd had a small taste of that other kind of lust now and, whilst it was disturbing, it was also incredibly exciting and unbelievably seductive. How would it feel to surrender herself mindlessly to a man, just once?

Surely she could handle one night of unbridled passion without totally losing it afterwards. Common sense was bound to return, once the cold light of day arrived and the heat of the moment was over.

Courtney stopped washing her hands and stared up at herself in the vanity mirror. The girl who stared back looked no different from the Courtney Cross she was used to. Her eyes often glittered like that. And her cheeks... Well, so what if they were a bit flushed? She'd just had a run-in with Superbitch!

This last thought made up Courtney's mind for her. No way was she going to let that arrogant, smirking woman get her hooks back into Jack again. No way!

With a saucy toss of her head, Courtney whirled on the heels of her black riding boots and deliberately went out to court big trouble.

CHAPTER FIVE

WHEN Courtney emerged into the late-afternoon sunshine once more, Katrina had already drawn Jack over to one side and was whispering frantically to him.

Jack's face was unreadable, but Katrina's was very animated. Almost anguished, at one point.

Courtney couldn't decide if this was a good sign or a bad one. Jack certainly wasn't contributing to this one-sided tête-à-tête. But he wasn't walking away either. Or telling her to get lost. He was listening intently.

As for Katrina's hapless husband, he was at that moment engaged in conversation with one of the club's committee men, blissfully unaware of his darling wife's attempts to seduce Jack practically under his nose.

On sighting Courtney coming across the lawn towards them, Katrina terminated whatever it was she was saying and hurried back to hubby.

'What did *she* want?' Courtney demanded to know.

Jack looked taken aback. 'Excuse me?' he said. 'You don't ask people about their personal conversations.'

'Why not?'

'Because it's rude.'

'Well, *she's* rude. She was *very* rude to me in the ladies' room just now. Called me a cypher and a second-rate substitute. Claimed you were still in love with her and she could get you back just like that.' And she snapped her fingers as Katrina had done.

'I see,' he said coldly.

'Can she, Jack?'

He laughed. 'Never in a million years.'

'That's what I told her. I said she was history. I said all you felt for her was contempt.'

His smile was one of dark satisfaction. 'Good.'

Courtney smiled her own satisfaction. 'As I said before…you're better off without her.'

He didn't answer, his rock-hard gaze following the rapidly departing Mr and Mrs Axelrod.

Consumed with a sudden longing to make this man forget that creature once and for all, Courtney slid her hand into his. 'Jack,' she said softly.

His eyes jerked back to hers. For a few seconds, they looked flat and dead and she thought, *Oh, God, he really does still love her.* But then slowly the life came back into them. His fingers interlinked with hers, then curled over, squeezing tightly.

Her stomach did likewise.

'What are you doing tomorrow?' he asked with seductive softness.

'What are you doing tonight?' she countered.

'Sorry. I have other plans for tonight.'

Her racing heart skittered to a panicky halt.

'Doing what?' she asked almost accusingly.

His smile was sardonic. 'Not what you're thinking. I have some business matters to attend to.'

'On a Saturday night?'

'Yes.'

'You're not going to tell me any more, are you?'

'No.'

'That's cruel. I'm dying of curiosity.'

He smiled. 'And you're going to badger me to death till I tell you.'

'Yes.'

'The fact is, Ms Cross,' he said, lifting her hand to his

lips and kissing the back of it lightly, 'I think I know just the man who'd be an excellent partner for you. But I have to check out a few things first.'

Courtney blinked. 'Are you serious?'

'Would I lie to you?'

Courtney extracted her hand from his. As much as Jack was a distractingly attractive man, and she couldn't wait to discover if his performance in bed matched his reputation, finding the right partner for Crosswinds had to be her first priority. 'Who is he?' she asked. 'Remember, I don't want anyone who's going to interfere in the running of Crosswinds.'

'This fellow will have no interest in interfering.'

'Then who is he? What's his name?'

'I'm not at liberty to say right now.'

'Why not? What's the big secret?'

'No big secret. Just client confidentiality. For now. Meanwhile, don't let Lois go chasing up anyone else. Give my client first crack at it, okay?'

'Suits me. As I said, I don't want any of her horse-mad contacts, no matter how rich they are. I want a big city slicker with absolutely no yen for breeding horses and more money than sense.'

Jack smiled. 'That's exactly what you'll be getting.'

Courtney could hardly believe her luck. Both her problems solved at once. Her debts. Plus her rather disturbing desire for this man.

She'd been wondering how she could confine any fling with Jack to one time only if she stayed down here in Sydney for a whole week. Jack wasn't the sort of man who would let her run the show as she usually did. If he was as passionate and powerful a lover as he was a kisser, then he'd be the one directing the action, and deciding when enough was enough.

Which was partly the point, of course.

Courtney wanted to feel what it would be like, being made love to by a dominating and possibly demanding man. She didn't, however, want to become addicted to the experience. She had no doubt Jack intended to seduce her tomorrow, but hopefully, by Monday, she could escape back to the normality of home, never to see him again. After all, business contracts were handled by electronic mail these days, as were cash transfers. There would be no need for any further personal contact. Bill could handle the details, and any follow-up business.

She beamed up at him. 'Wait till I tell Lois. She's going to be so pleased.'

'Tell me what?'

Courtney swung round to find a happy Lois standing there, clasping her trophy. Jack's was still on the table.

'Jack thinks he knows just the right sucker to save Crosswinds.'

'Partner,' Jack corrected drily. 'Not sucker.'

'*Silent* partner,' Courtney countered. 'He won't open his mouth, just his wallet. Isn't that right, Jack?'

'Not quite. He's no fool, Courtney. He'll want to know exactly what he's getting himself into. After a recent, rather unfortunate experience he had, he'll want me to go up to Crosswinds and check everything out firsthand. There *are* tax concessions for investments in thoroughbred breeding, but I'm going to have to assure my client that Crosswinds is a going concern with potential for a steady future income and return on his investment.'

'Oh… How long would you have to stay?'

'I'll need a few days to be totally satisfied,' he confirmed. 'You did say it was a large concern. I'll also need to speak to your accountant and see the books. If you haven't any other business to do here in Sydney, we could drive up there together tomorrow.'

'Well, I…er…' Courtney wasn't usually tongue-tied, but Jack's suggestion had totally routed her own nice safe plan which would prevent any chance of any sexual addiction or, heaven forbid, an emotional involvement.

Courtney had no intention of ever succumbing to either. But she had wanted to let her hair down, so to speak, just this once.

Now, any such experience was out of the question. No way would Courtney invite Jack into her bedroom at Crosswinds and risk any of her staff finding out. It was hard enough to maintain their respect as their boss with her being female and attractive and only twenty-five. Impossible if they thought she was an easy lay.

Courtney had never had sex with any of the men working at Crosswinds. Well…not since her first time, five years before. But Larry had been leaving the next day, so the risk hadn't been great. And she hadn't been the boss back then.

'Fine,' she said, irritated by this turn of events.

'I thought you were out of the investment brokerage business, Jack,' Lois remarked.

Lois wasn't sure what was going on between these two, but something was up. She wasn't blind. She'd seen that kiss in the stands. It hadn't been an impromptu peck on the cheek, either. It had been a full-blooded, open-mouthed, French kiss. Then, at the presentation, they'd been all over each other like a rash.

Jack obviously had more on his mind than just finding Courtney a business partner. His intention of staying at Crosswinds until he was *totally satisfied* could be construed two ways.

'This chap is by way of being a personal friend of

mine,' Jack attempted to explain, and Lois's excellent antenna for male deception twanged. She hoped there really *was* a potential partner, and this wasn't some plan for a rebound or revenge affair. Lois had seen Jack with Katrina on many occasions and she knew just how wrapped in her he'd been. It seemed far too coincidental that this sudden passion for Courtney had come about on the very day Jack's ex had been around.

'Why doesn't he want his identity known?' she challenged, scepticism in her voice.

'He likes to play a close hand. He'll be up front with Courtney, if and when he goes ahead with the partnership. You have my word.'

'That's good,' Lois said.

Lois didn't really think Jack was the type to rip Courtney off in any money sense. As far as their personal relationship was concerned...well, she supposed Courtney could look after herself in that regard. Hilary might have been a man-hater, but her daughter was rumoured to be a real man-eater. The horseworld grapevine was second to none, and men invariably talked. There'd been this horse-breaker a few years back. And a rep who sold horse vitamins. And a chap who drove for a horse transport company. And they were only the ones Lois had heard about.

Maybe the person she should be worrying about was Jack...

CHAPTER SIX

SUNDAY dawned crisp and clear, with the promise of another warm winter's day. Courtney, as befitted her habit of years, was up at first light. Lois had still preceded her by a couple of hours, overseeing her charges on the training track well before the sun's first rays peeped over the horizon. Her horses were back in their mucked-out stables long before most Sydneysiders opened their Sunday morning papers.

Lois still insisted on cooking Courtney breakfast, treating them both to bacon and eggs and lashings of toast and brewed coffee, serving all of it up on the round wooden table which dominated the homey kitchen in her red-roofed, three-bedroomed, fifties-style brick-veneer house. She'd inherited it—plus the stables—from her horse trainer father, who'd died of a stroke after one of his charges had come back with a positive swab and his licence had been taken away from him. Her mother had passed away a few years before or she, too, would have died of shame, Lois believed.

Lois, thirtyish at the time and in the throes of divorce, had taken up the challenge of making a success of the career she'd always wanted but which her mother had talked her out of in favour of marriage to a Macquarie Street specialist with two huge cars and a house on the harbour. All he'd needed to complete his perfect lifestyle was a beautiful wife and two beautiful children.

Lois hadn't been able to have any children, however, which was one of the reasons her marriage had failed.

That, along with the loneliness and boredom of being a doctor's wife. Her horses were now her children, which perhaps explained why they could never do any wrong in her eyes. No matter what fault they had—even being too slow—she was always sure she could fix it. The funny thing was, often enough she could.

'Sleep well?' Lois remarked over their second cup.

The girl looked tired, she thought. Though still beautiful. How was it that when you were only twenty-five dark circles under your eyes looked sexy, but once you passed forty you just looked wrecked?

'Fine,' Courtney lied. She'd tossed and turned for most of the night, unable to get out of her mind that Jack might have lied to her, that he was, at that very moment, making mad, passionate love to the awful but stunningly gorgeous Katrina.

Her emotions had kept alternating between anger and jealousy, though who exactly she was most angry with she wasn't sure. She still wasn't. Probably Jack, for even falling in love with such a creature in the first place. My God, didn't he have any taste? The woman was a witch, a manipulative, gold-digging, heartless witch.

Who was probably brilliant in bed.

More than brilliant.

Bad.

Men liked women to be bad in bed. They liked it a lot. Courtney knew that for a fact.

'It's Jack, isn't it?' Lois said abruptly.

Courtney's darkly bruised eyes whipped up from where she'd been staring blankly down at her plate. 'What?'

'Jack Falconer. You fancy him.'

Courtney shrugged. 'Who wouldn't?'

'I don't. He's not my type at all.'

Surprise that Lois even *had* a type must have shown in her face, for Lois laughed.

'You think I don't have a sex life?'

'I...I guess I never really thought about it at all.'

'Typical. The young think sex is only for the young.'

'No, I don't,' Courtney denied. 'I just thought you were totally wrapped up in your horses and didn't want or need a man in your life. Mum said you were divorced, and I guess I jumped to conclusions. The *wrong* conclusions, I see,' she added, feeling both curious and intrigued by this woman who had been on the fringes of her life for many years but whom she'd never bothered to really get to know. Yet she liked her. She liked her a lot. 'So what *is* your type, Lois? Tell me.'

'Hard to describe, exactly. But I know it when I see it. He's usually of average height. I don't like men to tower over me. Nicely built without being muscle-bound. Elegant in his movements. A good rider,' she said, her smile wicked. 'And with dark eyes. I adore dark eyes.'

'How old?'

'Age is immaterial. I've had lovers in their twenties and in their fifties.'

'And where do you find these men?' Courtney knew how hard it was to have a relationship with a man when you worked with horses. It was a seven-day-a-week job.

'I hire them.'

Courtney tried not to look shocked, and almost managed. 'You...hire...them,' she said slowly, her mind whirling. 'As in...how? From an escort agency?'

Lois chuckled. 'Lord, no. I mean I hire them to work for me. You must know how often grooms come and go in this business. When I'm interviewing new staff, if I see a fellow who appeals to me physically, I hire him.'

'Good grief. And does he…um…they…um…always come across?'

'Most of the time. I'm the boss, after all.'

'Wow!'

'You're not too shocked?'

'No! Heavens, no. But don't these men…um…talk?'

Lois shrugged. 'Not often. They know what side their bed is buttered on. To be honest, I'd prefer a permanent relationship, but not many men can handle a woman as strong as myself on a day-to-day basis.'

'I know what you mean.'

'What about you, Courtney? Will you be looking to get married one day?'

'Never.' She'd never met one single married man who didn't want to be the boss of his wife. Not one. And she knew she could never handle that.

'What about children? Don't you want children?'

Courtney had always pushed the issue of children to the back of her mind. 'I'll probably have a child one day. I'd like someone to leave Crosswinds to. But I don't have to be married for that. And I don't see any rush. I'm only twenty-five.'

'True. But the years have a habit of slipping away from you. You wouldn't want to wake up one day and find out it's too late.'

The telephone began ringing.

'Excuse me a moment,' Lois said. 'It's probably an owner. Sunday is visiting day.'

She swivelled round in her chair and reached for the mobile phone which was resting on the kitchen counter. She pressed the button and swept it up to her ear.

'Lois Wymouth speaking,' she said sweetly. 'Well, if it isn't Jack Falconer!'

Courtney stiffened in her chair.

'You're up bright and early. Did our mystery investor come to the party...? Wonderful...! He doesn't...? God, talk about super-secretive... She's upstairs... I'll go and get her for you...'

She cupped her hand firmly over the phone. 'Looks like you have your sucker. But he still wants to keep his ID a secret till he signs on the dotted line. Anyway, lover-boy wants to talk to you personally. Would you like to take the call somewhere more private?' she whispered.

'Just give me the phone, Lois. Nothing of that kind will be going on between me and Jack now that I'm doing business with him. Unlike some people, I don't mix business and pleasure.'

'Oooh. That's power talking for you. But will you be able to sustain your good intentions when you have Jack all to yourself up in that big old house for a few days *and* nights? I don't see him playing gentleman for that long. Not when he fancies you as much as you fancy him. And he does. I do have eyes, girl.'

Courtney had been worrying about exactly the same thing herself. 'I'll have Biggs sleep on my bed.'

'That old mongrel? Your stable cat is a better guard dog than him.'

'Maybe. But Biggs looks fiercer.'

'Well, take my advice and get in a good supply of condoms. Don't want any unexpected little filly or colt arriving next year, do we?'

'As if I'd ever let myself accidentally get pregnant to any man. Don't you think I learnt anything from my mother? Now *give* me the darned phone!'

Lois sighed, and handed it over. Courtney rose and walked into the lounge-room, away from prying ears. 'Jack! Lois said you have some good news for me.'

'I surely do. It's all systems go. My client is happy to

invest the four million in Crosswinds you need, provided everything is shipshape.'

Courtney frowned. 'Er…what does he mean by shipshape? I did explain to you the place is looking a bit rundown. That's why I wanted the four million instead of the three I already owe the bank.'

'I'm not talking about surface appearances. I'm talking about the land itself and the quality of your stock. The brood mares and the stallions you have standing at stud. Especially the latter.'

'We have three stallions at stud, two older well-formed stallions and one exciting new prospect.'

'Goldplated,' he said before she could.

'You *know* about him?'

'I looked him up last night. He's impeccably bred, the full brother to a Golden Slipper winner. He never started in a race after an accident on the training track, though he had won two well-documented trials in brilliant fashion. He stood his first and only season at a stud in Victoria, with an amazing fertility strike-rate of one hundred per cent. Which raises the question of why did they sell him?'

'That's easily answered. That stud stands his full brother as well, the Golden Slipper winner. They felt it wasn't commercially sensible to keep two stallions of exactly the same blood lines. But they were wanting to use Goldplated just once on some of their own mares before they let him go. I think you'll find he didn't service any outside mares.'

'They sold him at a bargain basement price.'

'That's because he's still a risk. It'll be two more years before his first crop reaches the track. A lot can happen between now and then.'

'I hope he's insured,' Jack said.

'Do I look like a fool?' Courtney thanked God for Bill, or she would have.

'Right, well, I'll want to know exactly how many mares Goldplated is booked to cover this season, how much you currently charge for his services, and how much you might be able to charge in the years to come, if his progeny start winning good races. This is obviously a long-term investment and my client will want to know what Crosswinds' prospects are, long-term.'

Courtney frowned. 'You've certainly done your research.'

'Amazing what you find out on the internet.'

'Is that what you were doing last night? Finding out what you could about breeding racehorses?'

'Partly.'

Courtney pulled a face. He sure liked to play his cards close to his chest. 'I see. Well, Sarah will be able to give you all the facts and figures on all our brood mares and stallions.' She'd already decided to turn Jack over to as many other people as she could during his stay at Crosswinds. 'Sarah's the office manager at Crosswinds. She's been there for yonks and probably knows more about those things than I do.'

Which was just so much bulldust. There wasn't anyone at Crosswinds who knew more about the horses there than Courtney.

'When can you be ready to leave?' Jack asked. 'I was thinking of a ten o'clock start. Would that be too early for you?'

Courtney glanced at the chiming clock in the corner of the lounge-room. It was ten to nine. She was already up, showered, dressed and breakfasted. Packing would take all of five minutes.

'I'm ready now,' she said, and he laughed.

'I guess I'm used to a different type of female. Katrina needed at least a day's notice of intent to go anywhere.'

Courtney thought of Katrina's perfect hair and exquisitely made-up face. No doubt the rest of her required as much time-consuming pampering. Her clothes selection for each occasion probably took hours. And she'd have to race out and buy something new if she didn't have *just* the right thing.

'Speaking of Katrina,' Courtney couldn't resist saying, 'did she happen to accidentally show up at your place last night?'

'No,' he said without hesitation. 'She did not. Happy now?' he added, a cool amusement in his voice.

Courtney realised she'd just made her first mistake, if she wanted to keep this man at arm's length. 'Just checking to make sure you weren't too exhausted to drive all day,' she said drily.

'It's only about six hours to the Upper Hunter Valley. Longer if we stop. Which we will, of course.'

'Oh?'

'For lunch.'

Reasons for stopping other than for lunch had flashed into Courtney's mind.

'I'll bring a picnic,' he said.

The vision of them lying together on a rug on some sun-drenched riverbank was not conducive to Courtney's rapidly disintegrating peace of mind.

'Please don't do that,' she said sharply.

'Why not?'

She decided to nip things in the bud.

'This is a business trip, Jack, not some romantic getaway. I'm sorry if I gave you the wrong idea yesterday. I *am* very attracted to you, I admit. But I don't mix business with pleasure, and that's final.'

'That's telling me straight, isn't it?'

'It's better to be up front. Saves trouble later on.'

'What kind of trouble are you referring to?'

'Having to handle men who think I'm going to be a push-over in my business dealings with them just because I'm sleeping with them.'

'And that's happened to you in the past?'

'In a fashion.' That vitamin rep had expected her to buy swags of his stuff, just because she'd spent one wretched weekend away with him.

'Does it occur to you that all the power in this case is on your side?' Jack said drily. 'Sleeping with me might get me to overlook any shortcomings in Crosswinds.'

'I don't believe that for a moment.'

'Why not?'

'Because any man who paid back all his partner's debts out of his own purse when he didn't have to is not going to play deceitful with a client.'

'There's always the first time,' he said wryly.

'No, Jack. That's not you.'

'Not me,' he repeated slowly. 'I doubt you know the real me, Courtney.'

'I have a pretty good idea. I'm quite a good judge of character. I have every confidence that you won't put the hard word on me, if I ask you not to. But if you're ever tempted, I'll have Biggs by my side.'

'Who the hell is Biggs? Some kind of bodyguard?'

'My trusty guard dog. He's a cattle dog cross. He comes with me everywhere.' A slight exaggeration. Mr Biggs, who was rising ten, spent most of his days snoozing on the swing seat on the front veranda. Only occasionally did he wander around the farm with her nowadays. And he *never* went in the ute with her any more, ever since she'd run into a ditch the previous year and he'd been thrown out of the passenger window, landing in a freshly deposited cow-pat. His dignity had been seriously offended.

'Thanks for telling me,' Jack said ruefully.

'I thought it only fair to warn you.'

'In that case, it's only fair that I warn you in return.'

Courtney stiffened. 'About what?'

'I don't take orders very well.'

'Meaning?'

'Just that. See you at ten. *With* a picnic basket.' And he hung up.

CHAPTER SEVEN

'WOULD you like to have a turn behind the wheel?' Jack asked an hour into the trip. They had not long crossed the Mooney Mooney bridge, and were heading north on the F3 freeway which connected Sydney to Newcastle. Traffic was light, compared to what was heading south towards Sydney.

Courtney shot Jack a surprised glance. When he'd first pulled up outside Lois's place in a red sports convertible with the top down and a personalised number plate—JF2000—on it, she'd been agape with shock. When she'd questioned how he could afford to even *insure* such a car, he'd shrugged and said that he'd bought it to celebrate the new millennium. And what the heck? You only lived once.

Courtney's sentiments exactly. She adored sports cars. Always had. She was sure she would adore driving one, but had never had the chance. Till now.

'You mean it?' she asked, her heart thundering.

To show her he did, he immediately pulled over to the side of the road, leaving the powerful engine growling impatiently whilst he jumped out and strode round the low, sleek front of the car.

Courtney ogled him every step of the way, thinking he looked even more hunky in casual clothes than he did in a suit. His long legs, narrow hips and compact butt were just made for jeans, and his big chest and broad shoulders impressively filled out his navy blue pullover. He would look damned good in the buff, she couldn't help thinking.

68

'Well, what are you still sitting there for, girl?' he chided when he yanked open her door. 'Hop to it.'

Courtney snapped out of her lust-filled reverie, leapt out and raced round before he could change his mind, telling herself that if she couldn't enjoy his body then she was darned well going to enjoy his car!

'Don't forget there's a one-ten speed limit on this road,' Jack warned when she roared off.

'Do you think they'd book me at one-twenty?'

'Yes. So stick to one-fifteen. Max.'

'Okay, boss.' She flashed him a happy grin.

'That'll be the day,' he muttered, and Courtney laughed.

The next hour was thrilling! So much better than driving the ute. Courtney hummed happily as she sped along the expressway with the wind in her face and her ponytail streaming out behind.

'This must be what it felt like riding Big Brutus down the straight yesterday,' she shouted at one stage. 'Fan-bloody-tastic!'

The turn-off for the New England highway came up all too quickly, with Jack asking her to pull over shortly afterwards.

'Can't trust you to slow down for all the little towns we go through on this road,' Jack commented once he was behind the wheel again. 'I can see you're a speed freak.'

'I am,' she said, nodding agreement. 'I just love anything fast. Always have.'

'And what else do you love?' he asked, his sexy blue eyes slanting her a seductive glance.

Courtney's stomach curled over, making her realise that driving Jack's car had undermined her defences where he was concerned. It was high time to get herself under control again. In a few short hours they would be at Crosswinds and this would never do, having her insides flip over every time he looked at her.

'I love being behind the wheel,' she said firmly, 'in *everything* I do.'

'That can be exhausting. Aren't there ever times when you just want to lie back, relax and let someone else be responsible for things?'

She glared over at him. Was he a damned mind-reader?

'Turn in here,' she ordered abruptly, and noted with triumph that he did as he was told. Sometimes.

It was a rest area in the middle of nowhere. There wasn't any babbling brook. Or any softly grassed bank. Just a small clearing carved into the scrubby roadside bush and a few straggly trees left to provide shade for a couple of picnic tables and benches.

'Why do you want to stop here?' Jack asked, scowling.

'I'm hungry. I thought this would be a good spot for our picnic lunch.'

The corner of his wide, firm mouth lifted in a smile of considerable irony. 'As good as any,' he agreed, 'under the circumstances.'

Courtney almost regretted her decision to lunch there when she saw Jack's truly beautiful picnic box and its simply delicious contents. Fortunately, he had a checked tablecloth which covered the rickety table.

'You shouldn't have gone to all this trouble,' she chided as he set everything out on the cloth.

'No trouble at all. I rang and ordered it from the local deli after my call to you this morning, then picked it up on my way.'

Courtney gazed at the delicious selection of cold meats, salads, cheeses and breads. There was even a chilled half-bottle of white wine along with two classy-looking glasses. 'It must have been very expensive,' she said with a frown.

'Reasonably. But please don't fuss. Just enjoy. Think of it as your commission for tipping me Big Brutus. Believe me when I say I still have plenty of change left from my winnings.'

To continue complaining would have been ungracious in the extreme, so Courtney shrugged and tucked in.

Having given in, she ate her fair share and drank most of the wine, which went straight to her head.

'Brother!' she exclaimed when she felt her head begin to spin. 'What percentage alcohol is in this?' She picked up the bottle and read that it was twelve per cent. 'Pretty potent drop. You trying to get me tipsy?'

'If I was, I'd have bought a whole bottle.'

'True,' she conceded.

'Would it make any difference? Are you a sure thing when you're tipsy?'

'Not too often.'

'But sometimes?' He looked hopeful.

'I hope you haven't come on this jaunt hoping I would be.'

'No.'

'You think you can talk me into it, is that it?'

'But of course. I wouldn't be a normal red-blooded heterosexual male if I didn't.'

Exasperation with him brought heat to her face. 'I thought I told you that's not on!'

Jack remained annoyingly cool. And terrifyingly confident. 'I know what you told me. But, as I said, I don't take orders. And your reasons for not sleeping with me don't wash, Courtney. You're not doing business with me personally. You're doing it with my client.'

'Other people won't see it like that,' she argued.

'There's absolutely no need for anyone at Crosswinds to know, if that's what you're afraid of. I can be very discreet. What happens behind closed bedroom doors is our business only. Though, to tell the truth, I'd prefer an open relationship with you. But if you insist on secrecy, then I won't give the game away.'

His eyes met hers and held them effortlessly.

Her whole world tipped sidewards, then whirled. She was like a spinning top that he'd suddenly set in motion—that he would always be able to set in motion with the touch of his hand or, as now, with that devilish gleam in his eye.

A scary thought. But oh…so thrilling. More thrilling than driving his car. More thrilling than anything she'd ever known.

She thanked God the wide wooden table lay between them or she'd drag his deliciously macho mouth onto hers right then and there, and Lord knew what would happen then. Passing traffic might start running off the road on spotting them making love on the table, with picnic things scattered everywhere!

'I'll think about it,' she said abruptly, and reefed her eyes away to start stacking up the empty containers.

She could feel his eyes still on her but she simply refused to look back at him, refused to let him see how much power he already had over her.

'You do that,' he drawled, then began to help.

CHAPTER EIGHT

THEY didn't stop again, or really talk again; the next few hours were agonisingly long for Courtney. Jack commented once on the scenic countryside, and complained occasionally over some fool's driving, usually a truck driver. He also put the radio on and sang softly along with a few songs, but they were only minor distractions for her increasingly panicky thoughts.

I'm a goner, she finally accepted a few minutes away from their turn-off. Come tonight, I'm going to end up in bed with Jack Falconer. No point in fighting it any longer.

Better to go willingly, she decided, than to act like Biggs when he had to go to the vet.

She almost burst out laughing at the image of herself with a lead around her throat, being dragged into Jack's bedroom, her heels digging into the polished wooden floor while she whimpered in fear.

As it was, an amused little giggle escaped.

No, that was not her. She was not a coward. Or a victim. She made the rules in her sex life. She would stick to those rules again tonight, and if Jack wanted to try anything other than her usual she would tell him that didn't work for her and he could just like what she was offering, or lump it!

She had no doubt he would like it. Every man she'd ever known had, and had come begging for more.

'Want to share the source of your return to good humour?' Jack asked.

'No,' she returned blithely. 'Take the next turn on the left.'

'Queenswood, ten kilometres,' he read on the sign as he turned. 'How far is your place from there?'

'About fifteen kilometres the other side of town. But I'd like to stop in Queenswood, if you don't mind. I've got a couple of things to pick up. If there's anything you need at the shops, I suggest you get it now. You don't want to be running back and forth for minor provisions. The road to Crosswinds is not the best. The tar gives way to dirt pretty quickly, and the surface is very rutted at the moment after all the rain we've had this last winter.'

'Too much rain?'

She shrugged. 'A lot of rain in winter is a double-edged sword. You do get good grass in the spring but it drowned some of the oats we planted. Still, I'm not complaining. We can always plant some more.'

'You know, you have an optimistic spirit. I like that.'

'Not as optimistic as Lois. That woman cracks me up sometimes.'

'Is that another warning about Big Brutus's chances in the Melbourne Cup?'

'No! Lord, no! I wasn't even thinking about Big Brutus.'

'What were you thinking about, then?'

'Nothing specific.' But she had been. She'd been thinking of Lois having the hide to employ men she fancied, then coercing them into bed with her because she was the boss. Courtney had always thought herself bold, but Lois left her for dead.

At least Jack *wanted* to go to bed with her. He had no ulterior motive or secret agenda. For him, it was simply a matter of sex.

And that was how she was determined to look at tonight. Simply as a matter of sex. No different from any of the other encounters she'd had with men in the past.

'Ah, here we are,' she said, feeling marginally better.

Queenswood was typical of most Australian towns, with a very wide main street lined by shops, a nice little park on entry and exit, a pub on one corner, a post office on another and the town hall in the centre, usually sporting a clock tower.

Queenswood's clock told Courtney it was five past four. Jack had made very good time, even without going over the speed limit.

'Just park anywhere there in the middle,' she told him. 'There's plenty of spaces. Not too many people in town at this hour on a Sunday afternoon. All the shops will be closed by now, except for the supermarket and the chemist. You need anything?'

'No. I don't think so.'

'Fine. Won't be long.'

Courtney bowled into the chemist shop with every intention of buying a packet of condoms. It wouldn't have been the first time. But the chemist's wife, Maggie, was serving at the counter and she was the town's resident gossip. So Courtney picked up the first thing that came to hand—a can of muskily perfumed deodorant—paid for it quickly, and left, after which she dashed into the supermarket.

Fortunately, the cashier was a gum-chewing magazine-reading adolescent girl whom Courtney didn't recognise and who hardly stopped reading when Courtney went through with her purchase.

As she hurried out, Courtney popped the box of condoms inside the opaque paper bag containing the deodorant, secretly glad there weren't too many people around to stare at her getting into a red sports car driven by a very handsome stranger. Gossip was the bane of country life, and discretion was necessary if you cared what other people thought.

Till recently, Courtney hadn't given a damn what people thought of her. Other than her mother, that was. But her mother was gone now and the responsibility for Crosswinds lay on her shoulders and hers alone. She *had* to care what some people thought, whether she liked it or not.

Jack had climbed out of the car whilst she was gone and was leaning with his back against his door, his arms folded and his ankles crossed. His head was tipped back slightly, his eyes were shut and he was soaking in the last of the afternoon sun. He looked totally relaxed and totally irresistible to Courtney.

She couldn't stop her eyes running over him in a decidedly lascivious fashion, lingering on the bulge in his jeans. Lord, now that was impressive. *Very* impressive.

Her eyes finally lifted to find that his eyelids had done likewise during her highly intimate perusal. 'I see you've been thinking about it,' he drawled.

She swallowed, but kept her eyes steady. Don't let him get cocky. Don't let him be sure of you.

Her small smile was just enough to make him stand up straight, his body language showing a measure of frustration. His lower body too, if she wasn't mistaken.

'As I said yesterday,' he muttered, yanking open his car door, and hiding his arousal from her, 'you run a close second in the Superbitch stakes, Courtney Cross.'

'I never run second in anything,' she retorted, stung by his putting her in the same breath as that calculating cold-blooded cow. 'No crime in a girl looking. But I did warn you, Jack. I don't mix business with pleasure. You should have believed me.'

'I'm beginning to appreciate that fact.'

'You can't win them all, you know.'

'Just get in the car, damn you.'

'Fine!'

They climbed in and banged their car doors simultaneously. Courtney threw her package at her feet, sorry that she'd even bothered to buy the darned things now. All that rampant desire she'd been feeling for Jack had well and truly disintegrated with their spat. Which was just as well, since she'd just told the man sex was definitely not on.

Jack shot out of his parking spot like a spurred quarterhorse, racing up the main street and out of town. When he hit the dirt road his back wheels slewed round, throwing up a cloud of dust which would have covered Lake Eyre.

'Careful,' Courtney bit out. 'I ended up in a ditch last year driving too fast along this road.'

'Pity you didn't break your beautiful neck in the process.'

Courtney was torn between feeling offended and complimented. She hadn't had her neck described as beautiful before. Probably because it wasn't, she decided. It was too darned long.

'Flattery will get you everywhere,' she snapped.

'Will it, now?'

His blue eyes glittered harshly as they flicked over her body, encased that day in blue jeans and a red and blue checked flannel shirt. With her hair up in a ponytail and no make-up on, Courtney knew she was as far removed from the glamorous and perfectly groomed Katrina as a woman could be. But Jack was still looking at her with the most corruptingly intense hunger.

'In that case you have beautiful eyes as well. A beautiful mouth, beautiful legs, beautiful breasts, and, oh, yes, a really beautiful backside. So how far has that got me?' he mocked. 'Through your bedroom door yet? Or do I need to mention your refreshing personality, your feisty spirit, your earthy sensuality and your wicked sense of humour?'

Courtney couldn't help it. She burst out laughing.

He grinned also and, thankfully, slowed down to a less neck-risking speed. She really did want to get home in one piece.

'You lied to me,' he said, but with a smile.

'About what?'

'About flattery getting me everywhere. It hasn't made the slightest bit of difference, has it?'

'No.'

'And I suppose they aren't condoms in that packet down there, as I was stupidly hoping?'

'Sorry, just deodorant for me and some headache tablets for Agnes,' she said with a perfectly straight face.

'Pity.'

'Them's the breaks.'

'That was your last chance to give in gracefully. From now on it's war, where all sorts of dirty tactics will be employed.'

'Such as?'

'You don't expect me to telegraph my punches, do you? That's not how the game is played.'

'War is not a game.'

'It can be. I played war games a lot as a kid. And I know all the right moves.'

'I'm sure you do,' she said ruefully.

'Them kind of moves, too,' he agreed with a devilish waggle of his brows. 'I've had loads of practice.'

'Start young, did you?'

'Fourteen, or thereabouts.'

'Disgusting.'

'I'll bet you weren't far behind, you little hypocrite. Country girls are notorious for being sexually active young. Something to do with seeing all those animal matings from an early age. Sex holds no mystery.'

'You're right there. Sex certainly held no mysteries for me, which is why I was twenty before I bothered.'

He threw her a startled look.

'It's true. Before then I wouldn't even kiss a boy. If anything, seeing stallions servicing mares all the time made me even more determined not to succumb to such a male-orientated activity. It's not pretty to watch, you know. Or sexy. The mare is tied up and quite often reluctant. But she has no choice. The stallion is brought in and he mounts her whether she likes it or not. Virgin mares whinny with the pain. Others freeze with shock.'

'But surely not all mares react like that.'

'No. There are born sluts, even in mares. Or so my mother used to say.'

Jack frowned. 'Surely *you* don't think that, do you? That a female is a born slut if she enjoys sex?'

'Not any more I don't. But I did for a long while. I hated the idea of a man on top of me, forcing part of his body into mine. I couldn't understand how it could be pleasurable, let alone bearable.'

'But you obviously don't think that now,' he said, still sounding a bit shocked.

'No. I don't think that now. Thanks to Larry.'

'Larry,' he repeated thoughtfully. 'Larry who?'

'Larry Mason. He was a horse-breaker. Specialised in difficult fillies.'

'Very funny. Were you in love with him?'

She laughed. 'Good Lord, no. But he was very attractive in a John Wayne sort of way.'

'And?'

'And I fancied him rotten.'

'And?'

Suddenly it all came back to her, like a slow-motion movie. She'd gone down to the far feed shed for something and walked in on Larry and one of the stable girls, having sex. Larry had been lying across some bales of straw and the girl had been sitting astride him, totally unaware of her surroundings as she'd risen and fallen on her lover's body, her eyes tightly shut, moaning cries escaping her wide open mouth. She hadn't seen Courtney standing there, frozen but fascinated.

Larry had, however. He'd even winked at her. She'd watched for a full five minutes before running away.

She hadn't told anyone what she'd seen, but after that, whenever she'd run into Larry, he'd stare at her and she'd go hot all over. She'd thought about him constantly, had dreamt of him at night: dreamt of sitting astride him as that girl had done. Dreamt of clutching his shoulders and riding him till she too cried out with the kind of orgasm she'd witnessed that afternoon.

Courtney had read all about orgasms. She just hadn't ever wanted one before.

But after that she had. With Larry.

Yet she hadn't dared approach him, fearing her mother might find out. But then she'd heard Larry was leaving the next day, going to work at a stud in South Australia. That had been her chance. And she'd taken it, dredging up the courage to go to him and tell him what she wanted, even whilst she'd been shaking inside.

That night it had been *her* in the far shed with him, not that stable girl. Her being shown how to do what she'd seen, and more. Much more. Larry liked assertive women, as it had turned out. He liked them being on top. He liked being made love to by the female.

Courtney had liked it too. Because she'd been in control. There'd been no question of male domination. Or of losing her head. The next time she'd met a man she fancied, she'd known exactly what to do. Not that there'd been all that many. Three or four over five years. Hardly a harem.

'You must have fancied this Larry one hell of a lot,' Jack persisted, 'if he got past all your obvious defences. Either that or he was the best seducer since Casanova. Which was it?'

Courtney suddenly realised Jack's questions had become very intimate indeed.

Time to terminate this conversation!

'I fancied him one hell of a lot,' she said. 'Watch this next corner. This is where I ran off the road.'

Jack's car took the corner as if it was on rails, and in a way it was, the deep, rain-worn ruts keeping all four wheels securely within their walls. But when the low-slung bottom of the car scraped the top off the hump of dirt in the middle, Jack groaned.

'I can see why people have four-wheel drives out here,' he grumbled.

'It'll be better once the council brings in the grader. They do that a couple of times a year.'

'You should get on their backs to do more. Put some road base down or something. This is appalling.'

'This is the country, Jack, not the city.'

'Still...'

Always sensitive to male criticism, Courtney was now on the alert for more, their arrival at the official entrance into Crosswinds making her smother a groan as she suddenly saw it through Jack's eyes.

The once proud iron archway, which had the word 'Crosswinds' emblazoned across it, was rusty, as was the cut-out drum sitting on a fence post, which served as their mailbox. Not an auspicious entrance for a property looking for an investor.

Courtney waited for Jack to make a detrimental comment but he didn't. He just drove through the open gateway without saying a word.

At least the driveway up to the house was gravel, she thought, and not rutted or potholed. The tall poplars on either side looked impressive, too, though the trees hadn't sprouted their leaves yet. Which was a pity. Their greenery would have distracted from the fences behind, whose greying paint seemed to have disintegrated further in the short time she'd been away.

Still, the land beyond the peeling fences did look good, the lushly grassed paddocks and green hills beyond presenting a panoramic picture of surface prosperity. Peaceful mares grazed in yards on the left, whilst healthy-looking yearlings frolicked on the right. The various barns and buildings in the distance didn't look as shabby as they would up close.

Hopefully, Jack's first impressions overall would be good. After all, she'd warned him about the recent lack of money to attend to what were really superficial things. He was the one who'd said it was the quality of the land and stock that mattered.

Jack continued up the winding driveway at a sedate pace, his head swivelling left and right, his intelligent eyes drinking it all in.

When his head stopped swivelling and his eyes stared straight ahead, Courtney's own gaze followed.

Satisfaction filled her soul at the sight that had trans-fixed him. Her home, perched on the hill at the far end of the driveway, looking magnificent.

'What a fantastic old house,' Jack said warmly.

'I'm so glad you think so.'

She smiled as her eyes moved lovingly over the house's stately grandeur, shown to advantage under the golden rays of the setting sun. The grey iron roof shone, and the white iron-lace balustrades which ran round the upstairs veranda sparkled. Any lack of recent painting certainly didn't show in the flattering afternoon light.

'My great great-grandfather built it back in 1852, when he first bought the land and started up the stud. He was a merchant from Scotland and quite wealthy. The walls are made out of a local sandstone and all the woodwork is Australian cedar. The lead light panels in the doors and windows were made in Melbourne and transported up by bullock wagons. The marble tiles in the front hallway were shipped out from Devon and the brass light fittings were manufactured somewhere in the north of England. I can't remember where exactly. He filled the whole house with wonderful European furniture, but unfortunately we only have a few pieces left.'

'That's a shame.'

'You can say that again. I wouldn't have come begging to Sydney if I'd still had them. I'd have just auctioned off the damned lot and paid off my debts. But Mum beat me to it. Over the years, every time she wanted to buy a brood mare she couldn't afford, she sold off a piece of furniture and replaced it with a cheap reproduction. As it is, all we have left is an ancient four-poster bed which stayed because it couldn't be moved out of the room without being totally taken apart.'

'*We*?' Jack probed. 'I thought you were an only child.'

'I was. I'm talking about me and Agnes.'

'The housekeeper?'

'I shouldn't have called her that. She's much more than a housekeeper. She's another reason why I'll do everything in my power to keep Crosswinds a going concern. She'd be lost if she ever had to move out and find somewhere else to live. The house is her life. And me too, I guess. We have a bit of a love-hate relationship at times, me and Agnes.'

'How old is she?'

'I have no idea. She's strangely coy about her age, but she looks about sixty. Sixty-five, maybe. She's one of those thin, wiry women who's always on the go. Indefatigable, my mother used to call her.'

'She sounds a character.'

'She is. And a sweetie underneath her brusque exterior. Tell her you like her cooking and she'll be your slave for life. Ah, there she is, waiting for us on the front veranda. I rang her this morning after you called, to let her know we'd be home in time for dinner.'

'She looks closer to seventy to me,' Jack said as he swung the car round to the base of the front steps.

Courtney's eyes narrowed on the slump in Agnes's shoulders and the curve in her back she hadn't noticed before. Jack was right. Agnes was older than she'd thought, and looking it.

Courtney's heart squeezed tight. Poor old thing. The death of her best friend had really knocked her for six; that and worrying about Crosswinds' debts. Courtney had told her the truth before she'd left to go to Sydney. No one else, however. Just Agnes.

It had been great to give good news this morning.

Courtney was out of the car in a flash and up the sandstone steps. 'Hi, there, Aggie!' she said, planting a peck on Agnes's gaunt cheek. No hug. Hugging had never been allowed around Crosswinds. 'You can stop worrying now. I'm back safe and sound.'

Agnes squared her shoulders, her faded eyes showing a mixture of reluctant fondness and annoyance. 'I gave up worrying about you almost twenty years ago, girlie. Now, why don't you have some decent manners for a change and introduce me to our guest?'

Courtney turned to find Jack right behind her, carrying her small duffel bag and his much larger suitcase. He was smiling a devilishly charming smile. Damn, but he was almost irresistible when he smiled like that!

'If we waited for Courtney to find her manners,' he said teasingly, 'we'd be here all night. I'm Jack Falconer, investment broker to the rescue.' He dropped the cases at his feet and stretched out his right hand. 'And you must be Agnes, the heart and backbone of Crosswinds. Courtney has told me so many wonderful things about you.'

Agnes beamed whilst Courtney rolled her eyes.

'Well, isn't it nice to meet a true gentleman for once?' Agnes said. 'But, my, you're a big fellow, aren't you? I think we'll have to put you in the front room with the four-poster.'

Courtney opened her mouth to protest, because that big old bed had been the focus of her wilder sexual fantasies over the past few years and she didn't want to push her luck. It was going to be hard enough resisting Jack without thinking of him lying naked and spread-eagled on top of that burgundy velvet bedspread, feet and hands bound to those four perfectly positioned bedposts.

But she could hardly say that, could she? And she couldn't think of any other reason why Agnes shouldn't put Jack in that particular guest room.

When her mouth snapped shut again, Jack gave her a small, strangely triumphant smile, as though he knew what was going on in her head.

To add insult to injury, Biggs chose that moment to wake and jump down from the swing seat he'd been snoozing in, sauntering over to sniff Jack's hand, totally ignoring Courtney. Jack gave him a scratch behind the ears, whereby the traitorous animal practically drooled.

'Nice dog,' Jack said.

'Getting old now,' Agnes said. 'Like we all are.'

'Not you, Agnes. You're just a spring chicken.'

It was a corny line but Agnes loved it, brightening up no end. 'I've a good twenty years in me yet, young man,' she told him.

'What's that delicious smell?' Jack asked, sniffing the air. Biggs sniffed with him.

'I'm cooking a leg of pork. I hope you like baked dinners.'

Jack groaned the groan of a true baked-dinner devotee. '*Do* I like baked dinners? I'd kill for one, but I haven't found anyone who could cook them like my mother. My darling mum's been passed away for a good few years now. But if my memory serves me correctly, her baked pork dinner smelt just like that. What's the secret, Agnes?'

'It's the sage and onion you cook with it,' Agnes revealed smugly. 'Some people like apple with their pork, but apple's not a patch on sage and onion.'

'I couldn't agree more. I can't wait to eat it.'

'Dinner's at six on the dot. But you must be thirsty from your trip. Would you fancy a nice glass of sherry? I always have one around this time of day.'

Jack grinned at her. 'Agnes, you wicked corrupter,

you! Just let me drop these bags in the right rooms and I'll join you in that sherry.'

'Courtney, you take Jack upstairs and show him where everything is. Oh, and get him some fresh towels out of the linen press. Those big blue bathsheets Hilary bought last Christmas would be best. Jack's going to need something large, by the look of him. I'll go check the dinner and we'll meet up in the front living room in ten minutes or so.'

'Great,' Jack agreed.

Agnes bustled off, leaving Jack to face Courtney's droll expression. 'I know who's the wicked corrupter around here,' she said drily.

'And I'm glad to see your guard dog is on such good form,' Jack countered, still stroking Biggs behind the ears. When the dog suddenly dropped down and rolled over onto his back, offering his stomach to be rubbed, Jack obliged.

Courtney scowled at her pet, but Biggs was too deep in doggie heaven to notice, or care.

'Oh, for pity's sake,' she snapped, sweeping the cases up from where Jack had dropped them. 'Do stop spoiling that infernal dog and come along.'

CHAPTER NINE

BIGGS trotted into the house with them, slavishly staying by Jack's side and looking up at him with doleful eyes as they mounted the stairs. Jack resumed petting him behind the ears.

'You're not doing him any favours, you know,' Courtney remarked tartly as they reached the top landing. 'He'll start howling when Agnes puts him out tonight.'

'I thought you said he slept on your bed.'

'I lied.'

His blue eyes gleamed. 'You're afraid of me.'

Courtney glared at him. 'Too right I am. You know I fancy you and, being a typical male, you're not above using that fact to your advantage.'

'Like Larry did?'

'No, not like Larry did,' she snapped. 'For your information, I propositioned Larry, not the other way around.'

'That's pretty daring behaviour, for a virgin.'

Her chin lifted. 'I'm a pretty daring sort of girl.'

'I know. I'm depending on it.'

'See? You're doing it already. What's next? Are you going to dare me into going to bed with you? Or will you grab me and kiss me once we're alone, thinking I'll melt. Well, I won't melt, buster,' she warned. 'I'll knee you in your pride and joy so hard you won't be any good to any woman for quite some time.'

He grimaced. 'I'll keep that in mind if I ever feel like grabbing you and kissing you.'

'Do that!' She stalked off along the upstairs hallway,

dropping her bag by her door before carrying his case into the front room and dumping it at the foot of the dreaded bed. One glance at the velvet spread had her swivelling round to leave straight away. Unfortunately, Jack was at that moment sauntering through the door; his devoted dog-slave at his heels.

'Now, that's some bed,' he said as he walked towards her.

Courtney stiffened and backed into one of the bed-posts, her hands flying up ready to fight him off. 'Don't start, Jack,' she warned.

'I won't. I just wanted you to know that my offer's still open, in case you change your mind later tonight.' He stopped at a short arm's distance, reaching out to pick up a stray curl and loop it behind her ear. The feel of his fingers brushing against her ear broke the surface of her skin out in goose-bumps.

'I won't use any dirty tactics,' he went on, his eyes never leaving hers. 'Or pressure. Or passes. Though I suspect if I did you just *might* melt, and you know it. But that's not what I want from you.'

'And what is it that you want from me, Jack?' she asked, her voice strange. It wasn't like her to sound like that, all soft and husky.

'Everything,' he returned, and there was nothing soft in *his* voice. It was hard and determined and oh, so sexy.

The temptation was acute. To say *Yes, yes, you can have everything. Do* everything. It's what I want, what I need, what I crave.

Suddenly, it wasn't Jack tied naked to that bed in her mind but herself, helpless and mindless, writhing under his mouth, his hands, his body, moaning and groaning, crying out, begging.

The begging bit saved her.

God, the very thought of it. *Begging* some man. Begging *Jack*. No, no, no, that was not on!

'I'll just get you those towels,' she said, pleased to hear her voice had returned to normal. 'And, Biggs, you get yourself back downstairs. If Agnes catches you up here in the bedrooms, you'll be exiled to the stables.'

Biggs, who was terrified of the stable moggie, did a bolt for the stairs.

'And you,' she added, swinging back to Jack. 'You can get your mind back on the reason you came here.'

Jack smiled. 'If you insist.'

'I insist. Now...that brand spanking new door over there leads into your *en suite*, a recent addition for privileged and usually married guests. I'll be back with the towels in less than a jiffy, then we'd best get downstairs too. I don't want Agnes thinking things.'

'Would she?'

'There's nothing Agnes doesn't think me capable of, Jack. Having a quickie with a handsome hunk like you would probably come low on her list of my many sins.'

'Then why worry?'

'Because I care what the old dear thinks of me, especially now, with Mum gone and her future in my hands.'

Jack frowned. 'Ah, yes. Agnes's future...'

'If I ever had to sell Crosswinds, it would kill Agnes.'

'And you, Courtney? Would it kill you?'

'Probably. But not before I killed every single person who made it happen!'

'That was simply wonderful, Agnes,' Jack complimented as he sipped the last of his after-dinner cup of tea. 'I haven't had a meal like that in years.'

You'd be right there, Courtney thought tartly. Not too many fancy Sydney restaurants serve up baked pork and crackling, with pavlova for afters. And I can't imagine darling Katrina specialised in home cooking. Her talents would have lain elsewhere, with the emphasis on *lain*.

Irritated by her sarcastic thoughts, Courtney stood up abruptly, scraping back her chair on the polished wooden floor. 'If you'll excuse me, I have to go see if any foals are due tonight. No, don't get up, Jack. You stay here. It's pitch-black and pretty cold outside. Far better you tour the place with the benefit of daylight and sunshine. I shouldn't be too long. But, if I am, don't worry. Foals don't always do as they're told.'

'Fine.' Jack shrugged those broad shoulders of his. 'I'll give Agnes a hand while you're gone, loading up the dishwasher.'

'We don't have a dishwasher,' Agnes informed him.

The surprised look on Jack's face annoyed Courtney.

Actually, everything about Jack tonight was annoying her. His charm. His kindness to Agnes. But most of all the way he could make *her* feel, without any effort on his part. He only had to be in the same room now, to set her heart pounding and her mind racing in erotic directions.

The dining room at Crosswinds was not a small room, the table large by any standards. Eight high-backed chairs could easily be accommodated around it. And there was still room for a selection of corner cabinets and sideboards.

Courtney had dashed in and set the table earlier whilst Jack had been busy drinking sherry with Agnes in the front living room. She'd placed Jack down the end near the fireplace, herself right at the other end not far from the door. She'd even strategically positioned a bowl of flowers, the blooms big enough to block any direct view of the ever increasingly attractive Jack.

But it had been a futile gesture. Jack had simply whipped the vase away on entering, dumping it on a sideboard with the witty aside, 'Roses are red, violets are blue, but I'd really much rather look at you.'

And look at her he had. Curiously. Speculatingly. Seductively.

Physical passes weren't the only way to seduce a woman, she was beginning to realise. The right man could do it with words, or his eyes, or simply by being under the same roof.

Courtney decided then and there that she would stay down at the brood-mare barn for a good few hours, whether a mare was foaling or not.

'Agnes likes to wash her own dishes,' she told Jack coolly, 'but I'm sure you could help by drying up. Now, if I *am* held up, there's always the TV for entertainment. We have satellite. And there are plenty of books to read.' The shelves in the living room had an eclectic mix, from biographies to novels of all genres, as well as books on everything to do with horses and horse breeding.

'Don't worry about me,' Jack replied with annoying nonchalance. 'I'll be fine. Agnes and I are going to play Scrabble. Naturally, you're welcome to join us, if and when you return.'

'Courtney doesn't like games,' Agnes said.

'Really? Why not?'

'Too much luck involved,' Courtney said sharply.

'Actually, luck only plays a small part in most games,' Jack countered. 'Winning depends more on concentration and skill.'

'You're skilled at Scrabble, then?' she asked archly.

'Never played it before in my life.'

Agnes chuckled as she rose and started clearing the

table. 'Let's get this done in a hurry, then, young man. After which you can come into my parlour...'

Jack stood up, laughing, his teeth flashing white. Courtney groaned silently and fled the room.

As it turned out, a mare *was* foaling when she arrived at the brood-mare barn, so she stayed and helped the night manager deliver the stylish bay colt. It was good to put her mind to something else for a couple of hours, other than that infernal man.

The birth was slow, and a bit tricky, and she was covered in blood by the time the new arrival slipped out into the waiting bed of straw.

'Glad that's over,' Fred said with a relieved sigh. 'I hate it when their legs get all tangled up like that. The mare panics. It was great to have an extra pair of hands to keep her calm. You're damned good at that, Courtney. You have just the right touch.'

The right touch...

The longing was back straight away, and so was the need, so sharp she almost cried out. In sheer desperation she stared at Fred. He wasn't a bad-looking man. Not the brightest, but still male. He wouldn't knock her back. Maybe if she...

Bile rose from her stomach to sting her throat. She gulped it down, even more panicky now. Because now she knew, knew that the thought of touching any man other than Jack revolted her so much that it made her sick.

Oh, God...

'Something wrong?' Fred asked.

Courtney shook her head. 'Just wool-gathering. You be all right by yourself for the rest of the night?'

'Sure. Nothing else doing here tonight. Next week things'll begin to hot up a bit, though. Then you might be losing some sleep. You'd better get back up to the house and to bed while you got the chance, I reckon.'

Courtney wished he hadn't said that.

'I think I'll go for a walk first,' she said. 'I like looking at the horses in the moonlight.'

It was chiming midnight on the grandfather clock in the hall by the time she tiptoed up the stairs. A light still glowed under the door of Jack's bedroom, which didn't exactly help her state of mind. Wretched man! Why couldn't he have been sound asleep, with everything in darkness? Why did she now have to contend with the thought of him lying there, still wide awake, his beautiful body ready and willing?

Gritting her teeth, she crept into her own room opposite his, snatching up a nightie from underneath her pillow and creeping back down the hallway to the far bathroom, hoping against hope that Jack wouldn't hear the shower running. She was careful in closing the old wooden door, then turning the big brass key in the lock.

Washing herself under the shower proved a torment. Her breasts felt full, her nipples electrified, and the area between her legs on fire. She tried to be quick, and not linger over sensitive spots, but the second she slid the soap over her private parts, she groaned. The temptation to keep doing it was acute. All she had to do was close her eyes and think about Jack, and surely...

'Damn it all, no!' she muttered. 'This is not what I want.'

She wanted Jack. Only Jack.

The soap clattered to the floor and her hand shot up to snap off the shower. She didn't bother with her nightie. A towel would do, wrapped tightly around her wet, heat-drenched body. Her hair hung in damp curls around her bared shoulders but she didn't give a fig about her hair.

She was past the point of no return, past caring about anything but finding some peace for her poor, pathetic, frustrated flesh.

How she had the forethought to return to her room for the box of condoms surprised her. At least she wasn't that far gone that she couldn't think of protection.

Her hesitation over the knob on Jack's door irritated the death out of her. Having made her decision, any lack of courage at this stage was not to be tolerated. It was just that he'd be so annoyingly smug and triumphant!

Too late to worry about that, she resolved boldly.

Opening the door, she slipped inside his room.

CHAPTER TEN

HE WAS asleep. Sound asleep. Sprawled out on the bed, one of the lamps still on, a book lying open on the pillow beside him. The remnants of a fire smouldered in the marble fireplace, making the room quite warm, which was possibly why he'd thrown back the sheets and was lying there wearing nothing but a pair of navy blue satin boxer shorts with some kind of jazzy red design all over them.

Feeling even more frustrated, Courtney stalked over and glared down at it.

Hearts, they were. Red hearts. Not the sort of thing a man would buy himself. Probably a Valentine's day present from a woman. No…from Superbitch.

Courtney practically ground her teeth. Did he think of her every time he put them on? Did he like sleeping in them, remembering how good she'd been in bed? Or how deliciously bad?

Piqued by her thoughts and by the fact that Jack hadn't tossed and turned into the night with wanting *her*, Courtney snatched up the book, snapped it shut and glared at the title.

'*How To Breed Champions*,' she read aloud, then glared at *him*. 'Breeding champions is not your job, buster,' she muttered, tossing the book onto a nearby dresser. 'Your job is to stay awake long enough for me to change my mind and take you up on your offer.'

'Your wish is my command…' His eyes flicked open as he rolled over and looked up at her through long dark lashes. 'Mmm. Glad to see you didn't overdress for the occasion.' And, reaching out, he tugged at the bottom of her towel.

It dropped to the floor, leaving her stark naked before him, clutching a box of condoms.

'You were awake all the time!' she accused.

'Not quite. But I certainly am now.' His hooded gaze travelled slowly over her from head to toe, drinking in every inch of her stiffly held nudity.

Do something, she ordered herself. Don't just stand there like some undressed dummy in a shop window.

'You are one beautiful woman, Courtney Cross,' he said thickly. 'Now, come here…'

It was a softly voiced order. A seductive order.

How easy it would have been to fall into his arms and let him do as he willed.

It was a struggle to find the boldly assertive creature she usually became when she wanted sex. Because it wasn't just sex she was secretly craving this time, was it? It was the mindless ecstasy of total surrender.

Which made it all the more imperative that she follow her usual path.

'Now, Jack,' she said firmly, and busied herself ripping the Cellophane off the box of condoms. 'I told you. I like to be at the wheel. Besides, you must be tired after all that driving today. That's why you fell asleep with the light on. So just lie back, relax and let *me* take responsibility for everything. You'll enjoy it. Trust me.'

The Cellophane gone, she flipped open the box and tossed it onto the bedside table before pushing Jack onto his back and climbing up onto the bed beside him.

He looked taken aback when she immediately started pulling down his boxer shorts. 'Hey! What the heck do…?'

Too late. His shorts were already off.

'Do be quiet, Jack. Agnes is not a heavy sleeper. We don't want her coming in to find out what all the noise is about, do we?'

His dark brows lifted but he eventually lay back and shut his mouth. Which was good, Courtney told herself. She didn't like her men to talk. She wasn't there for a tête-à-tête. She was there to soothe her galloping hormones, or whatever it was Jack had evoked in her to such a maddeningly compulsive level.

'Now,' she murmured, straddling his wonderfully muscular thighs then sitting back on his knees. 'Let's have a look at you...'

If she'd been struggling for control before, now was the real moment of truth, with Jack naked and immobile beneath her, his magnificently macho body on full display for her hungry gaze.

And hungry she was. Oh, so hungry. As her eyes raked over him she wanted to ravish him on the spot. Every single bit of him.

Courtney tried telling herself his body was no better than any she'd seen before. Just bigger. And bigger wasn't necessarily better.

Or so some stupid fool had told her once. Some people simply had no idea.

'You are one beautiful man, Jack Falconer,' she murmured, and leant forward to run her hands all over his wonderfully hairy chest, his smooth-as-satin shoulders, his strong upper arms. Her breathing became ragged as she moved back to his chest again, where her fingers splayed sensuously within the mass of soft dark curls.

He gasped when they grazed over his nipples.

When his hands reached for *her*, she grabbed his wrists and pushed them into the pillows on either side of his head, a position that unfortunately had the tips of her breasts brushing against the hair of his chest. For a second or two, she almost lost it.

His smiling at her snapped her back to the potential disaster of this situation.

'I'm the driver tonight, remember?' she whispered harshly against his lips. 'Not you. No touching,' she commanded. 'No moving. No nothing. Do you think you can manage that for once?'

'Yes, boss,' he replied, but he was still smiling.

She kissed him, deep and hard, a powerful punishing kiss which was supposed to tell him who, indeed, was boss. But once again it was herself in danger of losing control. If he'd been able to put his hands on her, she might have. As it was, she kept her head. Just.

As for Jack, he was breathing very heavily by the time she wrenched her mouth away from his and straightened up again. His eyes had darkened to slate and he was no longer smiling. His erection spoke for itself, lying huge and high against his stomach.

'You sure you know what you're doing, here?' Jack muttered thickly when she reached to encircle it with both her hands.

She sucked in a steadying breath, swallowed, then gave him what she hoped was a cool smile.

Her hands began to move and his eyes widened, his body flinching each time her thumb grazed over the soft velvety tip. Finally, his hips began to lift slightly from the bed, his buttocks squeezing tightly together.

'You'd better stop doing that,' he growled.

Courtney stopped, squeezing him in exactly the right spot so that he immediately subsided. Jack looked stunned whilst she tried to hide her own rattled state. She hadn't meant to let things go quite that far with just her hands, but she'd become mesmerised by his responses to her touch, by his actually becoming longer and thicker and harder. She'd thought he was fully erect.

'Courtney, *no.*' Jack groaned when she bent her mouth to where her hands had been. 'For pity's sake!'

But pity was not an emotion Courtney was feeling at that moment. Her whole being was consumed by the most compelling need to possess him again. Utterly. And far more intimately. There was no cohesive thought on her part. Just the sense of herself falling into a black abyss from which there was no escape.

Her heart lurched as her lips closed over him, her head swirled and, finally, she was lost to the darkness.

His abrupt pulling her off him and up to his mouth came as a shock, much like someone suddenly shining a blinding light into your sleepy eyes.

'Time to change driver, honey,' he grated out.

Dazed and disorientated, Courtney was like a rag doll as he rolled her over onto her back, his mouth crushing down onto hers. This time it was *his* tongue darting deep, *his* hands holding her arms out wide and *his* body pressing her down, down, down.

Panic had her struggling to break free, her mouth twisting from his with a harsh cry of protest.

'Hush up,' he ground out. 'You can be on top another night, but right now you're going to be made love to by a real man for a change, not some bloody puppet you can pull around by the strings. My name's not Larry, honey. It's Jack. And, like I said, I don't take orders. Now, are you going to be co-operative and quiet? Or do I have to kiss you till you are?'

Her eyes were like saucers, but her mouth stayed silent.

'Good.'

He still kissed her, over and over, kissed her till she was reeling, and then...then he started kissing her all over. Her throat. Her breasts. Her stomach. Her thighs. Between her thighs.

'Oh, God,' she moaned, and spread her legs wider for him.

This was one of the things she'd feared; what she'd worried might happen to her. That she would be powerless to stop him doing whatever he liked. And here it was, happening to her.

Yet the reality wasn't anything to fear, she eventually realised. It was...bliss.

'Don't stop,' she choked out when he did.

His laughter was dark. 'Can't have you getting too addicted to that. Or coming too soon.'

She groaned. She'd been awfully close.

He kissed his way back up her body till he got to her breasts again. There, he sucked on her nipples till they were so sensitive just breathing on them made her tremble and arch her back.

By the time he reached for the condom she was quivering, and panting. She could not wait for the moment when she could feel him entering her, filling her totally. She bent her knees in readiness, breathless with anticipation.

'You like it like that?' he asked, sounding surprised. 'In the missionary position?'

She blinked, startled that he was stopping to discuss positions at this stage when she was just dying to have him inside her, any old way.

'Sometimes,' she lied, and he shrugged.

'Not many women do. But that's okay. I'm easy.'

She gasped as he entered her, his thick, hard length thrusting home in one solid surge. Her legs automatically lifted to wrap themselves tight around him, as did her arms, winding around his big broad back, holding him close, pulling him even deeper into her.

The sensation was incredible. 'Oh, Jack...'

'I know,' he muttered. 'I know. I feel it too.'

Did he? she wondered dazedly. Did he really?

She'd never known anything like it. Not just the physical pleasure, but something else. A wave crashing through her, a wave of emotion so strong it took everything with it, especially all her preconceptions and misconceptions about making love with Jack.

Her heart filled with it, overflowed with it. She hugged him to her and wanted nothing but to stay that way forever, their flesh fused, their hearts beating as one.

This had to be love, she realised in her rapture, that long-scorned emotion that she scarcely believed in and told herself she would never fall victim too.

Love. Glorious, wonderful, overwhelming love.

Jack began to move, making her gasp and forcing her mind back to the physical reality of the moment, which was Jack, thrusting powerfully into her, Jack, having sex with her.

It wasn't love for him, was it?

Everything inside her contracted, with emotional pain not sexual pleasure. Yet it possibly felt the same to him, for he moaned and stopped momentarily. She stared up at him with hopeless longing, and he stared back down at her, an odd expression crossing his already strained face.

And then he did something that threw Courtney into total despair. He closed his eyes, and sighed.

He's thinking of her, she agonised. Maybe even pretending I'm her. That's what that weird look was all about. And that sigh.

Immediately, she wanted him gone from her. Away. Out of her body!

But no sooner had that angry thought swept through her than he began to move again, and she gasped, stunned at the pleasure he could still bring, even when she knew what she was to him. A cypher. A stand-in. A second-rate substitute.

Suddenly she understood her mother's bitterness towards her father. She must have fallen in love with him too. But he hadn't loved her back. That was his crime, not loving her back, whilst still being able to enjoy her body and forcing her to enjoy his.

Courtney tried not to enjoy Jack's body. Tried to switch off. But it was too late. Either that or she was too weak. Loving Jack was making her weak. Terribly weak.

Finally, she didn't even try to fight her feelings. Impossible, anyway. They were consuming her with a heat and a passion so strong that nothing short of a bomb falling on this bed was going to stop her seeing this out to its inevitable end.

Her first spasm had her sucking air sharply into her lungs. She might have screamed out, but his mouth crashed down on hers again, muffling her cries into soft moans, making her head spin even as the spasms went on and on and on. His big arms wrapped round her and he scooped her up from the bed, clutching her hard to him as he came too, shuddering and shaking. He buried his head in her hair, muttering things she couldn't quite make out.

Finally the tempest was over, and an awkward stillness descended on both of them. An awkward silence as well.

Jack's rather weary sigh spelled things out for Courtney.

Hard to keep pretending once the heat of the moment

was over and cold reality returned. Reality being a simple country girl with long dark hair, not a glamorous city-smart blonde who no doubt didn't fancy the missionary position at all, but all sorts of other exotic and erotic ways.

Courtney had used to think she knew it all when it came to seducing men. Yet what did she really know, other than being on top along with some elementary oral techniques? Hardly the stuff sex goddesses were made of.

Courtney's despair deepened. *Jack is never going to fall in love with me, not after Katrina. All I can hope for is a superficial friendship, sex every night he's here, and maybe the odd one-night stand whenever I come to Sydney.*

An hour ago Courtney could have coped with that quite well.

Now it would hurt her more than she could ever have envisaged. Yet, at the same time, she knew she wouldn't say no. She'd be there, at his beck and call, for as long as he wanted her.

That was the truth of it. Better to accept the harsh reality of a one-sided love, otherwise she might end up as bitter and twisted as her mother.

Besides, Jack was not a bad man. Just the opposite. He was a very nice man. He wasn't out to deliberately hurt her, or to callously use her. He thought she was on his wavelength, wanting nothing more from their relationship than what he'd offered right from the start.

An affair.

Now it was up to her to keep that status quo, as well as her pride. There would be no dramatic confession of love. No desperate tactics to try to get him to fall in love with her. Hell, no. She wasn't playing sweet little thing for any man. Or *femme fatale*, either. She was what she was and he could take her or leave her.

Which meant he would probably do both.

It would hurt, but she'd survive. Of course she would. She'd been brought up tough.

But first, how to extricate herself from Jack's arms without his twigging to anything being wrong?

Their position was still highly intimate and extrication potentially embarrassing. Jack was sitting on his haunches in the middle of the bed with her clasped tightly against his torso, her buttocks resting on his thighs, their bodies still intimately locked together.

'Er…um…Jack…?'

'Mmm?' His head remained buried in her hair.

'I…I need to go to bed. I have to be up early.'

He groaned, and lifted his head, his blue eyes soft and dreamy. 'I don't want you to go,' he murmured. 'I want you to stay with me.'

'I can't,' she replied, trying not to show alarm. Because she wanted to, oh, so much, wanted to wallow in his arms and in his lovemaking, if not for the rest of her life, then at least for one whole night.

But Agnes was an early riser and she simply didn't dare.

'I don't know about you, but I'm exhausted,' she went on, using every ounce of her will-power to sound cool and calm. 'We can spend more time together tomorrow night.'

His smile was wry. 'Can I trust you not to change your mind again?'

Oh, God. Little did he know.

'After that magnificent performance?'

'Same time tomorrow night, then?' he suggested.

'A little earlier perhaps.' She knew she wouldn't be

able to wait till midnight a second time. 'I never could resist a bargain.'

Surprisingly, he didn't laugh at her joke. Instead, he frowned. 'What about Agnes?'

'Agnes is usually in bed by ten-thirty.'

'What kept *you* so long tonight?'

Fear of coming back and falling in love with you.

'A foal. A gorgeous little colt.' Her face softened at the thought of it, valiantly struggling to its feet so soon after birth. 'A darling thing. But he gave the mare a bit of a hard time. I had to sit there in the straw for ages, stroking her neck and telling her it was going to be all right.'

'Which it was?'

'Oh, yes. Mother and baby doing fine.'

He gave her an odd look, as though he wanted to say something but wasn't sure if it was a good idea. 'Courtney...'

'Yes?'

'Just now, when we were making love...' His hesitation brought a tightening to her heart.

'Yes?' she asked warily. *Don't you dare tell me that,* her eyes informed him. *I don't need to know. That would be cruel.*

He sighed again. Damn, but she hated those sighs. 'Nothing. It was fantastic. That's all. *You're* fantastic. I just wanted you to know that.'

She smiled through her heartbreak. 'Thanks, lover. But you're the one who was fantastic. I can't wait till to-morrow night.' And wasn't that the truth? 'Meanwhile, don't forget your promise to be discreet. No giveaways, please, when other people are around. No sneaky little kisses or hand-holding, or any of that mushy stuff. I mean...we don't have to do that, do we? We both know the score here. It's not as though we're besotted lovers. We're adults, enjoying a nice little discreet fling. Isn't that right?'

Deny it, she willed wildly as she looked up at him. *Tell me it isn't so. Tell me you're madly besotted with me, that you can't keep your hands off me, that you want me by your side till we die!*

The feverish desperation of her thoughts disgusted her, and she looked away. Love had turned her into a fool. A stupid, romantic, female fool.

Oh, Mum. I know what you suffered now.

But she hated the thought of becoming bitter like her mother. Somehow, she had to stop that happening.

'I really must go now, Jack,' Courtney said truthfully enough, calmer eyes swinging back up to his.

The most seductive passion glittered in his eyes.

'And I really don't want you to go.'

'That's very flattering, but I really think that—'

His mouth obliterated the rest of her words.

Courtney was to be appalled later to realise it took him all of five seconds' flat to change her mind.

CHAPTER ELEVEN

COURTNEY rolled over, blinked blearily, and finally focused on her bedside clock.

'Good grief!' she exclaimed, and leapt from the bed. 'Ten-thirty!'

Seven minutes later she was showered, dressed and hurrying downstairs, her hands scooping her hair up into a ponytail on the way. She burst into the kitchen, startled to find Agnes, Jack and Sarah sitting at the kitchen table, sipping cups of tea.

The trio glanced up at her as she rushed through the door, both Jack and Sarah saying good morning and smiling whilst Agnes rose to move over to the stove. Sarah was especially effusive in her greeting, which was not like her at all.

A widow, Sarah Pearson had come to work at Crosswinds twenty years before, shortly after her gamblerholic husband had shot himself, leaving her with three teenage daughters to raise on her own. At the time of his suicide, Reg Pearson had been working at Crosswinds as a general handyman, and the stud had been a much smaller concern. Hilary had taken pity on the destitute Sarah and had created a job for her as secretary and office manager, even though Sarah hadn't been able to type back then.

Now fifty-seven, Sarah was still not the greatest typist in the world. Neither was she a great man-lover. Her bright smile, plus the colour in her plump cheeks this morning, made it apparent Jack had already been working his effortless charm on her.

The silly stab of jealousy this thought evoked made Courtney resolve to avoid Jack during daylight hours, confining her weakness for him to those private moments behind closed doors. She would not be able to function properly as the boss of Crosswinds if she kept thinking about him and the ease with which he had seduced her to his will last night.

She hadn't returned to her own bed till after three. No wonder she'd slept like the dead.

But what of the man himself? He had to be some kind of machine to do what he'd done and pop back up this morning looking perkier than a buck-rabbit in springtime.

There he sat, sipping tea and smiling up at her over the rim of his cup, looked totally refreshed and relaxed. Yet it was clear he'd been up for some time, if the empty breakfast plates beside him were any guide. He was wearing the stone-washed jeans he'd worn the previous day, but with a different top, a blue Sloppy Joe which made his eyes look bluer than the bluest outback sky.

'Someone should have woken me up,' she said to no one in particular as she set about making herself a mug of instant coffee.

'Jack thought you deserved a sleep in,' Sarah said.

Courtney finished making the black sugarless coffee before slowly turning, a cool smile hiding her pounding heart.

'Really?' Her eyes met his directly.

His eyebrows lifted ever so slightly in what she saw as a wickedly knowing gesture, and suddenly she was back in his bed, boneless after another mind-blowing orgasm, begging him to stop, then begging him not to.

Truly, she'd never known such orgasms existed. What

she'd been experiencing all these years paled by comparison.

Being in love with your lover certainly made a difference. As did the skill of that lover. Jack was everything Courtney had dreamt, yet feared he'd be. Demanding, yet giving. Dominating, yet not selfish. A sensualist of the first order, infinitely tender and gently coercing. It had been so easy to close her eyes and pretend that he loved her. No man could have been more loving in his lovemaking. That was the most seductive part of all.

But he didn't love her. She really couldn't afford to forget that, or Lord knew what other stupidities she might fall victim to. Being his love slave every night of his stay was going to be bad enough!

'You had a very long weekend,' he said, his eyes never leaving hers. 'The trip down to Sydney on Friday, the races on Saturday, driving back on Sunday. Then a late night last night on top of that. You had to have been exhausted.'

Courtney decided she wasn't going to indulge in word games or *double entendres*. Jack might like that kind of thing, but she didn't.

'Yes, I was very tired,' she said. 'You're right. But now it's Monday morning and time to get back to business. Have you had the opportunity yet to ask Sarah about all those things you wanted to know?' Presumably, by now, Sarah had been informed of the lie of the land.

'We've only just touched the surface, haven't we, Sarah?'

'Oh, yes. Barely. It's going to take most of the day, if Jack wants a detailed history of every horse you own. At last count, Crosswinds had over sixty brood mares. And then there's the three stallions, the yearlings and all those horses Hilary leased out for racing.'

'No worries,' Courtney said. 'I'm going to be busy all day myself, doing the rounds with Ned. It's busy, busy, busy at this time of year, isn't it, Agnes?'

Agnes glanced around from where she was cooking Courtney her usual breakfast of scrambled eggs on toast. 'It certainly is. And, speaking of Ned, he was here looking for you a little while ago. I said you'd go see him as soon as you'd had breakfast. He said to tell you he'd be at the breeding barn.'

'Right.' Courtney started sipping her mug of steaming coffee. 'Did he say what he wanted me for?' she asked, and a tiny icicle of apprehension trickled down her spine.

'No. But he didn't look all that happy.'

'I wonder what he's doing down at the breeding barn? I mean...the season hasn't started yet.'

'Maybe the roof has sprung a leak,' Sarah piped up. 'It's pretty old, you know. Most of the buildings have leaky roofs, the office included.'

'Yes, I know,' Courtney said grimly, her mind well and truly back on the problems at Crosswinds. She'd forgotten them for a while, there. 'Let's hope we can do something about that soon,' she added, and turned a matter-of-fact face Jack's way. 'How long do you think it will take to get the money, if your investor decides he's in?'

'Barely any time at all. He might have to sell a few stocks and shares, but that only takes minutes.'

'In that case, how long do you think before you'll be able to give him the go-ahead? And before you say it, yes, I know you'll want to be satisfied Crosswinds is a going concern with potential for future profits first. I'm assuming you'll be happy with what Sarah shows you. And what you see here in general. As I said before, shabby fences and leaky buildings mean nothing. They are not the value in a stud. It's the land itself, plus the brood mares and stallions. And ours are second to none.'

'I appreciate that. Look, it shouldn't take me too long. After Sarah's input today, I'll need to speak to your accountant. Perhaps you could arrange an appointment for tomorrow? Then I'd like to spend the rest of the week just getting the feel of the place, seeing how things run on a more personal level. I often rely on my gut instinct, not just facts and figures, when it comes to an investment. I'd say by next weekend I should be satisfied, one way or another.'

Courtney frowned and wondered if she was reading between the lines correctly here. What did he really mean by 'the feel of the place', and 'on a more personal level'? Exactly what kind of satisfaction was he referring to? Was he implying that if she kept him happy in bed all week he'd recommend the investment?

Shock at this last thought held her speechless for a split second. She hadn't expected such scurrilous behaviour from a man who'd nobly paid off debts he hadn't personally incurred. But she supposed men could never be trusted when it came to matters of sex and ego.

As for herself... She was a goner anyway when it came to resisting him sexually. So she might as well use that to secure her investor. But it put a nasty taste in her mouth. Hopefully, she was wrong about this. But if she wasn't?

Courtney smothered a sigh. Who did she think she was kidding? She would still do whatever was necessary to save Crosswinds.

A knock on the back door interrupted her troubled thoughts.

It was Ned, looking more than a little worried.

Although only forty-four, Ned's outdoor lifestyle in the

Australian sun, plus his hatred of hats, had left him with a very lined face. But some of the lines at that moment were clearly coming from stress. Or *dis*tress.

Serious alarm bells started ringing in Courtney's head. Ned was not a man easily rattled, or upset. He had a laid-back, laconic style which suited the handling of highly strung horses.

'What is it, Ned?'

'We have a serious problem with one of the stallions, boss.'

Courtney liked it that he called her boss, the same as he'd called her mother. Not that she expected it from anyone else around Crosswinds. Most just called her Courtney.

'Which one?'

'Goldplated.'

Oh, no…

'He's not sick, is he?' she asked, feeling sick herself at such a prospect.

'Nope. Nothing like that.'

'What is it, then?'

'Best come and see for yourself.'

She heard a chair scrape back on the wooden floor behind her.

'I'll come with you,' Jack said, materialising by her side.

'Very well,' Courtney bit out. She could hardly refuse. There was also no point in keeping the reason for Jack's presence here a secret any longer, though Ned needn't know the *full* extent of her debt. 'This is Jack Falconer, Ned. He's a financial expert, up here from Sydney to look over Crosswinds with a view to finding me a business partner. You know how strapped for cash we are around here. So get used to seeing him around this week. Jack, this is Ned Meggitt, my stud foreman.'

'Pleased to meet you, Ned,' Jack said, holding out his hand.

Ned looked impressed with Jack's handshake.

'Same here,' he replied. 'Know anything about horses?'

'They kick one end and bite the other?'

Ned glanced at Courtney. 'He doesn't look like a city-slicker, but he sure sounds like one. Which is perhaps just as well...'

With this last cryptic remark, Ned turned away abruptly to start walking down the back path which led past the rose garden and down towards the stud proper.

'After you,' Jack said, waving Courtney ahead of him through the wire-screen door.

'Looks like breakfast will have to wait, Agnes.' She dumped her coffee and snatched up the fawn Akubra which was hanging on a peg near the back door. Planting it firmly on her head, she set off after the rapidly disappearing Ned. Jack caught up quickly to stride out beside her.

'You look like a cowgirl in that hat,' he said, slanting her an admiring glance. 'A very sexy cowgirl.'

She ground to a brief but very necessary halt. 'Let's get one thing straight, Jack. Keep the flattery for the bedroom. It'll work very well there. Out here, however, I'm nothing to you but a business client. I told you this before. Have I made myself perfectly clear this time?'

'Crystal,' he bit out, not looking pleased at all. Which was just too bad. He couldn't have *everything* his way.

'Good,' she snapped, then marched on after Ned, leaving Jack in her wake.

It was quite some distance from the house to the breed-

ing barn. The wide gravel path wound its way down between the large brood-mare yards on the left and grazing
pastures on the right. Overhead, it was another sunny day,
but not exactly warm at this hour in the morning. Nights
in the valley were colder than in Sydney and the air on
clear winter days always stayed crisp till after lunch.

Courtney didn't feel at all cold, however, as she hurried along. She was too preoccupied to feel anything as
mundane as cold. Guilt was worming its way into her
head and heart. Yet why *should* she feel guilty about
putting Jack back into his place? He knew the score. Just
now he'd been deliberately trying to cross the line she'd
drawn for him. And she just wouldn't have it!

Being in love with him made it all the more crucial
she not let him take advantage of that fact. Of course, he
didn't *know* she was in love with him, but he knew she
fancied him: fancied him so much that all he'd had to do
last night was start kissing her again and all her will had
dissolved.

Courtney groaned at the memory, and strode out all
the faster, her head down, her thoughts in a whirl. She
didn't realise Ned wasn't alone outside the breeding barn
doors till she practically ran into the stranger standing
next to him.

'Oh!' she gasped, stepping back, then staring at the
man with startled eyes. He stared right back at her, his
appraisal as curious and as thorough as the one she gave
him.

He was of average height and an elegant build, with
jet-black eyes, deeply tanned skin and close-cropped
iron-grey hair. Though obviously middle-aged, he had the
air of one much younger, possibly because he was
dressed in tight black jeans and a black leather jacket. If
he'd been less handsome, he might have looked stupid

wearing such gear, like some aging biker who didn't know when to quit. As it was, he looked interesting and quite sexy, if you liked that type.

Courtney immediately thought of Lois. If these were her stables and this fellow was looking for a job, he'd be hired on the spot.

'And who are you?' she asked brusquely. 'Ned, you know we can't hire any more grooms at the moment.'

'The name's Sean, ma'am.' He had the most attractively lilting Irish accent. 'Sean O'Flannery.'

'Courtney Cross,' she returned as she took his hand and shook it.

'Yes, ma'am. I know who *you* are. And no, I haven't come here for a job. I wanted to see you.'

'*See* me?'

'He's got some information you're not going to like,' Ned said gruffly. 'About Goldplated.'

Courtney glanced over her shoulder to see where Jack had got to. He was leaning on the fence just behind her, watching and listening.

Her gaze swung back to her visitor. 'Not good news, I take it?' she said.

'Not the best.'

'Out with it, then.'

The man's eyes moved in Jack's direction. 'I don't think this is news you'll want spread around.'

'Don't worry about Jack. He'll have to know, sooner or later,' she added drily.

'Fine. Look, I'm really sorry to have to tell you this, but all the mares supposedly serviced by Goldplated at his first season were artificially inseminated. He didn't cover a single one. He refused to.'

Courtney went cold all over. My God, if this was true…

'How do you know this?' she demanded to know.

'I was working there at the time. I was Gold Fever's personal groom last season.'

'Goldplated's full brother?'

He nodded.

Courtney's mind whirled with all sorts of dreadful possibilities. 'They used *his* sperm instead of Goldplated's?'

'No. Goldplated's progeny are all genetically his, all right. But unless there's been a radical change in your new stallion's behaviour since last year, he won't willingly perform this year, either.'

'Oh, my God.'

'You can say that again,' Ned growled. 'When Sean told me all this, I couldn't believe it. So I thought I'd give the horse a trial run, so to speak. I got one of the stock mares who's in season and tied her up in the breeding barn. Then I went and got Goldplated out of his yard. He was like a lamb till I took him inside the barn. He got one sniff of the mare and just went berserk. I've never seen anything like it. Frightened the poor mare to death. Frightened *me* to death too. I was lucky to get her out of there before any damage was done. I left Goldplated in there till he calmed down and saw there wasn't anything to fear in the barn itself.'

Courtney could only shake her head in despair. No wonder her mother had bought the horse at that bargain price. Whatever was she going to do now? Crosswinds always provided a photo of the actual service with any outside booking, a guarantee for owners that they were getting what they paid for.

Jack tapped her on the shoulder. 'Can you sue the people who sold you the horse?' he asked.

'Maybe. But suing takes lots of money and time. And

it's always dicey, especially when the other party is so rich. The owners of Gold Fever are billionaires.'

'So why on earth would they do something as dishonest as this?'

'They didn't know,' Sean revealed. 'It was the stud master's doing. Plus his fault in the first place.'

Courtney frowned. 'What do you mean?'

'That's the right word. Mean. Mean and stupid. When Goldplated first arrived at stud he was still a very young horse, all hyped up from the track. The stud master didn't give him enough time to let down, and calm down. I gather Goldplated kicked him the first time they tried to get him to cover a mare. Probably more out of excitement than anything. It was just an accident. But the stupid fella lost his temper and lashed out with a whip.'

'You're joking!' Courtney was appalled.

'Unfortunately, no.' Sean looked totally disgusted as well. 'As if you can teach a young horse stud duties with a whip! It's no wonder the poor animal goes off his brain when he's brought near a mare in heat. He's probably expecting his handler to turn on him at any moment. If you look, you'll find two deep scars across his forehead. They're quite high, under his forelock.'

Courtney groaned. 'They said he'd done that rearing up in the starting gates.'

'Yeah, they would. But that's not the case. You've got yourself a fine young stallion in Goldplated, Ms Cross, but he's been badly mishandled. Personally, I believe he could still come good, but it'll take patience and some lateral thinking.'

'Why did you decide to tell me this?' she asked, puzzled. 'You didn't have to.'

'I felt badly when I heard your mother had been the one who bought Goldplated. She has a fine reputation in the horse world. I didn't like to think of her being cheated like that.'

Courtney looked at him thoughtfully. He'd taken his time coming to tell her, then. It had been months since her mother had bought the horse. Maybe he'd come because he *did* want a job.

'I gather you're no longer Gold Fever's groom?'

'No. I usually move on pretty regularly. I get bored staying in one place for long.'

'How good *are* you with stallions, Sean?'

His smile was wry. 'Damned good. Even if I say so myself.'

'Do you think you might be able to do something with Goldplated by exercising some of that patience and lateral thinking you spoke of?'

'I'd sure like to try.' His smile widened.

Darn, but he was a good-looking man for his age. Lois would go ape, if she ever saw him. Which she just might. She was due up soon.

'You're hired, then,' Courtney said, and smiled.

'But boss,' Ned protested, 'you just said we couldn't afford to hire any more staff.'

'One more isn't going to make much difference.' She wouldn't draw any salary herself for a while. She didn't need anything, anyway. Courtney turned to face Jack. 'Besides, if we don't get Goldplated serving mares the natural way this season, there might not be jobs for anyone at Crosswinds before long. Isn't that right, Jack?'

'I'm afraid so. I couldn't possibly advise anyone to invest here with a cloud hanging over Goldplated's ability to perform.'

Her chin rose. 'In that case, we'll just have to make sure he *does* perform. Sean, do you think you might be able to work a major miracle in less than a month?'

He didn't bat an eyelid. 'No sweat, Ms Cross. I already have a plan in mind.'

Courtney was surprised by his cool confidence, yet for some reason she had faith in the man. Maybe it was his eyes. He had clever eyes. 'That's wonderful,' she said, smiling up at him. 'And it's Courtney, please. Not Ms Cross or ma'am. We don't stand on ceremony here. Ned, show him up to the office and get Sarah to sign him on as a casual. Now, Sean, you have the option of bed and board here or perhaps finding a place in Queenswood. A lot of my staff are locals anyway, but some do live in.'

'I'll live in.'

'In that case I'll apologise in advance for the staff's quarters. They're in urgent need of a make over.'

'Well, I'm a dab hand with a paintbrush,' he offered. 'Fact is, I'm a bit of a jack of all trades. So don't hesitate to ask if you need anything else done around the place.'

'That's a very generous offer, Sean,' she said. 'I'll certainly keep it in mind, but your first priority is Goldplated. Perhaps we might have a chat later this afternoon over what you have in mind for him. Okay?'

'Fine by me.'

'See you later, then. Oh, and take Jack with you, Ned,' she added sharply. 'He has business with Sarah.'

'What about you?' Jack retorted.

'I have breakfast to eat, an accountant to ring up and a million and one other jobs to do. I'll see you tonight at dinner, Jack. Have a good day.'

Courtney turned her back on him and marched off. But not before she'd seen the stiffening in his jaw muscles, and the harsh resolve in his narrowed eyes.

Till tonight, honey, they seemed to say. *Then we'll see who's boss...*

CHAPTER TWELVE

IT WAS a long, long day.

Courtney skipped lunch, partly because she was avoiding Jack and partly because she didn't have much of an appetite. She wasn't sure if it was the problem with Goldplated causing her to feel so churned up, or the thought of the night ahead, with Jack.

Whatever, she went from job to job, frantic to keep busy. She did some trackwork on a horse they were trying to get fit after a long spell, the one Lois would be coming to pick up soon. She delivered and spread out fresh straw in the outdoor stables. She checked all the water troughs in the yards. She helped mix up feed. She also had a long and interesting chat with the new man, and thought his plan to cure Goldplated was so stunningly simple it just might work.

But even after that she felt no calmer inside, despite now having some real hope that Crosswinds might avert this new crisis.

So the problem had to be Jack.

Her problem was always going to be Jack from now on, wasn't it? Courtney conceded.

The sun had set by the time she gave in and returned to the house, the darkness of night rapidly descending as she kicked off her dusty boots at the veranda, then hung her equally dusty hat on the peg beside the front door.

A light was shining in the window of the main living room, which suggested that Jack and Agnes were already in there, sipping pre-dinner cream sherry and chatting away like old friends, a fact confirmed when Courtney popped her head in the door.

'I'm home,' she said.

'We were just going to send a search party out for you,' Jack said, looking relaxed in the big chintz armchair by the fire. Biggs was lying asleep at his feet, and didn't even raise an eyelid at his mistress's voice.

Miserable traitor, Courtney thought, before remembering Biggs was a boy dog. *Never trust a male,* her mother had always said. *They have no sense of loyalty. Their only priority in life is their own pleasure.*

And wasn't that the truth!

'Dinner is in fifteen minutes on the dot,' Agnes warned. 'But you don't have to set the table. Jack and I did it together.'

'Thanks,' she said, throwing Jack a sickly sweet smile. 'Won't be long. Just have to grab a shower and change.'

She trudged upstairs, muttering away to herself. Why it should bother her if Jack was nice to Agnes, she had no idea. It wasn't jealousy. Perhaps it was resentment that he might not be being sincere, that he was playing with Agnes, as he was playing with her. She hated the thought that this was all a game to him, whereas her feelings for him were dead serious. She loved the man to distraction.

As if to confirm just how much in love she was, she put her hair back in Lois's gold clip after her shower, and sprayed herself liberally with the perfumed deodorant she'd bought the previous day. She also donned not her usual jeans but a pair of figure-hugging black cut-offs and a soft V-necked black jumper which Lois had given her at the weekend.

'No more black clothes for me,' Lois had said. 'So you might as well have these too.'

Courtney had to admit she looked—and felt—quite

sexy in them, especially since she'd left off her bra. This wasn't as bold a move as it might have been if the jumper had been a lighter colour. Her nipples, despite feeling tight and tingly, weren't obvious at a glance. But her unfettered breasts moved like jelly as she hurried downstairs, making her intensely aware of her body, and how turned on she already was.

She loved—and loathed—the feeling. One part of her hated being powerless to control her passion for Jack, but the greater part of her wanted to wallow in it, to experience all there was to experience whilst he was here, to make memories which were probably going to have to last her a lifetime.

This last thought brought such a sharp pain to her heart that she stopped abruptly with a gasp, and clutched at the balustrade.

Jack chose just that moment to walk out of the room and catch her standing there, looking stricken. To give him credit, his eyes mirrored immediate concern. 'Are you all right?' he asked worriedly, and dashed around to leap up the stairs and put a gentle hand around her shoulder.

She just stared up at him. She'd heard of people dying of a broken heart. Was that going to be her fate when he left?

'What is it?' he demanded to know, eyes searching her strained face. 'Are you ill?'

'A…a pain,' she said truthfully. 'Like a vice. Here…' And she lifted a shaky hand from the balustrade to cover her heart.

He looked even more alarmed. 'You have some kind of heart trouble?'

'Not…not that I know of…' At least, not in any physical sense.

'Your mother died of a coronary, though, didn't she?' She nodded.

'You should get yourself checked out, Courtney. Have an ultrasound. And an ECG. These things can sometimes be congenital.'

Agnes came out into the hallway. 'What is it? What's wrong?'

'Courtney had some kind of turn. It could be angina.'

Courtney swiftly pulled herself together at the shock on Agnes's face. She hadn't realised till that moment just how much the old lady loved her. 'It's not angina,' she insisted. 'More likely heartburn. I get that sometimes when I forget to eat.'

Jack didn't look entirely convinced, but Agnes looked relieved and then annoyed, as loved ones do after a fright. 'We noticed you didn't have any lunch,' Agnes said tartly. 'Next thing, you'll be getting anorexic. As if we don't have enough things to be worried about around here. Jack told me about that darned fool stallion Hilary bought. A flop, like the last one.'

'Goldplated's not a flop,' Courtney defended. 'And neither was Four-Leaf Clover. He died. That was hardly his fault. His progeny are now coming good. Lois thinks Big Brutus could win the Melbourne Cup. Do you know how much money the Melbourne Cup is worth?'

Agnes gave a scoffing laugh. 'Lord preserve us. I thought you had more sense than to believe a word that woman says when it comes to trophy races, or to start relying on horse winnings to get Crosswinds out of debt.'

'I'm not. I'm relying on Jack.'

'Well, Jack can't do miracles,' Agnes pronounced bluntly. 'I can't see any sensible investor putting his money into Crosswinds now, not with Goldplated being damned useless at his job.'

'Now, Agnes,' Jack intervened gently but firmly, his arm still around Courtney's shoulders, 'let's give the poor horse a chance. I have a hunch that the new groom Courtney hired today will bring Goldplated around to perform as required.'

'I'm pretty sure he can,' Courtney joined in. 'I was talking to him later this afternoon and he says the main problem to be avoided is setting off the bad memories the horse has in his head. So he's going to put Goldplated in a large yard with an experienced mare who's in season, and let nature takes its course without any interference from anyone. There is to be no handling at all. Sean believes a colt as young and as healthy as Goldplated won't be able to resist. He thinks that, once he gets a taste for it, he'll gradually be able to introduce some careful human handling till Goldplated won't give a hoot who's holding him, or where he's doing it.'

'Disgusting,' Agnes snorted. 'But that's the male animal for you. Still, it's not a nice topic of conversation. Do you think we could talk about something else over dinner? Speaking of dinner, I'll just go get it out of the oven. I've made the most delicious lamb hotpot, even if I say so myself. You two go and sit down. I won't be too long.'

Agnes hurried off, leaving Courtney alone with Jack on the stairs.

'Let's go,' she said straight away, feeling self-conscious at the way Jack immediately started looking her over, his eyes not missing a trick.

'You're not going out later dressed like that, are you?' he asked, an accusing edge in his voice.

'Like what?'

'Naked, under your clothes.'

'I am not naked!'

'You're damned well close to it!'

'Don't be ridiculous.'

'I'm far from being ridiculous. I'm an intelligent man. You haven't come down in that sexy gear for me. That, I know. So, who's it for, I ask? There's only one possible explanation. The new man. Sean. I saw the way he stared at you today. And I heard the way you talked about him just now. You think he's the ant's pants, don't you? You fancy him. You've arranged to meet him after dinner, haven't you? You'll make some bloody excuse about a foal when really you'll be off with that smooth-talking Irishman.'

'Now you're being *really* ridiculous,' she snapped. 'The man's old enough to be my father!'

'Still handsome, though. And fit as a fiddle, by the look of him. You like him. Why don't you admit it?'

'I like him, yes. But not in that way. He's not my type at all.'

'And what's *your* type?' he snapped.

Jack's outburst of jealousy was so typically male. Courtney had experienced male possessiveness before and after she'd had sex with a man. Yet they hadn't loved her, any more than Jack did. They'd just wanted her to be exclusively theirs till *they* decided it was time to move on.

Courtney never gave a man a chance to do that. She always sent them packing first.

Jack, of course, was a different kettle of fish. Jack, she loved. Jack, she would *never* send packing.

This frustrating realisation did not make her behave well.

'*My* type?' she threw up at him. 'I thought you were intelligent. *You're* my type, Jack. You should have noticed that by now. Or do you think I make a habit of crawling naked into men's beds at night? I wore these clothes for *you*, not Sean. I'm half-naked under them for *you*!''

His eyes immediately darkened, his arms snaking round her waist then yanking her hard against him. 'You little tease. Do you have any idea how much I've missed you today? How hard it's been, waiting for you to come back to the house?'

'Wonderfully hard, by the feel of things,' she taunted softly, her mouth barely centimetres away from his, their hot breaths mingling.

He sucked in sharply when she began making provocative little side to side movements with her hips.

'Stop that,' he hissed.

'Make me.'

He did, with astonishing ease, grabbing her wrists and bringing them down behind her back, lifting them upwards till she winced with the pain.

'I told you that one day someone was going to take you in hand,' he ground out through gritted teeth, an angry slash of red across his cheekbones. 'In the old days I'd have put you over my knee and paddled you till you behaved yourself. But it isn't the old days, unfortunately. Since beating you is out of the question, I'll have to use the only weapon I have: the fact you want me as much as I want you. So while you're eating your dinner think about this. Later tonight, I'm going to make love to you so much you won't be able to sit down properly for a week. There won't be a position untried, nor any foreplay forbidden. You like being on top? Be my guest. It's a great position. Leaves a man's hands free to do all sorts of things, touch all sorts of places. And there's the added bonus of being able to see every inch of your totally naked body, to watch your face twist, your eyes widen, your mouth fall open, to witness that moment when you forget where you are and who you are.'

Courtney gasped at the image of herself in such a state. And the thought of Jack, watching her.

His dark threats should have disgusted her, but they didn't. They thrilled her and excited her. Unbearably.

'For Pete's sake, where are you two?' Agnes called out from the dining room. 'Dinner's on the table!'

'Be right there, Agnes,' Jack called back, as cool as could be.

He let her wrists go, turning her and pushing her in the small of her back in the direction of the dining room. She stumbled, not because his shove was all that hard but because her legs had gone to jelly. When he reached out to steady her from behind she shrugged him away, pulling herself together and striding on ahead into the dining room. As wickedly turned on as she was, no way was she going to give Jack the satisfaction of seeing that fact.

Yes, she loved him. And, yes, she always lost her head when he was making love to her.

But she didn't have to lose her pride, or her self-respect.

Her face was as cool as his by the time she sat down at the table. She was nicely in control. Till Jack spoke.

'Did you remember to ring your accountant?' he asked.

She hadn't, of course. It had gone clear out of her mind.

'No, I didn't,' she had to confess, an embarrassed colour tingeing her cheeks. 'I forgot.'

Something close to triumph gleamed in his eyes. 'Not to worry,' he said lightly. 'You can ring him tomorrow. There's no real rush, is there? The next day will do just as well.'

'I guess so,' she mumbled, and fell to silently eating her meal.

Jack didn't try to draw her into conversation after that, a manoeuvre, she suspected, that was not out of kindness. He didn't want her to have any distraction from thinking about what he'd said out on the stairs, from thinking about that moment after Agnes had safely gone to bed and she would present herself in his room once more, not just naked this time, but already cruelly aroused.

She tried to find some will-power to fight him with, but once again the only weapon she could find against his power was a façade of boldness. She would go to him with a bang, not a whimper!

Dinner was over far too quickly, leaving several hours before Agnes's usual bedtime of ten-thirty.

If Courtney had thought the day was long, then the evening proved interminable, with Jack not letting her get away with anything. When she offered to clear up and do the washing-up, he jumped up to help her. When she settled on the sofa to watch television, he sat right beside her, instead of in the armchair he'd occupied before dinner. The only reason she didn't say she had to check on something down at the stud was because she knew Jack would come with her.

Yet she knew he wouldn't touch her. Not at that point. He would just stay with her, watching and waiting, as he was secretly watching and waiting now. She could feel it in her rapidly heating blood. He thought she'd been teasing him today, and he was paying her back in kind. And to very good effect. Inside, she was a right mess.

She didn't look a mess at ten-forty-five that night when she entered Jack's room without knocking. She was still fully dressed, for starters, which was one over Jack, who was propped up against the headboard, his chest bare against a mountain of pillows. She couldn't see the rest of him. The bedclothes were pulled up to his waist. But she suspected all of him was bare as well.

She swallowed at the thought of it, but covered her excitement with a cool smile.

'No fire tonight?' she remarked as she strolled over towards the dead hearth.

'No.' He placed his book down on the bedside table. 'I thought we would be hot enough without one.'

She arched her dark winged eyebrows and reached up to undo the gold clip in her hair. 'Did you, now?' she said, and placed it carefully on the marble mantelpiece before shaking out her hair.

'Uh-huh.'

When she turned to face him, Courtney was gratified to see tension had crept into the set of his shoulders. He looked less like a cat playing with a mouse, and more like a starving lion, desperate for a kill.

'Are you going to just stand over there all night?' he grated out.

'No.' Crossing her arms, she picked up the bottom of her black jumper and reefed it over her head in one movement, tossing it aside as though she did this sort of thing every day: stripped off before men without a qualm.

Which she possibly had, on occasion. But things were different with Jack. Everything was different with Jack. Her usual boldness was mixed with an uncharacteristic vulnerability. His hungry gaze alternately excited, then embarrassed her. Suddenly she wanted to cover herself, to not let him see her naked breasts and their rock-like nipples.

But pride had her walking brazenly towards him, her chin lifting as she tossed her curls back from her face. Unfortunately they fell forward again, as they always did when not anchored back in some way, a riotous mass of raven curls and waves which defied taming, as *she* was trying to defy taming.

'What about the rest?'

She stopped and complied, without fuss. For that would have given him all the more power.

'So what now?' she challenged once she was totally nude. 'Am I to do cartwheels? Be tied to the bedposts? What, O lord and master.' Mockery was always a good defence.

'All I want,' he growled, 'is you…in here…with me.' And he threw back the quilt.

Courtney stared at him. He was naked. And stunningly aroused.

She really should not have fallen into bed with him so eagerly, or let him plunge into her without any foreplay, or cry out his name quite so often during that first torrid mating.

But she did, and he liked it. Too much, she worried.

When he started making love to her again, she thought she acted far more restrained, until he hoisted her on top and proved to her that, with him, her being on top bore no correlation to being on top in any other way.

She tried so hard not to come, or to lose control, or to cry out his name again, but failed on all counts.

There was some comfort in Jack's lack of control as well, and the fact it was her name he cried out at his moment of release. Not Katrina's. And he didn't close his eyes once, or sigh any sad sighs.

If nothing else, Courtney could remember that fact for the rest of her life: that for one wonderful, erotic night, the man she loved thought only of her.

CHAPTER THIRTEEN

'I RANG Bill,' Courtney relayed to Jack at ten past nine the following morning. 'I told him about you, and that you wanted to see him about the stud's financial status.'

Jack was sitting at the kitchen table, having another mug of coffee after breakfast. 'And?'

'He said for us to come in straight away.'

'*Us?* I thought I'd go in alone. You said you were flat-out here. And, let's face it, I could hardly get lost. There's only the one road into Queenswood and I'm sure Mr Sinclair's office shouldn't be too hard to find. Didn't you say it was over the hardware store?'

'Yes,' Courtney admitted curtly. 'Look, it wasn't my idea we both go. It was Bill's. He sounded...odd.'

Jack put down his mug. 'In what way?'

'Stressed.'

'What's odd about that? Everybody gets stressed occasionally these days. He might have had an argument with his missus.'

'Bill doesn't have a missus. He's a crusty old bachelor. He's sixty if he's a day and married to his job and his golf clubs. No, I have an awful feeling that the bank's called in the loan.'

Jack's straight dark brows shot upwards. 'What makes you think that? Have you been getting letters of warning?'

'No.'

'Then that would be very unlikely. Still, if that *was*

132

the case, surely your Bill would have said something over the phone.'

'You don't know Bill. He hates relaying bad news over the phone. He prefers to do business face to face.'

'Ah…an old-fashioned gentleman, is he?'

'Yes.'

'I think I'm going to like Bill.'

This statement brought considerable irritation. Jack wouldn't be around long enough to form any real relationship with Bill. Even if his mystery client came to the party as her silent business partner, Courtney couldn't see Jack whizzing all the way up here to Queenswood on any regular basis. Face-to-face transactions were really a thing of the past, as Jack himself had just noted.

'Courtney, darling, do stop worrying,' Jack said smoothly. 'There's no point in crossing your bridges before you come to them. If your accountant has bad news, we'll deal with it together, okay?'

Courtney was taken aback, not only by the casually tossed 'darling', but his reassurance of support, no matter what. Surprise swiftly gave way to exasperation. She might be a push-over in bed where he was concerned, but she wasn't a total fool out of it!

'I don't see how,' she snapped. 'If the bank *has* called in the loan, I can't see you recommending Crosswinds as an investment at this point in time, can you? I doubt even the best sex in the world would change your mind on that score.'

'Stop jumping the gun, Courtney. Not to mention jumping to conclusions. Wait and see what Bill has to say.'

'I know what he's going to say. I can *feel* it.'

Jack rose from his chair. 'Then let's get going and see if you're right.'

Everything inside Courtney tightened. 'I'll just tell Agnes we're off.'

Bill read the letter from the bank one more time. Damn Hilary, he thought. She should have told him the bank had been sending her letters of warning. He could have advised her.

But she hadn't. She'd lied to the bank instead, saying that in November she was going to cash in a couple of large insurance policies to repay the loan. She'd even quoted company names and policy numbers. Naturally they'd hung off sending any more letters after her death, thinking those insurance policies would have definitely covered the loan, since death pay-outs were always higher than any premature pay-out figure. But a belated phone call to Hilary's named insurance company had finally shown there were no such policies.

What on earth had Hilary hoped to achieve with her lies? Time? Time for what? Winning the Lottery?

Now it was too late. The bank was closing the Queenswood branch and any pull he might have personally had with the manager there was now gone. Courtney's only hope was this investment broker she'd told him about on the phone. Jack Falconer.

But he'd have to come up with the money pretty darned quickly. The bank had only given her one miserable month to repay the loan in full, after which they were threatening to repossess and auction off Crosswinds, lock, stock and barrel. And it was no idle threat. Banks were no longer in the business of philanthropy and public relations. They played hard-ball business these days.

Bill rose wearily from behind his desk and walked over to the window to stare blankly down at Queenswood's main street, his mind wandering back to Hilary and her extraordinary behaviour. It wasn't like the woman to be such a dreamer. Or was it? Maybe her aggressive feminist manner had all been a façade. Maybe, underneath the toughness, she'd been the biggest dreamer of all.

The sight of a red convertible sports car zapping into a central parking spot directly in his line of vision snapped Bill out of his musings, his eyes widening when he finally recognised Courtney as the female passenger who climbed out.

Okay, so she was still wearing jeans. But there was no checked shirt. No dusty hat. And no unflattering ponytail. Her glorious hair was down and she was wearing a fluffy figure-hugging cream jumper with a softly rolled collar.

Never in all the years had he seen the girl looking so utterly gorgeous and feminine.

Bill's surprised eyes swung to the driver, who was at that moment striding round the front of the car to join Courtney. A tall broad-shouldered man, he had short dark hair, cut army style, and an air of decisiveness in his walk which Bill immediately liked.

He suspected Courtney must like him too, to have bothered with her appearance. Never had he known it to happen before. Jack Falconer had achieved in a few short days what no local lad had in twenty-five years.

Admittedly the man was impressive, Bill conceded as he watched him take Courtney's elbow to steer her across the street. Ruggedly handsome in looks, a gallant gentleman in manner and city-sophisticated in his dress. The trendy fawn trousers and long-sleeved open-necked black shirt he was wearing with such panache were not the sort of clothes often seen around Queenswood.

Bill's mood immediately perked up. He'd thought he'd heard something in Courtney's voice when she'd been telling him about this miracle man she'd found. Now he knew what it was. She'd fallen for him, like a ton of bricks.

If this Jack Falconer had fallen for Courtney in return then he would bend over backwards to get her an investor. Men in love liked nothing better than to come to the rescue of their fair damsel when in distress.

Of course, till this moment Bill would never have described Courtney as a fair damsel in distress...

Bill watched them disappear from view under the street awning before hurrying back to his desk and awaiting their arrival with a little more optimism than he had a few minutes before.

'Probably grasping at straws,' he muttered to himself as the seconds ticked away. 'When she finds out what Hilary and the bank have done, she'll start acting like her usual difficult, stroppy self, and her miracle man will be speeding back to Sydney before I can say Jack Falconer!'

She didn't. She just sat there in one of the two chairs he'd set out for them, looking utterly defeated.

'So that's it,' she said flatly at last, her shoulders sagging, her eyes dead. 'I'm done for. Crosswinds is done for.'

'Not necessarily,' he said, and glanced over at Jack. 'Let's hear what Mr Falconer has to say. The bank calling in the loan shouldn't change his feelings on Crosswinds as an investment prospect.'

'You don't understand, Bill,' Courtney broke in before the miracle man could answer for himself. 'We have this problem with Goldplated. It'll probably take more than a month before we know if he's going to be any good.'

'What do you mean? Anyone who knows anything about horses knows it'll take a good couple of *years* before you know if a new stallion's any good.'

When Courtney told him what the problem was with

Goldplated, his heart sank to rock-bottom level. 'Damn and blast,' he muttered. 'That's torn it all right.'

'Might I say something now?'

It was the miracle man who'd spoken, as cool as you please.

'Of course,' Bill said politely.

'You're both right about one thing. I couldn't advise a client to invest in Crosswinds in its present circumstances. But I have an alternative solution to Courtney's problems.'

'You *have*?' Courtney exclaimed, head swivelling round, dark eyes wide.

'What?' Bill asked.

'I will repay the loan personally.'

Bill heard Courtney's sharp intake of breath, as well as his own. When this man came to the rescue, he sure did it in style. He must love Courtney a lot!

'And before you say anything,' Jack went on swiftly, slanting Courtney a stern glance, 'yes, I can afford to. I did hint to you on several occasions that I was far from broke, but you weren't listening, and in the end I decided to drop the subject. You seemed happy believing I was practically on the breadline and, to be honest, I rather enjoyed not having the matter of money enter into the picture for once.'

For a few seconds Courtney looked like a stunned mullet, but then some kind of enlightenment came over her face, an enlightenment which clearly infuriated her.

Oh-oh, Bill groaned silently. Hilary's daughter was about to look a gift-horse in the mouth!

'There never was a mystery client willing to invest in Crosswinds, was there?' Courtney threw at Jack. 'It was you all along. You, worming your way into my good books, and then into my bed!'

Bill blinked at this news. So they were lovers already? That was good news. Very good indeed. This was just a lovers' spat, then. Nothing to be concerned about.

Clearing his throat loudly, he rose from behind his desk. 'Perhaps I should leave you two alone to discuss things. I'll just pop along to the Bluegum Café for a spot of morning tea. Be back in say…fifteen minutes?' He glanced first at a fuming Courtney and then at a splendidly composed Jack.

'Thanks, Bill,' Jack returned. 'I think that might be a wise move.'

Bill resisted smiling, for fear it would rile Courtney all the more. But the moment he was safely alone he had a good old chuckle. It seemed the girl had finally met her match!

'Now, Courtney,' Jack began calmly as soon as Bill was gone.

'Don't you "Now, Courtney" me!' she exploded, jumping to her feet and stalking across the room to the front window, where she whirled and glared at him from the safety of distance. 'You deliberately tricked me and deceived me. Lord knows what for. Do you get off playing games with other people's lives? Do you?'

'No, of course not.'

'I think you do. You've been having a great time. You yourself said how much you enjoy playing games.'

He stood up from the chair. Her hands immediately balled into fists at her sides. She was so angry she could hardly see straight. Finally she crossed her arms, because if he came near her at this moment she'd be tempted to deck him one.

'Courtney,' he said as he started walking towards her. 'There are games and there are games. Yes, I have been having a great time. I admit it. But I don't think paying off a three-million-dollar debt could qualify as a game, do you?'

His cool reasoning flustered her. 'How would I know? Maybe you get off on paying other people's debts as well! You did it before, when you didn't have to.'

His face grew serious as he reached for her, his large hands curling over her stiffly held shoulders. 'But I *did* have to,' he insisted, his eyes searching hers. 'Surely you must see that. I couldn't have lived with myself knowing all those people had lost their life savings because of my partner's greed. Just as I couldn't live with myself now if I let you and Crosswinds go under. I care about you too much for that.'

Her heart just stopped. Was he saying what she suddenly hoped he was saying. That he loved her?

'But it's not charity I'm offering you,' he continued. 'It's a deal.'

'A deal,' she repeated, dismay clutching at her heart.

Not love...

A deal...

'I will clear your debts if you do something for me in return.'

'For heaven's sake, what?' It had to be something huge for three million dollars.

Jack looked worried for a second. 'This might be a bit of a shock, coming so quickly after we've met. But I'm quite sure on my part. In fact, I've never been more sure of anything.'

'Jack, for pity's sake, *what*?'

'I want you to have my child.'

Courtney was simply poleaxed.

A child. He wanted *her* to have *his* child. In her wildest dreams she would never have thought of that.

'You mean as…as some kind of surrogate?' she asked, still stunned.

'Good Lord, no. I mean we have a child together. Like any normal couple.'

The idea moved her as she would never have imagined. All her life Courtney had believed there wasn't much of the maternal in her, but the thought of having Jack's baby seemed to call not only to the woman in her but the mother.

Yet the reality of having Jack's child was fraught with more risk of future hurt than being secretly in love with him. She really shouldn't even consider it. And he shouldn't have asked her. It wasn't right.

'So what do you think?' Jack persisted when she just stood there, staring up at him.

Courtney gathered herself to answer. 'I think you have a hide,' she stated, her outer coolness a cover for her inner agitation. Because she knew that no matter what she said to him, her final answer was always going to be yes.

But she couldn't give in that easily, could she?

His smile was soft. 'Which makes us well-matched, don't you think? Any child of ours would be able to take on the world.'

Courtney's heart lurched at his words. 'I'm sorry, Jack,' she said stubbornly, 'but my answer has to be no. I would never bring an illegitimate child into this world, not after having been one myself.'

Jack shrugged. 'Marry me, then.'

The nonchalance of his proposal staggered her. Till she realised that marriage to her was just a means to an end to him. He must want a child very badly.

But he'd backed her into a clever corner with his counter-move. She'd thought her bringing marriage into things would put a spanner in the works. Instead, she was now in deeper trouble than ever.

Marry me, he'd said. Dear Lord, she'd *die* for him.

'The only reason I didn't mention marriage first,' he went on, 'was because you didn't seem the marrying kind.'

Courtney bristled, despite the accuracy of his observation. Had he been talking to Agnes about her? 'Well, I'm not,' she confessed grudgingly. 'But if there's going to be a child involved...'

'Then you will?' His hands tightened on her shoulders, his eyes lighting up with genuine delight. 'You won't regret it, Courtney. I promise you. I'll be good to you. And to our child. You won't need to worry about anything ever again. God, I—'

'I haven't said I will yet,' she broke in before he got totally carried away and took her with him. 'First, I'd like to ask you a few questions. But, before I do, do you think you could let me go?' She never could think straight when he was this close.

His hands dropped away from her shoulders and she walked back over to sit on the corner of Bill's desk, a nice distance between them. 'Right,' she began firmly, crossing her legs and clamping her hands over her top knee to stop her legs from shaking. 'I want to know when you decided to ask me this? And please don't give me any bulldust. Did you have this idea in your mind all along when you invented your mystery investor and wangled coming home with me?'

'Good Lord, no,' he denied. 'No!'

'When, then? Today...now...right here in this office?'

'Not quite. The thought did occur to me briefly the first time we made love. But I dismissed it as fanciful. I didn't think you'd agree. But today, when the idea came to me again, I felt that perhaps you would, under these new circumstances.'

'I shouldn't,' she muttered. 'It isn't right.'

'What's not right about it?'

'I'd have to be a mercenary bitch to agree to marry a man and have his baby in exchange for three million bloody dollars,' she threw at him. 'And you'd have to be a cold-blooded bastard to propose it in the first place!'

'Come now, Courtney, my offer isn't at all cold-blooded and you know it. We might not be in love with each other but we like each other one hell of a lot. The heat we generate together would put a furnace to shame. A lot of besotted couples aren't as compatible in bed as we are.'

'That's just sexual chemistry,' she argued. 'The sort which is highly unstable, I might point out. Give it six months and, poof, it will all burn out.'

'I doubt that very much.'

'Well, forgive me, but experience tells me it will. The truth is we don't know each other well enough for such a big step as marriage and a baby.'

'I know everything I need to know about *you*,' he insisted.

'In four days?' she challenged back.

'I've learnt more about you in these past four days than I knew about Katrina after four years of living with her. And I like what I've learnt. Very much so. I think you've gotten to know me pretty well, too.'

Only in the biblical sense, she thought unhappily.

Jack's frustrated sigh snapped Courtney back to the sight of him running his hands agitatedly through his hair. 'Still,' he said, an edge on his voice, 'there *are* things about me you can't possibly know, and perhaps you should. I don't want you to ever say that I tricked you or deceived you in any way. So let me put you in the total picture.'

'The total picture?' she echoed, a dark dread pooling deep inside her.

He began pacing back and forth across the room, talking and glancing over at her as he went. 'A year ago, the idea of getting married and having a child was the last thing on my mind. I thought I had everything a man could possibly want. A business which was making me millions. A house in the right part of Sydney. A glamorous lady who seemed crazy about me. A lifestyle of five-star pleasure-leisure. Then, in the space of a few months, everything changed. My partner did a flit. My business went down the tubes. I lost a fortune. Then, to top it off, my girlfriend left me for another man...'

Jack stopped his pacing to throw Courtney an uncompromisingly harsh glance. 'You believed Katrina's defection was because of money. And you know what? You could be partially right. Though that didn't occur to me at the time. I stupidly thought my still having a couple of million in the bank was enough play money for anyone. Still, the main reason Katrina left me was because I began pressuring her to have a baby.'

'You...you wanted Katrina to have your baby?' she choked out, feeling sick inside. In one fell swoop she was right back to being a stand-in for Katrina again. A second-rate substitute.

'Yes, I did,' he grated out. 'More fool me.' He shuddered at the memory, then began to pace the room once more. 'The disaster with my business partner changed me in more ways than you can imagine. Suddenly I saw the end result of living one's life for material gain and hedonistic pursuits. I started to appreciate that the simple family life my older brother led held much more satisfaction and real pleasure than my own so-called high life. I started hating the emptiness of it all. I wanted more. So I asked Katrina to marry me…and have a baby…' His pacing slowed to a halt, as did his voice.

Suddenly, his eyes were a million miles away. Such bleak, bleak eyes.

Courtney couldn't bear to think about what he was thinking about. '*And*?' she prompted harshly.

His head snapped round to her, his eyes still holding a cloud of remembered pain. 'She told me she loved me but had no intention of ever having children. She said she hated the thought of having babies. She wanted us to go on as we'd been doing, having no responsibilities except for each other's pleasure.'

Courtney didn't want to think about how well Katrina had given Jack pleasure, given he still wasn't over her.

'I told Katrina that if she wasn't prepared to settle down and have a baby, then we were through.'

Courtney was taken aback. 'You mean it was you who left her, not the other way around?'

'No. No, I have to confess that's not how it was. I arrogantly thought that, if she loved me, she'd give in to my demands. My ultimatum was a bluff. A dangerous one, considering Katrina's antagonism towards being forced to do anything at all. As you know,' he finished bitterly, 'she left me for Axelrod whom she subsequently married.'

Courtney could find no words to say at this juncture. Jack stared down at his feet for a few seconds before looking up again, his face grim.

'I won't deny I was devastated for a long time. I won't deny I came to the races last Saturday simply to see her again. Did I want her back? You may well ask. In all honesty, I don't know. I told myself I just wanted her to see that I'd survived, that I was as rich as ever. Richer, even. Yes, it's true. After Katrina left me, I began playing the stock market like some kind of self-destructive maniac, recklessly taking chances which would have given a wise investor nightmares. Perversely, I could do no wrong, and soon I had more money than before the fiasco with Graham.'

'I think you wanted to get her back, Jack,' Courtney stated, forcing *him* to face the whole rotten truth of his feelings for that woman. 'You still love her.'

'No,' he denied. 'No, I don't believe I do. Not any longer. The moment I met you, Courtney, the moment I started seeing Katrina through your very clear eyes, I knew I wanted nothing more to do with her. I also knew I wanted to get away from Sydney for a while. City life had begun to pall on me. Which is why I came up with the mystery client idea. I didn't deliberately deceive you. I was genuinely going to invest in Crosswinds if it looked like a going concern. I delayed revealing my identity so that I could spend more time with you as the man you thought I was, the not-so-successful Jack Falconer. It soothed my world-weary soul, and my badly bruised ego, to have you like me for myself. To *want* me for myself.

'You did want me for myself, didn't you?' he said softly, and began walking towards her, his eyes purposeful.

Panic had her sliding off the corner of the desk, her hands flying up to ward him off. But *his* hands were already reaching to cradle her face and his mouth was descending. Her palms ended up pressed flat against the hard wall of his chest, right above his heart.

Its thundering beat proved even more seductive than his kiss, for it showed Courtney that he wanted her for herself as well. He might still be in love with Katrina, but once *they* started making love, Courtney believed all thought of the dreaded Katrina was quickly banished from Jack's mind. If nothing else, he was hers when he was in her arms. Such thinking had her hands sliding up around his neck to pull him close. He groaned and kissed her even more hungrily, his lips prying hers apart, his tongue darting deep.

Courtney moaned, 'Oh, Jack...Jack, my darling...'

Bill's repeated clearing of his throat finally got through to the kissing couple. He wasn't surprised to find them in a torrid embrace when he returned. What did surprise him, however, was the way Courtney blushed once she saw him standing there.

To give her credit, she did her best to rustle up the girl of old.

'Fifteen minutes up already, is it?' she tossed his way as he walked over to his desk.

A sham, that boldness of hers, Bill decided. Just as Hilary's manner had been a sham. Underneath the surface aggression they were as soft and feminine as any other woman. At least, they were once the right man came along.

Bill sat down and beamed approvingly up at Jack. 'I take it you sorted things out between you?' he enquired.

'Perfectly,' Jack answered. 'If you give me the correspondence from the bank, I'll settle Courtney's loan this week.'

'Wonderful,' Bill said with genuine delight. 'And is this to be a loan on your part, or a gift?'

'A gift. You might as well know, Bill, since you're as much a family friend as an accountant. I've asked Courtney to marry me and she's said yes. That was a yes just now, darling, wasn't it?' he asked, an arm snaking possessively around her waist.

For one awful moment Bill thought she was going to say no. She'd stopped blushing somewhere along the line and he was sure he spotted a decidedly mutinous glint in her eye.

'Darling?' Jack prompted, giving her a squeeze.

She flashed him a somewhat brittle smile. 'Yes,' she confirmed, if a tad tautly.

Bill almost sighed his relief. 'Wonderful,' he said again. 'When?'

'As soon as it can be arranged,' Jack said, and Bill tried not to look shocked. What was the rush? Courtney could hardly be pregnant given she'd only met the man at the weekend.

Okay, so it was obvious they couldn't keep their hands off each other, but, given the brevity of their relationship and the fact they were already lovers, Bill would have thought it only sensible to have a longer engagement.

'And how soon would that be?' he asked Jack.

'Unless you get a special licence, you have to wait a month after you've lodged the appropriate form. So as soon as possible after that month is up. I thought a simple ceremony at Crosswinds, with a celebrant.'

Bill waited for Courtney to make some objection to Jack's plans, but she didn't. She just stood there, silent, but far from happy.

It suddenly came to Bill that maybe she hadn't fallen for Jack at all. Maybe she was just pretending. Maybe she was marrying this man for his money.

The thought shocked him. Courtney was capable of a lot of things but he hadn't thought deliberate deception was one of them. He frowned at her, and her chin shot up, her eyes suddenly as rebellious as ever.

'You've got some problem with that, Bill?' she said sharply.

'No. Not if you haven't. What about the other money you were going to ask for to bring Crosswinds up to scratch?'

'As Courtney's husband,' Jack inserted smoothly, 'I'll be only too happy to pay for any repairs and improvements necessary around our home.'

Bill saw Courtney stiffen, then throw Jack one of her blistering glances. 'What do you mean...*our* home?'

A lesser man might have wilted. But not this man. He stayed cool and composed under the fire of her eyes. 'I aim to live at Crosswinds with you, darling. We can hardly conduct a proper marriage with me in Sydney and you up here, can we?'

'I hadn't thought that far yet,' she replied tautly.

'We'll talk about it on the drive home.'

'Yes,' she bit out, 'we certainly will. Give Jack those letters he wants, Bill. We have to get going. Goldplated is having his first dry run today and I want to be there to see what happens.'

Bill did as ordered and watched with definite misgivings as Jack steered Courtney towards the door.

'Courtney,' he called out, partly in concern and partly out of curiosity.

She stopped and turned. 'Yes?'

'Could you spare me a moment, please? In private?'

'I'll wait for you in the car, darling,' Jack replied diplomatically before continuing out through the door.

'What is it, Bill?' she asked impatiently.

He waited till he was sure Jack was out of earshot.

'I hope what I'm thinking isn't true, Courtney Cross. I hope you're not marrying Jack just for his money.'

The minx laughed. 'Good God, Bill, how can you

sound so appalled when marrying a man for his money was your own idea, voiced in this office only last week?'

'But I didn't really mean it! Hilary would turn in her grave if she thought you'd do a thing like that.'

'You're wrong, Bill. Mum would probably applaud my boldness and daring. But please...do put your very decent mind at rest. I'm not marrying Jack *just* for his money.'

Bill could not contain his relief. He sighed expansively. 'Ah...so it *is* love. That was my first thought when I saw you two kissing. I said to myself, Bill, now there's a couple who are madly in love.'

Her laughter really shocked him this time. 'Heavens, you old romantic, you. Jack doesn't love me. He's still besotted with his ex, who upped and married another man. He wants me; that's all. I told you the only reason I'd ever marry a man and that hasn't changed.'

Sex? She was marrying him for the *sex*?

'The money is just an added bonus. See you at the wedding, Bill. And er...do keep this under your hat. No telling Agnes, especially. As much as Jack knows the score, I think he'd prefer everyone to think ours is the love-match of the century. I mean...it's a matter of male ego, isn't it?'

CHAPTER FOURTEEN

'WHAT did Bill want? Or shouldn't I ask?'

They had just left Queenswood, with Courtney still fuming over Jack's high-handed attitude in Bill's office. How dared he casually announce when and how they were getting married, not to mention where he was going to live, all without so much as consulting her? If this was the way he was going to act with her all the time once they were married, then he could think again. And if he thought she was going to come cap in hand for money all the time, then he could *really* think again. The man needed sorting out!

'He wanted to know if I was marrying you for your money,' she announced baldly.

'And what did you say?'

'I told him exactly what I told him last week when he himself made that suggestion.'

'*Bill* suggested you marry for money?' Jack's tone was disbelieving.

'Indeed he did. But I told him I'd never do that. I said the only reason I'd do something as stupid as marry a man was for the sex.'

Jack's amused laughter did not quell her rising temper.

'You don't believe me?' she said archly.

'I might…under other circumstances. Much as I might like to, I'm not going to fool myself into thinking my money didn't have a bearing on your saying yes…to *both* my proposals. But I'm happy that you liked me and fancied me *before* you knew I was filthy rich.'

'Just how filthy rich are you, exactly?'

'I'm no billionaire. But I'm worth a good ten million or so. Which reminds me, the day you marry me I'll have two million dollars transferred into your bank account for you to do all those things you want to do to Crosswinds. You don't have to answer to me. Spend it as you please.'

Jack's offer really took the wind out of Courtney's sails, and the heat out of her anger.

'That…that's very generous of you. But I don't really need that much. I mean I…I…'

'Of course you do,' he insisted. 'Crosswinds needs more than a coat of paint. It needs a complete update.'

'I don't know what to say.'

'I'll let you thank me tonight,' he said, slanting her a saucy smile.

The penny dropped. The extra million was a bribe to make sure she didn't change her mind about everything, and to keep her sweet in bed. Little did Jack know, but nothing short of Katrina getting him back would stop her marrying him. As for keeping her sweet in the lovemaking department…no amount of money could make her any sweeter.

In a way, she'd told Bill the truth. It was the lovemaking, rather than love, that had made her accept Jack's proposal of marriage. She could live without Jack's love. She had to. But she couldn't live without his lovemaking if she didn't have to.

And, as his wife, she wouldn't have to.

'I'm going to have to go back to Sydney tomorrow and attend to the business side of things,' Jack said. 'While I'm there I'll put in the form for a marriage licence, so you'd better give me your birth certificate before I go. I'll be back by the weekend, and this time I'll bring all my things with me.'

'You're really meaning to stay?' she asked. 'Permanently?'

'You have some objection to that?'

'No. But what are you going to do with your spare
time? I mean…Crosswinds has only one boss, and that's
me, Jack. I told you, I won't tolerate any interference in
the running of the stud.'

'Don't worry. I won't interfere. What the hell do I
know about horses, anyway? During the day I'll keep on
doing what I've been doing ever since I wound up my
consultancy business. I'll set myself up to trade on the
stock market on the internet. Do you have a room I could
use as an office?'

'You can use Mum's old study.'

'Great. That's all settled, then,' he said happily.

Courtney wasn't so sure. Life in the country was not
the same as in the city. It was very quiet. And remote.
There were no five-star restaurants within easy driving
distance. No theatres or international sporting events. No
fancy shops or galleries or wherever it was Jack had used
to go with Katrina. He said he didn't want any of that
any more, but old habits died hard.

'You'll get bored,' she told him.

'With you? Never!'

With me, she thought ruefully. With horses. And flies.
And the heat. With everything, long before any baby ar-
rives. Six months, she reckoned. Six months and he'd be
climbing the walls. Or, worse, interfering. She would put
money on it.

A silence fell in the car which didn't lift till they
reached Crosswinds and were driving up towards the
house.

'What are we going to tell Agnes?' she asked abruptly.

'What would you like to tell her?'

'Not the bald truth. And nothing about the baby business. You can admit you were the mystery investor all along but, after we fell in love, you decided on a different type of partnership. You can say you proposed to me on the way in the car this morning and I accepted. I don't want her knowing about the bank calling in the loan. I want her to think this is a true love-match. I'll give Bill a ring and make sure he backs me up in this.'

'Fine. But do you think she'll believe such a story? She knows you well, Courtney, and I gathered during our conversations about you that she had doubts about you ever marrying. Like mother, like daughter.'

Agnes might have thought that once, but she was not a stupid woman, and had twigged to something when Courtney came down to breakfast today wearing the jumper Sarah had given her last birthday. At the time, Courtney had confided to Agnes it was the sort of garment she wouldn't be seen dead in and was only fit for mushy girls in love. Agnes hadn't said anything when she'd spotted her wearing it, but the knowingness in her eyes had said it all. So had the barely hidden delight.

Courtney wasn't blind. Agnes thought Jack was the ant's pants. When he announced their engagement, Agnes would probably be over the moon.

She was. Utterly.

'Oh, my goodness!' she exclaimed, all of a flutter for once. 'Oh, heavens. And you're going to live here, Jack? How wonderful. And what about children? Might we eventually hear the patter of little feet?' she directed Courtney's way.

Courtney had been trying hard not to think about the baby bit, plus the fact she was virtually being paid to have Jack's child. It made her feel like some kind of expensive brood mare, selected for her genes and nothing else, a feeling added to when she recalled Jack's concern the other night about her possibly having heart trouble. Clearly, such a defect would have ruled her out as the mother of his child.

This shouldn't have hurt her, but it did. Everything about this marriage was going to hurt her in the end. Any physical pleasure she might garner from their union would come at a price.

But it wasn't fair to share any of her qualms with Agnes. After all the bad things that had happened lately, the woman deserved some happiness for a change.

'Jack and I intend starting a family straight away,' Courtney said, plastering a smile on her face.

'Oh, that's marvellous,' Agnes gushed. 'And who knows? Maybe Crosswinds will have a boy at long last.'

'You'd like a boy?' Jack asked later as they walked together down towards Goldplated's yard. Agnes had not let them go for ages, plying them with sandwiches and tea whilst asking about their plans for the wedding.

Naturally Agnes had made no objection to Jack's plans, as Courtney hadn't. There again, he'd made it all sound so romantic this time, even the getting married so quickly, especially here, on the property. Agnes had gone gaga over the idea and was already planning the wedding cake.

'Not particularly,' she replied. 'That was my mother's bent. Would you?'

'No. I don't care either way.'

'Are you going to invite your family to the wedding?'

'I don't think so. There's only my father and my brother and they both live in South Australia. Why? Did you want me to?'

'No, I guess not. Best we keep it small.'

'Who are you going to ask to give you away?'

The reality of having neither father nor mother at her wedding depressed her. 'I don't know,' she muttered. 'Does it matter?'

'You could ask Bill.'

'Yes, I could.' Which reminded her. She had to ring Bill later and clue him up on things. She could ask him then. 'Walk faster or we'll miss the mating. Sean said he'd be putting the mare in with Goldplated straight after lunch.' She hastened her step, Jack lengthening his stride to keep up with her with ease.

The yard Goldplated was stabled in was very spacious, used to agist stallions during the off season. It had a large lock-up stable in one corner and shady trees in two others. The ground was covered with good pasture, the lush green grass only worn out along the fences where the horses liked to run up and down. When Courtney and Jack arrived, both Ned and Sean were hiding behind the stable, surreptitiously watching proceedings. When she and Jack approached the fence just a few metres away from them, Sean put his fingers to his mouth in a shushing gesture.

'I just put the mare in with him. He immediately looked around to see where any people were so we skedaddled back here. Try to keep out of his direct line of vision.'

Courtney moved along the fence slightly till the stable blocked them from the horse's view. Jack moved with her, standing just behind her, his arms encircling her in what was really a very intimate and possessive position. Both Ned and Sean exchanged a knowing glance but Courtney decided not to make a fuss. They had to know how the land lay between her and Jack sooner or later, and she'd rather they too think her marriage was a love-match.

'Where did you get the mare from, by the way?' Courtney called over quietly, her stomach churning with nerves now that the moment of truth was at hand. She wanted Goldplated to perform quite desperately. It was no longer a matter of money, given Jack had come to the party, but a matter of pride. And justice. She wanted to stick one right up the ear of that person who'd done the dirty on Goldplated—and her mother—in the first place.

'Ned rustled her up from a neighbour. She's just a stockhorse. She's had five foals, and her owner says when she's in heat she's a right little tramp.'

'Good,' Courtney said. 'The trampier the better.'

'I just love the way you talk,' Jack whispered in her ear.

Courtney glanced up at him over her shoulder. 'This is business, Jack, not pleasure.'

'Yeah, right,' he said, smiling back at her.

'You'll see for yourself shortly. If we're lucky...'

The four of them fell silent whilst they watched. Initially, Goldplated was hesitant, and agitated. He wouldn't even go near the mare.

But she wasn't having any of that, the little flirt. She sidled over to him, sniffing him, then angling herself so that he could sniff her.

Goldplated must have got a good whiff of her hormone-laden scent, for, suddenly, he reared up and whinnied. Not in fear or panic, but in excitement, if the immediate state of his mating equipment was anything to go by.

'Good God,' Jack gasped.

'Shh,' Courtney reprimanded, but she too had been startled. Goldplated was obviously not one of those race-horses suffering from steroid overload. He was prime breeding material. A stud, in the most basic meaning of the word.

The mare took off, cantering around the yard, playing the tease to perfection. Goldplated was after her like a shot, giving her a tender love nip here and there, nuzzling into her neck when he could get close enough. And didn't she adore the whole ritual? Shaking her head and mane, then kicking up her heels and running off some more before finally letting herself be caught in the one empty corner. There, she backed away at first, acting like a reluctant virgin. But when Goldplated looked hesitant once more, the mare suddenly whipped around and backed up towards him, her tail swished to one side with tantalising frankness.

All right, big boy, her body language screamed. *I give in. Take me. I'm yours.*

Goldplated reared up on his hind legs and neighed his agreement.

Then, take her, he did.

For the first time in her life Courtney's mouth went dry as she watched a mating between horses. She could not take her eyes off Goldplated as he mounted the mare. The mare neighed once, then just stood there, trembling, the stallion keeping her captive with his front legs whilst his seed pumped deep into her body. It was obvious she was in a state of bliss, her flanks quivering, her back arching a little. No one witnessing such an incredibly primitive but pleasure-chocked display could doubt that a foal would result from this union, or that Goldplated would eventually get to learn to like his allotted career.

Meanwhile, Courtney had to endure the fact that Jack was pressed up against her behind with a quite stunning erection of his own. By the time the horses parted company Courtney's whole body felt stretched as tight as a drum. My God, she'd never been so turned on in her life! If only she could do what that mare had done, back up to Jack right here and now and whisper, 'Take me, I'm yours.'

But they weren't animals. They were human beings, constricted by standards of decency and decorum. They couldn't mate with no thought of where they were or who was watching. It just wasn't done.

With a struggle, she ignored her cripplingly aroused state and got on with her job as boss of Crosswinds.

'That looks promising,' she called over to Sean and Ned. 'What's your next move?'

'Ned's going to find him another experienced mare for next week,' Sean answered. 'I don't think we should overtax him to begin with. Best he wait a while. He'll be more eager that way. Then another couple of mares the following week, but with some handling involved. By then, hopefully, he should be ready to service some of your own mares.'

'That sounds great. Keep me posted.'

'Will do.'

'Come along, Jack,' she said, pushing him back from her with a brisk turn of her shoulder. 'We have work to do. A study to clean out and a birth certificate to find. Lord knows where Mum's put it. But it'll be in there somewhere.'

She was off, almost at a trot, Jack having to stride out to keep up.

'I don't want to go up to the house,' he said. 'Take me somewhere we can be alone. Right now.'

She ground to a halt and stared at him, heat zooming into her cheeks. Because she knew exactly what he had in mind. She could see it in his eyes.

'The far feed shed,' she said before she could stop herself.

'Come on, then.' He grabbed her nearest hand, began pulling her along the path.

'Not that way,' she choked out. 'This way...'

It only took them ten minutes, walking fast. Ten long, excruciating minutes.

The far feed shed had once been a grand old barn, but was now just a ramshackle building used to house straw and feed for the horses in the far grazing paddocks. With good grass in the pastures and fresh straw only being put into stables on a Monday the odds of anyone coming in there that afternoon were remote.

But it was possible.

When she told Jack this, he said he didn't give a damn and to just get her damned clothes off. *All* of them.

Did that add to her excitement, knowing someone might walk in on them?

Courtney didn't know. All she knew was she would have done anything he asked. She *did* do anything he asked. She took off every stitch she had on then bent over two bales of straw and let him take her as Goldplated had taken the mare, let him bite her on the neck, let him pump his unprotected seed in her.

It was over almost before it began, both of them climaxing together, Jack collapsing across her back, gasping. She lay underneath his heavy, heaving chest and slowly, very slowly, got her mind back.

'Jack,' she whispered at long last. 'You didn't use anything.'

He was, by this time, lying very still on top of her. Possibly exhausted, Courtney imagined.

'No,' came his rather cool reply. 'I didn't.'

A frisson of shock ripped down her spine at the

thought this omission had been deliberate, not the result of an uncontrollable passion.

'Does it matter?' he muttered. 'You did say you wanted to start a baby straight away.'

'You know I meant straight after the wedding,' she protested, panic in her voice at the realisation his timing couldn't have been better, if it had been his intention to impregnate her.

'I don't see what difference one month makes,' he said drily. 'Unless, of course, you're planning on changing your mind after you get my money.'

'You know I wouldn't do that.'

'No, Courtney. No, I don't know that, given this adverse reaction of yours to what was really a mutual recklessness. But it's good to hear you say it.'

He levered himself off her back, but when she went to rise up as well she realised he was still inside her. Not only inside, but not totally deflated. 'No, don't get up,' he said, his voice thick. 'I haven't finished yet.'

He pushed her back down with strong hands, then kept her there by massaging her shoulders and spine, swiftly bringing her back to a sensual awareness of her own not quite sated body. Her arms, which had been hanging limply down beside the bales of straw, lifted to fold and make a nest for her head. She just lay there, an odd mixture of relaxation and regathering tension. She could feel him expanding inside her but he remained still, only his hands moving, those clever, clever hands, caressing and stroking and exploring every intimate inch of her. When she began to moan and arch her back, those knowing hands grabbed her hips and lifted her up onto her knees.

'You do it,' he urged, and showed her what he wanted.

She groaned, but obeyed, rocking back and forth, making love to him with her body, her head still down on her forearms, her eyes squeezed tightly shut. If someone had walked in on them then she wouldn't have seen them, or cared. She was in another world, a world where nothing existed but what she was doing. She begged him to move also. But he didn't. Not till she was beside herself, till she was sobbing with frustration. Then and only then did he move, his knowing hands joining in once more, stroking her aching breasts before sliding down her stomach between her legs, touching that magical spot which shattered her apart.

She cried out his name, then just cried.

Oh, Jack...Jack...what have you done to me?

CHAPTER FIFTEEN

COURTNEY hung up the phone and walked disconsolately back into the kitchen. 'Jack's not coming back till Sunday, now,' she said drearily. 'He said it took him a lot longer to do everything than he realised. He also said he's got far too much stuff to fit into his car, so he's asked Lois to bring up the rest. She's coming up on Sunday as well, to pick up that horse, remember?'

Agnes glanced round from where she was standing at the sink, washing up. 'The one you've been trying to skinny up?'

'Yep. That one. You know, Jack must have one heck of a lot of clothes if he can't fit them in his car. Lord knows where he'll ever wear them all.'

Agnes pulled the plug in the sink. 'I don't think it's all clothes. He promised to buy me a dishwasher while he was down in Sydney. And he said something about a computer for Sarah.'

Courtney frowned. 'He never said anything to me about any of that.'

'He wanted it to be a surprise. I'm only telling you now to put your mind at rest. I'm pretty sure he's planning on buying you something special too, so you can stop pouting.'

'I'm not pouting.'

'Oh, yes, you are. You've been in a bad mood ever since Jack left.'

'I have not.'

'You can't fool me. You miss the man. And why shouldn't you? You're in love.'

'I don't think I like being in love,' she muttered.

'Yes, I gathered that too. But you'll get used to it, in time. Jack's a good man. You'll be happy with him, if you let yourself be. But if you start carrying on like your mother did with men you'll make yourself miserable.'

'I'm *not* like my mother!'

'You are in some ways.'

Courtney bristled. 'Truly, whose side are you on?'

'Does there have to be sides?'

'There are always sides where men and women are concerned.'

'Who said so? Hilary?'

'No, *me*. They always want the upper hand.'

Agnes shrugged. 'I don't think Jack's like that at all. He's a nice man. Kind and helpful. You should thank your lucky stars for the day he fell in love with you, because not many men would.'

'Well, thank you very much!'

Agnes shot her an uncompromising look. 'I only have your best interests at heart, girl. I'm worried you're going to do something to ruin this. Jack is the best thing that's ever happened to you, and to Crosswinds. So be careful. And behave!'

Courtney only just resisted throwing at Agnes exactly what sort of man Jack was. An opportunist, that was what. A man with a ruthless agenda. A man possibly driven by vengeance against a woman he was still besotted with.

He doesn't love me, she wanted to scream. *He's just using me. I'm no better than a brood mare, all paid for and properly serviced, according to plan. The bottom line is that only the baby matters to him. Not me. Not our marriage. They're totally irrelevant. He'll divorce me as good as look at me once I've had his precious child!*

This last thought brought Courtney up with a jolt. Actually, all her thoughts had jolted her. She hadn't realised they'd been lurking somewhere in her head.

Not that they changed anything. Even knowing the worst, she still wanted Jack, wanted him so badly that the wait till Sunday seemed an eternity. Yet it was only two days away. Two never-ending, miserably lonely days.

Everything inside Courtney seemed to tighten, then shatter. No wonder her mother had warned her about this kind of thing happening. It was hell. It was agony. It was unendurable!

'I'm going for a ride,' she announced abruptly.

Courtney reined the big bay gelding to a halt at the top of the highest hill on Crosswinds, a spot where the whole property was laid out before her. Her troubled eyes travelled slowly over all she owned, but, try as she might she couldn't muster up the passion she'd once had for it. All she could think about was Jack.

This was Sunday, the third day in a row she had ridden up here and just sat on her horse, thinking about him. They were terribly mixed up thoughts. One moment she clung to the hope that he did care for her, that he was done with Katrina once and for all and was genuine in his desire to embrace family life here at Crosswinds. Then, the next moment, doubts would crowd back in, fuelled by several recent incidents. First Jack's delaying his return. Then his vagueness over *exactly* what was taking him so long down there. Finally his taking an age to answer the phone last night, then sounding distracted when he did.

This morning her doubts far outweighed her hopes, due to an article in the Sunday paper that the minister for sport and his beautiful wife, Katrina, had parted company during the week and would be seeking a divorce. The article reported that Mr Axelrod had been tight-lipped about the split but it was rumoured there *was* a third party involved. Mrs Axelrod admitted she had left her husband's harbourside mansion and was currently staying with an old friend somewhere in Sydney.

The idea that Katrina was staying with Jack had taken hold on reading this, and simply wouldn't let go.

What would she do if Jack rang her today and said he wasn't coming back after all?

The sudden sighting of dust in the distance brought her bolt upright in the saddle, her neck craning, her heart pounding. *Yes!* It was coming from the road to Queenswood. A vehicle, speeding towards Crosswinds.

Yet Jack wasn't due for a couple of hours. Not unless he'd started with the dawn. Maybe it was Lois. She was known to get on the road very early.

The sun burst out from behind the clouds and Courtney spotted flashes of red between the trees lining the road. Red! It was a red car. It was Jack, hurrying back to her.

Courtney sobbed with relief, then kicked her mount into an instant gallop, tearing down the hill and across the paddocks, jumping any fences in her way. She vowed not to think such negative thoughts any more, or to worry that Jack didn't love her. He liked her. He desired her. And he'd come back to her. That would do for now.

She sailed over the last fence, which brought her onto the winding gravel driveway just as Jack drove through the main gate. He braked to a halt barely metres from the horse's dancing front feet, his handsome face darkening with instant fright. And a measure of fury.

'Courtney! Are you stark raving mad, jumping fences like that? What if you'd fallen?'

She grinned down at him, finding immense satisfaction in his angry concern. 'It wouldn't be the first time. You don't need to worry about me.' But it was nice that he did.

'But what if you're pregnant?'

All the pleasure in his return drained out of her. 'And if I am, am I to stop riding altogether?' she threw at him. 'Is my life going to come to a halt simply because I'm carrying Jack Falconer's child?'

'I would expect you to be sensible,' he ground out. 'So, yes, I'd prefer you to stop riding.'

'I'll bet you won't stop me riding *you* tonight, though,' she pointed out tartly. 'After all, I might *not* be pregnant yet. And that's your main priority, isn't it? Getting me knocked up.'

'Courtney, for pity's sake…'

'Pity, Jack? What's pity got to do with any of this? This is nothing but a deal, remember? Your millions in exchange for my womb. Did you think all that great sex had scrambled my brains? Oh, no, Jack, I know exactly where I stand with you now.'

'And where's that, Courtney?' he asked through clenched teeth, his knuckles white on the steering wheel.

'Nowhere of any lasting value.'

'That's not true.'

'Our marriage will be a sham and you know it. So why bother? Keep your two million pieces of silver. I'll still have your baby, since I probably already am knocked up. But I won't be marrying you. The price is just too high.'

He glared up at her for a long moment. 'Lois isn't far behind me,' he said, making an effort to be calm despite the stubborn set of his jaw. 'So let's keep this argument till later.'

'There'll be no argument later. My mind is made up. No marriage, Jack. And that's final!'

His face tightened. 'You don't mean that.'

'I do.'

'I thought you cared about me.'

'I thought *you* cared about *me*,' she countered, tears smarting her eyes. 'But you don't. Tell me, Jack. What took you so long to answer the phone last night? Have a visitor, did you?'

And there it was. That momentary flicker in his eyes.

Courtney paled. 'My God, Superbitch *was* there, wasn't she? You were in bed with her when I rang.'

'Of course I wasn't. Don't be ridiculous.'

Suspicion swiftly gave way to rage, a rage born of pain. 'Ridiculous, am I? I'll show you how ridiculous I am. I want you to turn right round and go back where you came from. Get the hell out of here and out of my life. I'll pay you back every cent, if I have to sell every damned horse I own. And let me tell you this, if I *am* having your baby, you are never going to see it. *Never!*'

Reefing on the reins, she dug her heels in and rode off even more wildly than she'd approached, uncaring of her safety, uncaring of anything. Tears streamed down her face as she jumped fence after fence, not stopping till she'd put plenty of distance between her and Jack, and only halting then because she could no longer see. She stopped she knew not where, slid down off the gelding's sweating back, then leant against him, clutching the saddle and sobbing her heart out.

'And why would a lucky lass like you be crying your eyes out like that?'

Courtney swung round, brushing her hair back from

her blotched face and blinking madly. Sean was leaning against a nearby fence, his dark eyes watching her.

Embarrassment put her immediately on the defensive. She dashed any remaining tears away with the backs of her hands, her chin lifting defiantly. 'Lucky, am I? How in hell do you figure that out?'

'You have this wonderful property. Hundreds of fantastic horses. Two very handy stallions and another who could be anything. On top of that, you'll soon be getting married to a man I hear is crazy about you.'

'Jack? *Crazy* about me?' She laughed. 'You have to be joking. All Jack cares about is himself!'

Sean looked genuinely taken aback. 'Are we talking about the same Jack here?'

'Who else?'

'Sarah said he was a real good bloke.'

'What would she know? She's as silly as Agnes. God, if only my mother was here. She'd understand. She'd be on my side. There again, Mum loved me,' she muttered.

'I love you too.'

Shock sent Courtney's eyes flinging wide. 'What? What did you say?'

'I said I love you too.'

'Are you mad? You don't even know me. Why, you're...you're old enough to be my...'

'Father?' he finished for her, smiling the strangest, saddest smile. 'That's because I am.'

'You are what?'

'Your father.'

She just stared at him, utterly speechless.

'I'm sorry,' he went on. 'I guess I shouldn't have blurted it out like that.'

All Courtney could do was stare at him, suddenly seeing the similarities between them. The eyes. The nose.

The jaw line. 'You're my father,' she said weakly. A statement of fact, not a question.

Courtney felt both dazed and confused. Where was the fury she'd always thought she would feel if her father ever *dared* show up again in her life?

He smiled softly again. 'Please don't be angry with me. I didn't desert you, you know. I always wanted to be a part of your life. But Hilary wouldn't let me. She wouldn't even let me *see* you. And you know your mother,' he added grimly. 'She could be like a brick wall.'

Courtney tried not to go to mush, because for all she knew he was lying. 'Why didn't you apply to the courts for custody rights, then?' she challenged. 'They would have granted you some as my father.'

'I had no proof, and this was before DNA tests, remember? No, that wouldn't have worked. Hilary would have fought me and it would have become ugly.'

'Well, of course Mum would have fought you. You broke her heart, don't you know that? Because of you, my mother *hated* men.'

'Hilary hated men long before I came along. It had something to do with her father rejecting her because she wasn't a lad. Look, I don't know what your mother told you about me, but I can guess. I seduced her because I had my eye on Crosswinds? I made her pregnant to trap her into marriage and get my greedy hands on her property and her horses? Am I close?'

'You left the bit out about being caught with one of the stable girls at the same time as you were sleeping with my mother.'

'Oh, lovely,' he said with a bitter twist to his mouth. 'I wasn't just a gold-digger, I was a serial seducer as well.'

'Are you saying none of this is true? That my mother lied?'

He shrugged. 'Maybe she convinced herself afterwards it was true. Maybe she thought that was the sort of man I was. Yeah, there was a stable girl. And, yeah, we were seeing each other. But that was *before* I slept with your mother. Look, I don't want to paint your mother out badly in your eyes, Courtney, but in all fairness I'd like to be telling my side of the story.'

'All right,' she said, still slightly dazed.

'Yeah, Hilary found me physically attractive, but she wasn't in love with me. She wanted an heir for Crosswinds and she paid me to sleep with her. Two thousand dollars.'

Courtney's eyes bulged.

'A pittance, you'll probably be thinking. But it was a fortune to me at the time. I was twenty-five and stony broke. The money bought me a motorbike.'

As her initial shock waned, Courtney conceded it was possible. It was the sort of thing her mother was capable of doing.

'Hilary chose me the same way she'd have picked a stallion,' Sean added bitterly. 'She told me I had all the right genes she wanted to pass on to her son. Good looking. Well-built. Nice eyes. And I was great with horses. Fearless, she said. She liked that most of all. She believed my being half-gypsy meant horses were in my blood, and my children would have that same blood. Which, I have to admit, turned out to be right. You can ride, lass. And you're fearless. Your mother got what she wanted in that, even if you did turn out to be a lass instead of a lad.'

Courtney couldn't help being fascinated by Sean's story. It was so bizarre it just had to be true. 'You're really half-gypsy?'

'Romany. On my father's side. My mother was Irish. My parents never married. I carry my mother's surname. My father used to leave her with regular monotony, only coming back when he needed a roof over his head, or some money, or some sex. My mother was besotted with him, but he was a wanderer.'

'If what you say about my conception is true,' Courtney said, 'why would you think my mother would ever let you have anything to do with raising me in the first place? You must have known she'd get rid of you once she was pregnant.'

Sean sighed. 'That was my plan too, at the start of things. I reckoned on one night and I'd soon be out of there with my two grand. But it didn't work out quite that way. Hilary was not a young woman. It took months before she fell. And by then things had changed. I fell in love with her.'

'But she was twenty years older than you!' Courtney protested. 'And hardly a beautiful woman.'

'I know that. But it was strange. After a while, I didn't notice any of that. She had a damned good body and she was very passionate. In the end, I couldn't stay away from her. When she finally told me she was expecting, I asked her to marry me.'

'My God! And what did she say?'

'She laughed, then fired me, with no references. You can imagine how I felt. I argued with her. I pleaded. I even made love to her one last time in some mad attempt to reach her. And I thought I had. She was…well, she was a wee bit upset afterwards. But then, suddenly, it was like she brought down some hard shell over her feelings. She turned on me, warning me that I had no real proof I was her baby's father, and that if I ever made any demands on her, or the child, I would regret it till my dying day. So I left, drove off on my well-earned motor bike. But not for her. For *you*,' he insisted, his dark eyes intense.

Courtney sucked in a deep breath, then let it out in a slow, shuddering sigh. Her father's eyes never left hers for a second.

'There wasn't a day that I didn't think of you,' he insisted, in a voice throbbing with emotion. 'Or wonder what you were like, what you were doing. I tried to keep an eye on you from a distance. I knew Hilary had a girl, and I knew she was a beauty. I used to hang around Queenswood, hoping for a glimpse of you. But it never happened, and in the end I had to get away. Right away. So I went to other states to work. Even then I used to hear things about Hilary Cross. She was a woman people talked about. When I found out she'd bought Goldplated, it bothered me. I didn't much care that *she'd* been cheated, but I cared for you. That horse was part of your inheritance. When I heard she'd died, I just had to come and help my little girl.'

Emotion mushroomed up from Courtney's heart like an atomic cloud, clogging her throat. 'That was very kind of you,' she managed. 'Thank you.'

'I didn't mean to tell you I was your father. I don't expect anything from you. I understand you don't know me, and couldn't possibly love me...'

Tears actually came into his eyes.

Courtney wasn't sure who made the first move, but seconds later they were in each other's arms, hugging and weeping.

'Oh, lass...lass,' he cried.

She couldn't speak. She just clung to him.

'So this is what's been going on since Jack went away. Courtney Cross, I'm ashamed of you!'

CHAPTER SIXTEEN

LOIS could hardly believe her eyes. She'd been shocked earlier this week when Jack had rung and announced he and Courtney had fallen in love and were getting married. But, once she'd got used to the idea, she'd thought they were a great match and their marriage the answer to everyone's prayers, hers included.

So she'd been doubly shocked on arriving at Crosswinds a little while ago to find that Jack was already in the process of leaving again, saying Courtney believed he'd been sleeping with Katrina while he was in Sydney and had told him to get lost, so he was going to, as soon as he'd unloaded everything.

Now she was triple-shocked to find Courtney in the arms of another man, making her accusation of Jack being unfaithful look very hypocritical indeed!

'This isn't what it looks like,' Courtney said shakily on pulling out of the stranger's close embrace.

Scepticism was Lois's first reaction once she got a good look at Courtney's bit on the side. This was a seriously sexy-looking guy, despite the fact he had to be well over forty.

'I'm not Courtney's lover, Ms Wymouth,' the sexy stranger said firmly.

Lois could not decide whether to be annoyed that he recognised her. Or flattered. 'Oh, really?'

'He's not,' Courtney insisted, her cheeks as red as her eyes. 'He's my father.'

Lois didn't usually gape. But this time she did.

173

'I...I didn't know till today,' Courtney went on, more flustered than Lois had ever seen her. 'Sean's been here this past week, helping us with Goldplated. You see he and Mum...they...oh, it's such a long story!'

'Too long to tell me now,' Lois said swiftly. 'In a few minutes Jack will be doing what you told him to do earlier. Are you quite sure that's what you want? Because, if it isn't, you'll have to hurry to stop him from leaving.'

Courtney stiffened. 'I don't care if he does leave. He doesn't love me. He still loves Katrina.'

'What a load of old rubbish. Jack doesn't love her. He loves you. He told me so himself.'

'He was just saying that. It's the story we agreed upon to tell everyone.'

Lois felt like slapping the silly little fool. 'You think I can't tell the difference between a made-up story and the truth? The man's crazy about you. I ought to know. I've spent the last few days being dragged from shop to shop whilst he bought you everything under the sun for your wedding. Rings. Clothes. Shoes. Lingerie. Perfume. No man goes to that much trouble for a woman he doesn't love. He told me he knows how busy you are up here at the moment and he wants everything to be absolutely perfect for you.'

'That's all very romantic-sounding, Lois,' the girl still argued, 'but nothing you've said changes anything. It's a game Jack's playing. Just a game. He's playing perfect fiancé. But he's not perfect. He was in bed with his ex-girlfriend last night. I know it.'

'He said that was what you thought, but it's not true. She was there at the house, admittedly, but she just showed up out of the blue and insisted on talking to him. He said he heard her out then sent her away again. He swears he never touched her. He said he can't stand a bar of her any more.'

'Well, he would, wouldn't he? He wants our marriage to go ahead.'

'Why would he want that, if he still loved Katrina?' Lois pointed out logically.

'Why? Because of the baby, that's why!'

'The baby!' both Lois and Sean exclaimed at once.

Sean turned Courtney to face him. 'You're having Jack's baby?'

'I…I might be. I don't know yet. But, yes…it's on the cards.'

His dark eyes blazed. 'And you're sending him *away*?'

'He…he doesn't love me, Dad,' Courtney cried. 'I can't bear it if he doesn't love me.'

'Oh daughter, daughter, don't do what your mother did. Don't send Jack away without talking things out with him. He might not love you as much as you love him, but he very well might. He might love you even more. You'll never know if you don't find out. You told me earlier your mother loved me. If she did, then she never said so. Maybe she was afraid to. Maybe she thought I was too young. Or maybe—like you with Jack—she thought I didn't love her back. If only she'd been honest with me, we might have married, or at least come to some kind of understanding, and I wouldn't have lost all those years of being your father. So for your baby's sake, if no one else's, go to your Jack and talk to him. Tell him how much you love him.'

'I…I can't,' she wailed, her face anguished.

'You *can't*? You, Courtney Cross, the most fearless lass I've ever known, *can't* tell a man she loves him? I've never heard so much balderdash in all my life. Now,

get yourself up to the house before your man gets away.
And don't walk. *Ride!*'

Lois was amazed at the man's strength. For someone
not all that tall or that big, he hoisted Courtney up into
the saddle as if she was a feather.

Great hands, Lois thought as she watched him. Great
eyes. Great buns too.

I wonder if he needs a job...

Courtney's head spun as she rode towards the house, her
heart pounding along with the horse's hooves. Too many
emotions were see-sawing through her. Too many contradictory thoughts.

*Jack doesn't love me. I know he doesn't. How could
he? How could any man?*

Yet Lois seemed so sure...

And then there was what Sean had just said to her.

*You don't really want to end up like your mother, do
you?*

She kicked the horse into a faster gallop and rounded
the last corner, which brought the house into view, only
to see Jack climbing in behind the wheel of the red sports
car.

'Jack, *wait!*' she called out. But he must have gunned
the engine at that moment for he didn't hear her. With a
spray of gravel, the car was off, and gone.

She took off after him, but the car was too fast for her.
Way too fast.

She'd never catch him, not even if she cut across the
yards. Yet she had to try, didn't she? She couldn't just
give up now!

It was madness, the speed at which she started taking
the fences. The horse only had to put one foot wrong and
they would fall.

The thought of actually losing Jack's baby, a baby she didn't even know she'd conceived as yet, jolted her so much that she immediately reined the horse in, and just watched Jack drive away. She watched till there were no specks of red through the trees. Watched till all the dust his car kicked up had dissipated and there was nothing left to show that he'd ever been there, nothing but a child, perhaps, already growing inside her.

It was a falsely calm Courtney that returned to the house and walked slowly upstairs to her room, where she found several boxes and plastic bags dumped on her bed.

With dry eyes, she opened them one by one, then carried them into the guest room where she laid them all out on the velvet spread. The lovely white lace suit. The matching picture-hat. The pearl high heels. The luxurious and quite sexy underwear. The huge bottle of perfume. The velvet box of matching wedding rings. And, last but not least, the beautiful ruby and diamond engagement ring.

She stared at that ring for a long time before clutching it to her heart and slowly sinking to the floor by the bed, her head coming to rest against one of the posts. She didn't cry. She was beyond tears. Way, way beyond.

She heard Agnes's footsteps on the staircase, and willed her not to come in to the room.

She didn't. It was Jack who walked in. Jack who came over and lifted her up into his arms.

'Now, you listen to me,' he said, cupping her face and looking deep into her eyes. 'I love you, Courtney Cross. *You*, not Katrina. And I know you love me. So don't you ever tell me to go away again. Because I'm not going to. I'm not going to leave you ever again. We're going to be married and we're going to have babies together. And we're going to live happily ever after.'

And, with that, he folded her against his huge chest, crushing her close, his lips in her hair.

'Now tell me you love me,' he insisted. 'No waffle. No bulldust. Just say, I love you, Jack.'

'I love you, Jack,' she choked out, still clutching the ruby ring to her heart.

He sighed. 'About time, too.'

EPILOGUE

'GUESS who I just saw in the ladies',' Courtney whispered to Jack on returning to the members' stand.

'Don't tell me,' he said drily. 'Katrina.'

'Got it in one! Would you believe she didn't recognise me at first with my glad rags on?' Courtney was wearing the glorious white lace bridal suit Jack had bought her, complete with picture-hat. Lois had suggested it, saying that such an outfit wouldn't look at all out of place at the Melbourne Cup meeting.

Now that she was there, Courtney had to agree, and she did look pretty good, even if she had to say so herself. Perhaps even better than on her wedding day, her figure having filled out somewhat now that she was three months pregnant. Did she have a bust, or what!

'And?' Jack probed.

'Once she realised who I was, she gave me a panicky look, then disappeared like a shot.'

'Good to see she took heed of what I told her that night.'

Courtney glanced up at her handsome husband, who was looking simply splendid in a light grey suit. 'Which was what, exactly? I never did ask you.' It was just curiosity asking. Courtney hadn't doubted Jack's love since the day he came back for her.

'After she came out with all that drivel about realising she'd made a mistake and that she still loved me, I told her she had absolutely no idea what love was, that all she loved was her own selfish self. I warned her that if she was ever to show up on my doorstep again, or ring me or try to contact me or do anything to destroy my relationship with you, then she had better emigrate. Fast! Then I told her to get her pathetic hide back to her husband, because soon her inner ugliness would show in her face and then no man would want her, not even one as stupid and shallow as George.'

'And did she? Go back to him?'

'I gather she did, which is why she's here today.'

'My God, her husband's not presenting the Melbourne Cup, is he?' As much as she wasn't undermined by Katrina any more, the less she saw of the woman, the better.

'No,' Jack confirmed.

Courtney sighed her relief. 'Not that we'll have to worry about that,' she went on. 'I mean, Lois has done wonders just getting Big Brutus into the race today. His win last week in the Werribee Cup was simply fantastic, but this race is so hard. As much as I'd be over the moon if he won, I can't seriously get my hopes up. A place would be lovely, though.'

'Mmm,' was all Jack said, and Courtney looked at him.

'You haven't put too much money on, have you, Jack?'

'What? Who, me? No, no...not all that much.'

'Mmm. Then why are you looking so worried all of a sudden?'

'I...er...well, the thing is, Courtney. I backed the darned horse each way. I hope you don't think I'm a wimp.'

She laughed. Him? A wimp? Her tower of strength? Her magnificent man? 'Don't be silly, Jack. Big Brutus is forty to one. And this is the Melbourne Cup. Everyone bets each way in the Melbourne Cup.'

'Not everyone,' he mumbled.

'What? What are you talking about?'

'Nothing. It's just that Agnes and Bill asked me to put a bet on for them both. And they didn't want it each way.'

'Yes, but they only bet small, whilst you, Jack, are a serious gambler.'

'*Me?*' He looked surprised.

'Yes, you. Only a serious gambler would have married someone like me.'

His eyes softened on her and Courtney smiled. She loved it when he looked at her like that. She loved everything about Jack. He was a wonderfully kind and big-spirited man and she couldn't wait till their baby was born. She rather hoped they'd have a son, but she wasn't stressing over it. A daughter would be just as welcome. Jack continued to insist he didn't mind either way, but she suspected he might like a little boy first.

A hush came over the crowd as it did in those tense moments in the Cup after the field had taken their place and the starter was on his stand, watching and waiting till the horses settled before he pressed the bell and the gates sprang open.

Surprisingly, Courtney wasn't as nervous as she'd been the week before, when she'd watched the Werribee Cup on the TV. Just getting Big Brutus into the Cup had satisfied her, and hopefully satisfied her mother, if she was up there, watching.

Courtney had felt very angry with her mother for quite a while after what Sean had told her, but it was hard to stay angry with a dead woman, especially when that woman was your mother. Besides, after all Courtney had recently been through, she realised it was impossible to judge another person's actions. Who knew what inner demons had fashioned her mother's thoughts and actions?

The roar of the crowd had her snapping back to the race. They were off!

Courtney stretched up on tiptoe and searched for Big Brutus's colours, amazed to find them not where she'd been looking, at the tail of the field, but out in front.

'My God, he's leading!' she gasped as they flashed past the post the first time.

Courtney shot a frowning glance over at Lois, who was standing on the other side of Jack, but Lois's eyes were glued on the track and she was clutching the arm of the man on the other side of her, a very handsome man in a very sexy black suit.

Courtney smiled an amused smile. Sean hadn't wanted to come to Melbourne with them. He'd had to be persuaded, both into the trip and the suit. But the moment he'd seen Lois, dressed fit to kill today, he'd been bewitched, and slightly bewildered, Courtney thought. Lois in race-day mode was a hard force to resist.

'He's gone further in front,' Jack groaned, and Courtney's eyes reefed back to the track.

He certainly had. Three lengths, in fact. Her stomach began to churn now as the butterflies of hope invaded. It wasn't impossible for a horse to lead all the way in the Cup, she reasoned. It *had* been done. And Big Brutus wasn't carrying much weight.

Still, these were daring tactics. Lois must have told the jockey to do this. He wouldn't have taken it upon his shoulders to ride such a bold race without being instructed to.

They were entering the back straight and Big Brutus went even further in front. Five...six lengths. Yet he was just loping along, his head on his chest.

Emotion welled up in Courtney's chest.

Are you watching this, Mum? This is your horse out there. You bred him. Isn't he just magnificent?

It wasn't till they swung into the straight, with Big Brutus still in front by four lengths, that the combination of hope and exhilaration overwhelmed Courtney. She started jumping up and down, screaming encouragement and instructions at the top of her lungs.

'Go, big boy, go! No, don't whip him. Just ride him. Hands and heels. You can do it, big boy. Not much further now. Yes, that's it. Stretch. Stick your neck out. Don't let them get you. Don't stop. Don't look. You can do it. This is your race. Your year. Your time. Yes, yes, *yes*!' As Big Brutus crossed the line, a gallant neck in front, Courtney threw her hands up into the air in victory.

'He did it, Jack,' she cried, turning to her husband. 'He did it!'

Jack's binoculars dropped back down onto his chest. 'My God, he did,' he rasped, looking a bit green around the gills. 'He really did.'

Courtney laughed, then hugged him.

People began tapping them on the shoulders, congratulating them. It reminded Courtney to do the same to Lois, but when she looked over at Big Brutus's trainer, Lois was otherwise occupied.

Jack's pressing what looked like betting tickets into her hand turned her attention away from her trainer kissing her father.

'What's this?' she asked.

'I found them in a secret drawer in your mother's desk.'

Courtney stared down at the tickets. Each was on Big Brutus to win the Melbourne Cup, placed months before, when Hilary had first entered the horse. Each was for thousands and thousands of dollars, and not for much outlay, either, since his price then had been huge.

'Your mother's insurance policies,' Jack said.

Courtney glanced up. A great big lump on her throat. 'Oh, Jack…'

He nodded. 'I didn't want to tell you, in case the horse lost.'

'You were protecting me,' she said, continually in awe of the many ways Jack showed her his love.

'I didn't want you to think your mother a total fool.' He inclined his head in the direction of where Sean and Lois were still glued together. 'You can't blame her, you know, for not trusting your dad. He was way too young. And way too good-looking. She did what she thought she had to do to survive, Courtney.'

'Yes,' she said, nodding. 'Yes, you're right.'

'Their romance was nothing like ours. We're well matched, you and I. True equals. True partners.'

Courtney knew what he meant. Now that she was secure in Jack's love, she wanted to share everything with him, even Crosswinds. She no longer saw his help as interference. Though he still had absolutely no horse sense.

But he was very smart with money.

'I was thinking, Jack, now that Goldplated's come good and I have all this spare cash, do you think you might like to become Crosswinds' financial manager? I mean…the stud's going to get pretty busy in the coming years, and I'm not going to have as much time once I become a mum.'

He just looked at her. And then he smiled.

'You are a wonderful woman, Courtney Falconer.'

'Yes, I agree. But will you?'

He grinned. 'I'd love to.'

Lois finally descended upon them, looking flushed and excited. 'That was simply fantastic, wasn't it?'

'Fantastic,' Courtney returned, not sure if Lois meant the race, or the kiss. 'And so are you, Lois.'

'Oh, no. Big Brutus deserves all the praise. And your mum. She bred him. Shall we go lead him in together?'

'I think the press might grab you first,' Courtney warned.

'Mmm, yes, they probably will. Do I look all right?'

'You look absolutely beautiful,' Sean said by her side, and Lois beamed up at him.

Courtney and Jack exchanged looks, their eyes dancing with knowing amusement.

'Guess who's not going to go to bed alone tonight?' Jack whispered in Courtney's ear as they pushed their way through the crowd.

'Golly. Who?'

'You, you sexy thing.'

Courtney's eighteen-week ultrasound showed she was having a boy. Nicholas Preston Falconer was born five days late on the seventh of May, weighing nine pounds five ounces. Agnes delivered him, with Jack her willing but slightly anxious helper. Sean and Lois were married the same day the baby was christened.

Jane Porter grew up on a diet of Mills & Boon®
romances, reading late at night under the covers so her
mother wouldn't see! She wrote her first book at age
eight and spent many of her high school and college
years living abroad, immersing herself in other cultures
and continuing to read voraciously. Now, Jane has
settled down in rugged Seattle, Washington, with her
gorgeous husband and two sons. Jane loves to hear from
her readers. You can write to her at PO Box 524,
Bellevue, WA 98009, USA. Or visit her website at
www.janeporter.com

**Don't miss the next intense and engaging story
by Jane Porter:
THE SHEIKH'S VIRGIN
On sale May 2005, in Modern Romance™!**

CHRISTOS'S PROMISE
by
Jane Porter

CHAPTER ONE

"You'D rather remain locked here in the convent than marry me?"

Disbelief echoed in Christos Pateras's voice. How could this girl—woman, actually, although she didn't look a bit like the twenty-five her father claimed she was—prefer living in the spartan convent over marrying him?

He was no barbarian. Compared to the Greek men she'd been raised with, he was downright civilized.

"You had my answer earlier," Alysia Lemos retorted coolly. "You needn't have wasted your time coming here."

He turned his back on the anxious nun hovering in the background, intentionally making it harder for her to hear. The abbess might have insisted on providing Alysia with a chaperone, but that didn't mean the sister needed to be privy to the conversation.

"You told your father no," Christos answered, his tone mild, deceptively so. "You didn't tell *me* no." He rarely raised his voice. He didn't need to. His size and authority generally were persuasive enough.

But Alysia Lemos's fine dark eyebrows only arched higher. "Some women might find such persistence flattering. I don't."

"So, your answer is…?"

5

Alysia's incredulous laughter contrasted sharply with the dark blaze in her eyes. "I know you're an American, but surely you can't be this much of an idiot!"

Her cutting dismissal might have crushed a man of lesser ego, but he wasn't just any man, and Miss Lemos wasn't just any woman. He needed her. He wasn't going to leave Oinoussai without her. "You dislike Americans?"

"Not all."

"Good. That should help ease the transition when we move to New York."

Her eyes met his, the dark irises all the more arresting against her sudden pallor. "I'm not moving. And I'd never agree to an arranged marriage."

He dismissed this along with her other protestations. "In case you're worried, I consider myself Greek. My parents were born here, on Oinoussai. They still call this home."

"Oh, happy people, they."

He almost smiled. No wonder her father, Darius, was feeling desperate. She was not an eager bride-to-be. "I don't know if they'll be happy with you for a daughter-in-law, but they'll adjust."

Bands of color burned along the curve of her cheek. "I'm sure your mother dotes on you."

"Endlessly. But then, most Greek mothers live for their sons."

"While daughters are disposable."

He gave no indication that he'd heard the hurt in her voice, the small wobble in her breath as she spat the bitter words. "Not mine. My daughters will be cherished."

At thirty-seven, he needed a wife, and Darius Lemos needed a husband for his wayward daughter. This was no love match, but a match made in a bank in Switzerland. "I'm an only child, the last of the Pateras in my branch of the family. I've promised my parents a grandchild before my thirty-ninth birthday, and I shall deliver."

"No, you hope *I'll* deliver!"

He bit the inside of his cheek to keep from smiling. "I stand corrected."

Alysia's hands balled. She longed to smack his smirk right off his gorgeous, arrogant face. She'd never met a man more sure of himself than he. Except for her father, that is.

She swallowed convulsively, her stomach heaving, as she struggled to understand why her father had reached across the Atlantic for a husband for her. Her father despised the new rich. Her father must be feeling desperate. Well, so was she. He was practically auctioning her off to the highest bidder, his sole heir up for grabs.

Hot tears rushed to her eyes but she held them back. Her mother would never have let her father do this.

"There are worse bridegrooms, Miss Lemos."

She felt the irony but couldn't even smile. "A husband is a husband, and I don't want one."

"Most women want to be married. It's the desire of every Greek woman."

"I'm not most women."

He laughed almost unkindly. "So say you, but I've learned one woman is not so different from another. You all have agendas—"

"And you don't?"

"Mine isn't hidden. I want children. I need children." He scrutinized her as though she were horseflesh. "You're young. You'd be an excellent mother."

She winced. "I don't want to be a mother."

He shrugged, unconcerned. "We can marry today. Here. It'll just be us. Your father is unavailable, I'm afraid."

"What a shame."

His mouth quirked faintly, revealing surprise, even intrigue. "You speak like a sailor."

"The closest I've come to my father's business."

"You're interested in business?"

"I'm interested in my competition." The industry her father loved above all else. Nothing came between him and his ships. Nothing had ever been allowed to interfere with the great Lemos fortune. Not her mother. Certainly not herself.

"I think the business would bore you," he said after a moment, jamming his hands into trouser pockets. "It's talks. Contracts. Number crunching. Tedious stuff."

"For my small brain?"

His eyes glimmered, her mocking tone had made him smile. "You shouldn't listen to everything your father says," he cheerfully drawled. "Only the good things about me."

She could easily have slapped his cheeky face. She knew exactly why Christos Pateras was marrying her. He wanted her dowry. Her dowry and her father's shipping interests. When Darius passed away, Christos would inherit Lemos's empire. "You're overly confident."

"So say my critics."

"You have many?"

"Legions."

She offered him her profile, grinding her teeth together. This was a joke to him and he toyed with her like a cat with a mouse. She struggled to contain her temper, her smooth jaw tightening. "You're mad if you think I'll marry you."

"Your father has already consented to the marriage. The dowry has changed hands—"

"Change it back!"

"Can't do that. I need you too much."

She turned her head, her brilliant gaze catching his. "Despite what you both think, I am neither mindless, nor spineless. Since you appear to have difficulty with your hearing, let me say it again. I will not marry you, Mr. Pateras. I will never marry you, Mr. Pateras. I'd rather grow old and gray in this convent than take your name, Mr. Pateras."

Christos rocked back on his heels and fought his desire to smile. Her father said she was difficult but he hadn't mentioned his daughter's intelligence, or spirit. There was a difference between difficult and

spirited. Difficult was unpleasant. Spirited was something a man quite enjoyed. Like a spirited horse, a
spirited chase, a spirited game of tennis. But nothing
was more appealing than a spirited woman. "Oh, I
think I quite like you," he murmured softly.

"The feeling isn't mutual."

His lips curved, and he watched as she threw her
head back, dark eyes challenging him.

With the sunlight washing her face, he suddenly
realized her eyes weren't brown at all, but blue. A
mysterious, dark blue. Like the sky at night. Like the
Aegean Sea before a storm. Honey wheat hair and
Aegean eyes. She looked remarkably like the pictures
he'd seen of her half-English, half-Greek mother, a
woman considered to be one of the great beauties of
her time.

"Hopefully you'll grow to tolerate me. It'd make
conjugal life…bearable."

A pulse beat wildly at the base of her throat. But
her eyes splintered anger, passion, denial. She was
going to fight him, tooth and nail. "I'd sooner let
you put a bit in my mouth and saddle on my back."

"Now that could be tempting."

Her cheeks darkened to a dusky pink, her gorgeous
coloring a result of the Greek-English heritage. Blue
eyes, sun-streaked hair, a hint of gold in her complexion. He felt desire, and possession. She was his.
She just didn't know it yet.

Alysia fled to a distant corner of the walled garden,
arms crossed over her chest, breasts rising and falling
with her quick, shallow breathing.

He followed more slowly, not wanting to push her too hard. At least not yet. Furtively he touched the breast pocket of his coat, feeling the crisp edges of the morning's newspaper. She wouldn't like the press clipping. He was the first to admit it was a power play, and underhanded, but Christos wasn't about to lose this deal.

He'd made a promise to his parents that he'd bring fortune to his beleaguered branch of the family, and every decision he'd made since then had been in the pursuit of that goal. Since he'd made that promise, the family fortunes had grown into a different league. Very different.

She must have felt him approach. "Have you no ethics?" Her low-pitched voice vibrated with emotion. "How can you marry a woman against her will?"

"It wouldn't be against your will. You have a choice."

"You disgust me!"

"Then go back inside. Call the nun over. She's dying to be part of the conversation."

Alysia glanced over her shoulder, spotted the nun and pressed her lips together. "You're enjoying this."

"It's my wedding day. What's not to enjoy?"

She took another step away, sinking onto a polished marble bench. He walked around the bench to face her. "Alysia, your father has sworn to leave you here until we exchange vows. Doesn't that worry you?"

"No. You are not the first man I've refused, and dare I say, nor the last. I've been here nearly a year, and the sisters have been wonderful. Quite frankly, I've begun to think of the convent as home."

The convent as home? He didn't believe her, not for a minute. Despite her refined beauty—the high, fine cheekbones, the elegant curve of her brow—her eyes, those indigo-blue eyes, smoldered with secrets.

She did not belong in the convent's simple brown smock any more than he belonged in priestly robes. And God knew he did not belong in priestly robes.

Christos felt a sudden wave of sympathy for her, but not enough to walk away from the playing table. No, he never walked away from the playing table, not that he played cards. He gambled in other ways. Daring, breathtaking power plays in the Greek shipping-industry which so far had resulted in staggering financial gain. He'd been wildly successful by anyone's standards.

"Your home, Alysia, will be with me. I've picked you. You are part of my plan. And once I put a plan into action, I don't give up. I never quit."

"Those admirable traits would be better applied elsewhere."

"There is no elsewhere. There is no other option. You, our marriage, is the future," he said softly, as a warm breeze blew through the courtyard, loosening a tendril of hair from her demure bun. She didn't attempt to smooth it and the golden-brown tendril floated light as a feather.

He liked the play of sunlight across her shoulders

and face. The sun turned her hair to gold and copper. Flecks of aquamarine shimmered in her eyes.

"I know who you are, Mr. Pateras. I'm not ignorant of your success." Her eyebrows arched. "Shall I tell you what I know?"

"Please. I enjoy my success story."

"A full-blooded Greek, you were born and raised in a middle-class New York suburb. You attended public school, before being accepted to one of the prestigious American Ivy League colleges."

"Yale," he supplied.

"Which is quite good," she agreed. "But why not Harvard? Harvard is supposed to be the best."

"Harvard is for old money."

"That's right. Your father left Oinoussai broke and in disgrace."

"Not disgraced. Just poor. Hopeful that there would a better life elsewhere."

"Your father worked in the shipyards."

"He was a welder," Christos answered evenly, hiding the depth of his emotions. He was fiercely loyal to his parents, but particularly to his father. His father's piety, unwavering morals and devotion to family had sustained them during times of great financial hardship. And there had been hardship, tremendous hardship, not to mention ostracism in the close-knit Greek-American community.

Quickly, before she could probe further, he turned the spotlight on her. "And your father, Alysia, inherited his millions. You've never lacked for anything. You have no idea what 'poor' means."

"But you aren't poor anymore, Mr. Pateras. You now own as many ships as Britain's entire merchant fleet. Despite your humble origins, it shouldn't be difficult to find a bride a...trifle...more eager to accept your proposal."

"I can't find another Darius Lemos."

"So in reality you're marrying my father."

She was smart. He smiled faintly, again amused by the contradiction between her serene exterior and fiery interior. He found himself suddenly wondering what she'd be like in bed. Passionate as hell, probably.

He watched the shimmering golden-brown tendril dance across her cheek, caress her ear, and Christos felt a sudden urge to follow the tendril with his tongue, drawing the same tantalizing path from her cheekbone to her jaw, from her jaw to the hollow beneath her earlobe.

His body tightened, desire stirring. He'd enjoy being married to a woman like this. Procreation would be a pleasure.

Alysia leaned back on the bench, her brown shift outlining her small breasts, her dark lashes lowering to conceal her expression. "How well do you know my father?"

"Well enough to know what he is."

She allowed herself a small smile, and Christos noticed the flash of dimple to the left of her full mouth. He'd taste that, too, after the wedding.

"My father must be quite pleased to have you in his back pocket. I can quite picture him, rubbing his hands together, chuckling gleefully.'' Her head cocked, her lashes lifted, revealing the dark sapphire irises. ''He did rub his hands after you made your deal, didn't he?''

Her tone, her voice, her eyes. He wanted her.

Abruptly he leaned forward, captured the coil of hair at her nape in his hand. Her eyes widened as his fingers tightened in her hair seconds before he covered her mouth with his.

Alysia inhaled as his lips touched hers, and he traced the soft outline of her lips with his tongue. He didn't miss her gasp, or the sudden softness in her mouth.

His own body hardened, blood surging. From the distance he heard a cough. The nun! Wouldn't do to get thrown out of here just yet.

Slowly he released her. ''You taste beautiful.''

Alysia paled and dragged the back of her hand across her soft mouth, as if to rub away the imprint of his lips. ''Try that again and I shall send for the abbess!''

He placed his foot on the bench, on the outside of her thigh. He felt the tremor in her body. ''And say what, sweet Alysia? That your husband kissed you?''

''We are not married! We're not even engaged.''

''But soon shall be.'' He gazed at her exposed collarbone and the rise of fabric at her breasts. ''Do you like wagers?''

She visibly shuddered. ''No. I never gamble.''

''That's admirable. But I like bets, and I like these

odds. You see, Alysia, I know more about *you* than you think.''

He caught her incredulous expression, and felt a stab of satisfaction. ''You won an academic scholarship at seventeen to an art school in Paris. You lived in a garret with a dozen other want-to-be artists, a rather bohemian lifestyle with small children running underfoot. When money ran out, you, like the others, did odd jobs. One summer you worked as a housekeeper. You did a stint in a bakery. Your longest job was as a nanny for a designer and his family.''

''They were respectable jobs,'' she said faintly, blood draining from her face.

''Very respectable, but quite a change from life with a silver spoon in your mouth.''

''Is there a point to this?''

His smile faded and he leaned forward, trapping her between his knee and chest. ''You've spent eight years of your life trying to escape your father.''

Her lips parted but no sound came out.

He watched her closely, reading every flicker in her eyes. ''For a while, you were free. You painted, you traveled, you enjoyed an interesting circle of friends. But then you became ill, and your obliging father placed you in a hospital in Bern. Since then, he's owned you, body and soul.''

''Body, maybe, but not my soul. Never my soul!''

Again the fire, the spirited defiance. He felt a kinship with her that he felt with few women. He softened his tone, appealing to her intellect. ''Think about it, Alysia. In Greece you're powerless. Your father is the head of the household, the absolute authority. He has the right to choose your husband. He has the right to leave you locked up here. He has the right to make your life miserable."

"I'm no prisoner here."

"Then why don't you leave?"

She held her breath, exquisitely attentive, her eyes enormous, her lips compressed.

"Now, if I were your husband," he concluded after the briefest hesitation, "you could leave. Today. Right away. You'd finally be free."

She didn't speak for a moment, studying him with the same intentness with which she listened. After a moment she exhaled. "Greek wives are never free!"

"No, maybe not the way you think of it. But I'd permit you to travel, to pursue hobbies that interested you, to make friends of your own choosing." He shrugged. "You could even paint again."

"I don't paint anymore."

"But you could. I've heard you were quite good."

She suddenly laughed, her voice pitched low, her body nearly trembling with tension. She wrapped her arms across her chest, a makeshift cape, a protective embrace. "You must want my father's ships very much!"

Christos felt a wave of bittersweet emotion, unlike anything he'd ever felt before. He saw himself exactly as he was. Driven, calculating, proudly self-serving. And this woman, this lovely refined young woman, knew she mattered only in business terms.

Her worth was her name. Her value lay in her dowry. For a split second he hated the system and he hated himself and then he ruthlessly pushed his objection aside.

He would have her.

Alysia slipped from beneath his arm, taking several steps away. She walked to the edge of the herb garden and knelt at the flowering lavender. "Ships," she whispered, breaking off a purple stalk. "I hate them."

She carried the tuft of lavender to her nose, smelling it.

"And I love them," he answered, thinking she should have been a painting.

The bend of her neck, the creamy nape, the shimmering coil of hair the color of wild honey, the sun's golden caress.

He wanted this woman. Deal or no.

She crumpled the lavender stalk in her fist. "Mr. Pateras, has it crossed your mind to ask *why* a man as wealthy as my father must give away his fortune in order to get his daughter off his hands?"

The sunlight shone warm and gold on her head. The breeze loosened yet another shimmering tendril.

"I'm damaged goods, Mr. Pateras. My father couldn't give me away to a local Greek suitor, even if he tried."

More damaged than he'd ever know, Alysia acknowledged bleakly, clutching the broken lavender stalk in her palm. Unwillingly memories of the Swiss sanatorium came to mind. She'd spent nearly fourteen months there, all of her twenty-first year, before her mother came, rescuing her and helping her find a small flat in Geneva.

Alysia had liked Geneva. No bad memories there.

And for nearly two years she'd lived quietly, happily, content with her job in a small clothing shop, finding safety in her simple flat. Weekly she rang up her mother in Oinoussai and they chatted about inconsequential matters, the kind of conversation that doesn't challenge but soothes.

Her mother never discussed the sanatorium with her, nor Paris. Alysia never asked about her father. But they understood each other and knew the other's pain.

Alysia would never have returned to Greece, or her father's house, if it hadn't been for her mother's cancer.

The mournful toll of bells stirred Alysia, and she tensed, lashes lowering, mouth compressing, finding the bells an intolerable reminder of her mother's death and funeral.

The bells continued to ring, their tolling like nails scratching down a blackboard, sharp, grating. Oh, how she hated it here! The sisters had done everything they could to comfort her, and befriend her, but Alysia couldn't bear another day of bells and prayers and silence.

She didn't want to be reminded of her losses. She wanted to just get on with the living.

Sister Elena, a dour-faced nun with a heart of gold, signaled it was time to return inside.

Alysia felt a swell of panic, desperation making her light-headed. Suddenly she couldn't bear to leave the garden, or the promise of freedom.

As if sensing her reluctance, Christos extended a hand in her direction. "You don't have to go in. You could leave with me instead."

It was almost as if he could feel her weakening, sense her confusion. His tone gentled yet again. "Leave with me today and you'll have a fresh start, lead a different life. Everything would be exciting and new."

He was teasing her, toying with her, and she longed for the freedom even as she shrank from the bargain.

She could leave the convent if she went as his wife.

She could escape her father if she bound herself to this stranger.

"You're not afraid of me?" she asked, turning from Sister Elena's worried gaze to the darkly handsome American Greek standing just a foot away.

"Should I be?"

"I know my father must have mentioned my... health." She gritted against the sting of the words, each like a drop of poison on her tongue. Unwilling tears burned at the back of her eyes.

"He mentioned you hadn't been well a few years ago, but he assured me you're well now. And you look well. Quite well, if rather too thin, as a matter of fact."

Her lips curved into a small, cold self-mocking smile. "Looks can be deceiving."

Christos Pateras shrugged. "My first seven ships were damaged. I stripped them to the hull, refurbished each from bow to stern. Within a year my ships made me my first million. It's been ten years. They're still the workhorses of my fleet."

She envisioned him stripping her bare and attempting to make something of her. The vivid picture shocked and frightened her. It'd been years and years since she'd been intimate with a man, and this man, was nothing like her teenage lovers.

Hating the flush creeping through her cheeks, she lifted her chin. "I won't make you any millions."

"You already have."

Stung by his ruthless assessment, she tensed, her slender spine stiffening. "You'll have to give it back. I told you already, I shall never marry."

"*Again,* you mean. You'll never marry *again.*"

She froze where she stood, at the edge of the herb garden, her gaze fixed on the ancient sun dial.

He knew?

"You were married before, when you were still in your teens. He was English, and six years older than you. I believe you met in Paris. Wasn't he a painter, too?"

She turned her head slowly, wide-eyed, torn between horror and fascination at the details of her past. How much more did he know? What else had he been told?

"I won't discuss him, or the marriage, with you,"

she answered huskily. Marrying Jeremy had been a tragic mistake.

"Your father said he was after your fortune."

"And you're not?"

Lights glinted in his dark eyes. It struck her that this man would not be easily managed.

He circled her and she had to tilt her head back to see his expression. Butterflies flitted in her stomach, heightening her anxiety. He was tall, much taller than most men she'd known, and solid, a broad deep chest and muscular arms that filled the sleeves of his suit jacket.

Her nerves were on edge. She felt distinctly at a disadvantage and searched for something, anything, to give her the upperhand—again. "Good Greek men don't want to be the second husbands."

"We've already established I'm not your traditional Greek man. I do what I want, and I do it my way."

CHAPTER TWO

IT STRUCK her then, quite hard, that two could play this game. All she had to do was think like a man.

Christos Pateras wanted her to further his ambitions. He was marrying her to accomplish a goal. This wasn't about love, or emotions. This was a transaction and nothing more.

Why couldn't she approach the marriage the same way? He wanted her dowry; she wanted independence. He wanted an alliance with the Lemos family; she wanted to escape her father.

Greece might be part of a man's world but that didn't mean she had to play by a man's rules.

She sized him up again, assessing the odds. Tall, strong, ridiculously imposing, he exuded authority. Could she marry him and then slip away?

No more Alysia Lemos, poor little rich girl, but an ordinary woman with ordinary dreams. Like a small house in the country. A vegetable garden. An orchard of apple trees.

She stole a second glance at Christos's rugged profile, noting the long, straight nose, line of cheek, strong clean-shaven jaw. He looked less ruthless than determined. Assertive, not aggressive. If she ran away from him, what would he do?

Chase her down? She doubted it. He'd have too

much pride. He'd probably wait a bit and then quietly annul the marriage. Men like Christos Pateras wouldn't want to advertise their failure.

He turned, caught her eye, his dark gaze holding hers. "Everyone thinks you've already married me."

"How can that be?" she scoffed.

Opening his coat, he drew a folded newspaper from the breast pocket and handed it to her.

Not certain what she was supposed to find, she unfolded the paper and pressed the creased pages flat. Then the headlines jumped out at her, practically screaming the news. Secret Wedding For Lemos Heir.

Anger, indignation, shock flashed through her one after the other as the headlines blinded her. How could he do it? How could he pull a stunt like this?

And then just as quickly as her anger flared, inspiration struck. For the first time in months she saw an open door. All she had to do was walk through it.

Marry him, and walk away.

It was all in place. The husband, the marriage, the motivation. She just needed to go along with the plans and then leave.

Perfect. Her heart did a strange tattoo.

Maybe too perfect. Christos Pateras didn't seize control of the Greek shipping industry by luck. He was smart. No, rumor had it that he was brilliant. A brilliant man wouldn't marry a young woman and then just let her slip away. He'd be prepared. He'd be alert.

She'd have to be very, very careful.

Alarm and eagerness tangled her emotions. She could do this, she could escape him, it was a matter of being just as smart as him.

Her heart began to pound faster and she felt heat creep beneath her skin. Excitement grew but she dampened her enthusiasm, not wanting to overplay her hand or reveal her true intentions.

She frowned, feigning surprise and shock. "You can't be serious."

"It's front page news."

"There's no wedding. How can there be a story?"

"Read it for yourself."

She obliged, skimming the front page story where her father had been quoted as saying he couldn't confirm or deny reports of the secret wedding, only that he knew that Greek-American shipping tycoon, Christos Pateras, had visited Oinoussai in the past several days and had visited his daughter at the convent. Other sources confirmed that Pateras had been seen in town, while another source mentioned the convent as the secret wedding location.

Her father's work, no doubt. The puppet and the puppeteer. Incredible. But this time, she was the puppeteer. She was in control.

She crumpled the paper for show. "You and my father make a spectacular team."

"Your father's idea, not mine."

"No one will believe this drivel."

"Everyone believes it. Media has descended on the harbor. They're expecting to see the blushing

bride and groom board the yacht later this afternoon.''

He looked so damn smug, as if he'd thrown a net
around her, trapping her in his scheme. *Sorry, she
silently apologized, but I win this one. Hands down.*

She was going to marry him. And then she'd leave
him. He could pick up the pieces. The fall-out with
her father wouldn't be her problem. If Christos
Pateras wanted to make deals with her father, then
fine, let him experience her father's wrath firsthand.

Guilt briefly assailed her. Then she ignored the
voice of conscience, reminding herself that Christos
and her father were the same kind of man. Selfish.
Unthinking. Lacking compassion.

Not once during her mother's horrible last year did
her father slow his schedule, put off a meeting,
change his travel plans. He never once attended her
radiation treatments. Never held her hand during the
chemo. Never checked on her at night when she lay
huddled with pain and fear.

Her father acted as if nothing bad had happened,
ignoring the terminal diagnosis as though it were a
spate of bad weather and simply charged ahead with
his plans for new ships, new routes, new alliances.

Damn her father, and damn Christos Pateras.

Alysia knew of no fate worse than that of being a
Greek tycoon's wife.

But she hid all this, focusing instead on her goal.
Independence. Peace. A life far from the wealthy
Greek shipping families. Maybe back to Geneva.
Maybe a little house south of London.

"When would we marry?" she asked, her pulse leaping in anticipation.

"Today. We'd marry here, in the chapel, and then sail this afternoon."

"And just what are your expectations?"

His dark gaze studied her, his expression blank, giving away nothing. "As my wife, you'll travel with me. When I entertain, you shall perform the duties of the hostess. And for my family functions, we'll appear together, behaving like a real couple."

"Versus a business liaison?"

"Precisely."

"For your parents sake?"

"Right, again."

He didn't want to disappoint his parents. She could almost admire him for that. Almost.

But fortunately, she needn't worry about his family, or his expectations. She wouldn't be around long enough to fulfill any such duties. If they married today, this afternoon, she was just hours from freedom, hours from starting a new life for herself far from Greece and the influential Lemos name.

"Anything else?" she demanded coldly, conscious that she could never let Christos Pateras know her intentions. Christos might dress fashionably, move with athletic ease and speak eloquently, but underneath the gorgeous veneer he was the same man as her father. And her father, ruthless, critical, unyielding crushed those close to him, destroying family as indiscriminately as he destroyed friends. No one was safe. No one was exempt.

"I expect us to have a normal relationship." He, too, had become detached, businesslike.

It struck her they'd moved to the negotiation stage. The deal would take place. It was just a matter of formalizing the details. He knew it. She knew it. A bitter taste filled her mouth, but she wouldn't back down now. "Define normal, if you would."

"I expect you to be faithful. Loyal. Honest."

She felt something shift inside of her, another whisper of conscience, but she dismissed it with a small sneer. Men had controlled her all her life. For once she'd take care of herself. "That's it?"

"Should there be more?"

He was testing her, too. He knew there should be more, would be more. They hadn't even discussed the physical aspect of the marriage and it loomed there between them, heavy, forbidding.

"This is a marriage of convenience, yes?" She cast a glance at him before looking too quickly away, but she caught the predatory gleam in his eyes. He wasn't nervous. He seemed to enjoy this.

"Marriages of convenience don't produce children. I need children."

Before she could speak, he continued.

"I'll do my best, Miss Lemos, to ensure you're satisfied. I want you to be happy. It's important we're both fulfilled. Sex is a natural part of life. It should be natural between us."

Fingers of fear stroked her spine, stirring the fine hairs on her nape, even as blood surged to her face, heating her cheeks, creating a frisson of warmth through her limbs. "We hardly know each other, Mr. Pateras."

"Which is why I won't force myself on you. I'm content to wait until some of the newness wears off and we've grown more...comfortable with each other before becoming intimate."

Another surge of heat rushed to her cheeks. His voice had deepened, turning so husky as to hum within her, warm and intimate. For a split second she imagined his body against hers, his mouth against her skin.

The very thought of making love with him made her inhale sharply. Every nerve in her body seemed to be alert, aware of this man and his potent masculinity.

Crossing her arms over her chest, Alysia tried to deny the tingle in her breasts, and the longing to be real again. It'd been forever since she'd felt like a woman.

She wouldn't look at him. "You're willing to commit to a loveless marriage?"

"I'm committing to you."

Oh, to have someone want her, to care for her...

She drew a ragged breath, hope and pain twisting in her heart, seduced by his promise and the warmth in his voice. What would it feel like to be loved by this man?

She drew herself up short. He'd never said anything about love, or wanting her. He wasn't even committing to her. He was committing to the Lemos house, committing to her father, but not to her. How could she allow herself to daydream? Hadn't she learned her lesson by now?

This is how Jeremy had broken through her reserve. This is how she'd offered up her heart. Well, she couldn't, wouldn't, do it again. Experience had to count for something.

Hardening her emotions, she reminded herself that Christos Pateras did not matter. His promises did not matter. The only thing that mattered was escaping the convent and her father's manipulations. It was what her mother would want for her. It was what her mother had wanted for herself.

Glancing up, her gaze settled on the high, whitewashed wall. All convent windows faced inward, overlooking the herb garden and potted citrus trees. None of the windows faced out, no glimpse of the ocean, no picture of the world left behind...

But she hadn't left it behind. Her father had ripped it from her just weeks after her mother's death. There had been no mourning for him. Just business, just money and deals and ships.

A lump filled her throat. For a moment her chest felt raw, tight. "If we are going to do it," she said after a long painful silence, "let's not waste time."

They were married in the briefest of ceremonies in the convent chapel. Rings, exchange of vows, a passionless kiss.

In the back of the limousine, Alysia clenched her hand on her lap, doing her best to ignore the heavy diamond-and-emerald ring weighting her finger.

Christos had already told her it wasn't a family heirloom, three carat diamonds had never been part of his family fortune. No, the ring had been purchased recently, just for her. But she wouldn't wear it long. By this time tomorrow she'd have it off her finger, left behind on a dresser or bathroom counter, she promised herself.

A strange calm filled her. For the first time in years she felt as if she were in control again, acting instead of reacting, making decisions for herself instead of feeling helpless.

With a swift glance at her new husband, she noted Christos Pateras's profile, his strong brow creased, a furrow between his dark eyes. He wore his black hair combed straight back, and yet the cowlick at the temple softened the severity of his hard, proud features.

He'd be surprised—no, furious—when he discovered her gone. He didn't expect her to deceive him. It wouldn't have crossed his mind. Just like a Greek man to assume everything would go according to his plan.

He sat close to her, too close, and she inched across the seat only to have his hard thigh settle against hers again.

She became fixated on the heat passing from his thigh to hers, panic stirring at the unwelcome intimacy. She wasn't ready to be touched by him. Wasn't ready to be touched by anyone.

She scooted closer to the door, pressing herself into the corner, willing herself to shrink in size.

"You're acting like a virgin," he drawled, casting a sardonic look in her direction.

She felt like a virgin. Years and years without being touched, not even a kiss, and now this, to sit thigh to thigh with a stranger, a tall, muscular, imposing stranger who wanted her to bear his children.

Stomach heaving, Alysia pressed trembling fingers against her lips. What had she done? How could she have married him? If she didn't escape him, surely she'd die. Despite her mother's wisdom, despite the gentle counsel of the sisters, Alysia didn't want family. No children, no babies. Ever.

She couldn't ever give Christos Pateras a chance. She wouldn't let him make a move. No opportunities for seduction. First chance she could, she'd leave.

"Relax," Christos uttered flatly. "I'm not going to attack you."

She opened her eyes, glanced at him beneath lowered lashes. He looked grim, distant. Gone was the laughter, the fine creases fanning from his eyes.

The luxury sedan bounced down the narrow mountain road, the street unpaved, lurching across a deep pothole. Despite the seat belt, Alysia practically spilled into Christos's lap. Quickly she righted herself, drawing sharply away. Christos's mouth pressed tighter.

The silence stretched, tension thick. Squirming inwardly, aware that she'd helped create the hostility, Alysia searched for something to say. "You like Oinoussai?"

"It's small."

"Like America."

The corner of his mouth lifted in faint amusement. "Yes, like America." The amusement faded from his eyes, his features hardening again.

She felt his dark gaze settle on her face, studying her as dispassionately as one studied a work of art hanging on a museum wall. "Have you ever been to the States before?" he asked.

"No." She'd always wanted to go, was curious about New York and San Francisco, but she hadn't had time, nor the opportunity. Thanks to her father, she'd been too busy enjoying the special pleasures of the sanatorium and the convent.

"I have a meeting in Cephalonia, which we'll sail to from here. And then I thought we could conclude our honeymoon someplace else, someplace you might find interesting before returning to my home on the East Coast."

Honeymoon. She tensed at the very suggestion. He'd said he wouldn't force himself on her, said he'd be content to wait. Honeymooning conjured up love-making and intimacy and...

She shuddered. This was a mistake. She'd made a mistake. He had to turn the car around, take her back to the convent now.

"We're not going back to the convent," he said, still watching her, dark eyes hooded.

Her head snapped up. She stared at him, shocked that he knew what she'd been thinking.

"My dear Mrs. Pateras, you're not difficult to

read. You wear your emotions on your face, they're all there, right for me to see.''

He tapped her hands, knotted in her lap. ''Try to relax a little, Alysia. I'm not demanding sexual favors tonight. I'm not demanding anything from you just yet. You need time. I need time. Let's try to make this work, learn a little about each other first.''

Angered by his rational tone, finding nothing rational in being coerced into marriage, she lifted her head, temper blazing. ''You want to learn about me? Fine. I'll tell you about me. I hate Greece and I hate Greek men. I hate being treated like a second-class citizen simply because I'm a woman. I hate how money empowers the rich, creating another caste system. I hate business and the ships you treasure. I hate the alliance my father has formed with you because my father detests America and American money—'' she drew a breath, shaking from head to toe.

One of his black eyebrows lifted quizzically. ''Finished?'' he drawled.

''No. I'm not finished. I haven't even started.'' But her outburst had leveled her, and she leaned heavily against the leather upholstery, exhausted, and suddenly silent.

She wasn't used to this, wasn't used to fighting, to speaking her mind. Her father had never allowed her to say anything at all. Her father never even looked at her.

''What else is bothering you?'' Christos persisted, his attention centered on her and nothing but her.

She shook her head, unable to speak another word.

''Perhaps we should leave our philosophic differences for a later date. Those big issues can be overwhelming, hmm?'' He smiled wryly, his expression suddenly human. ''Why don't we start with the small things, the daily routines that give us comfort. For example, breakfast. Coffee. How do you take yours? Milk and sugar?''

She shook her head, eyes dry, gritty, throat thick. ''Black,'' she whispered.

''No sugar?''

She shook her head again. ''And yours? Black?''

''I like a touch of milk in mine.'' He spoke without rancor, the tone friendly, disarmingly friendly. ''Are you an early riser?''

''A night owl.''

''Me, too.''

''Lovely,'' she answered bitingly. ''We should be perfect together.''

His expression remained blank, yet a hint of warmth lurked in his dark eyes. ''A promising beginning, yes, but I do think a week or two alone should help rub some of the edges off, take the newness away. And with that in mind, I've cleared my calendar and after this meeting on Cephalonia, will have the next couple weeks free.''

''How accommodating.''

''I try.''

Her exhaustion fed her fear. She felt a fresh wave of panic hit. What if she couldn't break away? What if he stayed too close, paid too much attention, to allow her to leave? She'd be trapped in this relationship, forced into marriage. The possibility made her almost ill, and a lump lodged in her throat, sealing it closed.

She couldn't afford to wait. She had to escape, and soon. Before boarding the yacht. Before appearing in public together.

He must have sensed her panic because he suddenly lifted her hand, examined the ring on her finger, before kissing the inside of her wrist. "You don't have to hate me."

A tremor coursed through her at the touch of his lips, her blood leaping in her veins. She tried to disengage but his mouth caressed her wrist in another sensitive spot.

"Please don't," she said, pulling at her wrist, attempting to free herself from his clasp.

"You smell like lavender and sunshine."

Anger hardened her voice. "Mr. Pateras, let me go."

He released her arm and she buried her hand in her lap. Her inner wrist burned, the skin scorched, her pulse pounding.

She hadn't realized she'd become so sensitive.

Alysia forcibly turned her attention back to the rocky landscape, watching the rough road as they snaked down the hill, kicking up dust and loose gravel. They were nearing the outskirts of town.

An unwanted thought suddenly crossed her mind. "Will I see my father in town?"

"No. He flew out this morning for a meeting in Athens."

Relief washed over her. At least she wouldn't have to deal with him right now.

"You don't care for him much, do you?" Christos asked, checking his watch and then glancing out the window again.

"No."

"He seems like a decent man."

"If you like maniacally controlling men."

His eyebrows lowered, his brow creasing. "He's tried to do what's best for you."

A lead weight dropped in her stomach. Christos Pateras didn't know the half of it! Her father had never done what's best for her. It'd always been about him.

She could forgive her father many things, but she'd never forgive him for neglecting her mother in the final weeks of her life. As her mother lay dying in that marble mausoleum of a house, Darius never once reached out to her; no acknowledgment of her pain, no interest in bringing closure, no awareness of her needs.

He should have been there for her. He owed that much to her. How could he not have cared?

A lump formed in her throat, and narrowing her eyes, Alysia concentrated very hard on the rocky landscape beyond her closed window.

"I wish I'd had the pleasure of knowing your mother."

The lead weight seemed to swell in size, pressing against her chest, making it hard to breathe. Gritty tears burned at the back of her eyes. "She was beautiful."

"I've seen photographs. She once modeled, didn't she?"

"It was a charity event. My mother was dedicated to her causes. I think if my father had let her, she would have done more." Her voice sounded thick with emotion.

"You must miss her."

Dreadfully, she thought, struggling to maintain her control. She was finding it almost impossible to juggle so many contradictory emotions at one time. The whole last year had been like this, too. The loss of her mother on top of the others...

It was too much. She sometimes didn't know where to go for strength and had to fight very hard to reach inside herself for the courage to continue.

"Your mother liked Greece?" Christos persisted.

"She tolerated it," Alysia answered huskily, patting her shift pocket for a tissue. Her eyes were watering, her nose burned, she felt like an absolute mess. And to top it all off Christos was looking at her with such concern that she felt as though she were covered in cracks, threatening to break in two.

"Too oppressive?" he mused.

"Too hot." She smiled for the first time all afternoon. Mother had hated the heat; she positively wilted in it. "Mum pined for the English grays and cool greens the way some pined for lost love."

Christos laughed softly, his expression surprisingly gentle. But his gentleness would be her undoing.

Alysia stiffened her spine, reminding herself that she couldn't trust his smile, or his warmth. He wasn't just any man; he was a man handpicked by her father and tainted.

Christos Pateras married her for money.

He was as bad, if not worse, than her father.

Flatly, no emotion left, she asked about her things. "Will I have any of my books or photos sent to me? And my wardrobe? What's happened to that?"

"Everything's already been transferred to the yacht. Your entire bedroom was boxed up and put in the ship's storage."

Shock rivaled indignation. "You're quite sure of yourself, aren't you?"

"I had your father's support."

"Obviously. But what I want to know is *how?* And why?" Her father had never liked Americans, and detested foreign money. "Why did he go to you? What made you so special?"

"I had what he needed. Money. Lots of it."

"And what did he give you in exchange?"

Christos's dark eyes gleamed at her, a faint smile playing his lips. "You."

"Aren't you lucky."

He shrugged. "Depends on how you look at it. Anyway, your father is happy. He won't bother you anymore." He turned a smoldering gaze on her. "I won't let him."

She heard the promise in his voice, and a hint of menace, too. For a moment Christos Pateras sounded like a street-boxer, an inner city thug, but then he smiled, a casual, relaxed smile, and she felt herself melt, her chilly insides warming, her fear dissipating ever so slightly. Truthfully she'd welcome a buffer between her and her father. He'd made her life nearly unbearable. She needed to get away.

Elegant whitewashed villas came into view, along with the sparkling harbor waters. The late-afternoon sun illuminated the bay. "There's my yacht," Christos said, leaning forward to point out a breathtaking ship of luxurious proportions.

She leaned forward, too, her breath catching in her throat. The yacht might prove to be just as confining as the convent and it crossed her mind that she might have bitten off more than she could chew.

No, she'd be fine. She'd figured a way out. She simply needed time.

Numerous fishing boats dotted the harbor, as did several yachts, but one moored ship dwarfed all others. The glossy white, sleek design only hinted at the elegant state rooms inside. The yacht would have cost him dearly.

She didn't realize she'd spoken the thought out loud until he chuckled softly, a twisted smile at his lips. "She was expensive, but not half as much as you."

Indignation heated her skin, hot color sweeping through her cheeks. "You didn't buy me, Mr. Pateras, you bought my father!"

But he was right about one thing, Alysia thought darkly as the limousine pulled up to the harbor. The media were out, and out in force. Reporters and photographers crawled all over town, jostling each other to take better position.

They surged forward when the car stopped and she sucked in a panicked breath. All those cameras poised...all the microphones turned on...

"It'll be over in a minute," Christos said, turning to her.

She felt his inspection, his dark eyes examining her face, her dress, her hair. He startled her by reaching up to pluck pins from her hair. The heavy honey mass tumbled down and he combed his fingers through it with unnerving familiarity.

"That's better," he murmured.

Just the touch of his fingers against her brow sent shivers racing through her. Repulsion, she told herself, even as the tight core of her warmed, softened. She didn't want him. Couldn't want him.

But when he tucked one long silky strand behind her ear, his hand caressing the ear, then the tender spot below, her belly ached and her limbs felt terrifyingly weak.

No one had touched her so gently in years.

Her need shocked her. She felt like a woman starved for food and warmth. Helplessly she gazed at him, hating herself for responding to him. "Are you quite finished?" she whispered breathlessly.

"No, not quite," he murmured, before his dark head lowered.

She stiffened as his head dropped, drawing back against the leather upholstery. *No!* No, no, no. He couldn't do this, couldn't kiss her, especially not here, not when she felt like this. Everything was too new, too strange, too crazy.

If he felt her resistance, he ignored it, clasping the back of her head, fingers twining in her long hair. She caught the glint in his dark eyes and a hint of rich, sweet spice. Not vanilla, not cinnamon, but some other fragrance so deep, and familiar, that it tantalized her memory.

His mouth took possession of hers and she breathed him in again, reminded of almonds, sweet baby powder, the heady musk of antique roses...

Somehow it all fit, he, this, the kiss. His mouth, the warmth of his skin, the strength in his arms. Tremor after tremor coursed through her veins, creating an intense craving for more sensation.

Even as his lips parted hers, another electric current shot through her, sparking awareness in every nerve in her body. More, her brain demanded, her lips moving beneath his, her tongue answering the play of his, more, more...

The kiss deepened, and unconsciously she moved against him seeking to prolong the contact, relishing the hard plane of his chest, the warmth of his skin, the heady sweet spice of his cologne.

As his tongue sought the sensitive hollows in her mouth, the inside of her lip, the curve of cheek, blood pooled in her lower belly, her veins pulsing. This felt, he felt...

Incredible.

Muffled voices penetrated her brain. Voices. People.

Her eyes flew open, reality returning.

Cameras pressed against the limousine windows, dozens of lenses, shutters snapping. ''Mr. Pateras, we have company.''

He raised his head, his mouth curving into a satisfied smile. He didn't even give the throng of reporters a second glance. ''Let them watch. After all, this is what they've come for.''

Panicked, she tried to bolt from the car, lunging out thinking only of running from the crowd and the cameras and Christos—

A hand clamped at her waist, biting into her skin, holding her still. ''Mrs. Pateras—'' Christos's husky voice pierced her panic ''—smile for the cameras.''

CHAPTER THREE

LEAVING the noisy media throng behind, Alysia stepped aboard the yacht, late-afternoon sun glinting off the water in the purest form of golden light.

Christos swiftly introduced her to his staff and crew, rattling off the dozen names, even as the yacht gently swayed in the harbor waters.

The emotionally intense afternoon, the numerous introductions, the strangeness of her new surroundings suddenly exhausted her. Or was it the stark realization that until they touched land, she was really and truly caught in this pretend marriage?

She might never get away.

She might be trapped forever.

Her head swimming, she gulped air, panic overriding every other thought. What had she done? What in God's name had she done?

"I can't," she choked, searching for the exit, her gaze jumping from wall to door to patch of blue sky outside. "I can't do this, I can't, I can't—"

"You can," Christos softly countered, stepping closer to her side. "You already did."

He cut the introductions short and took her by the elbow, steering her through the formal salon to an elegant stateroom decorated in the palest shades of blue. Just beyond the wide French doors, the ocean

44

shimmered a brilliant royal-blue. The effect was calming, indescribably peaceful, and she relaxed slightly.

"Do you need a drink?" he asked, sliding his suit jacket off.

"No."

"Brandy might help."

Nothing would help, she thought, not until she got off the yacht. But she couldn't say that, and she couldn't allow him to become suspicious.

Christos tossed his jacket across the foot of the bed. "Maybe a long hot bath would feel good. I can't imagine you were allowed such indulgences in the convent."

"No, definitely not. Cold showers were de rigueur."

He began unfastening the top button on his fine dress shirt. "Think you'll be comfortable here?"

Her gaze took in the massive bed with the bolsters and mountain of pillows. Soft silk drapes hung at the French doors. The same ice-blue silk covered a chaise lounge. Her fingertips caressed the silk chaise, the down-filled cushion giving beneath the weight of her hand. Her room at the convent had been so spartan. "Yes."

"Good." He continued unfastening one small button after another, revealing first his throat and then his darkly tanned chest with the crisp curl of hair.

Alysia sucked in a breath, the glimpse of his chest hair so personal she felt as if she'd invaded his privacy. Yet she found herself turning to watch him again, half-fascinated, half-fearful. Christos appeared utterly at ease as he slipped the shirt from his shoulders, the smooth muscular planes of his chest rippling.

"Your wardrobe's in the closet," he added. "Do change into something more comfortable. We'll have a light meal now on the deck and then supper later, closer to ten."

The typical Greek dinner hour. But not the typical Greek man. She quickly averted her gaze again.

Then his words registered. *Your wardrobe's in the closet.* "We share this room?"

His expression didn't change. "Of course."

She took a defensive step backward, bumping the edge of the writing table. She glanced down at the desk's polished surface, noting the neat arrangement of paper, inkwell, pen. "Mr. Pateras, you know the terms of our agreement."

"Sharing a bed isn't a sexual act, Mrs. Pateras."

"It's close enough."

"Surely you've shared a room before."

He didn't mention her former husband. He didn't need to. She knew exactly what he was thinking and she didn't like his presumption. "Regardless, I'd like a room of my own, please."

He walked toward her. She leaned back, her bottom bumping the desk. Without apology, he took her in his arms, his mouth covering hers.

Heat flooded her veins, heat swept through her middle, into her belly and deeper still. She felt hot and weak and when he parted her lips with his, she didn't resist. If anything she opened her mouth wider, arched closer, straining against the emptiness since her mother's death, and the years before.

His palm found her hip, pressed her more tightly against him. She felt the thrust of his arousal and her breasts ached, nipples hardening. This was too close but not close enough, too much sensation and yet too little, everything felt hot and flushed and yet it was wrong.

But she didn't pull away, couldn't pull away, riveted by the tumult of her feelings.

His tongue flicked against her inner lower lip before exploring the recesses of her mouth. Teeth grazed teeth, and then he bit once into the softness of her lip. Her protest sounded like a whimper, more desire than denial, and Christos made a sound low in his throat, rough, hungry.

He was tasting her, exploring, setting her body and limbs on fire. No pretend marriage for him. He'd have her naked and beneath him in no time.

Her legs were trembling and she felt the fire lick her ankles, her knees, between her thighs. It was, she thought wildly, a fire she didn't want, wouldn't be able to control.

Christos broke the kiss off, lifting his dark head to gaze into her eyes. He trailed a finger down her flushed cheek. ''Separate rooms?'' he said hoarsely. ''I don't think so.''

Christos left to speak with the captain and Alysia fled to the shower. Inside the glass stall, water streamed from the showerhead and she soaped her face vigorously, determined to wash away every trace of Christos's kisses.

Who did he think he was, kissing her, touching her, treating her like one of his possessions?

He might have made a deal with her father, but he hadn't made a deal with her! With another swipe of the soapy washcloth, she scrubbed her mouth again and then her neck, shoulders, breasts.

It had been ages since she'd indulged in a long, hot shower and she lathered her hair in the fragrant shampoo provided. The rich scent reminded her of a fruit cocktail with its fragrance of citrus, mango, papaya. It formed billowy suds and rinsed easily.

Christos Pateras spared no expense of anything. Yachts. Wives. Or bath necessities.

Suddenly the yacht hummed to life, the engine's vibrations shooting through the white ceramic floor tiles into the soles of her feet. They were leaving Oinoussai at last!

With one towel wrapped around her body, and another twisted turban-style around her head, she padded quickly to the bedroom.

Ambivalent emotions whirled within her, her breath catching in a mix of excitement and dread. She'd waited so long to leave Oinoussai, but to leave as an American's wife!

As the yacht pulled anchor she felt momentum shift in her own life. Anything could happen now.

Everything could happen now.

In mute satisfaction, she watched Oinoussai recede, the small island shrinking small, smaller, smallest until miles of water lay between the yacht and the rocky sweep of land.

Finally the island became just a speck in the sea, and then disappeared altogether. When the island was gone, and the horizon blue, just endless blue water and a low, gold sun starting to set, Alysia released the bottled air in her lungs in a rush, her eyes stinging, her heart thumping, lungs raw and bursting.

She inhaled another breath and suddenly it all became easier, freer, as if a weight had toppled from her chest.

Free. She was free. She might have been back on Oinoussai only two years, but those years felt like forever. It had been forever. Not just her mother's death, but the sanatorium, the horrible marriage to Jeremy, the baby...

The baby.

Alysia sank onto the bed, crushing the ice-blue silk coverlet. Groaning, she covered her face with her hands, pressing the heel of her palms to her eyes. Miniature yellow dots exploded against the blackness of her lids.

Her heart felt as if it were on fire and the pain consumed her. With a strangled sob, she rocked back and forth, stricken with need, tortured by the memory.

Alexi, I miss you, I miss you, I miss you.

It was too much, too sharp, too horrible.

She couldn't do this, couldn't give in to the terrible grief again. The doctors at the sanatorium had taught her to fight back, to keep the memories at bay.

Grinding her palms against her eyes, she pressed until she could see nothing, hear nothing, remember nothing.

Little by little she calmed, still rocking herself on the bed, unconsciously mimicking the motion she'd used to soothe Alexi when he couldn't get comfortable, when sleep seemed impossible. Back and forth, back and forth, until at last the monster inside her slept.

And slowly the grief receded until it lay still and silent, a great hulking giant at memory's gate.

Drawing a painful breath, she slowly lifted her head, catching a glimpse of herself in the large gold-framed mirror hanging above the antique chest of drawers.

Wide, wild eyes. Trembling lips. Terror there, hatred, too.

How could she not be full of hate? She'd done a terrible, unforgivable thing. She hated no one more than she hated herself.

Christos watched her appear on the deck, a vision in the palest shade of pink. Her long thin sleeveless dress clung to her breasts, brushed her ankles, sliding over her slim hips. With her long wheat and honey hair pulled into a knot at her nape, she looked incredibly feminine, very fragile, and he felt a wave of possession sweep through him. She was his now. She belonged to him.

He'd seen her before, years ago, at a gathering in Athens. She was young, even more blond, and she'd entered the room to tearfully whisper something to her father.

The men had hushed, the meeting interrupted, and Darius Lemos reacted in anger. He slapped his daughter in front of everyone, the sound of his palm loud, too loud in the suddenly silent room.

Christos had been twenty-seven and the foreigner, the interloper, alienated at the back of the room. Although he spoke fluent Greek, he hadn't understood all the innuendoes tossed his way. All he knew was that he'd had his fill of poverty, and powerlessness, and he'd never let anyone dictate to him again.

He'd been shocked when Darius struck his daughter, the savagery of the blow leaving a vivid handprint on the girl's face. But the girl hadn't made a sound. She simply stared at her father, tears swimming in her eyes, before wordlessly leaving the room.

The meeting resumed and all continued as if nothing happened.

But something happened. Something happened to Christos.

Alysia approached him now as slowly, as hesitantly as she'd approached her father all those years ago.

Silently he handed her a glass of champagne, noting as he did the spiky tips of her sooty lashes, the dampness at the corners of her startling blue-green eyes. She'd been crying.

"Second thoughts?" he murmured.

"And thirds, and fourths." She turned her head away, revealing more of her creamy nape.

Again he felt the urge to take her in his arms, to kiss her soft skin and make her warm in his hands. He'd know her better than anyone one day. He'd discover all the secrets she kept buried within her.

She rested her slender arms on the railing, the glass of champagne ignored, dangling in her fingers. The yacht was moving swiftly through the water and the wind lifted tendrils of hair from her smooth knot.

"Where are we going?" she asked.

"Where do you want to go?"

"Away from Greece."

"Done."

She turned her head just enough to glance at him over her bare pale shoulder. Her skin gleamed. Her blue eyes were dark, mysterious. "I don't even know where you live."

"We'll live outside New York most of the time. But I also have houses in London, Provence and on the Amalfi Coast."

"You sound restless."

Amusement curved his mouth. "See, you know me already."

The uniformed cabin steward stepped onto the deck, signaling that the light meal was ready. Christos held out a hand, gesturing for Alysia to follow the cabin steward to the table set on the far end of the deck.

Christos held her chair as she took her place at the

small table on the deck. "You look beautiful in pink."

She set her champagne glass down, pushing it across the linen cloth toward the floral centerpiece. She waited until the steward stepped away to speak. Very carefully she kept her gaze fixed on the yellow and white roses. "Let's not pretend this is anything but a business arrangement, Mr. Pateras."

"By its very nature, marriage is a business arrangement." He sat down across from her and leaned back in his chair. "But that doesn't mean it has to be sterile, or cold and intolerable. Nor does it mean we can't celebrate our union."

She grasped the stem of the champagne flute between two fingers. "And what are we celebrating, Mr. Pateras? Your new financial gain? Your alliance with Darius Lemos?"

"All of the above."

She made a move to set her glass down. "Then I'd rather not."

"What if we celebrate your beauty then?"

"I definitely won't drink to that."

"You don't think you're beautiful?"

"I know I'm not."

"I find you breathtaking."

"Perhaps you've lacked for company, lately."

He smiled, almost indulgently. "I've had exceptional company. But you, I must admit, fascinate me. You're a tormented beauty, aren't you?"

She paled, her eyes growing enormous, her blue

irises dark and flecked with bits of bottle-green. "This conversation makes me very uncomfortable."

"Sorry."

But he didn't sound sorry, she thought, fighting fresh panic, feeling increasingly trapped.

While dressing tonight she'd determined to keep her distance, to remain detached, to do everything in her power to keep him at arm's length but his power was insidious. She found herself drawn to him in ways she couldn't fathom.

He was a stranger. He'd been bought by her father. He only wanted Lemos money. So why did her heart stir and her emotions twist, why did she want what was absolutely wrong for her?

She half closed her eyes, reminding herself that he was a spider and he'd woven a web and if she weren't careful he'd eat her, the same way a spider ate a little fly.

This was about survival.

Alysia crossed one ankle behind the other, as if to fortify herself, become impenetrable. She'd shut him out, draw the line here. He wouldn't cross it. She wouldn't let him.

Christos stirred, lazily stretching out one long arm to drag her chair toward him. He had no intention of letting her escape. "No need to be frightened."

"I'm not." Good, frost glittered in her voice.

"Your pulse is racing. I can see it there, at your throat."

Her heart was racing. She felt breathless, dizzy, on edge. If he touched her, she'd scream. If he drew her any closer, she'd leap out of her skin. This was all going wrong, terribly wrong and there was nothing she could do now but play the cards she'd been given.

"It's not. I'm quite calm. You probably need glasses."

His lips tightened and then eased and she realized he was grinning. "My vision is perfect. Twenty/twenty. Neither my father nor mother wear glasses, either." His smile faded, eyebrows pulling and suddenly all laughter was gone and he looked hard, focused, determined. "Why do you think so little of yourself?"

The swift change of subject knocked her off balance. Alysia felt as though she'd run smack into a wall and she shook her head once, dazed by the contact with a reality she resisted.

Why, he asked? Because she'd committed an act so terrible, so vile that her husband had left her, her friends abandoned her, her mind had shut down. It had taken her time in the sanatorium to begin to recover.

"You're intelligent, beautiful, sensitive, possibly charming," he said, touching her on the cheek with the back of his hand. She averted her head. He took her chin in his hand and turned her back to face him. "Why so little pride?"

The kindness in his voice almost undid her. No one except her mother, and maybe the abbess, had spoken to her so softly, so gently, in years. He made her feel like a...human being.

Tears started in her eyes and she blinked them back. Clutching the champagne flute's slender stem even more tightly, she tried to break the intensity of his gaze. "Please, no more."

"I want to understand."

"There's nothing to understand. I am what my father says I am. Reckless. Disobedient. Rebellious."

His dark gaze moved searchingly across her face, examining every inch of her profile before dropping to her breasts and lower still. "Are you?"

"Of course. I'm my father's daughter."

She'd meant to be flippant but it came out dreadfully wrong, more despair than arrogance in her husky voice. Suddenly she felt completely naked, her dress no more protection than a sheet of plastic kitchen wrap.

Alysia clutched the champagne flute as though her life depended on it. What if he discovered the truth about her? What if he realized the kind of person she really was? "Let me go, please. You can keep the dowry, my jewels, my savings. I don't want anything."

"You couldn't survive poor. You've never tasted poverty. It tastes as bad as it looks."

"I'd rather be poor and free. *Please,* just let me go."

His dark gaze bored through her. He didn't speak for a long, tense moment. Finally he shook his head. "I can't. I need you too much."

Her slim body jerked, her hand convulsively tightened on the goblet and with an ear-splitting pop, she snapped the crystal stem in two. The champagne flute crashed in pieces to the table. A shard of glass lodged painfully deep in her thumb.

It was like slow motion, she thought, watching the blood suddenly spurt in a brilliant red stream. Christos swore violently, sounding every bit a native Greek, as he grabbed a linen napkin and covered the arc of blood.

"I'm fine," she protested weakly.

"You're not. You're a bleeding fountain." He lifted the napkin briefly to inspect the damage. "You might need stitches."

"It'll stop."

He cast her a scathing glance. "There's glass in it. Hold still."

Eyebrows flat, expression grim, his lips compressed, he probed the wound, gently working the sliver from her tender thumb. She winced at the pressure and he caught her grimace. Suddenly his expression changed. His eyes were so dark, so deep they looked bottomless. "I don't want to hurt you."

"You didn't hurt me. I did it myself."

"Still."

Still. As though he had the power to somehow heal all wounds, restore her peace of mind and soothe the cuts and bruises. Not just a groom, but a miracle man. Wouldn't that be something? Tears sprang to her eyes and she bit into her lower lip overwhelmed by the intensity of her longing to feel whole and rested, more herself again.

Christos tossed the glass shard onto the tablecloth.

"That should do it," he said, wiping away the drying blood and bandaging her thumb.

She held her breath as he tucked the ends of the linen cloth beneath the edge of the bandage. Something about his touch made her feel too warm, too liquid. He made her feel so…safe. What an illusion. Could anything be more unjust?

"Your father told me you're not to be trusted," Christos glanced up into her face, black lashes only partly lifting, his expression concealed. "But I didn't know he meant with my crystal."

His lips quirked, a black eyebrow arched, but beneath his ironic tone, she heard concern, then immediately chided herself. This is a deal, a marriage deal and you are a very expensive bride.

Her throat sealed shut. Unable to speak she stared at his hands, the backs very broad and tanned, his fingers long and well-tapered. His touch was so light, so deft, he could have been a carpenter, or a surgeon. Legally he was her husband. *Husband.* A shiver raced down her spine, and yet it wasn't fear creating havoc, it was anticipation. Her imagination was running riot. Nervously she glanced up into his face and her heart skittered sideways, as if she was a frightened country mouse instead of one of the wealthiest women in Greece. But money didn't equate with confidence, or happiness. No one knew that better than she. "My father…he told you I wasn't to be trusted?"

"Mmm."

A blush of shame rose to her cheeks. What else

had her father told him? She knew too well that her father's honesty could be brutal. He had hurt her, and her mother, countless times with his cutting appraisal. No one was good enough for him. Certainly not his family.

"Don't," Christos said, his voice unusually husky as he reached up to brush her flushed cheek with the tip of his finger.

A strange pain flickered through her and she pressed her bandaged hand to her belly. Everything felt so raw just then, so exposed. She could smell the sharp pungent salt in the air, the warmth of the night, the motion of the ship as it surged through the waves. "Don't what?"

"Think." Grooves formed on either side of his mouth, small creases fanned from the corners of his eyes. "You're torturing yourself again."

"Better me than you." She smiled as carelessly as possible, a devil-be-damned smile that hurt in every pore of her body. She'd fought her demons before and won. She'd win again. And she'd do it without Christos's help, or interference, whatever it might be.

"One more quick check," he insisted, taking her hand and lifting the edge of the napkin to examine the cut as if it were a wound of significance. "Maybe you won't need stitches after all."

"Thank you, Doctor."

"My pleasure."

He should have laughed, grinned, said something lighthearted. Instead he stared into her eyes, earnest and focused, deep furrows marring his high bronze brow. She swore he could see right through her. See her fears, her shocking secrets.

The blood drained from her face, the intensity of his gaze unnerving. What did he see when he looked at her like that? What did he possibly know? She felt threads of panic, hints of the past. ''Really, Christos, I won't fall apart over this.'' She'd meant to be funny, to ease the tension, but he didn't even crack a smile.

His jaw flexed, a small muscle pulling near his ear. ''First time you've used my given name.''

What was he doing to her? Softening her stony heart, breaking through her defenses, that's what he was doing. She couldn't allow it, wouldn't let him dismantle the high, hard wall she'd built around herself. No one came inside. Ever.

The sooner they reached Cephalonia, the better. Alysia pushed back her chair, and rose unsteadily. ''I don't think I'm hungry. If you'll excuse me, I'd like to return to my room.''

''Certainly. Why don't you go to our room and rest. I'll have dinner sent to you later.''

CHAPTER FOUR

AFTER her solitary dinner, Alysia changed into her satin lilac pajama set, the wide trousers and loose jacket style top covering her from ankles to collarbone. Of all her pajamas these were the least figure-flattering and not at all bridelike.

Bride. Even the word stuck in her throat, making her gag. But she wasn't a bride. She was an impostor and this time tomorrow she'd be gone. Christos could have the marriage annulled and they'd both put this embarrassing episode behind them.

Alysia crawled into bed and tried to sleep, but sleep didn't come. Moonlight flickered through the gap in the curtains and the rocking of the yacht was doing funny things to her insides. She felt deceptively warm, and alive, nerve endings alert, senses sharp. Turning onto her side, she closed her eyes and listened to the slap of waves against the yacht's hull, the groan and creak of wood and the low hum of the engine. Would Christos put in an appearance? Did he intend to share the bed?

How could she think she could manage a man like Christos Pateras? She must have been out of her mind. He might not be exactly like her father, but he was close enough. He'd get what he wanted and he wanted children.

Her stomach cramped and she squeezed her eyes shut. Don't panic, she soothed. Tomorrow they'd dock in Cephalonia, the largest of the Ionian islands, and mountainous Cephalonia was diverse enough, busy enough, to allow her to escape and hide. She just had to wait for the right opportunity.

Calmer, Alysia relaxed, and gave herself over to the gentle roll and sway of the ship. The rocking motion soon lulled her to sleep.

Warmth permeated her dreams, as well as the realization that a very solid, very real presence was taking up more than half of the bed.

Opening her eyes she discovered Christos next to her, his long muscular body inches away, his arm outstretched, practically touching her.

Alysia stiffened, held her breath, as his palm moved slowly across her head to tangle briefly in the long strands of hair. As quietly as possible, she scooted away, creeping to the bed's edge and listening with satisfaction as his hand fell to the mattress.

Alysia gathered her hair, moving it from harm's way. His deep, steady breathing reassured her and little by little she relaxed. Just when she was close to drifting off again, Christos stirred.

Suddenly he moved against her, pressing his thighs to the back of her legs. Total body contact, hip to ankle, his knees fitting behind hers, his groin pressed to her bottom.

Despite the clamor of protest inside her head, her body came to life, nerve endings screaming as if electrified.

Opening her eyes, she gripped the downy comforter, and stared at the edge of the bed, then down at the carpet. There was nowhere to go. She bit her knuckle to keep from shouting out loud.

She wasn't ready for this kind of intimacy. She didn't know Christos, and couldn't bear to be pressed limb to limb with him.

As her senses flooded, responding to his heat and strength, her fear grew. She'd never met a man who aroused such contradictory emotions in her before. Awareness, mistrust, desire, dread.

Using her elbow, she pushed against his chest, trying to prod him backward. He didn't budge. She pushed again. And still nothing but his deep, even breathing, his warm breath bathing the back of her neck.

Damn him. Damn his incredible nerve. Damn his empire, too.

He had her trapped on the edge of the bed. She couldn't move forward, she'd fall on the floor. If she wiggled backward, and she tried, she came up square against his groin.

Suddenly she realized not all of him was asleep.

Part of him was definitely awake and his thin cotton pajama pants did nothing to contain his impressive length.

Mortified, she pressed a forearm across her eyes, trying to block out the pressure of his arousal against her bottom. But the more she denied the existence of his erection the more rigid his shaft became, enflaming her tender skin, creating heat and liquid desire between her thighs.

The tip of his erection strained against her nightwear, her thighs tingling, her innermost muscles tightening, clenching at air and nothing when he lay so dangerously close.

She'd never admit it in a thousand years, but she wanted him, wanted to feel more of him, and the carnal want was more than she could bear. She'd never been physical, never felt sexual in her life, but Christos Pateras was changing all that. He was making her ache for things she'd never fully experienced.

Alysia writhed. She couldn't help it. She only prayed he was so deeply asleep he didn't know the effect he was having on her. Wriggling, her hips shifted, and she brushed the tip of his shaft, tormenting herself.

In the dark, with her arms around herself, and his arousal square against her, she could imagine making love to him, imagine him inside of her, imagine the pleasure of being filled by him.

It was all she could do to not whimper aloud.

And still, he slept on.

Suddenly one of his arms snaked out and clasped her around the waist, holding her firmly against him. His chest pressed to her back. His hips formed a cradle for her bottom. His taut thighs shaped hers. His shaft nearly pierced her through the satin of her pajamas.

Her heart stuttered, her breath caught in her throat. Digging her teeth into her soft lower lip, she muffled a groan. This was torture. Exquisite torture of the best and worst kind.

"Go to sleep," Christos growled in the darkness, his voice pitched deep and rough.

"I can't."

"You can. Just close your eyes. Stop thinking."

Thinking! She wasn't thinking. She was feeling, and every nerve ending begged for more sensation. She felt wired for action and nothing was happening. Absolutely nothing. So how was she supposed to sleep?

It seemed as if she lay awake for hours, her lower belly aching, her inner muscles clenching at nothing.

Easy for him to say sleep, he wasn't the one about to explode out of her skin. But finally, painfully, she drifted off. When she next awoke, the sun was shining and Christos was gone.

Dressing in a slim taupe linen skirt and matching knit top, Alysia tried to deny the nervous thrill she felt at seeing Christos again. He'd made her feel desperate last night, his hard muscled body a torment, and yet he'd also been warm. And solid. And real.

She thrust her feet into strappy tan sandals and hurried upstairs to the deck. A steward met her, greeted her with a bow and showed her to the breakfast table overflowing with lavish platters of fresh fruit and sweet rolls, yogurt and coffee. But no sign of Christos.

She felt her excitement plummet, anticipation turning inside out. The disappointment was so strong that she felt furious with herself for caring so much about someone she knew so little. For heaven's sake, he was a stranger. She married him to escape her father, not for a stab at domestic tranquillity.

Alysia nearly dropped her china coffee cup. She wasn't falling for him, was she? She didn't really expect a happy-ever-after with him…did she? This wasn't a real marriage. It wasn't a honeymoon.

Wake up, she snapped at herself. *Grow up!*

Halfway through her croissant, her appetite well and truly gone, she spotted gleaming white bobbing next to the ship on the water. Pushing back from her chair she moved to the railing and looked down. A speedboat.

Sleekly designed, painted a glossy white and maroon, the speedboat hadn't been there before. Had someone come on board? Or was Christos planning a trip out?

Either way, there was a boat, and means for escape.

Her fingers tightened on the railing, the wood warmed by the sun. She felt a whisper of regret, but mocked her weakness and her attraction to a man so potentially dangerous. This wasn't the time to rely on her emotions. She needed to act.

Swiftly descending the flight of stairs that joined the two wraparound decks, Alysia slid over the bottom rail and into the low-slung speedboat. She reached past the steering wheel toward the gauges. A key dangled from the ignition. *Yes.*

A shadow darkened the deck, filtering the bright

morning sun. "Going somewhere?" a husky voice drawled.

Christos.

Her stomach fell so fast and hard she leaned against the speedboat's dash, fingers compulsively flexing.

Go, just go, a terrified voice screamed inside her head. Get out of here.

But she couldn't move, paralyzed by fear. She stiffened, expecting him to grab her, haul her from the boat. He'd be enraged. He'd be physical.

"You like the Donzi?" he asked, his voice husky, almost amused.

How could he be amused? She'd tried to run away.

"The Donzi?" she choked, her breathing ragged, her body weighted with fear, and dread. Her father would have broken her in two if she'd tried this with him.

"My speedboat. It's an American boat, made in Florida."

Tensing, she dragged her gaze up, an inch at a time. He was wearing faded khaki shorts that exposed every sinewy muscle in his thigh and calf and a white cotton T-shirt that had obviously seen better days.

He looked fearless, careless, distinctly American. A frisson of warmth shot through her. There was no anger in his eyes. No anger in the twist of his lips.

"Get your swimsuit," he said, stepping down into the boat, one long bare leg grazing hers. "I've got a favorite beach I like to visit whenever I'm near Cephalonia.''

She almost tripped in her haste to escape him. ''I'm not much for the beach,'' she fibbed, scrambling out of the boat, away from him, cursing her slim-fitting skirt that hindered her movement.

Christos watched her struggles with interest, arms folded across his chest, the white T-shirt pulled taut at the shoulders. ''This isn't an elective, Mrs. Pateras. It's a requirement. Get your suit. We're going swimming.''

Heaping Greek curses on his head, Alysia changed in the bedroom, stepping out of her panties and bra and into a two-piece bathing suit she hadn't worn in years. Except for the bare midriff, the tank-style suit was cut conservatively, a little high on the thigh, but not indecently so, the top more like a soft sports bra, ample coverage there, too.

This shouldn't do much for Mr. Pateras, she thought, glimpsing her slim pale limbs in the mirror, her arms too long, her legs too thin, her head looking ridiculously doll-like on her fragile body.

She didn't look much like a Greek woman anymore, her curves melting away. Nursing her mother had taken its toll, the long exhausting hours decimating what little remained of her appetite. No wonder the sisters were always telling her to eat. She wasn't just slender anymore, she was skinny.

Alysia resolved to eat better starting immediately. No more cups of black coffee and nibbles of croissant for breakfast. She'd eat more fruit and vegetables, take bigger portions, make sure she was getting enough of the healthy foods.

The telephone by the bed rang and Alysia started. It rang again and she reached for it.

It was Christos. "Are you coming up or do I need to fetch you?"

"I'm coming," she retorted grimly before slamming the phone back down. She was definitely going back up. The last thing she needed was to be alone with Christos in the bedroom again.

Christos untied the speedboat from the yacht and within minutes they were jumping the white-tipped waves, sending streams of water into the air. The wind whipped Alysia's long hair into a frenzy, and she grabbed at it, futilely trying to bring it under control.

The speedboat hit a big teal-green wave and Alysia threw her hands out to steady herself.

Grinning, Christos shot her a quick glance. "Too fast?" he shouted.

"No!" The speed dazzled her, nearly as much as the brilliant sunshine and intense sparkle of blue water. She felt immersed in sensation—the speed of the boat, the surge of the engine, the wind whipping through her hair. Could she feel any more alive?

"You must have spent a lot of time on the water with your father," Christos said, his voice breaking up in the wind.

"Not really. He doesn't really like sailing. He usually flies everywhere he needs to go."

They were flying over the water now. Salty spray

coating her skin, droplets dancing in her hair. The daring capabilities of the Donzi left her breathless. "This is incredible," she confessed. "I could get addicted to this."

Christos laughed, the sound deep, husky and something turned over in Alysia's chest. She could see herself cradled in his arms, snuggled against his chest as she'd been last night. He'd been so warm and strong, his hard body a refuge.

Fiercely she squashed the image, reminding herself that he'd forced her into this marriage, manipulated her into taking vows. This wasn't a real relationship. He'd *bought* her.

Her pleasure in the boat ride faded and she sat numbly for the remainder of the trip. When Christos slowed the Donzi to steer into a protected little bay, Alysia felt tears prick her eyes. He made everything seem so interesting. His voice resonated with warmth and she found herself responding to him over and over again.

It made her mad. No, furious. And not just at him, but at herself. Didn't she have any sense? What about her self-control?

The boat motored closer to shore. The bay, shaped by massive rocks and backed by rugged vegetation, looked utterly private. No roads, no other boats, no people. Just the crescent beach with powdery ivory sand and the gentle lapping of waves.

They were alone. Completely alone.

Panic shot through her. Panic because this secluded little beach was nothing short of a lover's paradise. Picnic lunch, leisurely swim and exquisite lovemaking on the pristine sand.

Christos shifted and turning she caught a glimpse of him pulling his T-shirt over his head. His lifted arms tightened his chest, his rippled abdominal muscles contracted. His flat stomach was so lean and hard she itched to trace each sinewy muscle with her finger. A peculiar sensation rippled through her.

More desire, fresh desire flooded her, her breasts lifting with her swift intake. She felt an ache at the juncture of her thighs, her body suddenly hot and weak all over. She wanted something from him no man had ever given her. Wanted something that until now she didn't even know existed.

Tossing his T-shirt down, Christos looked at her, their eyes meeting. His dark gaze locked with hers, and in his eyes she realized he knew what she was feeling, and that he was feeling it, too.

Her tummy clenched, her nipples hardened, her mouth full and sensitive. All from just one look.

If he touched her she'd melt. She'd puddle at his feet and beg for release. She'd clutch his wrist and move his hand across her body, across her stomach, to cup her breasts and then down again, over her hips to her thighs. She'd show him every spot that tingled. She'd press her mouth to his, taste his skin, drink him in—

Good God, what was happening here?

Jerkily Alysia rose, turned, covered her parted lips and shook her head. No, no, no. Not like this, not here, not with him.

She felt the boat rock and then heard a splash. Christos was in the water. He waded to the beach, tied the speedboat to an iron ring drilled in one of the massive rock formations.

He returned to the boat and reach for her. "Let me give you a hand."

"Don't touch me!" Color washed her cheeks. She sounded absolutely terrified.

His eyes narrowed, thick black lashes concealing his expression. "You okay?"

No. She wasn't okay. She was anything but okay. Her heart felt strange and her emotions were wild and she didn't know what was happening to her but she was losing control, felt sickeningly out of control, and this wasn't supposed to happen. Not with him.

It'd been over four years since her marriage to Jeremy ended and in all those years she hadn't been with another man. Four years had passed since she'd last been touched, kissed, caressed. Four years of nothing and now she felt absolutely crazy with sensation.

"I can manage," she choked, resenting the fact that he stirred her up, that he *mattered*.

Christos shrugged, his lips compressed, and without a word gathered the picnic basket and towels from inside the boat and headed back to shore.

Alysia sat in the tethered boat, hands knotted in her lap and watched him drop the basket and towels into the sand before he returned to the water to swim. As the boat bobbed she followed his progress. He was a strong swimmer, his long, toned arms slicing through the waves, his dark head turning at regular intervals for air.

He'd covered the bay, reached the far end of the cove and prepared to turn around. Alysia pulled off her skirt and top and dived over the edge of the boat, swimming quickly to shore. The water actually felt wonderful, not too warm or too cold, just refreshing.

On the beach she toweled off, and then spread her towel to dry. She sat down on her damp towel and watched Christos's approach. He was on his back now, lazily swimming along the shore. His dark head was thrown back, his muscular arms rotating in impossibly smooth arcs.

Poseidon. God of the Ocean.

Suddenly another boat motored into the bay and anchored not far from Christos's Donzi. The group piled out, several families it seemed, mothers spreading blankets and towels on the sand, while the children splashed in the surf. The fathers sat together, a circle of male authority and Alysia darkly noted that while the men sat, the women did all the work. Typical.

Christos waded out of the ocean, water streaming, dark hair curling wetly on his muscular chest. He dropped to the sand next to her. Instinctively she scooted over, needing more space. Christos gave her a peculiar look. "Nervous?" he asked.

"No!"

"Good. Because we are married, Alysia. This is going to be a real relationship."

Her pained expression didn't go unnoticed. Christos's jaw tightened as he watched her from beneath lowered lashes. Her face was like a canvas, storm after storm crossing the finely drawn features.

He scooped a palm of sand, letting the warm grains trickle between his fingers. "Why did you marry me? What changed your mind?"

Her head jerked up, long blond hair wet, clinging to her slim shoulder. "What?"

"You changed your mind about marrying me. Why?"

She didn't answer and he reached out, opened his palm, trickling the soft sand to fall onto the inside of her arm. Alysia snatched her arm away and the warm grains slid to her inner thigh.

The pale grains of sand on her taut thigh were too irresistible to ignore. He lightly brushed the trail of sand from her thigh. Alysia gasped and jerked her knees closed, trapping his hand. He felt the smooth plane of muscle in her thigh, the heat of her body, the silky satin of her skin.

A faint tremor coursed through her. He felt it ripple through him and glancing at her, he arched one eyebrow. "This is nice."

Pink color darkened her cheeks, a blush of mortification. Her knees opened and she shoved his hand away from her leg.

"I rather liked it there," he drawled.

"Keep your hands to yourself."

"I want a marriage, Alysia. I want you."

"You said you'd give me time."

"I am. I have. But how much more time is necessary? You're attracted to me—"

"You've quite an imagination, Mr. Pateras, if you honestly believe that!" she interrupted, her head lifting, scorn flashing in her dark blue eyes.

He grinned, enjoying the flash and fire in her eyes. He liked it when she was angry, liked the fury and the challenge he saw buried there. "I do have a rather vivid imagination and I've a number of ideas I'd like to try with you."

"I might not be a virgin, Mr. Pateras, but I'm afraid I lack your level of sexual expertise. You might be better off finding a partner that could better satisfy your needs."

"I don't want a mistress. I want you."

"*No.*"

"Why can't I want you?"

"Because you don't even know me." She dug her hands into the sand, burying her skin to the wrist. "And you can't want someone you've only just met."

"Why not?"

"Because. It's just not right."

"Ah, your morals. I see. You'll marry a man to escape your father but you won't stoop low enough to want him."

"No, that's not it."

"That's exactly it. You'd find it a whole lot easier to accept our arrangement if you were forced to endure my touch, then you could blame it on me. But the truth is, you want my touch and that makes you angry.''

Alysia jumped to her feet and began brushing the sand from the back of her legs with tangible violence. ''I'm not attracted to you, I don't want you and I want nothing to do with you.''

''Little late for that, don't you think?''

Suddenly she stiffened, and raised a hand to shield her eyes as she stared out toward the water. Her lips parted in a silent oh, her focus entirely fixed on the tide. He felt her tension, her slender body taut, her breath bottled. She stood like that another couple of seconds before running frantically to the water's edge.

Alysia saw the small body floating face down, arms outstretched, legs apart. She heard a scream, someone was screaming and she lunged into the water, grabbing at the child, flipping him up.

Breathe, she shouted, breathe.

The little boy wiggled, blue rubber mask framing his dark startled eyes. The sea-green snorkel fell from between his clenched baby teeth.

He wasn't dead. He was swimming. Snorkeling.

Her legs turned to jelly and she nearly collapsed into the water, still clutching the little boy to her chest.

People surged towards her. Women, men, the other children, everyone yelling at once.

''Down,'' the little boy imperiously demanded, no longer frightened, just angry. ''Put me down now.''

Above the commotion she caught Christos's gaze,

his dark eyes fixed on her. There was no anger in his eyes, no expression at all. Weakly she set the child down, placing him on his feet.

A woman, his mother most likely, yanked him into her arms, turning on Alysia in a tirade of angry Greek. Alysia saw the woman's mouth move, flapping, flapping, flapping, but heard nothing the mother said, her brain dazzled by silence, stunned to stillness by the wretched memory of death.

Christos worked through the crowd, circling her shoulders with one arm, pushing the others away. "Shall we go?"

She nodded, her brain dimly aware of the pressure of his arm around her body, his size shielding her from the others nearby.

Her mouth felt parched, dry like the sand. They walked across the beach, leaving the others behind. Christos stopped briefly, bending over to gather their towels and shirts.

At the boat he undid the knotted rope. She waded to the boat, water surging around her thighs, swirling to her hips. She climbed up the boat's ladder and moved toward the driver's seat.

Christos glanced at her as the speedboat sliced through the ocean on the way back to the yacht, but he said nothing, and for that, she was grateful.

She couldn't look at him, couldn't talk to him, too mired in grief. Her stomach cramped, pain contorting in her belly. She clutched her hair in one hand and hunched over the side of the Donzi, throwing up into the saltwater.

Alexi.

Christos had seen the look on her face as she'd pulled the little boy up, snorkel, mask and all, it was a look of dread and terror, the expression of one who has seen a ghost.

Toweling off after his shower, Christos quickly dressed, donning black trousers and a fine white dress shirt.

She hadn't wanted to talk about what happened on the beach and he hadn't pressed for an explanation. It was enough that they both knew she'd run for the boy, seeing something else, thinking something else.

Christos saw enough today to feel worry of his own. Alysia's ghost would haunt her forever if he didn't try to help. He had to do something. But what?

He slid his arms into his black tuxedo jacket, grateful they'd be dining out tonight. They were dining on Cephalonia tonight, joining Christos's closest friends at Constantine Pappas's elegant villa, and he thought the party atmosphere would be good for Alysia, especially in light of what happened on the beach today.

He'd told her that dress for dinner was formal and while knotting his tie, Christos found himself wondering what she'd wear.

He imagined the long gowns she might pick from, beaded fabrics, velvet fabrics, delicate silk fabrics, but nothing he thought, could be more seductive than the conservative two-piece swimsuit she'd worn at the beach today.

Her suit, a pale pink tank-style with thin spaghetti straps, clung to her breasts and hips like a second skin. And wet, the fabric revealed the contours of her nipple, the cleft in her derriere, the protruding hipbones. He'd wanted to take her right there in the warm sand, pull her down beneath him and bury himself inside her.

Jutting his jaw to better see his collar, Christos knotted his black bow tie, then snapped off the bathroom light. Time to check on his bride.

CHAPTER FIVE

"YOU didn't tell me we were joining other shipowners for dinner!" Alysia stared at Christos in dismay, her thin silk shawl folded over her arm, her small beaded purse clutched in her fingers. She'd imagined a quiet dinner alone with Christos. Instead they'd be spending the evening with old, powerful Greek families, families that knew too much of her family history.

"I thought I'd mentioned it."

"No, you did not."

He inclined his head, his black hair gleaming like polished onyx, his white shirt a perfect foil for his dark, hard features. "I apologize, then. It must have slipped my mind. We've been invited to Constantine Pappas's for dinner. You know him, I believe?"

Oh, she knew Constantine Pappas very well. Not only had he once been her father's best friend, but he'd created tremendous, and lasting, controversy in the Greek shipping industry by inviting foreigners to invest in his company, investors like Christos.

Suddenly it dawned on her, that Christos might very well be Constantine's silent foreign investor. "You're not...you don't...with Mr. Pappas?"

"Are you asking if I'm his business partner? The

answer is yes. I've backed his business for nearly ten years.''

''Constantine and my father are enemies.'' But she saw from Christos's expression he already knew that. ''But my father doesn't know that, does he?''

''No. I've always been a silent investor. And I've had my own business. Your father only knows me as an American holding company.''

''He doesn't really know you, does he?''

''We're business acquaintances. Not friends.''

She felt a bubble of hysteria. ''So how did you make the deal? Did he ask to see your stock portfolio? Your savings accounts, what?''

''I sent him some income tax statements.''

''Income tax statements. Amazing. You had money, he had a daughter, a deal was struck.'' Shock made her tongue thick. Tears welled in her eyes. ''How many men did he go through trying to find one rich enough?''

''I don't know, Alysia, it doesn't really matter anymore, does it?''

''Not to you, because you won. You got Lemos's name, Lemos's ships, Lemos's business and Lemos's daughter.'' The shame of it made her skin crawl. What kind of man sold off his only child? What kind of man would sell her to a virtual stranger? Christos wasn't even Greek. He was American. He was everything her father despised and yet it didn't matter because Christos was rich, filthy rich, appallingly rich.

''I hate you!'' She swung her beaded purse, swiping him in the chest. "I hate that you'd do this to me. To *us*."

The moment she'd said "us" she'd realized why she felt so crazy the past few days. If she'd met Christos anywhere else, in any other situation, she would have fallen in love with him, fallen for his impossible good looks, his strength, his sensuality. Instead marrying him like this destroyed everything. He was a mercenary and all the charm in the world couldn't change that one horrible fact.

"I'm sorry." There was no emotion in his deep voice, nothing at all.

"I'm not going with you tonight," she said, blinking away the tears, her chest tender, her throat sore. "If you want to celebrate your victory, you go without me."

"Constantine is throwing the party for us. It'd be a slap in his face to not show up."

"I can't go there. I can't face everyone."

"Why not? Because you feel like an outsider? Guess what, darling, I've spent my life on the outside. I know what it's like to be the subject of constant speculation. I've heard the criticism about my past. But I don't care what others think. I don't need to please anyone but myself."

"Obviously," she flung back. He might consider himself Greek, but he was still an American. He'd been born in another country, raised with another society's values. As much as he wanted to think of himself as Greek, he was still alien, would always remain alien, despite his marriage to her. "I'm not going tonight. I want no part of this. You've made your deal with my father. Now leave me alone.''

He shrugged, unmoved. "You made a deal with me, too, and I expect you to hold up your end of the bargain.''

"It's not a fair bargain!''

"You should have thought about it earlier. But since you are a Pateras now, you shall do I as ask.''

"Ask?''

"Insist.'' His dark eyes narrowed, his jaw jutting harshly, hinting at emotions he so far hadn't revealed. "As my wife you will go with me tonight and treat Constantine Pappas with respect, indeed, reverence. Is that clear?''

The yacht slowly motored into the harbor, pulling up alongside the dock. Alysia and Christos didn't speak as they stepped ashore, and the silence continued once they were seated in the waiting Rolls-Royce.

In the car Alysia wondered how much Christos actually knew about her father's relationship with Constantine. The two had once been best friends, growing up together on Oinoussai and attending college together. It wasn't until they'd both gone to work in the shipping industry that their friendship changed. Always competitive, they grew suspicious of the other. Suddenly a lifelong friendship turned into a bitter rivalry, exploding one summer into wild accusations of cheating, stealing, lying, and petty crime.

The chauffeured car pulled up in front of

Constantine's enormous villa, the white marble building glimmering with light, and Alysia brought herself to speak. "Mr. Pappas must be shocked by our marriage."

"Everyone's a bit intrigued," he answered.

And that was putting it mildly, she suspected. Alysia gripped her pale blue silk shawl and drew the fringed edges to her breast, her dress the color of aquamarine. "People will gossip."

"They do anyway."

"Yet everyone knows he was trying to find a husband for me. He'd practically advertised in all the Greek papers!"

Christos's white teeth gleamed in the darkness. "You forget, everyone believes ours is a love match. We had a secret wedding. Most people will assume we've gone behind your father's back."

"My reputation."

"Is in tatters," he agreed, reaching out to touch the slender sapphire-and-diamond bracelet encircling her wrist.

The chauffeur swung the back door of the Rolls-Royce open and stepped back, silently attentive.

But Alysia couldn't bring herself to move. She felt tricked somehow, outwitted into this game. All her life she'd been manipulated by her father and now she was married to a man who intended to do the same. A lump formed in her throat. "I thought you might have been different."

Christos's jaw tightened, a small muscle popping. He ignored the chauffeur, his full attention on her.

"Sometimes we have to bend the rules to get ahead."

"Bend the rules? You mean, break them, don't you? You play every bit as underhanded as my father."

She felt the weight of his gaze. "Perhaps, but my motives are different."

"So you say!"

"I guess you'll just have to trust me."

"Trust you?" Slowly she shook her head, disbelief coloring her speech. "I'd trust my father before I trusted you. At least I've known him all my life. You, I just met."

Christos's large, callused palm clasped her clenched fists, gathering them into his hands. He kissed her clenched fists and then released them. "Sometimes strangers can be blessings in disguise. Now come, it's time we went inside."

Alysia had to admit that Constantine was a better host than her father would have been. He greeted her warmly, kissing her on both cheeks, congratulating her on her marriage. If he felt acrimonious toward her, there was no sign of it. She found herself struggling, though, to answer his polite inquiries about her father with equal enmity. Clearly Constantine sought to put past tensions behind them. She could do no less.

"Well done," Christos whispered into her ear, as they moved from Constantine and his wife to another couple.

She tried to hold herself aloof as Christos discussed business with the other man, but he snaked an arm around her waist and drew her firmly against his side. His fingers kneaded softly into her waist, moving down slightly to caress her hip.

Alysia attempted to draw away, and his arm only tightened, holding her more firmly. An escape was impossible.

Throwing her head back, she parted her lips to protest but caught the warning light in his eyes. Remember where you are, his expression said, remember who we're with.

Men. Businessmen. And Christos was conducting business.

She swallowed the bitterness in her mouth, unwillingly flashing back to a time she'd impulsively interrupted one of her father's meetings to ask if she could join a group of teenagers heading to an Athens disco. She'd never been to a disco, never been dancing. It had sounded exciting and despite her mother's warning, she'd gone to her father, desperate for permission. Her mother had been right. Her father was furious at the interruption, slapping her sharply across the face in front of a dozen men. He'd slapped her and sent her to bed.

Instead of dancing she'd wept for hours, trapped in her loneliness, and her shame.

Her father had crushed her feeble attempts at independence, refusing to permit her even the smallest of freedoms, wanting the traditional Greek daughter.

The slow circle of Christos's thumb against her hipbone permeated the cloud of memory and with a small jolt, her attention returned to the business discussion and the warmth of Christos's hand on her hip.

Heat shimmered within her, a spark of awareness that made her tingle from head to toe. And again she felt desire stir, languorous need awakening, threatening to possess her rational mind.

As Christos and the other man discussed the European market and the American economy, Alysia's head began to swim, dazed by the tension flooding her limbs. As the conversation continued, she heard fewer words, too aware of the blood surging through her, the tightening in her belly making her thoughts race in a dangerous direction. She'd never felt desire like this. It made her desperate to answer the emptiness aching inside her.

Just when she thought she couldn't stand it anymore, the couple moved on and she caught his fingers in one hand, lifting them from her hip.

"Don't," she gritted, undone by the intimacy, overwhelmed by her hungry response.

"We're supposed to be happy. We're newlyweds in love."

She stiffened in silent protest, hating how powerless she felt, helpless with needs she couldn't control. If he could make her feel this way in public, what would happen tonight when they were alone?

She couldn't let him make love to her. She wasn't on birth control, she doubted he'd wear a condom. He'd made it clear that he wanted children and he wanted them soon. One of these nights he'd push to consummate the marriage. Maybe even tonight.

She had to leave, couldn't afford to wait for another opportunity.

She had to go. Immediately. The party was the perfect cover. So many beautiful people coming and going, music playing, a hum of activity. Christos wouldn't even know she'd gone until too late.

Afraid she'd lose her resolve, she turned to him, murmured an excuse, a pretense of needing to use the ladies' room. Quickly she moved away, out of the white-and-gold ballroom, down the hall, continuing to a narrower passage, one that cut through to the kitchen.

She ignored the kitchen staff, her head high, her purse dangling carelessly from her wrist. She didn't run. Just kept her gaze fixed on the door before her.

The driveway, lined with a dozen expensive imported cars, Bentleys and Rolls-Royces, Mercedes, Jaguars and Ferraris, looked like an exotic car show. Alysia passed the parked cars with barely a glance, nodding briefly at the cluster of drivers who stood in front of a marble lion smoking.

One driver—her driver?—called out to her, asking if she needed a ride. She shook her head and continued on, knowing that a taxi would be the safest option.

She flagged the taxi, a four-person Mercedes, not far from the Trapano Bridge at the south end of Argostoli. Close to the harbor, she could smell the pungent salt in the air, and the hum of the ocean.

''Where to?'' the driver asked.

''Sami,'' she said, directing him to the island's other port, a small village with ferry access to other islands, as well as the mainland. And Sami lay miles from bustling Argostoli with its community of wealthy shipowners who knew too much about her and the Lemos family. No one in Sami would know her.

Alysia pawned her diamond-and-sapphire bracelet in Sami for necessary cash. Out of the money she'd gotten for the bracelet she paid for her ferry ride to Lefkas, and then on Lefkas, was able to buy a one-way plane ticket on Olympic Airways for Athens.

How ironic, she thought with a small twist of her lips, that the bracelet, a gift from her father on her sixteenth birthday, should now buy her freedom.

If only she'd taken the bracelet to Paris, pawned it there. She could have used the money. It might have saved Alexi.

Suddenly she saw Alexi's perfect face, his silvery blond curls, his small arms outstretched, floating.

Floating.

Alysia squeezed her eyes shut, pressed her knuckles against her mouth and fought to erase the memory. For a long moment she sat hunched, her insides frozen, her body rigid with endless, wordless grief.

To think that a bracelet could save her baby's life.

To think that a bracelet could have saved her sanity.

But, no, she couldn't think like that. She'd promised her mother she wouldn't think like that. Those thoughts were the dark ones that ate her alive. Those thoughts nearly destroyed her before. She had to live in the moment. There was only the moment. The past was gone. And the future lay ahead.

In Athens she called an old childhood friend, Lalia, to see if she couldn't perhaps stay with her for a few days until she arranged for a new passport.

Lalia, who'd always been very modern, so far forgoing marriage to pursue a career as a textile designer, was more than happy to accommodate Alysia, especially as she was preparing to fly to London on business and was anxious to find a housesitter for her high-strung cat.

"Zita's very sensitive and he hates disruption," Lalia said, gathering her travel bags and taxi fare together. "Don't be disappointed if he won't play. He'll probably hide until I come home. Just feed him and pretend everything's normal."

Alysia checked her smile. "How like a man."

"Speaking of men, I thought you were married?"

"Rumors." Alysia held the door open for her friend. "Now go, before you miss your flight. And don't worry about a thing. Zita and I will get along just fine."

The first day alone Alysia did nothing but sleep, and read, and sleep some more. The second day she made some calls. The government office handling passports couldn't help her without a copy of her birth certificate, which would require her coming into the office in person to fill out the necessary paperwork.

She hung up the phone and reluctantly conceded that she'd have to visit the government building in person. She'd hoped to avoid going out in public but perhaps if she donned a hat and sunglasses she'd pass unrecognized.

Zita, the onyx-colored, tailless cat, poked his head out from beneath the lace curtains at the window and gazed at her through narrowed eyes.

Alysia imagined she saw disapproval in Zita's slitted eyes and turned her back on the cat. Everything's fine, she firmly told herself. Don't let a cat put your nerves on edge.

The labyrinth of government offices exercised Alysia's strained patience. An afternoon spent waiting in long lines, filling out paperwork in duplicate, only to be sent to another endless line, turned a beautiful autumn afternoon into sheer torture.

Three hours after entering the government building, Alysia left, having been informed that the passport, even if rushed, would take two weeks to process.

Two weeks.

Alysia let herself into Lalia's apartment. Closing the door with one hand, she kicked off her leather loafers and dropped her purse on top of the shoes.

Barefoot she padded down the hall and into the kitchen, opening the refrigerator door for a bottle of chilled mineral water. "Zita," she called. "Hungry?"

The cat didn't answer. Of course, she hadn't expected it to answer, but people were supposed to take to their cats, right?

With her bottle of water in hand she headed toward the living room, richly patterned rugs—all Lalia's design—beneath her bare feet. "Zita! Where are you? Still hiding?"

She stopped short. A man, a tall, broad-shouldered man, sat on the sofa—no, dominated the sofa—with a tailless black cat curled in his lap.

Christos.

CHAPTER SIX

"HELLO, Mrs. Pateras," Christos said, his tone disarmingly conversational as he caressed Zita's dark head. "How was your day?"

She stared at the broad tanned hand cupped over the cat's head, strong fingers slowly, deliberately scratching behind Zita's short, pointy ears, and began to tremble. Her legs suddenly went nerveless, turning into mush.

The bottle of water almost slid from her fingers. "Christos."

"You remembered," he retorted with a savage twist of his lips. He rose so swiftly from the couch that he nearly dumped Zita on his feet. "I wasn't sure if you would. But then, I'm only your *husband.*"

He smiled at her, and yet there was nothing remotely kind in his expression, his features granite-like, his dark eyes glittering.

Zita meowed a protest at being so unceremoniously dumped from his comfortable resting place, but Christos ignored the cat, and clenching his fists, took a quick step toward her before checking himself.

She felt his anger, his barely controlled temper, and a sick tremor coursed through her. "Ahh…"

"What was that, sweetheart? Cat got your tongue?"

His joke went in one ear and out the other. She couldn't speak, her tongue wooden, her jaw taut, fear turning her inside out. Instead she helplessly shook her head, her gaze darting to the door and then back at Christos.

"I wouldn't try it. You won't get away and you'll only make me angry."

"And you're not angry now?" she flashed, finding her voice, and simultaneously stunned by the weakness in her knees. She felt as if her legs would buckle beneath her any moment now.

"Oh, I'm angry all right, I'm fit to be tied. But my father has persuaded me to show you mercy."

Mercy. What an odd, terrifying, and yet incredibly Greek thing to say.

Christos moved toward her, closing the distance between them. She was forced to tilt her head back to see his face, realizing belatedly she'd forgotten his height, and the sheer size of him.

"How did you find me?"

"You didn't think I would?" A black eyebrow lifted, expressing surprise.

"You didn't know I was on the mainland. You don't know Lilia."

"But I know you." His eyes gleamed, dark and hard, fixing on her face with predatory instinct. His smile deepened and it was the coldest, most malevolent smile she'd ever seen. "I knew you'd apply for a passport. I knew you'd try to leave Greece."

Her tongue thick and heavy, wouldn't form words. Instead she stared at him, dry-mouthed, wide-eyed, unable to think a single coherent thought. Fear pummeled her brain, melted her bones. "No..." she whispered helplessly. "It couldn't have been so easy."

"Sweetheart, it was too easy. Like taking candy from a baby." He stopped in front of her, reached out and lifted one gold strand from her shoulder, sliding the tendril through his fingers as if silk. "You see, sweet Alysia, I have a home here in Athens. I spend a great deal of time here. New York may be my headquarters, but I maintain offices in Athens, too. I have employees in Athens, and they've been watching you, from the moment you flew into the airport to the moment you just walked in the door."

Horror filled her. He'd had her followed the past few days. She'd been under surveillance. A prisoner, his prisoner, and she didn't even know it.

Slowly he coiled the tendril around his finger, wrapping it into a honey ribbon. He wrapped it tighter then gave a little pull, making her wince.

"You made a fool out of me," he murmured with another small tug. "In front of my colleagues and friends. You humiliated me at the Pappas's, created quite a stir. You should be punished. How shall I punish you? Any suggestions?"

Her tongue continued to cleave to the roof of her mouth. Her heart hammered. "No."

One of Christos's thick black brows lifted. "No suggestions, or no to punishment?"

All this time she thought—believed—she was free. These past several days had felt like heaven. Instead she'd been his, remained his possession. It made her want to weep with frustration. "Why did you think I'd want to leave Greece?"

"You hate Greece. You feel trapped here. I imagine you wanted to fly to England, look up your mother's family." Carefully he unwound the tendril.

"You're awfully clever, aren't you?"

"No. You're just awfully predictable."

"Go to hell!"

Almost absently he caressed her cheek. "Don't be childish, Alysia. It's not becoming."

She flinched at his touch, drawing sharply away. "I can't believe you had me followed."

"How could you think I wouldn't protect my investment?"

The softness in his voice, the husky tone, contrasted cruelly with his expression. His eyes said it all. She'd betrayed him.

He reached into a pocket and withdrew the diamond-and-sapphire bracelet she'd recently pawned. "Here. Put it back on."

She cringed at the bracelet, hating the reminder of the power Christos held over her. "No."

"Do it. Or I will." Without waiting for her to answer he took her hand, flipped her wrist open and snapped the glittering bangle onto her slender arm.

It looked completely incongruous with her leather loafers and casual clothes yet it felt heavy, like iron, he was shackling her to him, taking control of her life again.

"Do not take it off," he said curtly, "and do not think of running away again."

"I refuse to be an object, Christos!"

"You're no object. You're my wife." He tilted her chin up with one of his fingers, his dark eyes searching her mutinous expression. "I erred in judgment once, but I won't make the same mistake again. It's time I exerted my rights in this marriage and time you behaved like a proper Greek wife."

She knew, a split second in advance, that he was going to kiss her. Yet there was no escaping him. His mouth crushed hers, grinding her lips apart, his tongue boldly thrusting inside her mouth, stabbing at the softness with ill-concealed contempt.

But even as his tongue lashed at her sensitive contours, her body warmed, her innermost muscles tightening in anticipation. Despite everything, she wanted him.

Christos's dark head lifted and he gazed into her eyes, a mocking smile etched on his lips. "I'm beginning to understand why your father found it necessary to keep you locked up. You're wild. You're utterly wanton."

Heat burned in bands across the tops of her cheekbones. She tried to take a step back but his hands clasped her at the waist, fingers dipping into the small of her spine.

Again his mouth crushed hers, his tongue raking the sensitive contours of her mouth, thrusting at the hollow of her cheek, beneath her tongue, even tracing the roof of her mouth.

She clung to him, clasping his arms, her legs without strength. She felt mindless with wanting and helplessly opened her mouth wider to him, her tongue finding his, teasing.

He moved to strip her of her jeans, but his hand stilled on her tummy. "Stop me, now—" he muttered thickly, but she didn't speak, and she didn't answer him.

With a groan he tugged her jeans down and then her panties, pulling them off her ankles and casting them to the ground. She felt him grind his hips against hers, his erection creating friction between her thighs.

He worked his zipper down, dropped his own trousers even as his fingers slid between her legs, finding her heat and to her shame, her eager moisture.

Christos dropped her to the ground and parted her legs with his knees. He held her bottom in his hands and without a word, drove into her.

She gasped at the thrust, her body forced to accommodate his size, and she buried her knuckles into his back, overwhelmed by the intensity of his body filling hers, joining them intimately together.

He shifted, easing slowly out of her and then with a kiss on her neck, entered her again, filling her once more, making stars sputter against her tightly closed eyes.

And he made love to her without a word, without

another kiss, just moving inside her slowly, deeply to pull out and enter again, and again, and again.

He felt long, hard, thick, and yet his skin was as smooth as silk, his hips hard and narrow, in her hands. She clung to him as he moved inside her, scarcely daring to breathe, caught up in the pictures he was painting in her head. Him, her, the constellation of stars.

She felt him tense, a soft groan coming from his lips, and as he surged forward, deeper into her, she felt herself step out into the darkest night and fall, silently, blindly into waves of sensation. She rode the waves with desperation, clasping Christos's shoulders, burying her face against his broad chest.

There was no one but them. No place but now. Nothing but this.

Him, her, his body still straining, his hands now cradling her head.

She'd never come before. Never had an orgasm.

"I'm sorry," Christos said thickly, untangling his limbs, his skin still damp, his black hair disheveled. He drew away, rubbed his face with one hand, stood up.

He was sorry and he was done. So that's how he felt. It wasn't what she'd imagined, wasn't what she'd experienced. Nothing beautiful for him. Just a physical act. A form of exercise.

She sat up slowly, realizing they both still wore their shirts but not pants.

Thank goodness she'd just had her period. Thank

God she shouldn't be fertile now. She couldn't, wouldn't, conceive.

He stepped into his underwear and then his pants. "Did I hurt you?" he demanded, his voice pitched low, almost rough.

"No." She wanted to tell him it had been incredible, that even without love, it was the most sensual experience of her life. She'd answered each of his thrusts by lifting her own hips, wrapped her arms around his neck to draw him even closer, wanting it all, wanting him. But now...no pants, the dampness of him inside her, the obvious disgust on his face...

Good thing there was no love between them, no love lost, either.

What had they done? What had she been thinking?

Christos raked a hand through his dark hair, attempting to comb it into submission. "Dress. It's time to go. My driver is downstairs waiting."

He didn't speak on the short drive home. He felt Alysia's revulsion. It mirrored his own.

He was appalled by his actions, stunned that he'd forced himself on her. He'd taken her without regard to her feelings, or her needs.

Christos was grateful when the limousine drew in front of his estate, the palatial marble villa rising from behind iron gates and exotic greenery.

The gates magically slid open and the car continued up the driveway, the powerful engine vibrating like a great beast. He couldn't wait to get out of the car and as far from Alysia's accusing eyes as possible.

He'd promised to respect her, promised to never force himself on her, and yet what did he do but throw her onto the ground and bury himself inside her?

Alysia cast a desperate glance behind her at the high wrought-iron fence and gatehouse before turning to face the dozen employees gathered on the villa's front steps.

Christos nodded at them and then gestured toward Alysia, his expression grim. ''The wife,'' he announced curtly, before continuing up the sweeping circular staircase, leaving her to follow like a child in disgrace.

She flushed, and wordlessly trailed after him, aware of the cool scrutiny of his employees.

Reaching the top of the stairs Christos showed her into a lofty room that was obviously his own private quarters. Desk, leather armchairs, reading lamps.

He closed the door, motioned her to one of the leather chairs. She sat gingerly on the edge of one, wondering what would come next.

''I'm sorry I lost my temper. I behaved like a brute. It won't happen like that again.'' His speech was sharp, and short. He leaned against the shut door, his arms crossing over his chest, muscles tight, tension emanating from him in great silent waves. ''Your father warned me you'd try to run away. He said you'd go the first chance you got. I thought I was prepared. Yet I let down my guard at the party.''

She squirmed inwardly realizing how humiliated he must have been at Constantine's. Everyone looking for her. Everyone aware that his new bride had deserted him.

"Your father called," he continued. "He offered his services, apologized for your behavior."

She ducked her head, even more mortified. Her father calling to offer *his* services!

"I told him no thank you, of course." Christos's dark gaze met hers, his expression flinty. "I said you'd be back in no time and soon fulfilling your duty, providing me with sons."

Her heart beat faster. Her throat threatened to seal close. And still she didn't speak so he plunged on. "We will make love until you conceive. We will start that family. You will prove to your father—and the other Greek ship owners—that my faith in you isn't misplaced, that you know and accept your responsibility."

"No."

Her voice was but a whisper and yet he heard it. "No what, Alysia?"

"No, I will not give you children." She lifted her head, looked him in the eye. "No sons. Not even daughters. No heirs."

"Is this a philosophical issue for you? Part of your rebellion against Greek society?"

"A personal issue."

"Ah, then we can work through this."

"No, we can't work through this. You married the wrong woman. You chose the wrong wife. A hundred women could have filled my position. A hundred women would have begged to bear your children. I, on the other hand, will not.''

His smile had all but disappeared and she slid instinctively backward, hips hugging the chair, even though he hadn't moved from the door. ''I have tried to be patient, Alysia, tried to understand your feelings, but my patience is about gone. We need to move forward. We need to start our future.''

He approached her quietly, crouching at her feet, his palms sliding up her shins, over her knees, electrifying her legs. Awareness exploded in her middle, tension coiling in her lower belly making her thighs tremble.

Christos's dark gaze momentarily met hers and he smiled—if the slight twist of lips could be called a smile—acknowledging her unwilling response.

His palm shaped her outer thigh and followed with his body. She felt the press of his chest against her knees as he parted them, moving between her legs.

Blood pumped through her veins, heat searing her face, shredding countless nerve endings beneath her skin. It shocked her that she could still want him, shocked her that she could feel so raw and physical even after what had taken place at Lilia's apartment.

''Not again,'' she gritted as his thumbs caressed the lean line of her thigh.

''And just what do you think I'm going to do?'' he drawled, his voice never more husky, never more American than now.

Her mouth felt so dry that it cleaved to the roof of her mouth. She stared into his face, drowning in sensation, painfully aware of the size distinction between them.

"You're going to want more...sex," she retorted, her voice more breathy than angry, her body so traitorously warm she despised herself.

"I'll take more time, this time, I'll take it slow." He dropped a fleeting kiss against the side of her neck, just beneath her earlobe.

She tried to kick him again. He held her tighter. "You are the worst kind of man."

"The worst kind? Lower than your father?" He pressed another equally brief, equally tantalizing kiss to the outline of her breast, just brushing the taut, aching nipple. "That is a shame."

Warmth surged through her, traitorous warmth and she wanted to weep with frustration. She couldn't believe she'd want a man she hated so much, and yet her body, her stupid wretched, needy body was responding to him in hungry, wanton desperation.

His lips found her nipple again, closing around the exquisitely sensitive bud, suckling it through her blouse. She squirmed helplessly, fire and need rolling through her in great waves. For a half second she clung to him, closing her eyes and giving herself over to the pleasure of desire. She allowed herself to feel it all—the throb of his muscular body, the heat simmering beneath her skin, the insistent need between her thighs—and then when the craving became too strong, she wrenched away, rolling out from beneath Christos's arm to stand across the room, facing the window.

''You don't like me, I understand that,'' he said quietly, his voice devoid of all emotion, ''but we're married. We have to make this work.''

She squeezed her eyes closed as if to shut out his voice. ''You will never get what you want from me.''

He rose, yet he didn't leave. She felt his presence as if he still held her in his arms. ''I don't know what happened between you and your first husband, but Jeremy Winston did something to you—''

''No.''

''He put a curse on you, froze your heart, trapping you like Sleeping Beauty in the tower.''

''You don't know what you're talking about.''

''I know enough. I know your marriage ended with heartbreak. I know you spent nearly two years in Switzerland, after you left the Sanatorium, trying to find yourself again.''

Alysia's head felt light, so light that it tingled at the top. ''I can't talk about it.''

''Why not? What happened, Alysia?''

''Nothing happened.''

''Something did—''

''No!''

''Something so dark, so terrible—''

The words surged around her, words sweeping, blurring until the room spun with words and she heard nothing more.

Christos had called a doctor and the doctor, after a thorough exam, recommended rest, vitamins and more iron. Women, the doctor said, are often anemic and if they wanted to conceive, it would be wise for Alysia to increase her iron intake.

"I'm not that anemic," she protested, a day after the doctor had been called, and facing her third steak in a row. "I can get iron from spinach. I don't have to eat a platter of steaks."

"We can't have babies if you're not strong."

"I am strong, and I don't have to gorge on meat to conceive. Now back off with the bully routine. I won't be intimidated."

Christos visibly fought to control his temper. "I'm not trying to intimidate you. I just want you to be careful."

"I am careful. I'm also bored. I'd like to get some fresh air. If that's all right with you, of course."

He muttered something beneath his breath and shook his head, obviously eager to end the discussion. "You may go to the pool. I'll have the maid put towels on a lounge chair for you. But don't stay out in the sun too long. You don't want to burn."

Alysia dragged the chaise lounge from beneath the umbrella closer to the pool where she could enjoy the sparkle of the sun on the clear, aquamarine water. She'd brought a book downstairs with her but it turned out to be a rather dry historical account requiring more concentration than she could muster at the moment. After a half hour of reading, she tossed the hardback aside and gave herself over to the pleasure of nothing.

The sun felt wonderful on her back and unhooking the bikini top, she wiggled into the towel, drinking in the steady warm sunshine and promptly fell asleep.

Sometime later, she had no idea how long, she felt a touch, a lovely caress, like feathers or velvet dragged gently across her bare spine.

Sighing she nestled into the towel, not wanting to lose the delicious sensation. The leisurely caress repeated itself, and her lower tummy tightened, warming. She breathed in slowly, not wanting to open her eyes and lose the dreamy sensation.

The velvetlike touch played at the edge of her bikini bottoms, lingering over the line of skin just above the patch of fabric. She wiggled a little, teased by the touch and yet disappointed by the brevity.

Suddenly it clasped her bottom, no tentative touch, but a large hand firmly cupping the curve of cheek.

This was no dream.

Alysia leaped up, snatching her bikini top even as she struggled to cover herself. "Christos!"

The tall shadow shifted, creating a sliver of sunlight where darkness had been. He sat down on the lounge chair next to her. "You should have put lotion on. You've been out here hours and burned yourself to a crisp."

She glanced at her wrist, no watch, and then up at the sun. It had moved. A great deal, actually. A quarter of the way through the sky. "What time is it?" she demanded, struggling to get her bikini top back on without exposing herself.

"Quarter to four."

"*What?*"

He watched her fumble with the flimsy fabric with interest. "Perhaps I should help you."

"I don't need your help."

"You need to put something on the burn. You don't want the skin to blister."

"It's never blistered before." Yet her trembling fingers made it almost impossible to adjust the scrap of fabric across her chest. She had a horrible sensation that one nipple, or the other, would pop out at any moment.

"Alysia, I have seen breasts before."

"But never mine."

His lip curled, a black eyebrow winged. Laughter tinged his husky voice. "I'm sure I can handle the shock."

Of course he'd say something smart like that. He was a born wit. Jumping to her feet, she grabbed her towel and slid into her robe with just the briefest flash of flesh. "Unfortunately I don't think I can."

The silk robe felt ice-cold against her hot back and she winced as she tied the silk sash around her waist. "What time is dinner?"

"Drinks at seven. Dinner at nine."

She'd promised to be there, had planned on meeting him, but Alysia hadn't counted on the extent of her sunburn. It was a livid sunburn.

The warm bath had helped, at first, but as soon as she'd lightly toweled off, her entire backside, from shoulders to her insteps, felt like fire.

She couldn't even pull a pair of panties on without tears starting to her eyes. Her bra straps sliced into her now-blistering shoulders. Nothing in her closet looked comfortable. She stripped off the bra, stripped off the underwear and carefully crawled between cool bed sheets.

To hell with dinner. She'd stay in bed instead.

Too proud to summon Christos, she simply didn't show up downstairs at seven.

Quarter after seven, he arrived at the bedroom door.

He didn't bother to knock. He just walked straight in. "Knowing your penchant for running away, I thought I'd check to see if you were still with us."

Alysia drew the bed sheet toward her chin. "As you can see, I'm still here."

"But in bed."

"Yes."

"Is that, by happy chance, an invitation?" His teeth flashed whitely in a crooked grin.

"No."

"But you appear naked."

"Because I'm too sunburned to dress."

"Show me."

Her stomach did a slow, peculiar curl. Heat prickled across the curve of her cheeks. "You want proof?"

"Please."

CHAPTER SEVEN

PRICKLES of awareness touched her spine, contrasting with the fever raging in her skin. Alysia struggled to deny the feeling. "I'm not going to pull the covers down just so you can see a sunburn."

"You haven't been in the sun for over a year. You could have second- or third-degree burns."

"You're exaggerating. I might be a little sore, but it's just a sunburn."

"I'll be the judge of that." Christos stalked to the edge of the bed and wrenched the covers from her clenched fingers, peeling the sheet back.

Alysia rolled over onto her stomach to protect her front, humiliated by his impersonal scrutiny. "Just a sunburn," she gritted, "I told you. Now will you please allow me some privacy!"

"You're fried to a crisp," he answered, touching the middle of her back.

She couldn't help wincing. It hurt, badly. "*Please*. The covers."

"Not until I put something on your skin first. I've some aloe gel with a topical anesthetic in it that should help."

"Can you at least let me cover my...bottom." She felt his gaze move to the aforementioned and she blushed from head to toe, acutely embarrassed.

''You are modest,'' he drawled, heading to the bathroom and returning with a hand towel and tube of ointment.

He spread the small towel across her bottom, going to great lengths to adjust it just so, his long fingers brushing the curve of her cheek not just once, but repeatedly, as he slid the small towel up, before tugging it down. To the left. Up a hair. Down a bit, and over to the right.

He was manhandling her and she found it degrading. But that didn't seem to keep her from responding, each brush of his fingers, each slip of the towel sending fiery arcs of feeling through her veins, coiling need in the deepest part of her, a need so strong, so insistent that she throbbed from the inside out.

''That's enough!'' she snapped, finding his touch nearly as unbearable as the ache spreading from her womb into her limbs.

His fingers trailed across the dip in her spine, and tugged the small towel higher on her cheek, leaving the underside of her bottom exposed to air. ''Are you sure? I wouldn't want to deprive you of your modesty.''

''Then perhaps a bigger towel would have been more helpful,'' she gritted from between clenched teeth.

''I was afraid a bigger towel would irritate the burn.''

The cool air seemed to caress her exposed bottom and it took every bit of her self-control to not wiggle.

Part of her felt humiliated and another felt shamelessly excited. "You're the one irritating the burn."

He merely laughed softly, the husky sound reverberating from his chest. Unscrewing the cap from the ointment tube, Christos took a seat next to her on the bed.

His thigh brushed her hip and she tensed, shoulders hunching around her ears. She was aware of Christos in every nerve in her body, feeling his strength and warmth as if he were the sun and she the moon.

He rubbed the aloe between his hands and she could hear the slick lotion slurp against his skin. It struck her as an indecent sound, sexual and raw, and the ache in her lower belly intensified. Pressing her inner thighs together, she tried to control her breathing and yet her heart raced, her senses enflamed. She wanted him to touch her even as she feared it.

"Lie still," he commanded, leaning forward, his sinewy thigh pressing against her own. "This might sting a bit."

Sting? The ointment felt like ice. Helplessly she bucked against his hand, wriggling to escape the prickly hot and cold sensations. But he didn't let her escape. He pressed her down against the sheet and continued applying the aloe gel in slow, steady strokes.

Little by little the anesthetic went to work, numbing the worst of the pain and again making her hopelessly aware of Christos's hands stroking her spine.

His hands moved over her body, down the length of her spinal column, into the dip of her lower back, and then up, over the flare of her hips.

Heat coursed through her, but this warmth had nothing to do with the sunburn and everything to do with his sensuous caress.

His fingertips explored the hollow just above the cleft in her cheeks and she wiggled, telling him to move away. He did, but only to move to her flare of hips, caressing up her waist, to the curve of her breasts.

Alysia couldn't breathe. His thumbs stroked the soft swell. Her nipples hardened, the soft flesh prickling with awareness. She wanted more sensation than feathers and butterflies, more than just this soft teasing touch.

His hands returned to her rib cage and then lifted altogether. She drew a short, shallow breath. "Thank you," she choked.

"Not quite done," he answered, lightly massaging her shoulders and nape.

"It's good," she replied, her voice sounding thick and slow.

But how could it be otherwise? His touch sent blood coursing through her veins with dizzying speed. She couldn't catch her breath. Her heart raced too fast. Her body quivered from head to toe, but the greatest tension coiled in her middle, hot and heavy, her inner thighs almost dancing with need.

"I haven't covered everything," he replied,

squeezing another dollop of gel onto the middle of her back.

She wanted to protest but no sound came from her mouth. Instead she closed her eyes, her lips parting, attuned to every shift of his body, every press of his thigh against her own.

Again his palms fanned the width of her rib cage and curved down to cup her breasts, thumbs flicking across taut, swollen nipples.

Mercy.

If there was purgatory, she'd found it. Caught between heaven and hell and she wanted him to stop just as much as she couldn't let him.

Swept away by touch, sensation, raw physical hunger. Years of being nothing but skin and bones and suddenly she was all nerve endings. Alive, humming, hot liquid desire.

Forget prayers and penance, she'd take sin any day.

He stroked down again, his warm, hard hands moving beneath the towel, shaping the curve of her bottom. The liquid heat between her thighs threatened to consume her. She pressed her legs together tighter, trying to deny the tingle in her flesh, but Christos applied more pressure, deeply kneading the muscles in her bottom and she felt equal waves of shame and craving.

''Don't,'' she muttered, humiliated and yet sinfully aroused.

''Do you want me to stop?''

''N-n-no.'' The confession cost her but it was the truth.

Even without being able to see his face, she could feel his smile. But for once she didn't care. The sensations filling her body were too lovely, too consuming to interrupt.

His fingertips discovered the sensitive line between bottom and thigh and he caressed that, too, awakening a river of longing in the only place that hadn't been burned. The teasing of her sensitive flesh created the most awful awareness of her body and needs. She felt huge in that moment, voracious.

She ought to have more control, ought to tell him in scathing tones that she wouldn't put up with such liberties, but oh, liberties had never felt so wonderful. She was quite dizzy with want, and she took in air in short, shallow gasps, afraid to breathe, afraid to distract him, afraid that this pleasure would end.

Pressing her open mouth to her forearm, she shuddered as Christos's fingers slid inward, tracing the cleft of her bottom down, until he'd discovered the tight protective curls and her hot, wanton dampness.

She was on fire, truly, but this had nothing to do with her sunburn and everything to do with need. Suddenly she'd become all liquid and hunger, like molten lava.

No one had ever touched her with such tantalizing intimacy, not even Jeremy who'd been a timid—and dare she admit?—unsatisfying lover. For Jeremy sex had been just that: a brief coupling and then uncoupling. It hadn't crossed her mind to assert that she had physical needs.

When Christos's fingers slid across her slick, sensitive flesh, she trembled, biting her arm to keep from arching against his hand. She couldn't lose control, couldn't betray herself with him. But when he stroked the engorged bud, a thousand nerve endings danced and her hips lifted, as if of their own volition.

He caressed her again, and again, and each time he touched the acutely sensitive bud, she felt as though he was winding her tighter and tighter like an old-fashioned wood top.

More, faster, tighter.

Brilliant color filled her mind, painted stripes of red and green and white against the polished wood.

Stroking her, he wound her tighter still, drawing her in and out of herself, aware of his hands, his warmth, her heat, her labored breathing.

She couldn't catch her breath and the intensity of it made her long to scream. And then when she felt quite mad and mindless, he put her over the edge, setting the coiled wooden top on the ground, fingers stroking faster, faster, faster.

He let her go. And suddenly she was flying, flung across the floor, spinning wildly out of control.

The speed and strength of the climax stunned her. She bit her forearm, choking back a scream, muffling the intensity of her response.

Hell, hell, hell!

She'd thought she'd had an orgasm yesterday, but that…that was nothing like this. This…it was unreal.

Incredible. Unbelievable. One could get addicted to feeling this way.

Her open mouth pressed to her arm drew her back to the moment. Christos stirred and she suddenly remembered him, and his part in this.

He'd brought her to a climax with his hand. Good God, how impersonal. How crude. She longed to bury her face in the pillow and hide but that wouldn't exactly work. He was waiting for her to speak. Waiting for something.

Slowly she turned her head, her eyes feeling heavy, sleepy, and she stared up at Christos. His own gaze looked slumberous, his dark pupils almost black.

He'd enjoyed this, she realized, startled, overwhelmed. He'd enjoying making her fall apart in his hands.

She dampened her bottom lip, overwhelmed by her weakness. And still he waited for her to speak. She grasped at the first thing that came to mind.

"That was nice."

His lashes lowered, concealing his emotions. "I must be out of practice. I'll have to work on that." And with a nod in her direction, he left, leaving her naked and alone in bed.

Sleeping that night was excruciating, her skin so hot she felt as though a fire had been lit beneath her skin. Once she woke to find Christos at her side, aspirin in his hand. She gratefully accepted and allowed him to spray a topical pain relief across her back. He avoided mentioning what had taken place earlier and after he left she fell into a deeper, more restful sleep.

A maid brought a breakfast tray to her in bed and Alysia ate her melon and sweet roll sitting up in bed, moving gingerly, if at all.

Christos appeared briefly, dressed in a suit and tie, dark hair slicked back, accenting the hardness of his features. "How are you feeling?"

"A little better."

"I'd warned you about the sun."

Of course he did. He was the font of all wisdom. She gritted her teeth, resisting the urge to reply sarcastically.

"If you need me, you can reach me at my office."

"I won't need you."

He shrugged. "You say that, but your actions contradict your words." And with that, he was gone.

He was right, she realized, sinking back into bed. She felt completely split, two personalities inhabiting one body. One part of her craved purity, denial, discipline. Another hungered for heat and passion. It'd always been this way, too. As a child she'd felt so emotional, so hungry for affection, and her father's coldness, his critical manner, had made her ashamed of her feelings, turning a little girl's needs into something dirty and wrong.

Daughters were to serve. Daughters were to be silent. Daughters were to sacrifice.

Her father made it clear Alysia failed on all three accounts.

The older she grew, the more she struggled against

her passionate nature, fighting to deny herself, fighting to be what her father demanded of her. She'd always had a knack for drawing and she turned to her giant sketch pads, pouring her energy into endless charcoal drawings, portraits of the family servants, sketches of neighbor children, landscapes of the sea and rocky terrain.

Earning the art scholarship had been an answer to prayer. Her father had been furious that she'd even applied, but her mother somehow persuaded him to let her go. Once in Paris she embraced everything new, relishing the eclectic circle of artists and writers who talked about everything but making money. They were passionate and interesting, clever and original. Jeremy was one of them, always the life of the party, charming, handsome, completely irresponsible. She'd loved that about him. Loved the fact that he couldn't hold a job. Wouldn't hold a job. He was the least controlling person she'd ever known.

They didn't date long. A couple of nights after first making love he suggested they move in together. But deep down she was still a good Greek girl and she couldn't just live with a man. She needed to be a wife, and then a mother.

And so she had been. Both.

Alysia curled on her side, smoothed her hand across the cool cotton sheet. Paris seemed so long ago. Jeremy was just a name of a man she'd once known.

It was strange she thought, she'd lived lives that

didn't exist anymore. The good Greek girl was gone. Only the hedonist remained.

And the hedonist had decided she wanted Christos, wanted to remain with Christos, even if she had to bend the rules to make the relationship work.

He wanted a wife. She'd be his wife. She just wouldn't get pregnant. The doctor had given her a blue plastic case with a six month supply of birth control pills, to give her time to build up her strength before trying for a baby. So for the next six months she was safe. And then she'd see another doctor, and renew the prescription.

Late in the day, Alysia managed to bathe and dress, slipping on a soft cotton sundress and low-heeled sandals. She ate dinner alone in the formal dining room and wandered the garden grounds, hearing the distant horn of a car.

Footsteps sounded on the flagstone path. She turned, discovering Christos behind her. He'd changed from his suit into pale linen trousers and a smooth cotton shirt the color of butterscotch. The caramel color suited him, enhancing his bronze complexion and the gleam of his black hair.

"I'm sorry to have kept you waiting," he said. "There's been a problem at my head office in New York."

He sounded quietly ironic, as if everything between them was a joke. Hurt unfolded inside her chest, hurt because she understood that there was something intrinsically good in him, in them, but they couldn't seem to get around the obstacles.

"I've been all right. I'm quite good at entertaining myself."

He nodded slightly, comprehending her implied reference at learning to stay busy and out of her father's way. "I need to be in New York tomorrow. We'll leave tonight."

She felt a leap of excitement, and a peculiar sense of hope. Cynically she mocked her expectations. Starting over in a new place wasn't exactly starting fresh. The problems would follow. The conflict remained.

But maybe it didn't have to. Perhaps away from Greece they could start over, make something new. Here everything felt tainted. She felt tainted. But in America they could change, she could change. She would try harder. She'd please more.

"I've already instructed Housekeeping to pack. We'll be leaving soon." He hesitated, his expression grim. "There's something else. Your father wanted to stop over tonight, to say goodbye. I told him no. I hope that's all right with you."

Christos's private jet landed so gently that there wasn't even a bump as the plane's wheels touched the tarmac. They taxied to the executive terminal and immediately deplaned, exiting the jet only to be handed into the back of a waiting limousine.

Despite the early hour, dawn just breaking, Christos returned phone calls during the short drive to his country house in Darien, Connecticut.

Once during his conversation, he covered the receiver and leaned forward, pointing out a series land-marks to Alysia.

In the dim morning light it was difficult to see much, but she made out the shapes of ornate iron gates, stone walls and extensive grounds with endless manicured lawns. Although she'd grown up sur-rounded by wealth, the vast American country estates impressed even her.

Christos's house, rather than dominating the ver-dant landscape, nestled into a green knoll as if to take comfort in the undulating land with its views of the water and grove of majestic hardwood trees.

"It's not what you expected," Christos said, not-ing her expression as he hung up the phone.

And it wasn't. She'd expected something grandi-ose, another opulent mansion built of polished mar-ble. Instead this rambling two-story country house had been fashioned from clapboard and stone, fea-turing big beautiful bay windows and discreet cov-ered doorways. The soft morning light outlined the shingled roof, the sharp gables, the cascading roof-line. It was a fairy-tale house, the entry marked by a profusion of climbing roses.

An older woman answered the door, dressed sim-ply in a black jersey dress, her steel-gray hair coiffed in a severe knot. The housekeeper, Alysia assumed. She assumed wrong.

"Mother," Christos said, clasping the woman by the shoulders and kissing both cheeks. "What are you doing up at this hour?"

"I've been waiting by the door."

"So I see."

Alysia went hot, then cold. Not a housekeeper, but his mother. Abruptly the stone and whitewashed clapboard house lost its fairy-tale charm.

Christos made the introductions and his mother, greeted Alysia cordially, if coolly, which didn't surprise Alysia in the slightest. In Greece, mothers-in-law were notoriously hard on daughters-in-law. No woman was ever good enough for another woman's son. Greek mothers lived for their sons and considered it their duty to instruct new wives how to run the household, perform domestic duties.

The elder Mrs. Pateras turned to her son. "She's sick?"

"No, mother, she's just slim."

The gray-haired matron cast a skeptical glance over Alysia's slender figure and wan complexion. "You called a doctor in Athens, no?"

"Yes, Mother, but the doctor assured me she just needs iron. He prescribed some iron tablets and those will help."

Mrs. Pateras's dour expression grew darker. She tossed her hands in the air, gesturing with impassioned emphasis. "I thought you wanted family, Christos. Babies, no? A skinny wife isn't good for making babies. You need a good Greek girl, not a Lemos!"

Alysia expected a mother-in-law who'd been cool, perhaps even critical, but Mrs. Pateras's vocal attack left her speechless, the blood draining from her face, her body cold.

"Mama, gently, please," Christos quietly remonstrated. "You must give Alysia a chance."

"I know all about her. I know she's not the one for you. A good Greek girl, Christos, a *good* girl."

Christos glanced at Alysia, their eyes briefly meeting. "She is a good Greek girl," he answered, his expression blank, his dark eyes shuttered, before turning back to his mother.

"But she's Lemos's daughter."

"Yes."

"So how can she be the right one for you?"

CHAPTER EIGHT

His mother gone, Christos shut the door. "She'll be fine. She just needs time," he said flatly.

Alysia didn't dare contradict him, but knew better than most that time didn't always heal. Time just made some more bitter, but she couldn't say that to Christos, and she couldn't criticize his mother, either. Mothers, especially Greek mothers, were above reproach.

Aware that he felt awkward, she sought to alleviate some of the tension. "Would you like coffee?"

"Yes, but let me make it. You're the guest."

The guest. Not his wife, but the guest.

In the kitchen she watched as he ground the beans and filled the machine's filter. He glanced at her as he turned the machine on, his expression brooding. "Alysia, it would be best if you do not discuss your father here, or in front of my parents."

"I don't understand. Is there something I should know?"

"Yes. No. It doesn't matter. Just do as I say."

Alysia could hear his mother's scathing tone echo in her head. *A good girl, not a Lemos.* She shivered. "This is personal," she said numbly. "What happened? What did my father do?"

Christos shrugged, obviously uncomfortable. "It's a long time ago."

"Not so long ago if your mother can't look at me without cursing."

"It wasn't that bad."

"Close enough." She lifted her chin, horrified to discover she was on the brink of tears. She was suddenly scared. She'd begun to feel things for Christos that she'd never felt for any man, not even Jeremy. Christos had broken through that chink in her armor. Pulled the stone from around her heart. If his family hated her they were in serious trouble. "I have a right to know. As your wife, Christos."

"Your father made it impossible for my father to get employment on Oinoussai, resulting in my father being blacklisted. He couldn't get work on the island, not ever again."

A lump lodged in her throat. "How? Why?"

"Your father was engaged in unethical business practices—"

She closed her eyes, not needing to hear another word. So Christos did know. Her father, desperate to get ahead, hired men to damage other ship owners' vessels, sabotaging sailings. When the ships couldn't sail, her father rushed in and gathered the business. "Constantine told you?"

"No. I knew long before I ever went into business with Constantine. My father was one of the welders hired to dismantle Constantine Pappas's ships."

"He should have gone to the police," she whispered, sickened at the horrible things her father had done in the name of business.

"He wouldn't, out of respect to your mother."

She felt a cold knot form inside her. "Actually I think my mother would have thanked him."

"Don't worry. Constantine and I settled our debts with your father. That's why he and I went into business together. We both needed each other. And with his help, I've had my revenge." He leaned against the counter, and smiled, but there was no warmth in his eyes, no tenderness in the twist of his lips. "I have you."

And her father's fortune.

She closed her eyes, swaying. She felt like a fool. Here she was, falling in love with Christos, while he was exacting his revenge. What an idiot she was! She never had been able to separate her body and her heart.

"Your father desperately wants grandchildren," he added tightly. "And he'll get them, but they'll be Pateras, not Lemos. Never Lemos."

Freezing inwardly she wrapped her arms around herself. "What children?" she taunted. "And from where?"

"I know you've said you can't have children but you've never been to specialists. Doctors can perform miracles these days. There are procedures—"

"Stop telling me about doctors and procedures, and listen to me!"

"I'm listening but you're not saying anything."

"Yes, I am, but you just don't want to hear it.

You want me to be like your mother, you want me to stay home and take care of things here.''

''Yes. Exactly.''

''But that's what you want, not what I want. You can't dictate my life, Christos. I've a mind. I want to use it.''

''Use it by creating a home for us, a family for us—''

The back door opened, silencing him, drawing them both up short. A cheery voice shouted out a bright hello. Christos drew in a ragged breath, his hard features brittle with anger. ''Mrs. Avery,'' he announced, his voice clipped.

They stared at each other, visibly shaken. Christos drank from his coffee cup and Alysia smoothed a hand across her skirt, trying to steady her nerves.

He married her for her body. For her ability to bear him children.

Children she wouldn't have. Seven years ago, maybe. Now? Never.

The housekeeper's low-heeled shoes clicked briskly on the hardwood floor as she entered the kitchen. Her small, plump hands busily tied her apron over her bright red dress. ''Breakfast?'' she asked, before catching sight of Alysia.

''Yes, please,'' Christos answered grimly.

The woman's round face suddenly wreathed in smiles. ''The new Mrs. Pateras?''

Christos shot Alysia a dark glance. ''Yes, indeed, Mrs. Avery. And now that you're here, I'll leave the new Mrs. Pateras in your capable hands.''

Alysia heard the front door slam in the middle of Mrs. Avery's house tour. Alysia stiffened, turned toward the sound.

"Don't worry. It's just Mr. Pateras leaving for work." And with a bright smile Mrs. Avery continued showing Alysia around.

The original house was over two hundred years old and had been greatly expanded and remodeled at the turn of the last century. The rooms were all large and well proportioned, the ceilings eleven and a half feet high with enormous paned windows providing spectacular views and welcoming light.

But it was hard to feel the sun's warmth when she felt so cold inside. Hard to enjoy the comfortable luxury when she couldn't forget her last conversation with Christos.

What he wanted, she realized wearily, was a traditional wife. A wife like his mother. A wife to carry his children.

Just like she'd failed her father, she'd fail Christos. The things he wanted she couldn't give.

Christos called and left a message with Mrs. Avery, telling her he wouldn't be home until seven-thirty. Mrs. Avery usually left at six, but tonight she offered to stay and serve the dinner she'd already prepared. Alysia assured the kindly housekeeper that she could dish and serve just fine and sent Mrs. Avery home.

Alone, Alysia slowly set the table, using the good china and crystal, carefully folding the linen napkins. All afternoon she'd replayed the scene in the kitchen through her head, reliving Christos's revelation that his family had suffered at the hands of her father, reliving his own revelation that he'd married her not simply for her fortune, but to exact a price on the Lemos family, to take the Lemos name and make it his.

She'd paid the ultimate price for being her father's daughter.

Numbly Alysia lit the tall tapered candles on the table, shaking her hand to extinguish the match, even as Christos appeared in the dining-room doorway.

She turned, caught a glimpse of the fatigue etched in deep lines at his mouth and eyes. His gaze took in the fresh rose centerpiece and elegant place settings. "Mrs. Avery must think we're enjoying the honeymoon."

She heard the cynicism in his voice but refused to be baited. "Would you like a glass of wine? I've opened a bottle. Mrs. Avery said you enjoy wine with your dinner."

Reluctantly he nodded. "All right, then."

She poured him a glass, handed it to him. He avoided touching her fingers.

Christos wandered around the dining-room table, sipping his wine, studying her arrangement of flowers, the linen cloth, the gleam of crystal in the flickering candlelight. "We're not celebrating anything, are we?"

"No." She felt herself begin to flush, self-conscious and embarrassed. She'd tried to please him. "You don't like the table?"

"Seems like a lot of trouble."

"It was no trouble. Growing up we always set a formal table for dinner. Nice linens. Candles."

"Ah, yes, the lives of the rich and famous."

His sarcasm stung, sending blood surging to her face. "I can't change who I am."

"Just as I can't change who I am." He sipped from his goblet.

"It was not easy being Darius Lemos's only child."

"No, of course not. It must have been awful being rich."

"Spoiled rotten, I was." She smiled at him, her jaws aching with the effort. "Dining every night with crystal and candlelight."

"We couldn't afford crystal. Candles were frivolous."

She felt wound so tightly, her body so tense she was trembling inwardly. Jerkily she leaned forward, blowing out the candles she'd just lit. The blackened wicks smoked. "Better?"

"You didn't have to do that."

"I didn't have to do that, but it's what you wanted. You're going to punish me now, every chance you can get. You're going to use every opportunity to impress upon me how desperate you were growing up and how revoltingly rich we were. You, working so hard, making something out of yourself, and me, just a spoiled little rich girl in need of a hospital and doctors to fix my self-esteem."

"Is that why you were there? Low self-esteem?"

She laughed, even as her chest tightened with hurt and pain. "Wouldn't you like to know!"

"I would, yes."

"So you can figure out why my father couldn't marry me off to a real Greek?" She caught sight of his expression, his jaw jutted, eyes narrowed in anger.

She rushed on, fueled by his coldness and her acute loneliness. "You think you have the upperhand here, but I have news for you. You were bought, Christos, you were bought because you could be bought. A self-respecting Greek wouldn't have me. A self-respecting Greek would sooner put his eye out than look upon me. But you, hungry for ships and money and power, made a deal with my father, and now you're curious, dying to know why Daddy Darius couldn't get rid of me."

"I do have some questions."

"I bet." She trembled with rage. "You, Christos Pateras, like my father, love to play God."

He said nothing, his back rigid, his dark eyes narrowed, thick lashes lowered.

"But I'm tired of you and my father making choices for me, deciding who I am, what I'll do, how I should think. I've had twenty-five years of men making decisions for me and I will not put up with it anymore."

"You're making me out to be a monster."

"Aren't you? My father was a monster. He couldn't love, or forgive. Tell me, how are you different from him?"

He said nothing, his jaw popping, his body so tense she feared he might reach for her, punish her insolence with a quick backhand the way her father used to do. But he didn't move. Didn't lift a finger.

Suddenly her anger deflated, and she felt wretched. She didn't understand why she had to lash out at him and what she'd hoped to accomplish.

This wasn't the way to his heart, that much she knew.

But she'd never have his heart. Just as she'd never have his respect.

Fighting tears, she fled to her room.

Unable to calm herself, Alysia tackled her stacks of luggage, finishing the unpacking job Mrs. Avery had begun. She was still filling the drawers in her dresser when Christos opened the bedroom door.

She'd felt him in the doorway, felt him watching her, but he didn't speak and she didn't turn around.

Her eyes burned and she blinked hard, concentrating on her task.

She'd said terrible things to him, called him terrible names, and he didn't deserve it, not all of it, at least. She was angry with him because she wanted more from him but fighting wouldn't bring him closer. It would only push him farther away.

"I've dished up dinner," he said quietly.

A lump filled her throat. "I'm really not all that hungry."

"You need to eat. Come," he repeated, extending a hand. "Let's not waste Mrs. Avery's meal."

She didn't have the strength to fight him, nor the

energy to resist. She was hungry, and tired, jetlag catching up with her, and she followed, if only to avoid further conflict.

In the dining room the candles glowed on the table, the lightbulbs in the grand crystal-and-silver chandelier dimmed. The room shone pale yellow in the flickering light and the plates on the table were filled with Mrs. Avery's roasted chicken and buttery new potatoes.

They ate in silence, each contemplative, studiously avoiding conversation.

Finally Christos pushed his plate aside. "Fifteen years ago I made a choice," he said quietly, not looking at her, but at a fixed point on the table. "It was a difficult choice."

She looked across the gleaming table, her gaze fixing on his mouth, unable to meet his eyes. He undid her. He made her want things she thought she'd given up long ago.

"I had to choose between school and sports. I'd got into Yale on an athletic scholarship."

"Baseball," she murmured.

He nodded. "I loved the game, loved being outside, on the grass, and the camaraderie of being part of a team. But I wasn't a great player. I was good, and I might have made it to the pros, but I couldn't take the risk."

He lifted his wineglass, took a sip and set the goblet down again. "If I stuck with baseball there was a good chance I'd struggle for years. I wouldn't be able to take care of my parents, and I knew without my help, my mother would spend her life scrubbing other people's toilets. I couldn't bear it. My pride couldn't bear it. My family had been through so much. I wanted more for them, more for all of us.''

"So you pursued business instead.''

"I pursued your father,'' he corrected softly, self-mockingly. "Every decision I made, every contract I signed, every investment had one purpose—to get me closer to the day I'd crush your father.''

"You hated him that much?''

"I hated what he did to my father. As you can see, I'm not a very forgiving man.''

"You don't strike me as ruthless.''

"I wasn't always.''

Had there been a different Christos then, a younger Christos who wanted less, and perhaps loved more? "I might have liked you then.''

His dark head lifted and he gazed at her from beneath a furrowed brow. His cheekbones jutted, his jaw at an angle, and even though he stared at her, she was sure he was looking inward, seeing not her, but himself, and his expression haunted her. "Maybe,'' he answered in a deep, strangled voice. "Maybe.''

She rose from her chair, wanting to go to him, but halfway around the table realized he wouldn't want her, didn't need her, not that way.

Torn, she gathered the dishes, stacking the bread plate on the dinner plate and pushing the cutlery to the middle.

"There is one other thing.'' His deep voice stilled

her jerky motions. "I wouldn't mention it except I know my mother, and I know she will."

She glanced at him over her shoulder, waiting for whatever would come next. He smiled, but the smile didn't warm his eyes. "I was engaged earlier this year, before I married you."

Dishes cradled to her tummy, she struggled to make sense of what he was saying. "Engaged to whom?"

"A local girl."

"Someone from a family like yours."

His dark head inclined. "Our mothers arranged it."

With a flash she intuited what he was really saying. "Your mother was the matchmaker."

His gaze held hers. "Yes, and our families were thrilled. They made quite a big fuss."

"I can imagine." And she could. Christos Pateras, an American-Greek tycoon, a dazzling American success story, marries local American-Greek girl. It would have been a perfect match. Even the gods would have been smiling.

"You loved her?" she whispered, hating how her body responded with pain. Why did she care? Why did she have to feel so much?

"I loved her sweetness. I loved her gentleness."

"She wanted children."

"She dreamed of a big family."

Jealousy consumed her. Alysia didn't even know this other woman and she felt wild with envy. To be the woman Christos would cherish...

But she couldn't leave it at that. She had to know more. "Was there an accident?"

"No." Christos's black brows knitted, his expression grim. "I broke it off a couple of months ago, realizing she wasn't the one for me."

Sweet relief flooded her limbs. "What changed your mind?"

"Your father."

Alysia didn't know if she dropped the dishes or if they simply fell. Either way, they came crashing down, plates rolling, cutlery clattering, one fork bouncing. Nothing, she dimly realized, broke. How fortunate.

She struggled to gather the dishes but her fingers wouldn't cooperate.

All she could see was her father, pen in hand, scribbling staggering figures on paper, promising Christos ships, wealth, more power.

She sucked in air, scalding tears filling her eyes and grabbed blindly at the fallen silverware, unable to see, unable to think.

Her father cutting a check and Christos taking it all. The deal, the marriage, the business. Not for love. But for money. For revenge.

Christos's chair scraped back. He took her arm and she jumped back, his touch setting her skin on fire.

If only she'd been the poor girl from a poor emigrant family, engaged to Christos. To be chosen for one's goodness, to be chosen for one's rightness, to be chosen and loved!

''Don't,'' Christos said roughly, taking her arm again.

She opened her eyes, looked at him, unaware of the tears filling her eyes. Emotion darkened his own beautiful features. ''Don't what?'' she whispered.

''Don't say it. Don't want it. What we have is what I wanted.''

''Is it?''

''Yes.''

''But what we have is nothing.''

''That's not true. It's no better, no worse than any other arranged marriage.''

''I can't live like this.''

''Sorry. You don't have a choice.''

''Don't I?''

''No. Not anymore. Not as my wife.''

CHAPTER NINE

BEFORE he'd taken a step, she knew he was going to touch her, to take her into his arms and create havoc within her again. She wanted his touch as much as she dreaded it, fearing the loss of control, especially to him.

Alysia tried to escape but Christos was too quick, catching her by her arms and drawing her against his chest. His hands cupped her bottom, pulling her firmly against his hips. "All your life you've been the poor neglected Alysia. No one to love you. No one to want you."

He pressed her even closer to his hips, making her vividly aware of his arousal. "But I want you, I want you more than I've ever wanted anyone."

"You want me to punish my father—"

"I couldn't care less about your father. I want you." He kissed the side of her throat, his breath warm, his lips making her skin tingle.

His lips felt incredible, his mouth sending torments of feeling racing up and down her spine. He was turning her into something hot and dangerous. Her body felt electric, her nerves overly sensitized.

Helplessly she slid a hand across his chest, dazed by the warmth he created within her, and her desire to feel him, be a part of him, capture the passion she'd felt in his arms before.

"Careful," he mocked her, his voice deepening, "I might actually think you want me."

The warmth of his breath against her cheek, the mockery in his voice, the heat of his body against hers made her crave more.

As Christos's dark head dipped, she reached up, clasping his nape, a soft moan escaping her lips. She slid her fingers through his crisp, damp hair and inhaled his clean male scent.

His mouth parted hers, his tongue teasing the softness of her inner lip until her lips opened wider. She felt the core of her melt. Shameless in her desire, she shifted, rising slightly, encouraging him.

He pressed her backward, against the dining-room table, his kiss deepening, drawing her tongue into his mouth. He sucked on the tip of her tongue, creating a tight friction that echoed the throbbing in her belly and the ache between her thighs.

He sucked harder on her tongue before finding the inside of her lip. He bit the softness of her lip and she gasped, arching into him for relief.

"I do want you. I want you to make love to me," she begged, her voice thick, husky with passion.

It was all the encouragement he needed. Christos swept her into his arms and carried her up the stairs, pushing open the bedroom door, through the darkened room to his bed.

He found the warm, smooth flesh of her abdomen, unbuttoning her blouse with quick, sure fingers. His palms caressed the length of her torso, tracing the edge of her lace bra beneath the weight of each breast. Her nipples tightened, peaking with feeling, yet he grazed the nipples, bypassing them to kiss the hollow beneath. She squirmed, reaching for him, struggling to unbutton his shirt.

He helped her with his shirt, peeling the fabric from his shoulders to reveal the taut planes of his chest. Her palms slid down his hard abdomen to his belt buckle and with shaking hands she unfastened the buckle and then his trousers.

He sucked in his breath when she found him, her hand wrapping around his hard satin length. He drew her hand away, whispering, ''Not yet,'' and lowered his own head to savor the sensitive hollow between her breasts, his tongue drawing circles of fire, around and around until she clamped her knees together in futile desire.

He finished off her blouse, pushing the silk fabric aside, and then unhooked the lace bra, sending that to the floor as well. The air felt cool against her heated skin and she reached for him, drawing him back down to her.

When his mouth covered one tight bud, she responded blindly, helplessly dragging her nails down his torso, lightly raking the carved plane of his chest, and small hard nipples.

She was slick with need by the time he knelt between her thighs. ''No more anything,'' she whispered, ''I just want you.''

He entered her slowly, trying to give her time to

adjust to his body, but she didn't need much time, welcoming the exquisite sensation of fullness.

Her body felt lovely and alive, her muscles suffused with warmth, her skin incredibly sensitive. Every place he touched her glowed. Every kiss made her crave more.

"Am I hurting you?" he demanded hoarsely.

"No," she answered, pressing a finger to his lovely lips, stilling his speech. "Just love me."

And he did, bracing himself on his hands, thrusting deeply inside, first slowly and then faster, creating alternating torments of fullness and need, drawing them together, building the tension, building the reward.

His mouth returned to hers, and she answered his kiss with near desperation, lifting her hips to meet him, relishing the tenderness and passion.

She knew then she'd always love him, heart and soul, or the part of her soul not destroyed with Alexi.

"Christos," she whispered urgently, drawing him deeper inside her, opening her mouth, giving him all of her body since he wouldn't take her heart.

The vivid swirling sensations built to a feverish pitch, his thrusts harder, faster, and for long mindless seconds she was at an insurmountable peak, nearing climax, her body warm, damp, straining against his, but not yet set free.

Christos plunged into her yet again, moving deeply, and suddenly she was his, all his, exploding in brilliant, breathtaking pleasure. Her pleasure sent him over the edge, and they came together, their bodies shuddering with rippling sensation, satiated and exhausted.

Still tangled together, her heart racing wildly, Christos kissed her again, long and hard. "Mine," he whispered against her mouth. "Remember that." And then his tongue rasped against hers in one final mind-spinning kiss that drew shivers down her spine, warmth from her belly, and flexed her toes.

He settled her to one side of him, pulling her hip in against his, one palm cupping her breast. For a long moment neither moved, nor spoke, their warm, weary bodies relaxed.

Alysia felt herself spiral down, down, down, but she never crashed, just floated in lovely suspended sensation, aware of Christos's fingers trailing in the curve of her lower back, and gently caressing the swell of her hip.

"You are worth all the ships in the world," he murmured, his voice husky, and she turned her head to look up at him, surprised by his words, but before she could ask him what he meant, he was breathing deeply, black lashes fanning his cheekbones. He was asleep.

They made love again later, toward the end of the night. Neither spoke, their bodies communicating in wordless expression. But later, after they'd recovered from the intensity of the physical pleasure, Christos pressed a kiss to the top of her head and eased out of bed.

"Where are you going?" she asked, sleepily sitting forward, sheet drawn to her breasts.

"Work."

"Now? It's so early!"

"It's five. I've a lot to do. Better to get started."

She sat up higher, pushed a fistful of hair out of her eyes. "Can I come?"

"No. Go back to sleep. You need the rest."

She pushed back the bedcovers, pressed her hands to her knees. "I could help you. You could put me to work."

"You know nothing about the industry."

"So teach me." She was warming to the idea, realizing she could try to win him over. Christos was like her father. He equated business with success, and he respected successful people. If she could find a way to be useful, contribute to his business, he might see her as more than Darius Lemos's spoiled daughter.

He might realize she had a brain. He might respect her.

He might even fall in love with her.

"Please, Christos, give me a chance."

"This is not a good day for show and tell. Today I have important conferences scheduled. Union bosses waiting to rip my head off. It's a day of hard bargaining, a little bloodletting—hopefully not my own. You'd be in the way. You'd be a distraction."

His good mood quickly evaporated as his wife flung herself from bed, her slim figure lunging at the floor, grabbing for her clothes. "I wouldn't be a distraction. I wouldn't get in your way. Christos, please."

"Alysia, be serious."

Her hands shook as she picked up her panties and stepped into the tiny scraps of satin. "I am. Completely serious."

"Alysia, you're a woman."

Daggers flashed in her dark blue eyes and with a furious glance in his direction, she yanked her white silk blouse over her shoulders, forgetting her strappy lace bra, the fabric hugging her breasts, outlining the full, round shape. "I can't believe you just said that!"

"I watched my mother slave on her knees in other people's bathrooms. She worked her fingers to the bone and I vowed that when I married, my wife would never work, never be humiliated like that."

"I want to go into the office, not clean bathrooms." Her full, swollen nipples pressed tautly against the thin silk fabric and he felt his body harden, responding to her beauty and passion, unfazed by her anger.

"No. I will provide for us because I *can* provide for us. That is how it should be, and that is how it will be. Understood?"

With a strangled oath she flung her navy skirt at him. He caught it easily.

"Then go!" she spat, tossing her head, long silky hair swinging over her shoulders. "Do whatever it is you must do, but don't expect to come home and find me waiting!"

He stopped where he was, two steps from the foot

of the bed, desire dying. He hadn't heard right. She was threatening him again. Unbelievable.

One of his hands circled her slim upper arm and he dragged her toward him. Her bare legs kicked, her hands pounded on his chest. "What did you say?"

"You heard me."

Anger swept through him, anger and impatience. He tilted her head back, holding her face captive beneath his. His kiss was an assault as much as it was an insult. He kissed her hard, a savagery in the rake of his tongue and grind of his lips. He wanted her to feel his wrath, wanted to remind her that in this house, he was the man, and she, the woman.

But even as he probed her mouth, his hard embrace gentled, his fingers releasing her chin to cup her cheek. She felt unbelievable in his arms, tasted like honey and crushed almonds. She was sweet and damn it, she was his.

She'd been his ever since she'd interrupted her father's meeting all those years ago. He knew then he wanted her, wanted her to be his. He'd protect her. He'd cherish her. He'd keep Darius Lemos from hurting her again.

Alysia's swollen mouth trembled beneath his, her slim body quivering against his bare chest. His kiss softened and he caressed the length of her neck, stroking her satiny skin, her body shuddering at each slow, lingering touch, playing her tenderly the way one would play the violin. She was melting in his arms, melting into him, and gently he released her.

He exhaled slowly, his breathing ragged, his heart

pounding with the same fierceness that it surged through his limbs, gathering in his groin. God, he wanted her, wanted to take her and taste her, make love to her until she surrendered completely, admitting that she wanted no one but him, no life but theirs.

But she wouldn't meet him, not even halfway, and as much as he wanted to kiss her senseless, there wasn't time.

His brows flattened as he pressed the tip of his finger to her quivering mouth. "Do not, my rebellious wife, threaten to leave me again."

She heard the hardness in his tone and realized she'd pushed him too far. Shivering, she drew her blouse even tighter across her chest, wanting him yet again, craving him still. She should have more pride, want more from him than just sex, but desperate woman that she was, she took whatever he gave her, even the crumbs from his table.

Disgusted with herself, she lashed out. "I gave you what you wanted. You wanted me to perform my wifely duties, well, I did. I serviced you. Now give me what I want."

Christos stared at her, stunned, his expression revealing hurt, and betrayal. Then his dark eyes shuttered, leaving his chiseled features starkly remote. But she'd seen enough in his eyes to know her barb hit home. She'd wounded him.

Instead of joy, she felt remorse, and fresh shame. Before she could apologize, he was walking away, putting distance between them.

He headed for his bathroom, flicked on the lights and heat lamp before turning on the shower. She followed him into the bathroom, unsettled by what had just taken place between them.

The cold tile floor curled her toes. "Christos—"

Steam rose from the open shower door, fogging the white tiled bath. Christos turned to look at her. He was naked but completely uninhibited. "We have an expression in America. It's called 'low blow.' It means, you've hit below the belt. Do you understand what I'm saying?"

She swallowed hard, wondering how something so lovely, what took place in his bed, could now turn into something so ugly. "Yes, but—"

"Hitting below the belt is not acceptable. Not in this marriage. Not ever."

"I'm sorry, but you—"

"Like a child. So defiant. So unwilling to bend."

"Is that how you accept an apology?"

"Is that how you give an apology?"

She couldn't stand it, couldn't stand the way he made her feel so inadequate. "I hate you," she whispered, tears starting to her eyes. "I hate you and everything you stand for."

"Trust me. At the moment, the feeling's mutual." His dark lashes lowered, concealing his expression. "It didn't have to be like this, Alysia."

Tears shimmered in her eyes as she flung her head back. "Is that an apology?"

"No. A statement of fact."

"Why didn't you marry your good American-Greek girl and leave me in the convent?"

His mouth flattened, his dark eyes narrowing as his gaze raked her half-naked body. "I couldn't."

"You and my father are exactly alike. You love money before all else!"

"I tried to love you. But you won't let anybody near you. You won't allow someone to be kind—"

"Is that what you were showing me in bed? Kindness?" She laughed, her voice high and strained, a hint of hysteria in the thin pitch. "Well, from now on, I can do without your acts of kindness." She balled her hands into fists. "Call a spade, a spade. Our marriage is nothing but a business deal. Dollars. Numbers. A bank account. What happened in there, in that bed, was nothing more than a business transaction."

His cheekbones jutted against the pallor of his skin. His nostrils flared with each short, ragged breath. "Fine, it's business. But it's an ongoing business. I'll take you when I want, and how I want, and to hell with the kindness you despise."

He pulled her into the shower with him, holding her beneath the blast of jets, water soaking them both, drenching her blouse, outlining her breasts.

Turning, he shifted her body behind his to take the brunt of the water. Clasping her face in his hands, he covered her mouth with his, lips parting her, tongue stabbing at her mouth's softness, taking her without pretense of tenderness.

The water beat down around them, splashing their bodies, dripping down their legs.

When Christos finally lifted his head, he slowly pressed a kiss to the corner of her throbbing mouth. His black eyelashes were spiky wet, his jaw glistening with water. "From now on I'll expect you to be ready for me, just like my banker's always on call, ready for my business."

"You're an ass," she whispered, hurt, and yet hungry for more skin, more pressure, more of him.

"And you're my wife." He unbuttoned her soggy blouse, dropping it in a puddle at their feet.

She tried to climb out of the shower. He pulled her back in, blocking the door with his body. He picked up a bar of soap and began lathering it between his large hands. He worked the soap into thick white suds, and then held the bar above her body. The foaming suds spilled from his hands to her shoulders and dripped down her breasts.

His gaze lowered, his burning gaze following the path of the bubbles as they slid down the sweep of breasts, her taut aching nipples peeking through soapy foam.

Reaching out to her, Christos traced the bubble path, his firm sudsy palm against her breast and distended nipple. He drew his hands across her, spreading the soapy lather down her flat abdomen, into the soft mound at the apex of her thighs. He washed her clean, rinsed the soap off, and lifted her chin. "I've washed you, I've made you mine. Your life, Alysia, is with me."

Shivering, she left the shower and wrapped a towel around herself and squeezed the extra water from her hair. Christos stepped past her, his hips bumping her bottom and she quickly moved out of the way. Reaching across her, he pulled a towel off the bar. "You have a half hour," he said flatly, no expression in his voice.

"A half hour?"

He looked at her with anger, and scorn. "Until we go. I won't leave you here and give you a second chance to run away. So you win, Alysia. You're going to work with me even though I don't like it one little bit."

CHAPTER TEN

DURING the helicopter ride into the city, Christos avoided looking at her, and she kept her chin firmly lifted, refusing to let him see that her hard-earned victory tasted terribly bitter.

She'd wanted to be a part of his world, but not at this price. Never at this price.

The moment they arrived at his office, walking through the frosted glass doors into a modern office furnished in navy, burgundy and cream, they joined a meeting already in progress and remained in the conference room all day.

Christos didn't glance her way during the three-hour-long discussion with the shipworker's union boss. And the discussion, so heated that at times she feared the union boss would come to blows, made her incredibly uneasy. But Christos remained utterly calm. He addressed the others without rancor, and yet he didn't bend, nor did he compromise.

The meeting adjourned for ten minutes so all could move around the room, use the bathroom, stretch their legs. Christos stood up, walked to the phone on the corner table, a table just inches from her chair, and made a series of brief phone calls without once looking at her.

Concluding his calls, he returned to his chair, again without a glance in her direction.

It was as if he was telling her, without so many words, that she could push him all she wanted, but that would never change the way he felt about her. He despised her. Clearly she meant nothing to him.

A bitter pill for a bitter victory.

They were silent on the ride home in the helicopter, landing on the cement pad in Christos's estate only twenty minutes after having taken off from the Manhattan skyscraper.

A car waited for them at the landing pad, driving them the short distance to the house. Mrs. Avery opened the door, welcomed them cheerfully, offering an appetizer tray and cold drinks.

Christos took his glass, and Alysia's, thanking Mrs. Avery with a warmth that Alysia couldn't miss.

"Mr. Pateras, your mother called late this afternoon to let you know your father had to work late tonight. She didn't think they'd be here much before eight."

"Thank you, Mrs. Avery. I know you've had a long day. Please don't feel you need to stay."

"But I can, and then you and Mrs. Pateras could relax a little. Unwind before your parents arrive."

Christos shot Alysia a speculative look. "We'll relax, don't you worry about us."

The moment Mrs. Avery was gone Christos ordered Alysia upstairs.

Her eyebrows shot up. Her stomach a bundle of nerves. "Pardon me?"

"Can you walk, or shall I carry you again?"

"You want me to go upstairs now, just before your parents come?"

He smiled coldly, no warmth in his dark eyes. "We've a good solid hour."

"You've got to be joking."

"Sweetheart, I never joke about sex."

I never joke about sex. How much cruder could one be? Her eyes smarted. Her throat closed, bottling the air in her lungs. "I'm sorry, but I'm not exactly in the mood."

He tossed back his drink, and shrugged. "Then get in the mood, because we made a deal. Business, right, sweetheart? You wanted to be a part of my world, well, I'm going to be a part of yours. I want you. Now."

"Don't do this."

"Why not? You treat me with as much contempt." He made a rough sound in his throat, reaching forward to run his finger across her cheek. "Ah, there it is, the anger. The hatred. It's all there, just for me." Christos turned, began climbing the stairs. "Now come. Business is business."

She wanted to hate him, wanted to shout something at him, but her voice failed her and her heart ached, craving something else from him than this.

As he took the stairs, she watched the length of his back, the powerful legs, and despite the anger and anguish burning within her, she felt another emotion, one awakened by the caress on her cheek.

She wanted him. She wanted to feel him over her,

against her, the warm, hard planes of his body, her own warm acceptance. And slowly she followed him up the stairs.

They made love the first time with savage intent, nails raking, teeth nipping, kisses fierce and bruising. But after the first shattering orgasm, after the anger abated, Christos turned to her again, his touch softer, his expression almost gentle. He made love to her once more, this time giving rather than taking, kissing her through her second climax, holding her while she shuddered against him, murmuring assurances in her ear.

She nearly fell asleep in his arms but Christos stirred, and drawing back the covers reminded her that his parents would arrive in the next half hour.

He'd left the room and she bathed, but instead of dressing, she'd returned to the bed, curled on the foot in her towel.

She wanted more from Christos than skin. More than his mouth and fingers, his incredible satin and steel body. She wanted his heart, too.

But this marriage, their marriage, was paper and money, ships and inheritance. It wasn't love, would never be love. It was just business. Business and vengeance.

Her eyes burned, her throat sealed closed, and digging her nails into her palms she felt like the poor little rich girl again, the young Greek heiress whose fortune couldn't even protect her infant son.

God, how she hated her inheritance, hated the pampered world of nothingness.

The door to her room opened. Christos stood in the doorway, buttoning the sleeves of his crisp white shirt, the tail of it already tucked into dark wool trousers. "Alysia, you can't afford to dawdle. My parents will be here very soon. And trust me, you won't endear yourself to my mother if she finds you undressed."

She couldn't move, couldn't tear her gaze from him. He looked so cool and calm, so perfectly controlled, while she felt like a ball of warm wax, soft and changing, helpless in his hands.

She still felt him everywhere in her, on her, near her. She felt his mouth and hands, felt her body respond, and the dull pain in her heart.

Covering her heartache, she gave him a defiant glare. "Why not? You undressed me."

"Fine. I'll dress you. So much for independence, Mrs. Pateras." He stalked to her closet, plucking a silk skirt and cropped jacket from hangers.

"Wear these," he said, tossing them at her before digging through her drawers for appropriate lingerie. "My father loves lavender and my mother dislikes trousers. Wear your hair down but not too much makeup. I expect to see you downstairs in fifteen minutes tops. Am I clear?"

"Christos—"

"Am I clear?"

"Yes." She swallowed, gathering courage. "Your father, he must hate me very much."

He stopped at the door, but didn't turn around. "My father has no vendetta against you. My father is a compassionate man. A man far more tolerant than I.''

He glanced back at her, his hard, handsome features without expression, his dark eyes intent, focused on her, observing the sudden tension at her mouth. ''My father will be kind to you. Do not worry about him.''

''And your mother?''

''She answers to my father.''

Like a good woman should.

He didn't say the last part, but it hung there, unspoken between them. She smiled painfully. ''I'll try not to embarrass you tonight.''

''Just don't run away.''

Downstairs she found Christos uncorking a bottle of red wine. Headlights gleamed in the driveway, reflecting through the dining-room window.

''They're here,'' he announced unnecessarily.

She stiffened, frightened at coming face-to-face with people her father had hurt so deeply. ''Tell me what to say to your mother. Tell me how to act.''

''Just be yourself,'' he said quietly. Her head jerked up. Her eyes met his. ''My mother will be happy when I'm happy,'' he added more gently.

But I won't ever make you happy, she silently answered him, her heart aching, emotions so raw and new that she struggled to keep them in check. ''Christos, it's not all business, is it?''

''You mean between us?''

Silence stretched, a humiliation of its own. Car doors slammed outside. Footsteps on the brick steps.

Bands of color burned her cheekbones. "Yes. Between us."

More silence. The shockingly loud ring of the doorbell. The knowledge that his parents were there, waiting, just on the other side of the door.

He didn't even glance at the door. "No. It's not just business."

She felt a bubble of emotion rise, higher, fuller, hope and pain, tenderness, too.

He crossed to the door but didn't open it, his gaze still on her, as if able to read her chaotic emotions. "I didn't marry Maria just because your father offered me money, and I didn't marry you to punish your family. I married you because I wanted you." And then, just like that, he swung the front door open, inviting his parents in.

Dinner with his parents was less of a disaster than she'd expected. With his father present, Christos's mother was subdued, silently following the conversation while Christos's father discussed business and matters of the church with Christos.

The elder Mr. Pateras made efforts to include Alysia, listening thoughtfully to her point of view, and treating her with what seemed to be genuine warmth and respect.

Following dinner they shared a sweet liqueur, a drink Christos said was made locally by a Greek family. Then his parents left after Christos and Alysia saw them to the door.

They stood together in the entry, neither moving from the door. After a long moment Christos leaned forward to tuck a tendril of golden hair behind her ear. "That wasn't so bad," he said

"No. Your father is lovely."

"I don't know if lovely is the right word, but it's obvious he likes you. I'm glad. I'd hoped he would."

"But your mother…"

"My mother is notoriously hard to please. With babies, grandchildren, I promise you, she'll have a change of heart."

Her own heart twisted, feeling like a traitor. She should talk to Christos, really talk to him, but how? What would she say? How could she tell him the truth? In some ways he was modern, open-minded, strong. But in other ways, when it came to women and family, he was impossibly protective. Almost chauvinistic. If she confessed to him, she knew she'd lose him.

Christos lifted her face in his hands, his expression somber. Then his head dipped and he kissed her with heart-shattering tenderness, savoring her lips, promising a warmth and a tangible hunger.

She clung to him, needing him, and as she kissed him, tears slid from beneath her closed lashes, spilling onto her cheeks.

Christos drew back, forehead furrowing. "What's wrong?"

She couldn't tell him. Words would only destroy the tentative bonds between them. Instead she drew his head down to hers again, covering his mouth with her own.

His lips felt damp and tasted salty from her tears,

and a primitive emotion compelled her to kiss him deeply, sampling the trace of her tears on his skin. She tasted herself, and him, and it stirred dormant emotions, deep-rooted emotions of love and longing. She wanted him, to belong to him, not just now, but always.

The intensity of their lovemaking that night affected them both, but for Alysia, it was life-changing. She knew she'd never want any man, or love any man, the way she loved Christos. He was a perfect combination of strength and passion, pride and tenderness.

They made love again and his hands, body and mouth drove her to a shattering climax. Afterward, he kissed her on the damp brow before returning to her lips.

"You might not know it, but you need me, Alysia, just as much as I need you."

She lay on the crook of her arm, gazing at him in the dark. She could see his eyes and the flash of white teeth, and she leaned forward to kiss his mouth, closing the distance between them. "I know, at least the part about me needing you."

She felt him tense, his breath catching, holding. At last he exhaled, his hand rising to her face, stroking her cheek, her skin still glowing with the heat of passion.

"I want to have a baby with you. I want to make a family with you."

Fear gripped her heart and she pressed her fingertips to his mouth to keep him from saying more.

''But you know that,'' he said. ''You know it's what I want more than anything.''

''I'm not mother-material,'' she answered hoarsely.

''That's not true. You're just afraid you can't conceive, but I'm sure with the right doctors, with new treatments—''

''Christos, you don't know!''

''What don't I know?''

The truth... You don't know anything.

''Alysia, you're my wife. I want you. I want a family with you.''

Her eyes scalded, hot and gritty, and she tipped her forehead against his, hiding her face from him, hiding her past. If he knew the truth, he'd hate her, despise her.

''Talk to me,'' he whispered, drawing away and rolling her over onto her back. Lifting a strand of hair from the hollow of her neck, he pressed it to his mouth and then kissed her collarbone before kissing her mouth. ''Trust me.''

''I do.'' And she did, as much as she could trust anyone. *But what about the birth control pills?* A little voice whispered inside her head, stirring fresh panic. *He should know you're taking contraception.*

But another voice inside her protested. *He doesn't need to know now. You'll tell him someday, someday when he'll understand...*

''I'd do anything for you.''

''Shh, you can't say such things.''

''I can, because I love you.''

She lay still, frozen, not daring to breathe. He couldn't have just said what she thought he said. It was her imagination, her need for acceptance, and forgiveness. Because he couldn't love her, not the real Alysia. The real Alysia destroyed those she loved.

"Look at me," Christos urged, his voice husky, firm fingers on her chin, turning her face to his, not understanding the tears in her eyes or the pain snaking through her heart. "We'll make a baby, and we'll be happy. I promise."

The weeks passed quickly; Christos was attentive, his desire something tangible and real. They slept together, woke together, took their meals together, and still neither could get enough of the other, seeking each other's company, wanting more touch, more passion, more pleasure.

After that stormy first week they'd managed to become friends, developing a relationship out of the artifice.

Christos invited Alysia to join him once or twice a week at his office, making a point of including her in big meetings, and other times, bringing home business reports and financial statements to discuss with her.

She found Christos's perspective on business fascinating, yet was bored by the myriad of details. While she liked understanding why he made certain decisions, she didn't want to pore over numbers or challenge his economic predictions. The fact was, his business bored her. What's worse, the endless columns of numbers looked meaningless after a while, just number after number, like little ants marching across the page.

"I hate this," she muttered, slamming the proposal closed and tossing it at the foot of the couch. "I can't stand it. There's nothing about this business that I enjoy."

Christos turned from the window where he'd been admiring the sunset, his mouth twisting. "I wondered how long it'd take for you to confess." He plucked the spiral-bound booklet from the couch and flipped through it, briefly scanning the charts and graphs. "Why don't you paint again?"

His tone was deceptively mild. She glanced at him, frowned. "You know I don't paint anymore."

"We could build a studio for you here—"

"I don't want a studio," she interrupted, jumping from the couch to confront him. "I don't paint. I'll never paint again."

"I thought you trusted me."

"I do."

"Then perhaps you can explain these," he said flatly. Something had changed in his voice, his quiet tone taking an edge. "I found these in your bathroom drawer." He drew a small plastic case from his pocket, lifted them high and tapped the plastic case with a finger. "These pills aren't iron tablets, are they?"

She went hot, then cold. "No." They were her pills. Her birth control pills. He knew, too, what her bottle of iron tablets looked like.

"Where did you get them? When did you get them?"

"In Athens." She swallowed hard. "From the doctor that visited me at your house, after I fainted."

"You've been on birth control pills for the last month?" His voice echoed hard, brittle, just like his features.

"Yes." She lifted her head, flinched when she met his gaze, fury blazing in his dark eyes.

"You lied to me."

"I didn't lie."

"You weren't honest."

No, she hadn't been honest, and it was all going to come out. She saw that now. The skeletons, the nightmare, the terror. The bones were stacked too high against the closet door and the door had been opened, just a crack, but a crack was more than enough to destroy her fragile control.

She turned, opened the door to his study and began walking away, quickly, heading for the stairs and the sanctuary of her room.

Christos followed her to the stairs, and she ran up the steps, flying as fast as she could.

He covered the stairs in half the time, able to climb three steps to her one. Grasping her by her shoulders, he spun her to face him. "What the hell is going on?"

"You don't know, and you don't want to know."

"Damn it, Alysia, I've had it with your secrets and your cryptic answers." His fingers held her fast, no escaping him now. "No more riddles. I want answers. Truthful answers. Why didn't you tell me you were on the pill?''

''Because you'd have taken them away, or tried to talk me out of them—''

''Yes!''

''That's why.''

''But you knew I wanted children.''

''And you knew I couldn't give them to you!''

She yanked away, stepping blindly backward. She teetered on the top step, losing her balance. Christos caught her, pulling her roughly after him to the relative safety of her bedroom.

''No more pills, no more protection,'' he said, shutting the door behind them. ''Do you understand?''

''I understand what you're saying, but I can't do what you're asking me to do.''

''You mean you won't?''

She saw the hurt flicker in his dark eyes before being replaced by anger. ''Please, Christos, trust me—''

''Like you've trusted me?'' He turned away, covered his face with one hand. ''God, I am a fool.'' He shook his head, dropping his hand. ''Your father warned me you'd run away. He warned me you weren't very stable. But I didn't believe him. If only I had!''

''It would have saved us both a lot of trouble,'' she answered quietly, finding her pride, and her backbone.

She'd known from the beginning their marriage

wouldn't last. She knew he'd discover the truth sooner or later and the relationship would end, as swiftly, as painfully, as it had begun. Only she hadn't expected to lose her heart to him. She'd never meant to fall so madly in love.

He stared at her as if he'd never seen her before, his dark eyes stripping her to the bone. "You were never going to have my child, were you?"

"No."

"How long would you have let me wait?"

Forever, she heard the answer whisper inside herself, forever, if it meant I could be with you. Instead she shook her head. "I don't know. Until you pushed for the truth."

"So you would have continued taking the pills, getting your period, letting me believe we couldn't conceive."

"Yes."

"God, I hate you."

She shriveled on the inside, dying. "I know."

"You can't. You have no idea how much you disgust me."

"I have a faint idea," she whispered, knowing he couldn't break what was already broken, and her heart had been shattered years ago. But still he was digging a fresh hole, dirt for her grave.

He closed the distance between them, lifted his hand as if to strike her and instead caught her face in his hands, kissing her hard on the mouth. "Why?" he demanded against her trembling lips. "Just tell me why. Let me understand."

His mouth felt so warm against hers, his skin smelling of cologne and musk and she reached up to cling to his chest, needing him more than she'd ever needed anyone.

But he didn't want her touching him, and he caught her wrists, pulling her hands off him. "I'm waiting."

"You don't want to know, oh, Christos, it's bad—"

"I don't care. I just want the truth."

She gazed at him helplessly, knowing she'd lose him—no, she'd already lost him—but fear held her back. She'd kept her secret so long, told no one, not even her father, what had happened in that Paris studio that unbelievable afternoon.

"Tell me."

Her heart lurched, her mouth so dry, it tasted of cotton. Where to begin? What to say first? "I...I had a baby."

"You what?"

The adrenaline surging through her veins threatened to make her ill. She couldn't look at Christos, didn't dare take a glimpse into his face. "Had a baby. A little boy."

"When?"

"With Jeremy. We were married, had been married for a little over a year when Alexi was born."

"And?"

"I lost him."

"Stillbirth?"

"No." She shivered, chilled, wondering how

she'd ever get the words out, not wanting to see Alexi, not wanting the horrible pictures to fill her head again. "I delivered him, loved him, raised him. I took him on my jobs. He had his first birthday. And then…"

"And then what, Alysia?" Christos ground out, shaking her, almost violent in his impatience to hear the rest.

"I killed him."

CHAPTER ELEVEN

CHRISTOS couldn't believe it. He demanded the story again and again, ignoring her sobs, oblivious to her anguish, insisting she explain it all once more, from the beginning.

He struggled to piece her past together. She ran away with Jeremy after meeting him in Paris. They married thinking they could make a living by painting. That part made sense. That much was clear. But the rest of it...

"Christos, please, no more—"

He saw her cowering on the bed, but felt nothing for her. "How did the baby drown?" he demanded again.

"In water, in the bath—"

"You said the sink."

"Yes, in the sink. He'd been taking a bath."

"No, he wasn't taking a bath, you were giving him a bath."

"Yes."

"And what happened?"

"He drowned."

"How?"

"You know how! His little chair broke, I think. Or he wasn't in his chair—I forget, Christos, it's been so long."

"Not that long. Five years."

She closed her eyes, hugging herself. "Let me go," she whispered. "Let me go, let me go."

"I want to hear this. I want to know how you let your baby drown."

"I can't tell you."

"You can. You will." He stalked toward her, his face dark with anger. "Did the phone ring? Someone came to the door? How did you forget him?"

"Stop it!"

"How could you do it? How could you let your baby drown?"

"I was painting!" she screamed, her voice shrieking so high that it sounded like breaking glass. "I was painting."

"You were painting?" Christos stared at her aghast.

"I killed Alexi because I had to paint."

A doctor came, and Christos's parents. Alysia lay huddled in her darkened bedroom, unwilling to eat, or turn on a light. She wanted only to be left alone.

But the voices could be heard through her closed door, murmurs and exclamations, urgency in Christos, disgust in his mother's.

Sometime later the doctor entered her room, and despite her protests, turned on the light and checked her vitals. His examination was brief but thorough, shining a miniature flashlight into her eyes, listening to her chest, and taking her pulse yet again. Finally he asked her if she'd been taking any other medications lately, other than her birth control pills.

"No," she answered dully, just wanting him to go, wanting to be alone again.

But the doctor didn't move. "I understand you were in a hospital in Switzerland. Were you on something then?"

"Only when they first checked me into the hospital. It was a sedative...I fell apart at the funeral." Her shoulders lifted, a listless shrug.

The doctor didn't speak and lifting her head, her gaze met his. She expected revulsion in his expression. Instead she found only pity. Suddenly her eyes welled with tears and she begged him to go.

"I think you should rest," he said.

"I don't want to sleep."

The doctor sat down next to her on the bed. "Everyone makes mistakes."

"A mistake is burning toast."

"Good people can make tragic mistakes."

"Not like this." The tears filling her eyes clung to her lashes, blurring her vision. Every breath she drew felt like an agony. Every beat of her heart reminded her of what she'd taken from her own child. "I loved him," she sobbed. "I loved him more than I loved myself and yet look what I did—"

In her grief she hadn't heard the door open, or notice Christos standing silently in the doorway. She didn't hear when he stepped out again, soundlessly shutting the door behind him.

"I think," the doctor said quietly, gently pushing

her back, settling her against the pillows. "You must rest now. Tomorrow talk about the future."

Alysia woke to a sunlit room, the curtains drawn back to welcome the warm light. Her head felt heavy, her brain groggy, and slowly she slid from the bed to stagger to the bathroom.

She caught a glimpse of herself in the mirror. Pale face, dark, sunken eyes, white pinched lips. She looked like a corpse. Then suddenly she saw Alexi, floating face up beneath the water, eyes open, mouth open, tiny hands outstretched and her knees buckled as she screamed, shrieking at the flood of memory.

A woman in black appeared—Mrs. Pateras, Alysia dimly registered—to take her by the arm, and firmly lead her from the bathroom back to bed.

Muttering in Greek, she pushed Alysia down and handed her a cup of tea. "Drink."

Alysia's hand trembled as she clutched the hot cup. "Christos?" she whispered, disoriented by the intensity of her emotions and the realization that she'd probably lost Christos forever.

"Gone," Mrs. Pateras answered coldly.

"Where?"

The older woman pushed Alysia's legs under the covers and drew the sheet up, and then the feather duvet. "Business."

Business. "Where?"

"Greece. Something to do with ships."

Ships, there'd always be ships. Ships, contracts, profit and loss. Tears filled Alysia's eyes. How could life be so black-and-white when she lived in shades of gray?

She missed Christos, needed to see him, talk to him. He was the one person she trusted. The one she loved most. "When is he coming back?"

"I don't know."

"I'd like the phone number of his Manhattan office."

"He's not there," Mrs. Pateras answered sharply. "I told you that already, now rest, or I shall tell Christos how difficult you've been."

The bedroom felt cold after Mrs. Pateras left, the corners swathed in shadows. How difficult she's been. Same words her father used to say. Alysia the difficult. But was she really that difficult? Was wanting love such a bad thing?

Alysia closed her eyes but she couldn't sleep, consumed by memory, confused by time. How could she have turned her back on Alexi? How could she have forgotten him?

It didn't make sense. She'd been a good mother, or at least, she'd tried to be a good mother. She never let him sit in wet diapers. She never skipped on his naps. Never left him out too long in the sun. She'd been young, but she'd really tried her best.

Until that day. That one day...

All this time later and she could still feel the weight of him, feel his limp body as she pulled him from the sink. She'd run with him into the streets screaming, *God, someone, anyone, help me. Help my baby. Help my baby.*

The day of the funeral, she destroyed her easel and canvases, shredding the paintings with a pair of sharp scissors, slicing them like a madwoman into long, tangled shreds.

As she destroyed her work, she howled, her agonized cries drawing the neighbors, and then the police. It was then they gave her the shot to calm her, and bundled her off to the hospital in Bern. They said she'd been talking gibberish, but it wasn't gibberish. She'd been weeping for Alexi, promising him she'd never forget him, and never ever paint again.

And she'd kept that vow.

Alysia woke to bathe and eat. Mrs. Pateras was there, presiding over the house, overseeing Alysia's meals, her iron tablets. She determined the routine, making it clear she was the mistress of the house, not Alysia.

Alysia didn't have the strength to argue. She was still struggling to put together pieces of the past, wondering at the gaps in her memory, even as she dreaded reliving the pain. But there were too many holes in her memory, places where nothing fit and nothing made sense.

But now that the guilt had been fully awakened, she couldn't rest. Nor find peace. It felt as though she were on fire on the inside, her own form of hell.

Lying in bed was only making it worse. She had to get busy again, needed exercise, sunlight, work to do.

On the third day after the horrible confession Alysia appeared downstairs for breakfast. Mrs. Avery beamed with pleasure but Mrs. Pateras blocked the doorway to the dining room. "The doctor said you were to rest," she said stiffly.

Alysia felt a ball of tension form in her belly. She didn't want to fight with her mother-in-law, but she wasn't going to sit around any longer feeling sorry for herself. What had happened, had happened, and awful as it was, it wouldn't bring back Alexi.

"Mrs. Pateras, I appreciate all you're doing for me, but I think it's time I began to act like a normal human being again. Hiding in my room will not bring Alexi back, and it will not help me forget."

"Some things you'll never forget."

She met Mrs. Pateras' unforgiving gaze and flinched inwardly but held her ground. "It was a mistake, a dreadful mistake, but I'm not going to give up on life. I love Christos—"

"He doesn't love you. How could he?"

It was exactly her own fear, shouted at her in contempt. Alysia wavered, glanced at the stairs, and the front door behind her, then turned her back on the escape routes. There was no escape. She had to face herself, and the future. "It's none of your business," she answered quietly, far more calmly than she felt. "This is between your son and me."

The housekeeper disappeared into the kitchen and Mrs. Pateras took a step toward her, her finger pointed in accusation. "My son deserves better than you. He deserves a real woman."

"I am a real woman. I just happened to make a terrible mistake."

"You murdered your child. That's not a mistake, that's a crime!"

"I can't change the past. But I can promise Christos loyalty, and love—"

"Do you honestly believe my son will ever be happy with you? Do you think he'll ever trust you?"

Mrs. Pateras was right, Alysia realized with a shudder, she wasn't thinking about Christos's needs, just her own. Christos deserved happiness. He was a good man, a loving man, he deserved a wife he could trust.

Sick to her stomach, Alysia turned away, headed for the stairs, hurrying back to her bedroom. At her closet she yanked clothes from hangers, a long gray skirt and a loose-fitting cashmere sweater in a paler shade.

Mrs. Pateras followed her into the bedroom. "If you were smart, you'd go now, before he returns. He could get an annulment, have a proper marriage."

"Leave," Alysia choked, facing her closet, her voice failing her. "I do not want you in here, nor do I need you here. Please leave now."

"Yes, Mother, please leave now." Christos appeared in the doorway, a dark coat over his arm, a briefcase in one hand. He looked exhausted, and pained. "I heard you, Mother, all the way into the kitchen. You have no right to speak to my wife like that—"

"Your wife? She's no wife—"

He cut his mother short, his voice rarely raised now blistering with fury. "She is my wife, and I love her very much. If you have a problem with her, then you have a problem with me because Alysia is my heart. You speak to her like that again and I shall cut you off forever. Do you understand?''

Mrs. Pateras stared at her only child in shock, her mouth opening, eyes wide. And then she shook her head once, a slow, angry shake, before walking out of the bedroom and closing the door behind her.

Christos rolled up his shirtsleeves. "I'm sorry. I'm sorry she talked to you like that. I'm sorry I couldn't get back sooner.''

Alysia stood rooted to the spot. She clutched the clothes tightly, too astonished, too overwhelmed to speak. The cashmere sweater tickled her neck, the long skirt rough against her bare arms. She could smell a whiff of her perfume on the sweater, a sweet light floral, a hint of Spring.

"You should have called me," he said, his features tight. "I left my numbers with my mother.''

No point in telling him that his mother didn't share them. She swallowed, pressed the wadded clothes to her stomach. "Where were you?''

His dark gaze followed each jerky gesture, before lifting to her face, eyes searching hers. "I went to Paris.''

She took an unsteady step to the chaise in the corner of the room and sank down. "Paris?''

"Then to London. I spoke with many people. People you worked for in Paris, the police there, and then on to Jeremy. He lives in London now. In a small dirty flat overlooking the Thames.''

Jeremy alive, and well, Jeremy in a dirty flat near a river. But she didn't want to think of him, didn't want to be reminded of the grief they'd shared. Jeremy ruined her life once. She wouldn't let him ruin it again. "I don't want to talk about him."

"We have to."

"I can't, Christos, I can't. Please, not again. I told you everything—"

"No, not quite everything. You've forgotten the facts, Alysia, you've changed them."

She felt a tiny prick, almost like a beesting. "What do you mean?"

He moved across the room and sat down next to her on the chaise, drawing the bundled clothes from her arms. "It's time we talked about what really happened that afternoon in the apartment."

"I told you what happened."

"But that's not what happened. Look at me, Alysia. Look into my face." He waited until she dragged her gaze up, eyes meeting his. "The baby drowned," he said quietly, "but it's not your fault. You weren't even there. Somehow you've mixed the facts up, guilt and grief. You have to remember how it really happened, not the story you told me."

She couldn't speak, panic wrestling with hope and yet even as she dared to hope she remembered the truth. Alexi died, Alexi was dead, her baby, he was *her baby,* and it was *her fault.*

"Jeremy was the one watching him. You weren't home when Alexi drowned. You were painting—"

She struggled to rise but Christos caught her

around the waist, drawing her back down, onto his lap.

His arms circled her, holding her fast to his chest. "You loved your baby, my sweet Alysia. You loved that baby more than anyone could love a child and you didn't fail him."

"I should have been there. If I were there he wouldn't have drowned. I wouldn't have blinked, or moved a muscle. I wouldn't have turned my back, not for an instant, not for anything in this world!"

"I know. I know what a good mother you were. Your friends told me. Your neighbors told me. The police told me. That's what makes this such a tragedy. You did what you could—"

"It wasn't enough."

He stroked the back of her head, fingers detangling the long silky strands of hair. "Jeremy had been drinking. He claims he lost track of time."

"He drank too much," she whispered, awash in pain. It was awful, too awful to relive again and again and again. "He wasn't happy," she added dully, remembering his bitterness when he discovered that her father had cut her off, that there'd be no generous allowance, no financial support. He'd married her for her fortune and there'd been none.

"But were you?"

Her heart constricted. "I had my baby." She felt her throat close. "You see why I can't have children. And your mother is right. This marriage won't work. You must give the money back to my father. Find yourself a real bride."

"You are a real bride. You're my bride."

"But the dowry—"

"There was no dowry. Your father is bankrupt."

"Bankrupt?"

"I paid his debts, got rid of his creditors and set up a small nest egg in Switzerland for him. He needs something to live on."

Her mouth dropped open. "You mean, I have no inheritance? I've nothing?"

His lips twisted. "Nothing but me. I'm sorry, Alysia. I've been trying to figure out a way to break the news, but I didn't know how to tell you."

She felt a bubble of joy. This was actually wonderful news. She hated her father's money, had never wanted his money. Just his love. All she'd ever wanted from him was his love. "I don't suppose my father will give the money back to you," she said doubtfully.

"No, and I don't want it back, because I'm not about to give you up. I've waited for you for ten years. I first saw you over ten years ago in Athens, at a ship owners meeting. We were gathered in the living room and you interrupted the meeting to ask your father a question—"

"You were there?" she breathed.

His jaw thickened. "I hated what he did to you, I hated how he treated you. I vowed then and there to find you, to make you mine. I made a deal with your father, but it was for you, and me. I knew I could make you happy, and I will."

"How can you trust me after Alexi? Your mother, she hates me."

"I don't need her approval. I don't care what people think. I love you, and I want to be with you and that's all that matters."

"And there's really no inheritance."

"None. Zilch. You're as poor as a church mouse."

"That's too wonderful!" Tears filled her eyes, tears and a hint of laughter. For the first time in years she felt as though she could finally breathe. No inheritance, no pretense, no duty. Just love. And hope. "You really do love me?"

He stared deep into her eyes, his own dark depths full of emotion. "With all my heart and all my soul."

"Say it again."

"With all my heart, all my mind, all my body and all my soul. I was made for you, to love you, and only you." He kissed her then, stemming additional protests, silencing the intellect, letting emotion and sensation rule.

She woke the next morning nestled against him. It was early yet, not even six, and immediately her first thought was of Alexi, but instead of denying the flicker of pain, she drew a deep breath and said a prayer for him.

She did love him, she would always love him. As she finished her prayer Alysia felt a great wave of peace. The peace filled her, warm and light and bright, bringing tears to her eyes, but this time tears of happiness, and relief.

"Alysia?" Christos stirred, wrapped an arm

around her waist, drew her closer to him. "What's wrong?"

"I said a prayer for Alexi." Her voice broke. "But it's okay, I understand he's in God's hands, and I owe it to him to make my life matter, to make it better. I owe it to him to be strong."

"As long as you live, Alexi will live on, in your heart, and in your thoughts."

"Then I must live a good long life and never forget the blessings we've been given." She couldn't swallow around the lump in her throat, and burying her face in Christos's shoulder, her mouth pressed to his bare skin, she let go of the anger and the guilt and the shame.

She cried for those she'd loved and cried for those she'd lost. She even cried for the relationship she'd never had with her father.

Christos held her throughout. But at last, there were no more tears, and exhausted, she lifted her wet face. "I'm sorry," she sniffed, reaching for tissues. "That was rather appalling."

He kissed her brow, the tip of her nose, her tear-streaked mouth. "It's what you needed to do. Grieve. Love. Feel. Especially feel. You can't live all shut down. You're not a robot, you're a beautiful, smart, sensitive woman." He kissed her again, her lower lip quivering. "You can talk to me about Alexi as much as you want. And if you ever want to talk to someone else, you could do that, too. Whatever you want. Whatever you need."

She pressed her cheek to Christos's chest savoring the even beat of his heart. "You give me hope."

"Then believe, Alysia, believe we will have a wonderful life together, a new life that will be better than anything either of us have yet lived."

"Is it possible?"

"I know it is."

"How can you be so certain?"

"I just know, the same way I knew that day in Athens that I would find you again and make you mine. I was made to love you. And I shall. Always."

EPILOGUE

"CAREFUL! Watch out," Alysia called, jumping from the polished marble bench, shielding her eyes as she anxiously followed the toddler's progress down the flagstone path toward the fishpond.

"Gotcha." Christos laughed, swinging the wriggling little boy in the sailor jumper onto his shoulders. "I know where you were going."

"Fishies!" Two-year-old Nikos shouted, jabbing his father in the ear with a wet finger. "I wuv fishies."

Christos walked up the path, returning with the energetic toddler to the bench in the shade.

Alysia stood, arms outstretched to take the bouncing boy. Happily Nikos lunged into her arms, patting her face, kissing her cheek and then her mouth. "Mama."

Her heart turned over. "Yes, Mama loves you."

"Nikos wuvs fishies," he shouted, enthusiastically patting her face again.

"Careful with Mama," Christos said, reaching out to touch Nikos's small hand, gentling the tiny fingers.

"Mama," Nikos said again, kissing her cheek.

Alysia lifted her head, met Christos's dark gaze. "I'm fine," she whispered, even as the baby inside her moved. In just weeks there'd be another little Pateras running wild in the lovely rambling Colonial house.

Christos leaned down, placing a possessive kiss on her upturned lips. "You're so beautiful, especially now."

"You're blind."

"Not blind, just deeply in love." He kissed her again, over the top of Nikos's dark head. "How did we get so lucky?"

Her eyes burned and yet she smiled as tears welled up in her eyes, her heart brimming with happiness and love for Christos. It still staggered her, the joy she'd found with him. "I don't know. It's a miracle."

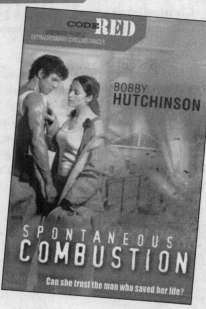

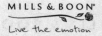

MILLS & BOON®

Live the emotion

0105/01b

Modern
romance™

THE VENGEANCE AFFAIR by Carole Mortimer

Beau Garrett moved to the village of Aberton for a more peaceful life. But he became the target of gossip when he employed female gardener Jaz Logan. Soon he acted on his attraction to Jaz – and that's when the poison pen letters started arriving…

THE BILLION-DOLLAR BRIDE by Kay Thorpe

Gina Saxton has been left half of the Harlow billion-dollar empire – but there is a major condition: she must marry the heir to the other half, arrogant Ross Harlow! It's easy – until Gina realises that she's falling in love with her convenient husband!

THE MILLIONAIRE BOSS'S MISTRESS by Madeleine Ker

Anton Zell, a top entrepreneur, needs a PA to be at his side night and day. Amy Worthington takes on the challenge. But she's determined not to become just another notch on her gorgeous boss's bedpost – no matter how hard he tries to seduce her…

THEIR SCANDALOUS AFFAIR by Catherine George

Beautiful but fiery Avery Crawford wants her affair with Jonas Mercer to remain private, but the handsome millionaire wants their relationship to go public, and he's determined to marry Avery. However, Avery has secrets that come at a cost even Jonas can't afford…

Don't miss out…

On sale 4th February 2005

Available at most branches of WHSmith, Tesco, ASDA, Martins, Borders, Eason, Sainsbury's and all good paperback bookshops.

Visit www.millsandboon.co.uk

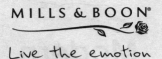

MILLS & BOON®

Live the emotion

His Boardroom Mistress

In February 2005 By Request brings
back three favourite novels by our
bestselling Mills & Boon authors:

The Husband Assignment
by Helen Bianchin
The Baby Verdict *by Cathy Williams*
The Bedroom Business *by Sandra Marton*

Seduction from 9-5...
and after hours!

On sale 4th February 2005

0105/05

MILLS & BOON®

**Volume 8
on sale from
6th February
2005**

Lynne
Graham

International Playboys

*The Unfaithful
Wife*

*Available at most branches of WHSmith, Tesco, Martins, Borders,
Eason, Sainsbury's and all good paperback bookshops.*

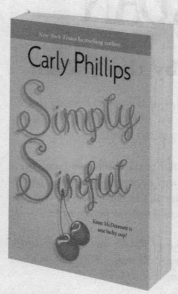

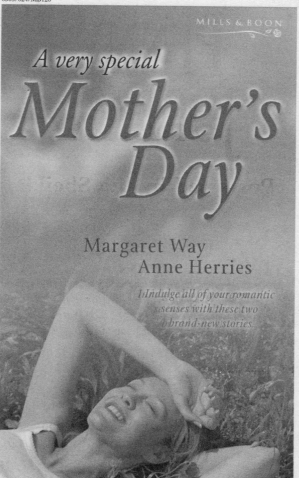

New York Times Bestselling Author

Vicki Lewis Thompson
Stephanie Bond
Judith Arnold

Three brand-new novellas!

Fool For Love

Available from 1st April 2005

*Available at most branches of WHSmith,
Tesco, ASDA, Martins, Borders, Eason, Sainsbury's
and most good paperback bookshops.*

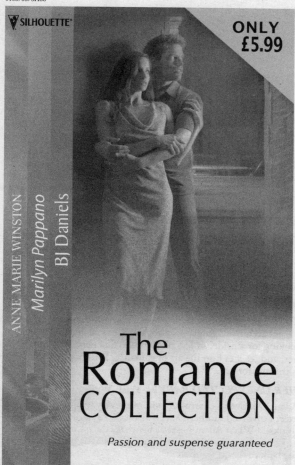

0105/02

Live the emotion

TO MARRY FOR DUTY by Rebecca Winters

(The Husband Fund)

Piper Duchess is worried she's been left on the shelf – her life is all work and definitely no play. She is ready to marry and she knows the man she wants: honourable aristocrat Nic de Pastrana. And, it seems that Nic needs her help – in fact his family's future depends on it...

HER WISH-LIST BRIDEGROOM by Liz Fielding

Having sworn off men for good, Juliet heads back home for a fresh start – only to bump into her childhood crush Gregor McLeod. Greg has been top of Juliet's wish-list since she was a little girl, but Greg has a few secrets... And she's sworn off men, hasn't she?

THE FIANCÉE CHARADE by Darcy Maguire

To save her struggling business Jess Thompson needs inside info on her arch rival: gorgeous, arrogant Alex Calahan. Alex is looking for a bride, so Jess plots a ruse. She persuades him to hire her, and teaches him the art of romance. But soon Jess realises *she* is the one for him...

HER UNEXPECTED BABY by Trish Wylie

Adam Donovan's charm can win over every woman in the world, except divorced mother Dana Taylor. She's immune, or so she thinks... When Adam poses as her date, the pretence becomes all too real – now she's pregnant! But Dana's been hurt before; can she believe Adam is different?

On sale 4th February 2005

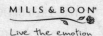

MILLS & BOON®

Live the emotion

Historical
romance™

A SCANDALOUS MARRIAGE
by Mary Brendan

William and June Pemberton are happily married – but the
longer they go without June's conceiving, the more concerned
she becomes. Especially since William's old flame is free to
marry again and, according to his mother, would make much
the better wife!

THE WAGERING WIDOW by Diane Gaston

Guy, Lord Keating, laden with his father's debts, elopes with
'heiress' Emily Duprey – only to discover she is as poor as he!
His only hope of saving his family is a return to the gaming
tables. Emily needs more money than she can win as Lady
Keating – so she becomes Lady Widow, a card-playing masked
seductress. And then Guy recognises her as his mousy wife...

THE DUMONT BRIDE by Terri Brisbin
Medieval 1194

A royal command to wed would restore all that Christian
Dumont had lost – but at what price? Marriage to the beautiful
Emalie Montgomerie presented no hardship, but his countess
harboured a secret dangerous enough to destroy them both.

On sale 4th February 2005